CERTAIN PREY

CERTAIN PREY

John Sandford

HEADLINE
FEATURE

First published in Great Britain in 1999
by HEADLINE BOOK PUBLISHING

A HEADLINE FEATURE hardback and softback

10 9 8 7 6 5 4 3 2 1

British Library Cataloguing in Publication Data

ISBN 0 7472 7414 2 (hardback)
ISBN 0 7472 7415 0 (softback)

Typeset by Avon Dataset Ltd, Bidford-on-Avon, Warks

Printed and bound in Great Britain by
Mackays of Chatham PLC, Chatham, Kent

HEADLINE BOOK PUBLISHING
A division of Hodder Headline PLC
338 Euston Road
London NW1 3BH

For Tom and Rozanne Anderson

Chapter One

Clara Rinker.

Of the three unluckiest days in Barbara Allen's life, the first was the day Clara Rinker was raped behind a St. Louis nudie bar called Zanadu, which was located west of the city in a dusty checkerboard of truck terminals, warehouses and light assembly plants. Zanadu, as its chrome-yellow I-70 billboard proclaimed, was E-Z On, E-Z Off. The same was not true of Clara Rinker, despite what Zanadu's customers thought.

Rinker was sixteen when she was raped, a small athletic girl, a dancer, an Ozarks runaway. She had bottle-blonde hair that showed darker roots, and a body that looked wonderful in v-necked, red-polka-dotted, thin-cotton dresses from K-Mart. A body that drew the attention of cowboys, truckers, and other men who dreamt of Nashville.

Rinker had taken up nude dancing because she could. It was that, fuck for money, or go hungry. The rape took place at two o'clock in the morning on an otherwise delightful April night, the kind of night when Midwestern kids are allowed to stay out late and play war, when cicadas hum down from their elm-bark hideaways. Rinker had closed the bar that night; she was the last dancer up.

Four men were still drinking when she finished. Three were hound-faced long-distance truckers who had nowhere to go but the short beds in their various Kenworths, Freightliners and Peterbilts; and a Norwegian exotic-animal dealer drowning the sorrows of a recent mishap involving a box of boa constrictors and thirty-six thousand dollars' worth of illegal tropical birds.

A fifth man, a slope-shouldered gorilla named Dale-Something, had walked out of the bar halfway through Rinker's last grind. He left behind twelve dollars in crumpled ones and two small sweat rings where his forearms had been propped on the bar. Rinker had worked down the bar-top, stopping for ten seconds in front of each man, for what the girls called a crack shot. Dale-Something had gotten the first shot, and he had stood up and walked out as soon as she moved to the next guy. When she

1

was done, Rinker hopped off the end of the bar and headed for the back to get into her street clothes.

A few minutes later, the bartender, a University of Missouri wrestler named Rick, knocked on the dressing-room door and said, 'Clara? Will you close up the back?'

'I'll get it,' she said, pulling a fuzzy pink tube-top over her head, shaking her ass to get it down. Rick respected the dancers' privacy, which they appreciated; it was purely a psychological thing, since he worked behind the bar, and spent half his night looking up their . . .

Anyway, he respected their privacy.

When she was dressed, Rinker killed the lights in the dressing room, walked down to the ladies' room, checked to make sure it was empty, which it always was, and then did the same for the men's room, which was also empty, except for the ineradicable odor of beer-flavored urine. At the back door, she snapped out the hall lights, released the bolt on the lock, and stepped outside into the soft evening air. She pulled the door shut, heard the bolt snap, rattled the door handle to make sure that it was locked, and headed for her car.

A rusted-out Dodge pickup crouched on the lot, two-thirds of the way down to her car. A battered aluminum camper slumped on the back, with curtains tangled in the windows. Every once in a while, somebody would drink too much and would wind up sleeping in his car behind the place; so the truck was not exactly unprecedented. Still, Rinker got a bad vibe from it. She almost walked back around the building to see if she could catch Rick before he went out the front.

Almost. But that was too far and she was probably being silly and Rick was probably in a hurry and the truck was dark, nothing moving . . .

Dale-Something was sitting on the far side of it, hunkered down in the pea gravel, his back against the driver's-side door. He'd been waiting for twenty minutes with decreasing patience, chewing breath mints, thinking about her. Somewhere, in the deep recesses of his mind, breath mints were a concession to gentility, as regarded women. He chewed them as a favor to her . . .

When he heard the back door closing, he levered his butt off the ground, peeked through a car window, saw her coming, alone. He waited, crouched behind the car: he was a big guy, much of his bigness in fat, but he took pride in his size anyway.

2

And he was quick: Rinker never had a chance.

When she stepped around the truck, keys rattling in her hand, he came out of the dark and hit her like an NFL tackle. The impact knocked her breath out; she lay beneath him, gasping, the gravel cutting her bare shoulders. He flipped her over, twisting her arms, clamping both of her skinny wrists in one hand and the back of her neck in the other.

And he said, his minty breath next to her ear, 'You fuckin' scream and I'll break your fuckin' neck.'

She didn't fuckin' scream because something like this had happened before, with her step-father. She *had* screamed and he almost *had* broken her fuckin' neck. Instead of screaming, Rinker struggled violently, thrashing, spitting, kicking, swinging, twisting, trying to get loose. But Dale-Something's hand was like a vise on her neck, and he dragged her to the camper, pulled open the door, pushed her inside, ripped her pants off and did what he was going to do in the flickering yellow illumination of the dome light.

When he was done, he threw her out the back of the truck, spit on her, said, 'Fuckin' bitch, you tell anybody about this, and I'll fuckin' kill ya.' That was most of what she remembered about it later: lying naked on the gravel, and getting spit on; that, and all the wiry hair on Dale's fat wobbling butt.

Rinker didn't call the cops, because that would have been the end of her job. And, knowing cops, they probably would have sent her home to her step-dad. So she told Zanadu's owners about the rape. The brothers Ernie and Ron Battaglia were concerned about both Rinker and their bar license. A nudie joint didn't need sex crimes in the parking lot.

'Jeez,' Ron said, when Rinker told him about the rape. 'That's terrible, Clara. You hurt? You oughta get yourself looked at, you know?'

Ernie took a roll of bills from his pocket, peeled off two hundreds, thought about it for a couple of seconds, peeled off a third and tucked the three hundred dollars into her back-up tube top: 'Get yourself looked at, kid.'

She nodded and said, 'You know, I don't wanna go to the cops. But this asshole should pay for what he did.'

'We'll take care of it,' Ernie offered.

'Let me take care of it,' Rinker said.

Ron put up an eyebrow. 'What do you want to do?'

'Just get him down the basement for me. He said something about being a roofer, once. He works with his hands. I'll get a goddamn baseball bat and bust one of his arms.'

Ron looked at Ernie, who looked at Rinker and said, 'That sounds about right. Next time he comes in, huh?'

They didn't do it the next time he came in, which was a week later, looking nervous and shifty-eyed, like he might not be welcomed. Rinker refused to work with Dale-Something at the bar, and when she cornered Ernie in the kitchen, he told her that, goddamnit, they were right in the middle of tax season and neither he nor Ron had the emotional energy for a major confrontation.

Rinker kept working on them, and the second time Dale-Something showed up, which was two days after Tax Day, the brothers were feeling nasty. They fed him drinks and complimentary peanuts and kept him talking until after closing. Rick the bartender hustled the second-to-the-last guy out, and left himself, not looking back; he knew something was up.

Then Ron came around the bar, and Ernie got Dale-Something looking the other way, and Ron nailed him with a wild, out-of-the-blue round-house right that knocked Dale off the barstool. Ron landed on him, rolled him, and Ernie raced around the bar and threw on a pro-wrestling death lock. Together, they dragged a barely resisting Dale-Something down the basement stairs.

The brothers had him on his feet and fully conscious by the time Rinker came down, carrying her aluminum baseball bat; or rather, t-ball bat, which had a better swing-weight for a small woman.

'I'm gonna sue you fuckers for every fuckin' dime you got,' Dale-Something said, sputtering blood through his split lip. 'My fuckin' lawyer is doin' the money-dance right now, you fucks . . .'

'Fuck you, you ain't doing shit,' Ron said. 'You raped this little girl.'

'What do you want, Clara?' Ernie asked. He was standing behind Dale with his arms under Dale's armpits, his hands locked behind Dale's neck. 'You wanna arm or a leg?'

Rinker was standing directly in front of Dale-Something, who glowered at her: 'I'm gonna . . .' he started.

Rinker interrupted: 'Fuck legs,' she said. She whipped the bat up, and then straight back down on the crown of Dale-Something's head.

The impact sounded like a fat man stepping on an English walnut. Ernie, startled, lost his death grip and Dale-Something slipped to the floor like a two-hundred-pound blob of Jello.

'Holy shit,' Ron said, and crossed himself.

Ernie prodded Dale-Something with the toe of his desert boot, and Dale blew a bubble of blood. 'He ain't dead,' Ernie said.

Rinker's bat came up, and she hit Dale again, this time in the mastoid process behind the left ear. She hit him hard; her step-dad used to make her chop wood for the furnace, and her swing had some weight and snap behind it. 'That ought to do it,' she said.

Ernie nodded and said 'Yup.' Then they all looked at each other in the light of the single bare bulb, and Ron said to Rinker, 'Some heavy shit, Clara. How do you feel about this?'

Clara looked at Dale-Something's body, the little ring of black blood around his fat lips, and said, 'He was a piece of garbage.'

'You don't feel nothing'?' Ernie asked.

'Nothing'.' Her lips were set in a thin, grim line.

After a minute, Ron looked up the narrow wooden stairs and said, 'Gonna be a load 'n half getting his ass outa the basement.'

'You got that right,' Ernie said, adding, philosophically, 'I coulda told him there *ain't* no free pussy.'

Dale-Something went into the Mississippi and his truck was parked across the river in Granite City, from which spot it disappeared in two days. Nobody ever asked about Dale, and Rinker went back to dancing. A few weeks later, Ernie asked her to sit with an older guy who came in for a beer. Rinker cocked her head and Ernie said, 'No, it's okay. You don't have to do nothin'.'

So she got a longneck Bud and went to sit with the guy, who said he was Ernie's aunt's husband's brother. He knew about Dale-Something. 'You feeling bad about it yet?'

'Nope. I'm a little pissed that Ernie told you about it, though,' Rinker said, taking a hit on the Budweiser.

The older man smiled. He had very strong, white teeth to go with his black eyes and almost-feminine long lashes. Rinker had the sudden feeling that he might show a girl a pretty good time, although he must be over forty. 'You ever shoot a gun?' he asked.

5

That's how Rinker became a hit lady. She wasn't spectacular, like the Jackal or one of those movie killers. She just took care of business, quietly and efficiently, using a variety of silenced pistols, mostly .22s. Careful, close-range killings became a trademark.

Rinker had never thought of herself as stupid, just as someone who hadn't yet had her chance. When the money from the killings started coming in, she knew that she didn't know how to handle it. So she went to the Intercontinental College of Business in the mornings, and took courses in bookkeeping and small business. When she was twenty, getting a little old for dancing nude, she got a job with the Mafia guy, working in a liquor warehouse. And when she was twenty-four, and knew a bit about the business, she bought a bar of her own in downtown Wichita, Kansas, and renamed it The Rink.

The bar did well. Still, a few times a year, Rinker'd go out of town with a gun and come back with a bundle of money. Some she spent, but most she hid, under a variety of names, in a variety of places. One thing her step-dad had taught her well: sooner or later, however comfortable you might be at the moment, you were gonna have to run.

Carmel Loan.

Carmel was long, sleek, and expensive, like a new Jaguar.

She had a small head, with a tidy nose, thin pale lips, a square chin and small pointed tongue. She was a Swede, way back, and blonde – one of the whippet Swedes with small breasts, narrow hips, and a long waist in between. She had the eyes of a bird of prey, a raptor. Carmel was a defense attorney in Minneapolis, one of the top two or three. Most years, she made comfortably more than a million dollars.

Carmel lived in a fabulously cool high-rise apartment in downtown Minneapolis, all blond-wood floors and white walls with black-and-white photos by Ansel Adams and Diane Arbus and Minor White, but nobody as gauche and come-lately as Robert Mapplethorpe. Amid all the black-and-white, there were perfect touches of bloody-murder-red in the furniture and carpets and even her car, a Jaguar XK8, had a custom bloody-murder-red paint job.

On the second of the three unluckiest days in Barbara Allen's life, Carmel Loan decided that she was truly, genuinely and forever in love with Hale Allen, Barbara Allen's husband.

Hale Allen, a property and real-estate attorney, was the definitive heartthrob. He had near-black hair that fell naturally over his forehead in little ringlets, warm brown eyes, a square chin with a dimple, wide shoulders, big hands and narrow hips. He was a perfect size forty-two, a little over six feet tall, with one slightly chipped front tooth. The knot of his tie was always askew, and women were always fixing it. Putting their hands on him. He had an easy-jock way with the women, chatting them up, playing with them.

Hale Allen liked women; and not just for sex. He liked to talk with them, shop with them, drink with them, jog with them – all without losing some essential lupine manliness. He had given Carmel reason to believe that he found her not unattractive. Whenever Carmel saw *him*, something deep inside her got plucked.

Despite his looks and easy manner with women, Hale Allen was not the sharpest knife in the dishwasher. He was content with boiler-plate law, the arranging of routine contracts, and made nowhere near as much money as Carmel. That made little difference to a woman who'd found true love. Stupidity could be overlooked, Carmel thought, if a woman felt a genuine physical passion for a man. Besides, Hale would look very good standing next to the stone fireplace at her annual Christmas party, a scotch in hand, and perhaps a cheerful bloody-murder-red bowtie; she'd do the talking.

Unfortunately, Hale appeared to be permanently tied to his wife, Barbara.

By her money, Carmel thought. Barbara had a lot of it, through her family. And though Hale's cerebral filament might not burn as brightly as others, he knew fifty million bucks when he saw them. He knew where that sixteen-hundred-dollar black cashmere Georgio Armani sportcoat came from . . .

Allen's tie to his wife – or to her money, anyway – left few acceptable options for a woman of Carmel's qualities.

She wouldn't hang around and yearn, or get weepy and depressed, or drunk enough to throw herself at him. She'd do something.

Like kill the wife.

Five years earlier, Carmel had gone to court and had shredded the evidentiary procedures followed by a young St. Paul cop after a routine traffic stop had turned into a major drug bust.

Her client, Rolando (Rolo) D'Aquila, had walked on the drug charge, though the cops had taken ten kilos of cocaine from under the spare tire of his coffee-brown Continental. The cops had wound up keeping the car under the forfeiture law, but Rolo didn't care about that. What he cared about was that he'd done exactly five hours in jail, which was the time it took for Carmel to organize the one-point-three-million dollars in bail money.

And later, when they walked away from the courthouse after the acquittal, Rolo told her that if she ever needed a really serious favor – *really serious* – to come see him. Because of previous conversations, they both knew what he was talking about. 'I owe you,' he said. She didn't say no, because she never said no.

She said, 'See ya.'

On a warm, rainy day in late May, Carmel drove her second car – an anonymous blue-black Volvo station wagon registered in her mother's second-marriage name – to a ramshackle house in St. Paul's Frogtown, eased to the curb, and looked out the passenger-side window.

The wooden-frame house was slowly settling into its overgrown lawn. Rain water seeped over the edges of its leaf-clogged gutters, and peeling green paint showed patches of the previous color, a chalky blue. None of the windows or doors were quite level with the world, square with the house, or aligned with each other. Most of the windows showed glass; a few had black screens.

Carmel got a small travel umbrella from the back seat, pushed the car door open with her feet, popped the umbrella and hurried up the sidewalk to the house. The inner door was open: she knocked twice on the screen door, which rattled in its frame, and she heard Rolo from the back: 'Come on in, Carmel. I'm in the kitchen.'

The interior of the house was a match for the exterior. The carpets were twenty years old, with paths worn through the thin pile. The walls were a dingy yellow, the furniture a crappy collection of plastic-veneered plywood, chipped along the edges of the tabletops and down the legs. There were no pictures on the walls, no decoration of any kind. Nailheads poked from picture-hanging spots, where previous tenants had tried a little harder. Everything smelled like nicotine and tar.

The kitchen was improbably bright. There were no shades or curtains on the two windows that flanked the kitchen table, and only two chairs, one tucked tight to the table, another pulled out. Rolo, looking smaller than he had five years ago, was dressed in jeans and a t-shirt that said, enigmatically, *Jesus*. He had both hands in the kitchen sink.

'Just cleaning up for the occasion,' he said.

He wasn't embarrassed at being caught at house-cleaning, and a thought flicked through Carmel's lawyer-head: *he should be embarrassed.*

'Sit down,' he said, nodding at the pulled-out chair. 'I got some coffee going.'

'I'm sort of in a rush,' she started.

'You don't have time for coffee with Rolando?' He was flicking water off his hands, and he ripped a paper towel off a roll that sat on the kitchen counter, wiped his hands dry, and tossed the balled-up towel toward a waste basket in the corner. It hit the wall and ricocheted into the basket. 'Two,' he said.

She glanced at her watch, and reversed herself on the coffee. 'Sure, I've got a few minutes.'

'I've come a long way down, huh?'

She glanced once around the kitchen, shrugged and said, 'You'll be back.'

'I don't know,' he said. 'I got my nose pretty deep in the shit.'

'So take a program.'

'Yeah, a program,' he said, and laughed. 'Twelve steps to Jesus.' Then, apologetically, 'I only got caffeinated.'

'Only kind I drink,' she said. And then, 'So you made the call.' Not a question.

Rolo was pouring coffee into two yellow ceramic mugs, the kind Carmel associated with lake resorts in the north woods. 'Yes. And she's still working, and she'll take the job.'

'She? It's a woman?'

'Yeah. I was surprised myself. I never asked, you know, I only knew who to call. But when I asked, my friend said, "She." '

'She's gotta be good,' Carmel said.

'She's good. She has a reputation. Never misses. Very efficient, very fast. Always from very close range, so there's no mistake.' Rolo put a mug of coffee in front of her, and she turned it with her fingertips, and picked it up.

'That's what I need,' she said, and took a sip. Good coffee, very hot.

'You're sure about this?' Rolo said. He leaned back against the kitchen counter, and gestured with his coffee mug. 'Once I tell them "Yes," it'll be hard to stop. This woman, the way she moves, nobody knows where she is, or what name she's using. If you say, "Yes," she kills Barbara Allen.'

Carmel frowned at the sound of Barbara Allen's name. She hadn't really thought of the process as *murder*. She had considered it more abstractly, as the solution to an otherwise intractable problem. Of course, she had *known* it would be murder, she just hadn't contemplated the fact. 'I'm sure,' she said.

'You've got the money?'

'At the house. I brought your ten.'

She put the mug down, dug in her purse, pulled out a thin deck of currency and laid it on the table. Rolo picked it up, riffled it expertly with a thumb. 'I'll tell you this,' he said. 'When they come and ask for it, pay every penny. *Every penny.* Don't argue, just pay. If you don't, they won't try to collect. They'll make an example out of you.'

'I know how it works,' Carmel said, with an edge of impatience. 'They'll get it. And nobody'll be able to trace it, because I've had it stashed. It's absolutely clean.'

Rolo shrugged: 'Then if you say "Yes," I'll call them tonight. And they'll kill Barbara Allen.'

This time, she didn't flinch when Rolo spoke the name. Carmel stood up: 'Yes,' she said. 'Do it.'

Rinker came to town three weeks later. She had driven her own car from Wichita, then rented two different-colored, different-make cars from Hertz and Avis, under two different names, using authentic Missouri driver's licenses and perfectly good, paid-up credit cards.

She stalked Barbara Allen for a week, and finally decided to kill her on the interior steps of a downtown parking garage. In the week that Rinker trailed her, Allen had used the garage four times, and all four times had used the stairs to get to the skyway level. Once in the skyway, she'd gone straight to an office with the name 'Star of the North Charities' on the door. When Rinker knew that Allen was *not* at Star of the North, she'd called and asked for her.

'I'm sorry, she's not here . . .'

'Do you expect her?'

'She's usually here for an hour or two in the morning, just before lunch . . .'

'Thanks, I'll try again tomorrow.'

Barbara Allen.

On the last of the three unluckiest days of her life, she got out of bed, showered, and ate a light breakfast of Raisin Bran and strawberries – with Hale for a husband, it paid to watch her figure. As the housekeeper cleared away the breakfast dishes, Allen turned on the television to check the Dow Jones opening numbers, sat at her desk and reviewed proposed charitable allocations from the Star of the North Charities trust, then, at nine-thirty, gathered her papers, pushed them into a tan Coach briefcase, and headed downtown.

Rinker, in a red Jeep Cherokee, followed her until she was sure that Allen was heading downtown, then passed her and hurried ahead. Allen was a slow, careful driver, but traffic and traffic lights were unpredictable, and Rinker wanted to be at least five minutes ahead of her by the time they got downtown.

Rinker had picked out another parking garage, also on the skyway system, a little less than a two-minute fast walk from the killing ground. She wheeled into the garage, parked, walked to her own car, which she'd parked in the garage earlier that morning, and climbed into the back seat. She glanced up and down the ramp, saw one man leaving, heading toward the doors. She reached down, grabbed the carpeting behind the passenger seat, and popped open a shallow steel box, which held two Remington .22 semi-automatic pistols, silencers already attached, on a bed of Styrofoam peanuts.

Rinker was wearing a loose shift, with a homemade elastic girdle beneath it. She pushed the .22s into the wide pockets of the shift, through another slit cut through the insides of the pockets, and into the girdle. The .22s were held tight against her body, but she could get them out in a half-second. With the guns tucked away, Rinker hopped out of the car and headed for the skyway.

Barbara Allen, a sturdy, German blonde with short, expensively cut hair, a dab of lipstick, a crisp white cotton blouse, a navy skirt and matching navy low-heels, went into the stairwell of the Sixth Street Parking Garage at 9:58 a.m. Halfway down, she met a small woman coming up, a redhead. As she passed her, looking down, the other woman smiled, and Allen, who knew about such things, looked at the top of her head and thought, 'Wig.'

That was the last thing she thought on the unluckiest day of her life.

Rinker, climbing the stairs, had mistimed it. She knew the lower ramp was clear, and wanted to take Allen low. But Allen came down the narrow steps slowly, and Rinker, now in plain sight, didn't feel she should stop and wait for her. So she continued climbing. Allen smiled and nodded at her as they passed and, as they passed, Rinker pulled the right-hand .22, pivoted, and fired it into the back of Allen's head from a range of two inches. Allen's hair puffed out, as though somebody had blown on it, and she started to fall.

The silencers were good. The loudest noise in the stairwell was the cycling of the pistol's action. Rinker got off a second shot before Allen fell too far; then stepped down to the sprawled body and fired five more shots into Allen's temple.

As she stepped away from the body, ready to head down the stairs, a cop came through the door in the stairwell above them. He was in uniform, a heavy guy carrying a manila folder.

Rinker had thought about this possibility, a surprise from a cop, though she'd never experienced anything like it. Still, she'd rehearsed it in her mind.

'Hey,' the cop said. He put up a hand, and Rinker shot him.

Chapter Two

Baily Dobbs' first day on patrol had taught him that police work was more complicated than he'd thought – and more dangerous than he'd expected. Baily had seen police work as a way to achieve a certain authority, a status. He hadn't thought about fighting people bigger than he was, about drunks vomiting in the back seat of the squad, about freezing his ass off outside the Target Center when the Wolves were playing. So Baily resolved to keep his head down, to volunteer for nothing, to show up late for trouble calls, and to get off the street as fast as he could.

He was inside in less than two years.

One Halloween, responding – late – to a domestic, he'd walked up a dark sidewalk, stepped on the back axle of a tricycle, flipped into the air, and twisted his knee. He was never exactly disabled, but it became clear that if he couldn't run, he couldn't work the streets. His hobbling progress around a gymnasium track baffled the docs and amused his former partners. The phrase, 'I'm gonna *baily* on that,' came into the vocabulary of the Minneapolis Police Department.

Baily went inside and stayed there. He still wore a uniform, carried a gun and got paid for being a cop, but he was a clerk and happy with it. Which is why he didn't respond as quickly as he might have, when he saw Rinker execute Barbara Allen. His cop reflexes were gone.

Baily's lunch started at eleven o'clock, but on this day he'd taken some under-time. He snuck out through the basement of City Hall, into the country government building, carrying a manila folder that contained a few sheets of paper addressed to a court bailiff – his cover-your-ass file, if he was spotted by his supervisor.

Once in the government building, he took a quick look around, then dodged into the skyway that went over to the Sixth Street parking garage. From there, he planned to take the stairs to the street level, cross over to the Hennepin Country Medical Center, which had a nice discreet cafeteria rarely visited by cops. He'd eat a cheeseburger and fries, enjoy a few cups of coffee, read the newspapers, then amble back to City Hall, just in time for lunch.

That perfectly good plan fell apart when he stepped into the stairwell.

Two women were in the stairwell below him, and one of them, a redhead, appeared to be sticking something in the ear of the other, who was lying on the stairs.

'Hey,' he said.

The redhead looked up at him, and in the next quarter-second, Baily realized that what she had in her hand was a pistol. The pistol came up and Baily put a hand out, and the redhead shot him. There wasn't much noise, but he felt something hit his chest, and he fell down backwards.

He fell in the doorway, which saved his life: Rinker, standing below him on the stairs, looking over the sights of her pistol, couldn't see anything but the bottoms of his feet. Baily groaned as he fell, and he dimly heard a man's voice call, 'Are you all right?'

Rinker had taken two quick steps toward him, to finish him, when she heard the new voice. Complications were increasing. Quick as a blink, she decided: down was safe. She went down, not running, but moving fast.

Baily struggled to sit upright, to crawl away from the stairwell; and heard a door bang closed in the stairwell below. His chest hurt, and so did his hand. He looked at his hand, and it was all scuffed up, apparently from the fall. Then he discovered the growing blood stain on the pocket of his white uniform shirt.

'Oh, man,' he said.

The other voice called again, 'Hey, you okay?'

'Oh, Jesus, oh, God, Jesus God,' said Baily, who was not a religious man. He tried to push himself up again, noticed his hand was slippery with blood, and started to cry. 'Oh, Jesus . . .' He looked up the ramp, where a man carrying a briefcase was looking down at him. A woman was beyond him, also coming toward them; he could sense her reluctance.

'Help me . . .' Baily cried. 'Help me, I've been shot . . .'

Sloan banged into Lucas Davenport's office and said, 'Baily Dobbs's been shot.' He looked at his watch. 'Twelve minutes ago.'

Lucas was peering glumly into a six-hundred-page report with a blue cover and white label, which said, 'Mayor's Select Commission on Cultural Diversity, Alternative Lifestyles and Other-Abledness in the Minneapolis Police Department: A Preliminary Approach to Divergent Modalities

[Executive Summary],' which he'd been marking with a fluorescent-yellow high-lighter. He was on page seven.

He put down the report and said, incredulously, '*Our* Baily Dobbs?'

'How many Baily Dobbs are there?' Sloan asked.

Lucas stood up and reached for a navy-blue silk jacket which hung from a government-issue coat tree. 'Is he dead?'

'No.'

'An accident? He shoot himself?'

Sloan shook his head. Sloan was a thin man, hatchet-faced, dressed in shades of brown and tan. A homicide investigator, the best interrogator on the force, an old friend. 'Looks like he walked in on a shooting, over in the Sixth Street parking garage,' he told Lucas. 'The shooter killed a woman, and then shot Baily. I figured since Rose Marie and Lester are out of town, and nobody can find Thorn, you better haul your ass over to the hospital.'

Lucas grunted and he pulled on the jacket. Rose Marie Roux was the chief of police; Lester, Thorn and Lucas were deputy chiefs. 'Anything on the shooter?'

'No. Well, Baily said something about it being a woman. The shooter was. The woman she shot is dead, and Baily took two rounds in the right tit.'

'Last goddamn guy in the world,' Lucas said.

Lucas was tall, lean but not thin, broad-shouldered and dark-complected. A scar sliced across one eyebrow onto his cheek, and showed as a pale line through his summer tan, like a vagrant strand of white thread. Another scar showed on the front of his neck, over his windpipe, just above the V of his royal-blue golf shirt. He took a .45 in a clip-rig out of his desk drawer, and clipped it inside his pants, under the jacket. He did it unconsciously, as another man might put a wallet in his back pocket. 'How bad is he?'

'He's going into surgery,' Sloan said. 'Swanson's over there, but that's all I know.'

'Let's go,' Lucas said. 'Does anybody know what Dobbs was doing in the stairwell?'

'The other people in the office say he was probably sneaking over to Hennepin Medical for a cheeseburger. He'd pretend he was going to the government center, then he'd sneak over to the hospital and drink coffee and read the papers.'

'*That's* the Baily we know and love,' Lucas said.

15

* * *

The emergency room was a warm four-minute fast walk from City Hall. A cop was shot, hurt bad, but life went on. The sidewalks were crowded with shoppers, the streets clogged with cars, and Sloan, intent on making it to the hospital, nearly got hit in an intersection – Lucas had to hook his arm and pull him back. 'You're too ugly to be a hood ornament,' Lucas grunted.

The emergency room was oddly quiet, Lucas thought. Usually, after a cop-shooting, thirty people would be milling around, no matter who the cop was. Here, there were three other cops, a couple of nurses and a doc, all standing around in the alcohol-scented reception area. Nobody seemed to be doing much.

'Place is empty,' Sloan said, picking up the thought.

'Word hasn't got out yet,' Lucas said. One of the three other cops was talking on the phone, while a second, a uniform sergeant, talked into his ear. Swanson, a bland-faced, overweight homicide detective in a grey suit, was leaning on a fluids-proof counter-top talking to a nurse, a notebook open on the counter. He saw Lucas, with Sloan a step behind, and lifted a hand.

'Where's Baily?' Lucas asked.

'He's about to go in,' Swanson said, meaning surgery. 'They already got the sedative going, so they can plug in the airway shit. He won't be talking. The surgeon's down the hall scrubbing up, if you wanna talk to him.'

'Anybody tell Baily's wife?'

'We're looking for the chaplain,' Swanson said. 'He's at a church thing up on the north side, some kind of yard sale. Dick's on hold for him now.' He nodded at the cop on the phone. 'We'll get him in the next couple of minutes.'

Lucas turned to Sloan: 'Get the chaplain going, send a car. Lights and sirens.'

Sloan nodded and headed for the cop on the phone. Lucas turned back to Swanson. 'What's going on at the scene?'

'Goddamndest thing. Woman was executed, I think.'

'Executed?'

'She took at least four or five in the head with a small-caliber pistol, short range: you can see the tattooing on her scalp,' Swanson said. 'Nobody heard a thing, which might mean a silencer. Everything in that stairwell echoes like crazy, off that concrete, and Baily told me he couldn't remember hearing the gun. Baily saw the shooter, but all he remembered was that it was a woman, and she was a redhead. Nothing else. No age, no weight, nothing. We figure the shooter was white, if she was a redhead, but shit, there're probably five thousand redheads downtown everyday.'

'Who's working it?'

'Sherrill and Black. I heard about it, first call, and ran over, took a quick look at the dead woman and then came over here with Baily and the paramedics.'

'So the dead woman's still over there.'

Swanson nodded. 'Yeah. She was way-dead. We didn't even think about bringing her in.'

'Okay . . . you say the doc's scrubbing?'

'Dan Wong, right down the hall. By the way, Baily says he was only shot once, but the docs say he's got two slugs in him.'

'So much for eyewitnesses,' Lucas said.

'Yeah. But it means that this chick is fast and accurate. The holes are a half-inch apart. Of course, she missed his heart.'

'If she was shooting for it. If it was a .22 . . . .'

'. . . that's what it looked like . . .'

'. . . then she might have been worried about punching through his breastbone.'

Swanson shook his head. 'Nobody's that good.'

'I hope not,' Lucas said.

Lucas brushed past a nurse who made a desultory effort to slow him down, and found Wong up to his elbows in green soap. Wong turned and said, 'Uh-oh, the cops.'

'How bad is it?' Lucas asked.

'Not too bad,' Wong said, going to work on his fingernails. 'He's gonna hurt for a while, but I've seen a hell of a lot worse. Two slugs – in the pictures, they look pretty deformed, so they were probably hollow-points. They went in at his right nipple, lodged under the right scapula. Two little holes, he hardly bled at all, though his body fat makes it a little hard to tell what's going on. His blood pressure's good. Looks like some goddamn gang-banger with a piece-of-crap .22'

'So he's gonna be okay?' Lucas could feel the tension backing off.

'Unless he has a heart attack or a stroke,' Wong said. 'He's way too fat and he was panicking when they brought him in. The surgery, I could do with my toes.'

'So what'll I tell the press? Wong is doing surgery with his toes?'

Wong shrugged as he rinsed: 'He's in surgery now, listed in guarded condition but he's expected to recover, barring complications.'

'You gonna talk to them afterwards?'

'I got a two o'clock tee-time at Wayzata,' Wong said. He flicked water off his hands and stepped away from the sink.

'You might have to skip it,' Lucas said.

'Bullshit. I don't get invited all that often.'

'Danny . .'

'I'll give them a few minutes,' Wong said. 'Now, if you'll get your germ-infested ass out of here, I'll go to work.'

Randall Thorn, the newly-promoted deputy chief for patrol, showed up ten minutes later. Fifteen cops stood around the emergency area now. The crowd was beginning to gather. 'I was all the way down by the goddamn airport,' he told Lucas. His uniform showed sweat rings under his armpits. 'How is he?'

Lucas briefed him quickly, then Sloan came over and said 'The chaplain's on his way to Baily's house. He oughta notify the old lady in the next five minutes or so.'

Lucas nodded and looked back at Thorn: 'Can you hold the fort here? I ran over because Rose Marie is gone and I knew you and Lester were out of the house. But he's sort of your guy.'

Thorn nodded: 'I'll take it. You going over to the scene?'

'For a minute or two,' Lucas said. 'I want to get a picture in my head.'

Thorn nodded and said, 'You know what picture I can't get in my head? Baily Dobbs getting shot. Last goddamn . . . '

'Guy in the world,' Lucas finished for him.

If the emergency room had seemed unnaturally calm, the Sixth Street parking ramp looked like a law-enforcement convention: a dozen homicide and uniform cops, medical examiner's personnel, a deputy mayor, the parking-garage manager and two possible witnesses were standing in the skyway-level elevator lobby and the stairwell above it.

Lucas nodded at one of the uniform cops controlling the traffic and he and Sloan poked their heads into the stairwell. Marcy Sherrill and Tom

Black were going through the victim's purse. The victim herself was lying on the stairs, at their feet. Her skirt was pulled up over her ample thighs, showing nude panty hose. One hand bent awkwardly away from her face – she might have broken her arm when she landed, Lucas thought – and her eyes were frozen half-open. A pool of blood coagulated under her still-perfect hair-do. Her face was vaguely familiar; she looked like she might have been a nice lady.

Sherrill turned and saw Lucas and said, shyly, 'Hi.'

'Hey,' Lucas said, nodding. He and Sherrill had ended a six-week romance: or as Sherrill put it, Forty Days and Forty Nights of Sex & Disputation. They were now in the awkward phase of no longer seeing each other while they were still working together. 'Looks nasty,' he added. The stairwell smelled of damp concrete overlaid with the coppery odor of blood and human intestinal gas, which was leaking out of the body.

Sherrill glanced down at the body and said, 'Gonna be a strange one.'

'Swanson said she was executed,' Sloan said.

'She was, big-time,' said Black. They all looked down at the body, arranged around their feet like a puddle. 'I can see seven entry wounds, but no exits. You don't need to be no forensic scientist to see that the gun was close – maybe an inch away.'

'Who is she?' Lucas said.

'Barbara Paine Allen. She's got a *notify* card in her purse, looks like her husband's a lawyer.'

'I know her face from somewhere, and the name rings a bell,' Lucas said. 'I think she might be *somebody*.'

Sherrill and Black both nodded and Sherrill muttered, 'Great.'

Lucas squatted next to the dead woman for a moment, looking at her head. The bullet wounds were small and tidy, as though she'd been repeatedly stabbed with a pencil. There were two wounds high on the back of her head, and a cluster of five in her temple. Her heart had kept pumping for a while after she landed; a thin stream of drying blood ran down from each of the holes. The seven thin streams were neatly defined, which meant that she hadn't moved after she hit the stairs. Professional, and very tidy, Lucas thought. He stood up and asked the other two, 'You got witnesses? Besides Baily?'

'Baily said the shooter was a red-headed woman, and we've got two people who say they saw a red-headed woman walking away from the scene close to the time of the shooting. No good description. She was wearing sunglasses, they said. Both of them said she was wiping her nose or sneezing into a handkerchief.'

'Covering her face,' Lucas said.

'I don't believe this shit,' Sloan said, looking down at Barbara Allen. 'People don't get hit.'

'Not in Minneapolis,' Sherrill said.

'Not by a pro,' said Black.

Lucas scratched his chin and said, 'But *she* did. I wonder why?'

'Are you buyin' in?' Sherrill asked. 'Could be an interesting trip.'

'Don't have the time,' Lucas said. 'I have the Otherness Commission.'

'Maybe if we find the shooter, we could get her to kill the commission.'

'They're not killable,' Lucas said gloomily. 'They come straight from hell.'

'We'll keep you updated,' Sherrill said.

'Do that.' Lucas shook his head, and looked back down at the cooling body. And he said, aloud, again, 'I wonder *why*?'

Chapter Three

Barbara Allen was killed a month to the day after Carmel Loan took out the contract on her. When word of the murder swept through the firm, Carmel immediately told herself that she had nothing to do with it. She'd made the arrangement so long ago that it hardly counted.

Carmel learned of the killing as she sat reading the deposition of a late-night dog-walker who claimed that he saw Rockwell Miller – her client – go into the back of his failing steak house with a five-gallon can of gasoline. The prosecution would argue that it was the same gas can found by the arson squad in the shambles of the restaurant's basement. The fire had been so hot that it had melted the fire extinguishers in the kitchen.

Carmel was looking for what she called a *peel*. If she could get her fingernails under some aspect of a story, or some aspect of a witness, she could peel the testimony back, and damage the witnesses' credibility. She'd begun to think that she could peel the dog-walker. He was divorced, and carried two convictions for domestic assault, which hurt any witness if there were enough women on the jury. She could get the women, all right. The problem was getting the assault conviction before the jury, since the average judge might mistakenly consider it irrelevant.

The dog-walker lived near the restaurant and knew the restaurant owner by sight. Had the dog-walker and his ex-wife ever eaten at the restaurant? Had they ever had an argument in the restaurant, when they were breaking up? Might the dog-walker have bad feelings about the restaurant, or its owner, even if they were unconscious?

It was all bullshit, but if she could implicitly ask, 'Can you believe the testimony of an admitted brutal wife-beater?' of twelve women good and true . . . That would be a definite peel.

She was dialing her client when her secretary stuck her head into Carmel's office, unannounced, and asked, 'Did you hear about Hale Allen's wife?'

Carmel's heart jumped into her throat, and she dropped the phone back on its base. 'No, what?' she asked. She was one of the top-three defense attorneys in the Twin Cities, and her face showed all the emotion of a woman who has been asked the outside temperature.

'She's been killed. Murdered.' The secretary couldn't quite keep the relish out of her voice. 'In a downtown parking garage. The police are saying it was a professional assassination. Like a mob hit.'

Carmel hushed her voice, while letting the natural interest show through. 'Barbara Allen?'

The secretary stepped in and let the door close behind her. 'Jane Roberts said the cops came and got Hale, and they rushed to the hospital, but it was too late. She was already dead.'

'Oh my God, the poor woman.' Carmel's hand went to her throat. And she thought: *I didn't do this.* And she also thought: *I was sitting right here, where everybody could see me.*

'We're thinking we should get some money together and send some flowers,' the secretary said.

'Do that. That's a good idea,' Carmel said. She found her purse beside her desk, and dug inside. 'I'll start it with a hundred.' She rolled the cash out on the desk. 'Is that enough?'

Late that afternoon, on the open-air balcony of her fabulous apartment, a gin-and-tonic in her hand, Carmel worried: gnawed a thumbnail, a bad habit she'd carried with her since grade school, chewing the nail down to the quick. For the first time since the infatuation with Hale Allen had begun, she stepped outside of herself, and looked back.

She'd often told her clients, those who were more-or-less professional criminals, that they could never think of all the possible ways to screw up a crime. However many ways you cover yourself, there's always some way that you are not covered.

Carmel had considered the possibility of killing Barbara Allen herself. She'd never killed anything before, but the thought didn't particularly bother her. She could pull the trigger, all right. But the devil was in the details, and there were too many details. How would she get a gun? If she bought one, there'd be a record of the purchase. She could use it and throw it away, but if the cops came asking for it, 'The dog ate it,' would be insufficient.

She could steal one, but she could get caught stealing it. And she'd have to steal it from one of two or three people she knew who had guns, and that might point a finger at her. She could try to come up with a fake ID – a crime in itself – but she was memorable enough that a gun-store clerk, asked later about the purchaser, might well remember her, especially if prompted by a photo.

Then there was the killing itself. She could do it. She could do anything she put her mind to. But, as she'd warned her clients, mistakes, accidents, or even random chance could ruin even the best-planned crime. With murder, in the state of Minnesota, a mistake, accident or random error meant spending thirty years in a non-fabulous room the size of a bathtub.

In the end, she'd decided the least risky way was to go with a pro. She had plenty of untraceable cash stashed in her bank deposit box, and she had Rolando D'Aquila, the connection. She also had a safety margin. Neither her connection nor the shooter could tell the cops about their involvement, because that would make them as guilty of first-degree murder as Carmel herself was. The shooter, even if she were eventually run down, would be eminently defensible in court: as a competent professional, she was unlikely to leave obvious clues, and would have no apparent previous connection with the victim.

So Carmel was probably safe; but after a few moments of reflection, drink in hand, she decided to stay away from Hale Allen for a while. Let him recover from the murder; let the cops talk to him – they would, of course. Since she'd never demonstrated her infatuation to Hale, there was no reason to think she'd become involved from that direction.

She was working out the various possibilities, her thumbnails red with blood, and raw, when Rinker called.

The line was Carmel's unlisted home-business number, and nobody called who didn't already know her. 'Yes?' she said, picking up the receiver.

'I need to get some money from you.' The woman on the other end had a dry, mid-south or Texas accent, the corners of words bitten off. But there was also an undertone of good humor.

'Are you okay?' Carmel asked.

'I'm just fine.'

'You make me a little nervous,' Carmel said. 'I'd prefer to see you in a public place.'

The woman chuckled, a pleasant, homey sound rattling down the phone line, and she said, 'You lawyers worry too much – and you ain't gonna see me, honey.'

'Maybe,' Carmel said. 'So how will we do it?'

'You have the money with you?'

'Yes, that's what Rolo said.'

'Good. Get in your Volvo, drive down to the University of Minnesota parking lot at Huron and Fourth Street. That's a big open lot, lots of students coming and going. There's a ticket-dispensing machine at the entrance. Park as far as you can from the pay booth, but park in a spot where there are other cars around you. Don't lock the driver's side door. Leave the money in a sack – one of those brown grocery sacks would be best – on the floor on the driver's side. Walk over to Washington Avenue . . . Do you know your way around over there?'

'Yes. I went to school there.' She'd spent seven years at the university.

'Good. Walk over to Washington, then walk down to the river. After you get to the River, it's up to you. Whenever you want, walk back to the car. I'll lock it when I leave it. And all the time, you'll be out in the open, in public. Safe.'

'What if somebody takes the money before you get there?'

Again, the pleasant chuckle: 'Nobody will take the money, Carmel.' The woman said 'CAR-mul,' while Carmel always pronounced it 'car-MEL.'

'When?'

'Right now.'

'How'd you know I have a Volvo?'

'I've been watching you off-and-on for a week or so. You drove it down to that Rainbow store the day before yesterday. I wouldn't have bought that sweet corn, myself; it looked a couple of days too old.'

'It was,' Carmel said. 'I'll be there in fifteen minutes.'

Carmel did exactly as Rinker asked, taking an extra few minutes in her walk along the Mississippi. When she got back to the car, the door was locked and the money was gone. She drove straight back to her apartment, and when she walked in, the phone was ringing.

'This is me,' the dry voice said.

'I hope everything went all right,' Carmel said.

'Went fine. I'm leaving town, but I wanted you to know that your credit is good. Do you have a pencil?'

'Yes.'

'If you ever need me again, call this number' – the woman recited a phone number with a 212 area code that Carmel recognized as downtown

Washington, D.C. – 'and leave a message on the voice mail that says, "Call Patricia Case." '

'Patricia Case.'

'Then I'll call you back within a day.'

'I don't think I'll ever need this.'

'Don't count on it; you lawyers have strange ways . . .'

'Okay. And thanks.'

'Thank *you*.' Click – and the dry voice was gone.

The phone rang again, before she had a chance to turn away.

'Carmel?' And for the second time that day, her heart was in her throat.

'Yes?'

'This is Hale.' Then, like she might not be able to sort out her Hales, he added, 'Allen.'

'Hale. My God, I heard about Barbara. How terrible.' She *leaned* into the telephone, vibrating with the urgency of the emotion. Tears started at the inner corners of her eyes. Poor Barbara. Poor Hale. A tragedy.

'Carmel . . . God, I don't know, I'm so screwed up,' Hale Allen said. 'Now the police think maybe I had something to do with it. The murder.'

'That's crazy,' Carmel said.

'Absolutely. They keep asking about how much money I'll inherit, and Barb's parents are saying all this crazy stuff . . .'

'That's terrible!' He needed help; and he was calling *her*.

'Look, what I'm calling to ask is, could you handle this for me? Could you deal with the police? You're the best I know . . .'

'Of course,' she said briskly. 'Where are you now?'

'I'm at home. I'm sitting here with all of Barb's stuff . . . I don't know what to do.'

'Sit right there,' Carmel said. 'I'll be there in half an hour. Don't talk to any more cops. If anyone calls, tell them to talk to me.'

'Won't that make them suspicious?' Not the sharpest knife.

'They already are suspicious, Hale. I know exactly where they're coming from. It's stupid, but that's the way they think. So give them my office number and this number, and do not, *do not*, talk to them.'

'Okay.' He sounded better already. 'Half an hour?'

Oh, God. The thing about Hale Allen, she thought, was his hands. He had these big, competent-looking hands with clean, square nails, and fine dark fuzz on the first joints of his fingers, a hint of the underlying masculinity. He had beautiful, thick hair, and wonderful shoulders, and his brown eyes were so expressive that when he concentrated on her, Carmel felt weak.

But it was the hands that did it. And did it one afternoon in a nice lawyer bar with lots of plants in copper kettles, and antique dressers used as serving tables. There'd been three or four of them sitting around a table, different firms, no agenda, just gossip. He'd been laughing, with those great white teeth, and he'd looked deep into her a few times, all the way, she felt, to the bottom of her panty hose. But the main thing was, he'd been drinking something light and white, a California Chardonnay, maybe, and he kept turning the wine glass in those strong fingers and Carmel had begun to vibrate. They'd been together two dozen times since, but always in social situations, and never too long.

She thought, though, that he must *know*, somewhere in his soul. Now with this call . . .

She took fifteen minutes with her makeup – making it invisible – and after applying the lightest touch of Chanel No. Seven, she went down to the parking garage and climbed into the Jaguar.

She forgot all about her resolution to stay away.

Hale Allen needed her.

Chapter Four

Lucas felt light: psychologically light. Nothing left to lose.

He hadn't spoken seriously with a woman since his break-up with Marcy Sherrill. And he felt good: he'd been working out, shooting some hoops, running through the neighborhood, though he could feel it in his knees if he did more than five miles. Age coming on . . .

Money in the bank. All bills paid. The job under control, except for the Cultural Commission. Even that had a calming effect on him. Like a boring concert, where the music never changed, the commission gave him three hours a week in which he had to sit still, his brain in neutral, his motor idling. He couldn't get away with sleeping during the meetings, but he'd managed to catch up on his reading.

Earlier in the year, before the Forty Days and Forty Nights, he'd felt himself on shaky ground, poised between sanity and another bout of depression. Marcy Sherrill had changed that, at least. He felt as good as he could remember, if somewhat detached, disengaged, floating. His oldest childhood friend, a nun who was also a professor at St. Anne's College, had gone on a summer mission to Guatemala, giving thanks for a successful recovery from a terrible beating; half of his friends were on vacation. Crime, improbably, was down across the board.

And it *was* summer: a good one.

Lucas had been working four days a week, spending the three-day weekends at his cabin in Wisconsin. Five years past, a Northwoods neighbor, a flat-nosed guy from Chicago, had stocked a pond with largemouth bass. Now the pond was getting good. Every morning, early morning, Lucas would walk a half-mile over to the Chicago guy's house, push an old green flat-bottomed john boat into the water, and throw poppers and streamer flies at the lily pads until the sun got high. The weight of the world dissolved in the mirror flashes of the smooth black water, the smell of the summer pollen, hot in the sun – the sun on his shoulders – and the stillness of the woods.

Barbara Allen had been killed on a Thursday. Lucas tucked the memory of her sightless, upside-down body into a large mental file stuffed with similar images, and closed the file. On Thursday night, he left for the cabin. He missed Friday's paper, but saw a *Pioneer Press* in a Hayward store window on Saturday morning: The main Page One story was headlined, 'Husband Questioned In Heiress Slaying.'

On Sunday, the *Star-Tribune's* front-page piece started under a headline that said, 'Allen Murder Baffles Police' while the *Pioneer Press* went with 'Allen Murder Puzzles Cops.' Lucas said to himself, 'Uh-oh.'

On Monday morning, he walked, whistling, into City Hall and bumped into Sherrill and Black. 'You were gonna keep me updated,' he said.

'That's right,' Black said, as they clustered in the hall. 'We were. Here's your update: we ain't got dick.'

'That's not entirely true,' Sherrill said, with an edge of impatience. 'There's a really *really* good chance that Hale Allen did it. Paid for it.'

'Well, good,' Lucas said, jingling his office keys. This was somebody else's job. 'Ship his ass out to Stillwater. I'll call ahead and reserve a cell.'

'I'm serious,' Sherrill said. 'We looked at him all weekend and we found out three things. One, the first thing he did after we talked to him is, he called Carmel Loan.'

'Ouch,' Lucas said. He knew Carmel. If you were a cop pushing a marginal case, or a difficult one, you didn't want Carmel on the other side.

'Which doesn't make him guilty of anything but common sense,' Black observed mildly.

'Second,' Sherrill said, 'He's gonna inherit something like thirty or forty million dollars, tax free. So much that we can't even find out how much it *is*. Her parents say the marriage was in trouble and the divorce was a possibility.'

'Nothing solid on the divorce?' Lucas asked. 'The way you said that . . .'

'Nothing solid,' Sherrill said grudgingly.

'The thing is, if Hale Allen is convicted of killing his wife, he can't inherit. The money would probably go to her parents, who don't need it, but would definitely like it,' Black said. 'Can't ever be too rich or too thin, as the Duchess of Windsor once told me, in a personal communication.'

'The money didn't come from them in the first place?' Lucas asked.

Black shook his head. 'Nope. The great-grandparents were timber barons here and land speculators in Florida. The money comes down through a whole bunch of trusts. It's hers. Her parents got theirs the same way. Hasn't one of them worked a day in their lives.'

'Third?' Lucas asked, looking at Sherrill. He added, 'The first two weren't so good.'

Sherrill said, 'Three, he's fuckin' a secretary in his firm. He's been doing it for a couple of years, and push was coming to shove. She was gonna go see the old lady, and tell her about the affair. Allen was stalling, but the hammer was comin' down.'

Lucas looked at Black. 'Now *that's* something.'

Black shrugged. 'Yeah. That's something.'

'Though they usually kill the girlfriend, not the wife,' Lucas said, going back to Sherrill.

Sherrill shrugged it off. 'Not always.'

'You look at the girlfriend?'

'Yeah. She was working when Barbara Allen was hit. Taking shorthand in a conference about some guy's will. She's got about six hundred and fifty dollars in her bank account, so we figure she probably didn't hire a pro.'

'Maybe she saw a movie,' Lucas said.

'Or read one of those *Murder for Dummies* books,' said Black.

'What about Allen? You hit him with the girlfriend?' Lucas asked.

'Not yet,' Sherrill said. She looked at her watch. 'We're gonna do it in about ten minutes.'

'By the way,' Black added, 'we should also update you on the Feebs.'

'The Feebs? Are they in this?' Lucas' eyebrows went up.

'Maybe. They want a meet, so we're walking over this afternoon,' Black said. 'Got some guy in from Washington.'

'The nation's capital,' Sherrill said.

'You wanna come?' Black asked. 'We could use some of that deputy-chief bullshit. That special shine.'

'They love you so much anyway,' Sherrill concluded.

'Give me a call,' Lucas said. 'I'll be around all afternoon.'

Carmel Loan, wearing bloody-red lipstick, arrived at City Hall to find Hale Allen sitting in the homicide office, across a grey metal desk from Black and Sherrill. The homicide office looked like a movie set for a small-town newspaper.

'Why are we here?' she asked, taking charge. She dropped her purse on Black's desk, pushing aside some of his papers; a calculated move – she was the important one here. 'I thought we covered everything on Friday. And when are you going to release Mrs. Allen? We need to make arrangements.'

'We'll release her as soon as the chemistry gets back, which should be this afternoon or tomorrow,' Black said. 'We're rushing it.'

'You know the sensitivity of the issue,' Carmel said, leaning into him. She had an effect on most men. Black was a not-quite-out-of-the-closet gay, and the effect was blunted.

'Of course,' Black said, with equanimity. 'We're doing everything we can.'

'So why're we here?' Carmel pulled a chair over from another desk, sat solidly in the middle of it, turned to Allen before Black or Sherrill could answer, and asked, 'How're you feeling?'

He shrugged. 'Not so good. I can't catch my breath. We need to get something going on the funeral.' He was absolutely gorgeous, Carmel thought. The weariness around his eyes added a depth he hadn't seemed to possess before; a certain fascinating sadness.

'So,' she said, turning to Sherrill. 'What?'

Sherrill leaned across the desk and asked Allen, 'Do you plan to marry Louise Clark?'

Allen sat back as though he'd been slapped. Carmel took one look at him, instantly understood the question, fought down a surge of insane anger, and blurted, 'Whoa. No more questions. Hale – out in the hall.'

When they were gone, Sherrill looked at Black and grinned: 'He didn't tell her.'

Carmel literally saw red, as though blood clots had drifted over her pupils. In the corridor outside Homicide, she grabbed Hale Allen by his coat lapel and shoved him against the wall. She was not a large woman, but she pushed hard, and Allen's shoulder blades were pressed against the stone.

'What the fuck are they telling me?' she hissed. 'Who is Louise Clark?'

'She's a secretary,' Allen mumbled. 'I've been . . . sleeping with her, I guess.'

'You guess?' Carmel demanded. 'You don't know for sure?'

'Yeah, I know, I should have told you,' Allen said. 'But I didn't think anybody would find out.'

'Jesus H. Christ, how dumb are you? How dumb? What else didn't you tell me? Are you fuckin' anybody else?'

'No, no, no, God, I hate that word. Fucking.'

Carmel closed her eyes for a moment: she couldn't believe this. She could believe that he was sleeping with another woman. She just couldn't believe that an actual lawyer could be this damn dumb.

'You have a law degree?' she asked, opening her eyes. 'From an actual college?'

'Carmel, I don't . . .'

'Ah, shut up,' she said. She turned away, took a couple of steps, then swung around to face him. 'I oughta quit. If I weren't a friend of yours and Barbara's, I *would* quit.'

'I'm sorry,' Allen stuttered. 'I've told you everything else, honest to God.'

Carmel let out a breath. 'All right. I can yell at you later. And I will. Now tell me about this Louise Clark. Are you gonna marry her?'

Allen shook his head: 'No, no, it was never like that. It was physical . . . She's really . . . into sex. She's a goddamn sex machine – what can I tell you? She kept hitting on me and finally one day we had a closing on a motel over in Little Canada and one of the rooms was unlocked . . .'

'Ah, man . . .' Carmel pressed the heel of her hand against her forehead. '*What?*'

'You've heard the word *motive*, right? It's a legal term, often used by lawyers?'

'I didn't know Barbara was gonna get murdered, for Christ's sake,' Allen said, his voice rising. A little angry now, flushing, tousled hair falling down over his forehead.

'All right, all right. Is it done with this woman?'

'If you say so,' Allen said.

'I say so,' Carmel said. 'But I've gotta talk to her.'

'All right. I'll call her.'

'We'll have to talk to the cops about it, sooner or later, but not right now. Maybe tomorrow.'

'How do we avoid it?'

'Gotta work 'em,' Carmel said. She chewed at her thumbnail, tasted blood, spit and chewed some more.

Carmel walked back into the Homicide office with Allen trailing behind. Black and Sherrill were still sitting at the desk, Black with his feet up.

31

Before Carmel could open her mouth, Sherrill asked, 'Wanna hear a horse-walks-into-a-bar joke?'

'Sure,' Carmel said.

'Horse walks into a bar, sits down, and in this sad voice, says, "Give me a bourbon, straight up." The bartender gets the drink, slides the glass across the bar and asks, "Hey fella – why the long face?" '

Carmel showed an eighth-inch of smile and said, her voice flat, 'That's fuckin' hilarious.'

'I don't get it,' said Allen, looking worried.

'Sit down,' Carmel said. To Black and Sherrill: 'My client tells me that he has had a sexual relationship with Louise Clark. He hadn't told me earlier because he assumed it wasn't relevant. He's right: it's not relevant. On the other hand, we can see how you might think it is. I've got to talk to him some more, and also to Louise Clark. If you don't leak any of this to the papers, we'll come back tomorrow and answer your questions. If you do leak it, then screw ya: we're done cooperating.'

'So come back,' Black said. 'Nobody's gonna hear about this from us.'

'Ten o'clock tomorrow morning,' Carmel said. 'I assume you've already talked to Louise Clark and suggested that she not talk to anybody about it. Including me.'

Sherrill nodded: 'Of course.'

'Of course,' Carmel said.

Sherrill called Lucas a little after three o'clock: 'We're going over to the bureau office, if you want to come.'

'Let's go,' Lucas said. He tossed the Equality Report on the floor. 'Let me get my jacket.'

The sunlight was blinding; another good day, Lucas thought, as he slipped on his sun glasses. A great day up north – a day to stretch out on a swimming float, listen to a ball game on a tinny transistor radio and let the world take care of itself.

'. . . thought she was gonna kill him,' Sherrill was saying.

Lucas caught up with the conversation. 'So Carmel didn't know?'

'No. She wasn't faking it, either. When we hit her with it, her eyes actually *bulged*,' Sherrill said happily. 'I didn't see what happened out in the hall, but when they came back in, he looked like a sheep that'd been shorn.'

'Huh . . . any vibe off the affair? Was he hiding it?'

Sherrill shrugged, but Black shook his head: 'I didn't get a goddamn thing. He looked surprised – like, surprised we'd even ask. He didn't look scared, he didn't look like he was covering . . .'

The heavily armed male white-shirt-and-tie receptionist rang them through into the FBI's inter sanctum, where they found a lightly sweating assistant agent-in-charge waiting in a conference room with a man who looked like an economics professor, a little harassed, a little unkempt, the lenses on his glasses a little too thick; on the other hand, he had a thick neck. He smiled pleasantly at Lucas, looked closely at Sherrill, and nodded at Black.

'I'm Louis Mallard,' he said, pronouncing it Louie. 'Mallard like the duck. You know Bill.' Bill Benson, the assistant AIC, nodded, said, 'Hey, Lucas.'

'What's going on?' Lucas asked.

'The Allen killing,' Mallard said. 'Anything at all?'

Lucas looked at Sherrill, who looked at Mallard and said, 'We're looking at her husband, a lawyer here.'

'Mafia connections?' Mallard asked, breaking in.

'No, nothing we've seen. You have information . . .?'

'Never heard of him,' Mallard said. 'Couldn't find any record of him at all, in our files – he never served in the military. Never even got a traffic ticket, as far as I can tell. A dull boy.'

'We've been looking at his wife, too,' Sherrill said, 'Trying to figure out something in her background that might get the attention of a pro, if this was a pro . . .'

'It was,' Mallard said.

'What . . .?'

'Go ahead with what you were going to say about the wife.' He had a precise way of speaking, just *like* an economics professor.

'We've been looking at her,' Black said, picking up for Sherrill. 'We've had some of our business guys looking over her assets, but there's nothing there. Her money's been managed for decades. No big losses, no big gains, just a nice steady eleven percent per year. No changes. We looked at this charity she works with, too. Her grandfather set it up, and she and her parents are on the board, with some other relatives. But it's mostly taking care of old folks. We can give you all the stuff, if you want it, but we don't see anything.'

Mallard looked at Lucas, then at Benson, the assistant AIC, then said, 'Goddamnit,' in a professorial way.

'Tell us,' Lucas said.

'The woman who did it is a pro,' Mallard said. 'She's not very tall – maybe five-three or five-four. She once lived in St. Louis, or the St. Louis area. She might have a southern accent. She became active about twelve or thirteen years ago, and we think she's killed twenty-seven people, including your Mrs. Allen. We think she's got some tie with some element – maybe just a single person – in the St. Louis Mafia crowd. And that's what we got. We would *really* like to get more.'

'Twenty-seven,' Lucas said, impressed.

'Could be more, if she's taken the time to get rid of some of the bodies, or if it took her a while to develop her signature – the silenced pistols, close up. But we're sure it's at least twenty-seven. She does good research, gets the victim alone, kills them and vanishes. We think she does her research to the point where she picks out the precise spot for the murder, in advance . . .'

'How would you know that?' Black asked.

'Because the caliber of the pistol is always appropriate for the spot. If it's out in the open, it's usually nine millimeter or a .40. If it's enclosed with concrete, like it was here, and a few other places, it's always a .22 – you don't want to be in a concrete stairwell with nine millimeter fragments flying around like bees. She uses standard-velocity .22 hollow points which turn the brain into oatmeal but stay inside the skull, for the most part.'

'That's it? That's what you've got?' Black asked.

'Not quite. We think she *drives* to the city where the hit takes place. We've torn passenger manifests apart for the airlines, all around the suspect killings, looking for anything that might be a pattern.'

'And nothing,' Black said.

'Oh, no. We found patterns,' Mallard said. 'All kinds of patterns. We just didn't find *her* pattern. We've looked at several hundred people, and we've got nothing.'

'She always works for pay?' Sherrill asked.

'We don't know what she works for. Some of the hits have been internal Mafia business – but some of them, maybe half, look like straight commercial deals. We just don't know. Twenty-seven murders, and there's never been a conviction,' Mallard said. 'There have been a couple of situations in which wives were killed, and we suspect the husband was involved, but there's nothing to go on. Nothing. In none of the cases was it even remotely possible that the husbands were present for the killing: they were always in some well-documented other place.'

'Can we get your files on her?'

'That's what I'm here for,' Mallard said. He reached into his coat pocket and took out a square cardboard envelope, and slid it across the table at Sherrill. 'Duplicate CDs: everything we've got on every case where she's been involved. Names, dates, techniques, suspects, photographs of everybody and all the crime scenes. The first file is an index.'

'Thanks.'

'Anything you get,' Mallard said. 'No matter how thin it is, *please* call me. I *want* this woman.'

Louise Clark decided that she could talk to Carmel only after Hale Allen convinced her it was okay. 'I'm a *lawyer*, Louise,' Allen said. 'It's *all right* to talk to Carmel – the cops are just busting our balls.'

'If you're sure,' Clark said anxiously. She was a thin, mousy woman with lank brown hair, a fleshy nose, and nervous, bony hands. 'It's just that the police said . . .'

Clark did not look like any sex machine Carmel had ever seen; but, she thought to herself, *you never know*. 'He's sure,' Carmel said abruptly. They were sitting in Denny's, and had been talking for ten minutes and the woman had started whining. Carmel didn't like whiners. She looked at Hale Allen. 'Why don't you take a walk around the block? I want to talk to Louise alone.'

So Hale Allen went for a walk, his hands in the pockets of his light woolen slacks, wearing a great blue-checked sportcoat over a black t-shirt. The coat emphasized the breadth of his shoulders, and both women watched him as he held the door for a woman coming into the restaurant with a child; the woman said something to Allen, who gave her the great grin, and they had a little conversation in the doorway.

After a few seconds, Allen continued on his way; and Carmel and Louise had their talk.

Carmel had a king-sized bed with two regular pillows and a five-foot-long body-pillow that she could wrap her legs around when she slept. Although she told people that she slept nude – all part of the image – she actually slept in an extra-large Jockey t-shirt and boxer shorts. With the shirt loose around her shoulders and her legs wrapped around the pillow, she lay in bed that night and re-ran mousy Louise Clark.

For the most part, Clark's story was the same ol' story. She and Allen spent time alone, in their work. They shared a lot of stress. His wife didn't understand him. They developed a relationship based on mutual respect, bla-bla-bla-bla. They fell into bed at the Up North Motel. Then the Mouse stuck it to Carmel.

'The first time I saw him naked in the motel there, it was afterwards. Really, after we made love, he was just so . . . beautiful. He's a beautiful man.' Then her eyes flickered, and she added, girl-to-girl, a little giggle, a half-whisper, 'And he's really large. Beautiful and really, really, large. He filled me up.'

Carmel squeezed the pillow between her legs and tried to squeeze the image out of her head. Hale Allen and the Mouse. Large.

The alarm went off at seven o'clock sharp. Carmel pushed out of bed, slow and grumpy, robbed of her usual sound sleep. Large? How large? She scratched her ass, yawned, stretched and headed for the bathroom. A half-hour later, she was drinking her first cup of coffee, eating her second piece of toast, and checking the *Star-Tribune* for leaks about Allen and Clark, when the phone rang.

'Yes.'

'Miz Loan? This is Bill, downstairs.' Bill was the doorman.

'What?' Still grumpy.

'We got a package for you, says Urgent. I was wondering if we should bring it up.'

'What kind of package?'

'Small one. Feels like . . . looks like . . . could be a video tape,' Bill said.

'All right, bring it up.'

Bill brought it up, and Carmel gave him a five-dollar bill and turned the package in her hand as she closed the door. Bill was right: probably a video. Plain brown wrapping paper. She pulled the paper off, found a note written with a ballpoint pen on notebook paper. All it said was, 'Sorry.'

Carmel frowned, walked the tape to the media room, plugged it into the VHS player, and brought it up.

A woman's image came up, and Carmel recognized it immediately. She was looking at herself, sitting in the now-understandably bright light of Rolando's kitchen, just a little more than a month ago.

The on-screen Carmel was saying, 'Only kind I drink.' And then, 'So you made the call.'

A man's voice off-camera said, 'Yes. And she's still working, and she'll take the job.'

'She? It's a woman?'

'Yeah. I was surprised myself. I never asked, you know, I only knew who to call. But when I asked, my friend said, "She." '

'She's gotta be good,' the on-screen Carmel said. The off-screen Carmel decided that the camera must have been in the cupboard, shooting through a partly open door.

'She's good. She has a reputation. Never misses,' the man's voice said. 'Very efficient, very fast. Always from very close range, so there's no mistake.' A man's hand appeared in the picture, with a mug of coffee. Carmel watched her on-screen self as she turned it with her fingertips, then picked it up.

'That's what I need,' she said on-screen, and she took a sip of the coffee. Carmel remembered that it had been pretty good coffee. Very hot.

'You're sure about this?' asked the man's voice. 'Once I tell them "Yes," it'll be hard to stop. This woman, the way she moves, nobody knows where she is, or what name she's using. If you say, "Yes," she kills Barbara Allen.'

The on-screen Carmel frowned. 'I'm sure,' she said. The off-screen Carmel winced at the sound of Barbara Allen's name. She'd forgotten that.

'You've got the money?' the man asked.

'At the house. I brought your ten.'

The on-screen Carmel put the mug down, dug in her purse, pulled out a thin deck of currency and laid it on the table. The man's hand reached into the picture and picked it up. 'I'll tell you this,' the voice said. 'When they come and ask for it, pay every penny. *Every penny*. Don't argue, just pay. If you don't, they won't try to collect. They'll make an example out of you.'

'I know how it works,' on-screen Carmel said. 'They'll get it. And nobody'll be able to trace it, because I've had it stashed. It's absolutely clean.'

'Then if you say "Yes," I'll call them tonight. And they'll kill Barbara Allen.'

Carmel, off-screen, had to admire her on-screen performance. She never flinched, she just stood up and said, 'Yes. Do it.'

The tape skipped a bit, then focused on a black telephone. 'I'm really sorry about this, but you know about my problem. I'm gonna have to have twenty-five thousand, like, tomorrow,' the man's voice said. 'I'll call and tell you where.'

The tape ended. Carmel took a long pull on her coffee, walked into the kitchen, poured the last couple of ounces into the sink, and then hurled the cup at one of the huge plate-glass windows that looked out on her balcony. The cup bounced, without breaking. Carmel didn't see it; she was ricocheting around the kitchen, sweeping glasses, dishes, the knife block, a toaster, silverware, off the cupboards and tables and stove and onto the floor, kicking them as they landed, scattering them; and all the time she growled through clenched teeth, not a scream, but a harsh humming sound, like a hundred-pound hornet.

She trashed the kitchen and then the breakfast area; and finally cut herself on a broken glass. The sight of the blood flowing from the back of her hand brought her back.

'Fuckin' Rolo,' she said. She bled on the floor. 'Fuckin' Rolo, fuckin' Rolo, fuckin' Rolo . . .'

Chapter Five

For the rest of the evening, Carmel worked her way through alternate rages and periods of calm; fantasized the painful end of Rolando D'Aquila. And finally admitted to herself that she was in a corner.

She called Rinker, left a number and said, 'This is really urgent. We've got a big problem.'

The next day, a little after one o'clock in the afternoon, Rinker called on Carmel's magic cell phone. She didn't introduce herself, she simply said in her dry accent, 'I'm calling you back. I hate problems.'

Carmel said, 'Hold on: I want to lock my door.' She stuck her head out into the reception area, said to the secretary, 'I need ten minutes alone,' stepped back inside and locked the door.

'All right . . .' she began, but Rinker cut her off.

'Is your phone safe?'

'Yes. It's registered under my mother's name – she's remarried, and has a different last name. Like the Volvo. It's good for . . . special contacts.'

'You have a lot of those in your job?'

'Enough,' Carmel said. 'Anyway, I'm calling about Rolando D'Aquila, who is the guy who put me in touch with you.'

'What happened?' Rinker asked.

Carmel explained, quickly, then said, 'I would have thought the people on your side would have been warned against this. You push somebody into a corner . . .'

'What? What would you do?' Carmel could feel the warning edge on the other woman's voice.

'I'm sure as hell not going to turn you in, or talk to the police, if that's what you're worried about,' Carmel said, defensively. 'But there has to be some kind of resolution. Rolo's a junkie. If I give him every dime I've got, he'll put it up his nose. When he's got every dime, he'll still have the tape, and he'll start looking around for somebody to sell it to. Like TV. Then I'm gone – and you, too. The cops will put Rolo through the wringer before they give him any kind of immunity, and you can't tell what'll come from that.'

'Maybe nothing,' Rinker said. 'He's off there on the edge of things.'

'Bullshit. Sooner or later, he'll give them the guy he called about you,' Carmel argued. 'Then they'll squeeze that guy. You know how it works. This is murder we're talking about; this is thirty years in the state penitentiary for everybody involved. That's a lot of squeeze. And believe me, I'm well enough known in the Cities that there'd be a hurricane of shit if this got out. This is not something the cops would let go.'

'When are you paying him off? This Rolo guy?' Rinker asked.

'I'm supposed to meet him in the Crystal Court tomorrow at five o'clock. I put him off as long as I could, told him it'll take time to get the money together. The Crystal Court is this big interior court . . .'

'I was there,' Rinker said.

'Okay. Anyway, I give him the money, and he gives me the tape. I insisted that he show up, personally. But the best he'll do is give me a copy of the tape. He says there's only one, but he's lying. He'll want to come back for more money.'

'You're sure about that?'

'He's a fuckin' dope dealer, for Christ's sakes.'

After a couple of seconds silence, Rinker said, 'There's a flight into Minneapolis tomorrow morning. I can be there at eleven thirty-five.'

'I don't know . . .' Carmel started. Then, in a rush, 'I don't know if I want to see your face. I'm afraid you'll have to kill me.'

'Honey, there're a couple of dozen people who know my face,' Rinker said. 'One more won't make any difference, especially when I know she paid me for a hit. I'd rather you *not* see me, but we've got to fix this thing. You're gonna have to help.'

Carmel didn't hesitate: 'I know that.'

'The thing is, we're gonna have to *talk* to him about where the tape is,' Rinker said.

'Yes. Talk to him privately,' Carmel said. 'I'd figured that out.'

'That's right . . . Why'd you insist that he meet you in person?'

'Because I thought you might want in . . . at that point,' Carmel said.

Rinker chuckled: 'All right. You ever kill anybody?'

'No.'

'You might be good at it. With a little training.'

'Probably,' Carmel said. 'But it doesn't pay enough.'

Rinker chuckled again and said, 'See you at eleven fifty-five. Bring the Jag. And wear jeans and walking shoes.'

* * *

Carmel hadn't known what to expect. A tough-looking, square-faced hillbilly with bony wrists and shoulders, maybe – or somebody beefy, who might have been a prison guard at Auschwitz. The next day, at noon, she looked right past the first passengers getting off the plane from Kansas City, looking for somebody who fit the assorted images she'd created in her mind. When Rinker's voice came out of a well-dressed young woman with carefully-coiffed blonde-over-blonde hair and just a slight aristocratic touch of lipstick, Carmel jumped, startled. The woman was carrying a leather backpack, and was right at Carmel's elbow.

'Hello?'

'What?'

Rinker grinned up at her. 'Looking for somebody else?'

Carmen wagged her head once and said, 'It's you?'

'It's me, honey. I checked a bag.'

As they started up the concourse, Carmel said, 'God, you really don't look like . . . you.'

'Well, what can I tell you?' Rinker said cheerfully. She looked past Carmel to her right, where a tall, tanned man was angling across the concourse to intercept them. 'Carmel,' he said, dragging out the last syllable.

'James.' Carmel turned a cheek to be kissed and, after James kissed it, asked, 'Where're you off to?'

'Los Angeles . . . My God, you look like an athlete. I never suspected you had jeans or Nikes.' The guy was at least six-six and looked good, with a receding hairline; like an athletic Adlai Stevenson. He turned to Rinker and said, 'And you're cute as a button. I hope you're not a raving left-wing feminist like Carmel.'

'I sometimes am,' Rinker said. 'But you're cute as a button your own self.'

The guy put one hand over his heart and said, 'Oh my God, the accent. I think we should get married.'

'You've been married too often already, James,' Carmel said drily. She took Rinker's arm and said, 'If we don't keep moving, he'll drown us in bullshit.'

'Carmel . . .'

Then they were past him and Rinker glanced back and said, 'Nice-looking guy. What does he do?'

41

'He's an accountant,' Carmel said.

'Hmm,' Rinker said. Carmel caught the tone of disappointment.

'But not a boring one,' Carmel said. 'He stole almost four million dollars from a computer-software company here.'

'Jesus.' Rinker glanced back again. 'They caught him?'

'They narrowed it down to him – they figured out that he was the only one who could have pulled it off,' Carmel said. 'He hired me to defend him, but he never seemed particularly worried. Eventually, the company came around and said if he gave the money back, they'd drop charges. He said that if they dropped charges, and apologized for the mistake, he'd tell them about the software glitch that they might want to patch up before their clients started getting ripped off, and they found themselves liable for a billion bucks or something.'

'They did it?'

'Took them a week to agree,' Carmel said. 'They hated to apologize – hated it. But they did it. Then he insisted on a contract that would pay him another half-million for isolating the bug. Said it was severance pay, and he deserved it. They eventually did that, too. I guess they got their money's worth.'

Rinker shook her head: 'Don't people just *work* for money anymore?'

Carmel didn't want to think about that question. Instead, she said, 'Um, listen, what do I call you?'

'Pamela Stone,' Rinker said. 'By the way, do you know how to get to South Washington County Park?'

'No, I don't think so.'

'I'll show you on a map,' Rinker said. 'We gotta get my guns back. Can't fly with them, you know.'

Carmel kept *looking* at Rinker as they headed out of the airport to the parking ramp; looking for some sign that she could be an executioner for the mob. But Rinker wasn't a monster. She was a *chick*, chattering away about the flight, about an airline-magazine article on body piercing, and about the Jaguar, as they pulled through the pay booths: 'I drive a Chevy, myself.'

Carmel listened for a while and then Rinker put a hand on Carmel's forearm and said, 'Carmel, you've gotta relax. You're tighter'n a drum. You look like you're gonna explode.'

'That's because I don't want to spend the next thirty years locked in a closet like some fuckin' squirrel,' Carmel said.

'They're locking squirrels in closets now?' Rinker asked.

Carmel had to smile, despite herself, and loosened her grip on the steering wheel. 'You know what I mean.'

'Ain't gonna happen anyway,' Rinker said. 'We'll get this Rolo fellow in a quiet place, explain the situation to him, and get the tape.'

'And kill him?'

Rinker shrugged. 'Maybe he's made three or four copies. If he tells us about two of them, and the third one is hidden somewhere . . . maybe if he's gone, it'll never be found.'

'We can't take the chance that there's the third one. We have to make sure we can get them all before we do it. Kill him.'

'We'll scare him,' Rinker said. 'I can guarantee that. But there's no way we can finally be sure . . .'

'How'll we do it?'

'Leave it to me. I'll pick him up with you, tag him, and when he's alone, I'll take him. Is there a farm store around here? Or a truck store? Or a big hardware place?'

'Yeah, I suppose.'

'We're gonna need some chain and a couple of padlocks and some other stuff . . .'

South Washington County Park was twenty miles south of St. Paul, a complex of hiking and skiing trails. Only two cars were parked in the entry lot, but their drivers were nowhere to be seen.

'Park down at the end,' Rinker said, pointing. Carmel parked, and they got out. Rinker, carrying her leather backpack, led the way down a trail along a tiny creek, then up a hillside covered with thick-trunked oaks. At the top of the hill, she took a long look around, then led the way off the trail, back into the trees. After a minute, they came to a fence separating the park from a farm field. Rinker turned down the fence, finally said, 'Here.'

She stepped away from the fence, knelt next to an oak, and probed between two of its roots. The dirt was soft, and came away easily. After a minute, she pulled two automatic pistols from the ground, the dirt still clinging to them.

At that moment, Carmel was aware that she was out of sight of everyone, in a nearly deserted park, with a killer who now had two guns.

43

If Rinker killed her, here and now, who would know, until some hiker *way* off the beaten path found her body? Rinker could take the Jag and park it downtown. Or who was to say that she hadn't somehow pre-positioned one of those cars in the parking lot down below?

The whole scenario flitted through Carmel's mind in a half-second. Rinker brushed dirt off the two pistols, put them in her leather backpack, and said, 'You worry too much.'

'I anticipate,' Carmel said.

'Why didn't you anticipate that Rolo was making a movie?' Rinker asked politely.

Carmel didn't dodge the question. She grimaced and said, 'I fucked up. I knew something wasn't right. I remember thinking that he wasn't embarrassed by the fact that he was living in a shit-hole, after years of being a big-time dealer. Wasn't embarrassed. That was wrong.'

'At least you know you messed up,' Rinker said. The guns clinked in the bag as she hung it over one shoulder. 'We need to get some oil. When we get the chains and padlocks. Oil for the guns.'

'Doesn't burying them . . . sort of wreck them?'

'Yeah, it would if I left them buried for more than a couple of days. In a week they'd be rusted wrecks. Then, even if somebody found them, there'd be no way to connect them to the death of Barbara Allen.'

'So you were just going to leave them.'

'Sure. You can get them for a couple hundred bucks apiece. I just didn't have time to deal with the airlines and all that.' Rinker glanced at her watch. 'Four hours to Rolo,' she said. 'We'd better get back to town.'

The Crystal Court is the interior courtyard of the tallest glass tower in Minneapolis, a crossroads of the Minneapolis Skyway system. Carmel met Rolo on the ground floor: she was furiously angry, which Rinker said was perfect. 'If you weren't pissed, he'd be suspicious. The madder you are, the better.'

'I can fake it if I have to, but I don't think I'll have to,' Carmel said. 'I hate this: being extorted, somebody else squeezing you like this, and you're powerless.' She ground her teeth, felt control slipping away; held on tight.

'Not powerless,' Rinker said. 'Just the appearance of it . . .'

'But he has to think I am. The goddamn humiliation, that cocksucker . . .'

There was nothing faked about her anger when Rolo showed up, carrying the videotape in a brown beer sack from a convenience store. She was carrying the money in a cloth book-bag.

'You fuck,' Carmel hissed at him. 'You piece of shit. I should have let you go down for life, you fuckin' greaseball.'

Rolo took it calmly enough: 'Just give me the money, Carmel. I got your little movie right here, and we're all done.'

'We'd better be all done,' Carmel snarled. A white-haired man in a golf shirt glanced at her face as she passed, and it occurred to her that she probably looked like a cornered wolf, her face twisted with hate, anger and maybe fear. She took a breath, straightened up, tried to pull herself together.

'Give me the tape,' she said.

'Give me the money first.'

'For Christ's sakes, Rolo, I can hardly grab it and run, can I? If a cop gets involved, I'm dead meat.'

Rolo thought about it for a minute, then said, 'Let me see the money.'

Carmel pulled open the top of the bag, let him look in. He nodded, grudgingly, and handed her the sack. She looked inside, saw the tape, shook her head and said, 'You fuck,' and he said, 'The money, Carmel,' and she handed him the bag.

'You'd better not be back,' Carmel said. 'I couldn't handle that.'

'Check the tape,' Rolo said, stepped into a stream of traffic, followed it to an escalator, and went up. A minute later, he was gone. The Crystal Court was five minutes from her apartment. Carmel had walked, because parking would have taken as long as walking, and now she hurried back, jay-walking when she caught a red light, wondering what was happening with Rinker.

Rolando D'Aquila had parked his broken-down piece-of-shit Dodge on the third floor of the Sixth Street parking ramp, the same ramp where Barbara Allen had been shot. Rinker was pleased: the situation had a nice symmetry, and she knew the ramp well, because of her previous scouting. Carrying her big green Dayton's Department Store bag, she'd stayed well behind Rolo in the Skyways, blending with the crowd of heading-home shoppers and white-collar office workers. When she realized where they were going, she closed up, and when they pushed through the Skyway door into the ramp, was a dozen steps behind, with two other people between them.

She followed Rolo down the ramp, making no effort to hide, but keeping a grey-suited man with a briefcase between them. Then grey suit turned off toward a black Buick, and she and Rolo continued on, single file. Rolo glanced back at her once, barely seeing her, and as he did, she glanced at her watch and looked diagonally past him, as if heading for a car at the end of the floor. But when Rolo turned off to the brown-shoe-colored Dodge, she was only two steps behind him. He didn't even notice until she was a foot away. Then he turned, key in his hand, and before he could open his mouth, Rinker took the last step and the muzzle of the pistol came up from the shopping bag she was carrying and she said, 'If you make one fuckin' noise, I will shoot you in the fuckin' heart. If you think about it, you will know who I am. And you'll know that I'll do it.'

Rolo stood stock-still for a long beat, then said, quietly, 'You can have the money back.'

'We'll take the money back, but we've got to talk for a while, you and Carmel and I.'

'Just take the money.'

'We're gonna get in the car, Rolo, and I'm gonna slide across the seat and you're gonna stand there, by the door, and if you make a noise, or make a move to run, I'm going to shoot you.'

'I don't think so,' Rolo said, trying to recover. 'There are too many people around.'

She shot him in the left leg. The little silenced .22 made a sound like a clapping hand, and Rolo's leg dipped and he slumped against the car, his eyes wide.

'You shot me,' he said, his voice almost a whisper. He clasped the money bag under one arm; his free hand felt down his left leg, and came away to his face, scarlet with blood; and he could feel more blood trickling down his leg.

Rinker glanced around: Two other people walking down the ramp, neither one paying attention to the two of them. The gun itself was below the level of the cars, where it couldn't be seen. 'Open the car door, Rolo,' she said quietly; but the quiet tone carried the menace of death. 'Or the next one goes right in your eye.'

The black hole on the end of the pistol came up, and D' Aquila was seized with the sudden conviction that he could see the head of the bullet that lay down its maw. He fumbled the key into the car lock, opened the door.

'Stand still,' Rinker said. She stepped close to him, so close that they might have been lovers sharing a car-side kiss before heading home, and she pushed the muzzle of the .22 under his breastbone and said, 'I'm going to get in. If you make a noise or try to run, I'll kill you. Do you understand that?'

'You'll kill me if I get in the car.'

Rinker shook her head. 'No. We can't be sure about the tape – how many copies you've made. But we figure you've got at least one, and we want that one. After that, you're on warning: if a third tape ever shows up, we're gonna kill you, no questions. But we want to make that clear to you.'

'My leg's killing me.'

'No, it's not. But I might be. Follow me into the car,' Rinker said. She sat down, the end of the muzzle never leaving his breastbone. She slid across the seat, and Rolo followed. 'Drive,' she said.

'Where're we going?'

'Home,' Rinker said. 'Your place.'

Carmel found them sitting in the front room, Rolo in an easy chair with a ripped sheet wrapped tightly around his left leg. Rinker was on a couch, her pistols held carefully across her lap. Carmel noticed that the pistols now had silencers attached to their muzzles. 'I had to shoot him a little,' Rinker said, her voice flat, uninflected, as though shooting Rolo was nothing at all. 'Did you look at the tape?'

'Yeah, I looked at the tape,' Carmel said. She was carrying her handbag and a sack from a hardware store, which clanked when she dropped it by her foot. 'It starts out with him telling me that it was only a copy, that he has another, and that he needs a little more money.'

'I'll give you the tape,' Rolo said. 'Just get me to the hospital.'

Carmel pulled a chair up and sat in front of his and said, 'Look at me, Rolo. How many tapes did you make?'

'Just two,' he said. 'Honest to God, I was gonna give you the only one, but then I got to thinking . . . so I made another one. Why would I make any more? As long as I got the original, I can make as many as I want.'

'Where is it? The second one?'

'Not here,' he said. 'I put it in my safe-deposit box. I figured if anything like this happened, you couldn't kill me. You'd have to take me to the bank.'

'You put it in a safe-deposit box?' Carmel asked.

'Yeah, at US Bank.'

'Look at me, Rolo.'

He looked at her, his eyes clear and honest.

'Where are the keys to the safe-deposit box?'

'Well, I . . . gave them to a friend to hold, this chick I know . . .'

'Oh, bullshit, Rolo.' Carmel looked at Rinker. 'He's lying.'

'I'm not lying,' Rolo protested. 'Look, I can call my friend . .'

She turned back to him. 'Yeah, you are. You wouldn't give the keys to anyone, you'd hide them someplace.'

'I'm not lying,' Rolo protested. 'Look, I can call my friend . . .'

'What's her name?' Carmel asked. 'Quick . . .'

Rolo's eyes went sideways and he stumbled over a couple of syllables. 'Um,m,m, Mary,' he said.

'Would that be the Virgin Mary?' Carmel asked sarcastically. To Rinker: 'He's lying.'

'Should I shoot him again? A little more this time?'

Carmel looked at Rolo for a moment, pulled on her lower lip, then shook her head slowly. 'Nope. I think we should just chain him up . . .' She touched the hardware store bag with her foot. '. . . See about this Mary. Tear the house apart. See if we find any safe deposit keys.'

'I don't think there is one,' Rinker said. 'I think I should shoot him again.'

'Jesus Christ,' Rolo said, listening to the argument.

'Let's just get him on the bed, so we don't have to watch him every minute, and try to work this out,' Carmel said to Rinker. She touched the bag again, with her foot, and looked at Rolo. 'We're gonna chain you to your bed and tear this place apart. Either that, or Pamela's gonna shoot you again, and *then* we're gonna tear this place apart. Are you gonna give us a hard time?'

'You're gonna kill me,' he said.

'Not if we don't have to,' Carmel said.

'You're both fuckin' crazy.'

'Which you should keep in mind.'

'Into the bedroom,' Rinker said, gesturing with the muzzle of the gun.

'My leg is killing me,' Rolo said.

Rinker dropped the muzzle toward his other leg and Rolo lurched forward, said, 'I'm going, for Christ's sake, I'm going.'

Rinker moved with him, just behind him, the gun pointed at his spine. 'Just stretch out on the bed,' she said, when they got to the bedroom door. 'No problems . . .'

They'd gotten a package of lightweight chain at the hardware store, the kind used for children's swings; a roll of duct tape at a pharmacy; and four keyed padlocks and two pair of yellow plastic kitchen gloves at a K-Mart. While Rinker leaned on the end of the bed, the gun ready, Carmel took a couple of turns of chain around Rolo's neck, wrapped the chain around the end of the bed and snapped on a lock. 'And his feet,' she said. She did his feet the same way.

'His arms,' Rinker said.

'Hmm,' Carmel said, looking at him, Finally she took a tight wrap of chain around one of his wrists, snapped on a padlock, leaned over the side of the bed, threw the chain beneath it, fished it out from the opposite side, took a wrap around Rolo's other wrist, and snapped on the last padlock. 'That's it for the chain,' Carmel said. She went back to the sack for the duct tape.

'What're you going to do with that?' Rolo asked.

'Tape up your mouth,' Carmel said.

Rolo thrashed a little against the chain, but it cut into his neck and he stopped and looked up at Carmel. 'Don't hurt me,' he said, his voice suddenly quiet.

'How many copies?' Carmel asked.

'Just the one,' Rolo said.

'And it's in your safety deposit box?'

'That's right. I'll get it for you.'

'Shut up,' Carmel said. She pulled off two feet of duct tape and wrapped it around his head, taping up his mouth.

Carmel and Rinker spent an hour ripping through the little house, working in the yellow plastic gloves. They dumped cupboards, closets, and dressers, looked through the small, dank, empty basement, poking their heads up into cobwebs and bug nests; they probed the equally empty ceiling crawl-space, which was stuffed with pink fiberglass insulation that stuck to their skin and tangled their hair. They dumped all the ice-cube trays out of the refrigerator, dumped all the boxes in the cupboard, looked in the toilet tank, ripped the covers off all the electric outlets. They found a half-dozen tapes under the television, but their labels said they were pornographic, and when they pushed them into Rolo's cheap VCR, pornography was what they got. They found two address books; checked his billfold and found more phone numbers. The video camera was on the floor of a closet: Rinker opened it, said, 'Empty,' and tossed it on the wooden floor, where it hit hard, and rolled. They also found a few tools, a lot of clothing, and odd bits of cheap jewelry.

They checked Rolo every few minutes. The chains immobilized him, and though he grunted at them, they ignored him and went back to pulling the house apart. After an hour, it had become obvious that they weren't going to find the tape.

'It might still be here,' Rinker said finally, after she'd torn out the under-seat lining of the couch and chair. 'We can't look everyplace – we'd need a wrecking ball.'

Carmel was in the bedroom doorway, looking at Rolo.

Finally, she walked around and ripped the tape off his mouth. He sputtered, and she said, 'Last chance, Rolo; tell me where the fuck it is.'

'In the bank,' he snarled. He'd won, he thought.

'Fuck you.' Carmel got the roll of tape and reached forward to slap it over his mouth, but he turned his head away. 'Turn your head this way,' she said.

'Hey, fuck *you*,' he said; and there was a tone in the way he said it.

'He's just achin' to be shot a little more,' Rinker said from the doorway.

'You'll kill me if you shoot me a little more,' Rolo said. 'I'm still bleeding from my leg. And if you kill me, the cops are going to open the safety deposit box . . . Hey!'

He said Hey! because Carmel had crawled on top of him. She sat on his chest, grabbed his head by the hair and pulled forward, hard, until he was choking on the chain. He thrashed some more, but had started making gargling sounds when she let his head drop. 'Keep your head straight,' she said, as he took a half-dozen rasping breaths. 'You fuckin' . . .'

He kept his head straight and she took a half-dozen wraps of duct tape across his mouth. 'Now what?' Rinker asked, as Carmel crawled off him.

'I'm very good at cross-examination,' Carmel said. 'One thing you could do is to get out a mop, and get the broom, and brush over every place we've walked . . .'

'We've walked everywhere,' Rinker said.

'Yeah, you don't have to clean it, you just have to stir it up good, so if the crime lab comes through, they won't know what's old and what's new.'

'The crime lab?'

'Yeah,' Carmel said. She leaned close to Rinker. 'It's pretty clear that after I cross-examine him, we're gonna have to kill him. Eventually they'll find him, and then the crime lab will come through.'

'What about the video tape?' Rinker asked.

'We'll have the tape,' Carmel said. They were in the kitchen, and she went to the tool drawer they'd dumped, and picked up the electric drill and a box of drill bits. 'We *will* have the tape.'

Carmel went back to the bedroom, and as Rolo strained to watch, plugged the drill into an electric outlet and said to Rolo, 'Did I ever tell you that I was crazy? I mean, absolutely fuckin' nuts? Well, I am, and I'm gonna prove it,' she said. She climbed back on the bed and sat on his legs: 'This is an eighth-inch drill bit,' she said. 'I'm now going to drill a hole through your knee cap.'

He flopped and strained against the chains and grunted, and she shook her head: 'No, no, no. No negotiation. We'd just waste more time screwing around. So I'll drill first.'

And she did it. He bucked against her, but with his neck and feet tightly chained, was unable to move enough to lose her. She rode his legs, and with brutal efficiency drove the drill bit through his knee cap, the drill whining and sputtering, bringing up flakes of white bone, and black blood, driving it in until the drill chuck touched his jeans. Rolo bucked against it, his screams muffled by the tape; at the end, with the drill silent, he made an eerie dying-animal sound, a high keening groan. Across the room, Rinker turned away, finally walking to the living room, where she sat down on a chair and put her hands over her ears.

When the drill bit had gone in as far as it would go, Carmel wiggled it, and said, 'Feel good, fucker? Feel good? Tape is in the bank? What a crock of shit . . .' A little spot of white saliva appeared at one corner of Carmel's eyes; Rolo fainted.

'Now, you probably think I'm just gonna take the tape off and ask you again; but I'm not gonna,' Carmel said, conversationally, when he was conscious again. 'I'm gonna drill a hole in your other knee instead.'

And she did it all over again, Rolo strangling himself on the chain, kicking his heels, Carmel riding his legs.

Then, 'You know what I bet would really hurt? A hole in your heels.'

51

And she drilled a hole through both of his heels, taking her time, developing a technique. Halfway through the first heel, Rolo fainted again; and again, halfway through the second.

'Get me some ice cubes out of the sink,' Carmel called to Rinker. 'If there are any left . . .'

There were a few, and Carmel dumped a bowl of ice water and cubes on Rolo's face. A minute later, his eyes flickered open.

Carmel said, 'A guy like you, you know what would really hurt? What would hurt a lot?' Her fingers went to his belt line and she unbuckled his belt, unbuttoned his pants, and started to drag them down. Rolo lay limp, unresisting. Carmel got his pants down on his thighs and then the animal keening began again, and Carmel stopped and said, 'What? You won't want me to drill out your dick? I'd be happy to do it . . .'

He went, 'Uh-uh, Uh-uh,' and Carmel asked, 'Are you gonna tell us where the tape really is?'

'Uh-huh, uh-huh.'

Carmel pulled the tape off his face and he turned toward her, his eyes glazed, and groaned. 'I'm dying,' he said. 'My heart busted.'

'Look, if you're gonna bullshit us, I'll put the tape back on and start the drill again. I could do this all night.'

'Tape's in the car,' Rolo said. 'In with the spare.'

Carmel looked at Rinker and she said, 'Oh, shit. How could we be that stupid?'

'I'll go get it,' Rinker said. 'You've got some blood . . .' Carmel looked down at her blouse: the droplets of blood looked like fine embroidery.

Rinker went out; another nice evening. She could hear music playing up the block, through an open window somewhere. She stopped to listen, but couldn't identify the music, then went to Rolo's car, popped the trunk, and pulled the cover off the limited-use spare. The tape was tucked behind it. She looked at it, weighed it in her hands, sighed, and went back inside.

'Get it?' Carmel asked.

'Got a tape,' Rinker said. She pushed it into the VCR. The picture came up immediately: and Carmel came to watch.

'Good light,' Rinker grunted.

'He had all the windows open. That's another thing I should have noticed. He's not an open-windows guy.'

'Boy . . .' Rinker said, as the tape wound out. 'You were *gone*, if the cops got this.'

'That's why I had to get it back.,' Carmel said.

'You think this is it?' Rinker asked.

'I don't know. I could go drill him some more,' Carmel said.

Rinker looked toward the bedroom. 'He looked pretty rough in there . . . I don't think he could take any more, and I don't think we'll get any more out of him. More'n what we've got.'

'So we gotta call it,' Carmel said.

'It's your face on the tape.'

Carmel looked at the bedroom door for a moment, then said. 'All right. We're done. If there's a copy, we'll have to deal with it later. But I think we're still gonna have to kill him. After the drill, he might be so pissed he'd go to the cops,' Carmel said.

'You wanna do it?' Rinker asked. 'I mean, you yourself?'

'Sure. If you want,' Carmel said.

'Not if you'd feel bad,' Rinker said.

'No, no, I don't think I would, not really,' Carmel said. 'What do I do?'

Rinker explained as they went back into the kitchen. Rolo saw them coming with the gun and didn't bother to struggle. 'See you in hell,' he said.

'There's nothing as silly as hell,' Carmel said. 'Don't you know that yet?' And then to Rinker, 'What, I just put it at his head, and pull the trigger?'

'Easy as that.'

Rolo turned his head away, and Carmel put the muzzle of the pistol at his temple and then waited a few seconds.

'Do it,' Rolo said.

'Made you sweat, didn't I?' Carmel asked. Rolo started to turn his head back; a little hope? She could see it in his eyes.

Carmel shot him six times; then the bullets ran out.

Rinker and Carmel spent another ten minutes in the house, closing up, obscuring anything that might even theoretically provide evidence against them.

'We can drop the guns in the Mississippi – I know a good spot down by the dam,' Carmel said.

'And burn the tape,' Rinker said.

'As soon as we get back to my place. We oughta go back to my place and change, and get rid of these clothes, and get showered off and everything.'

'Maybe we could go out someplace tonight,' Rinker said. 'My plane isn't until the day after tomorrow.'

'That'd be fun,' Carmel said. 'Maybe we could rent a movie or . . .'

She stopped in mid-sentence, looking back at the kitchen. 'What?' Rinker asked.

Without answering, Carmel went back to the kitchen, squatted next to the video camera that Rinker had tossed on the floor. Touched it, turned it over.

'What?' Rinker asked again.

'That fuckin' Rolo. This camera is a VHS-C. This tape . . .' She held up the tape they'd found. '. . . this tape is a full-sized VHS tape. If you were making a copy using your cheap-ass VCR and the camera, this is what you'd use to pick up the copy. So there's another tape – a VHS-C.'

'You're sure?' Rinker asked.

'Look,' Carmel said. She picked up the camera, turned it over, opened the cartridge compartment. The tape they had was at least twice as big as the compartment.

'Bad news,' Rinker said.

Carmel glanced at her, sideways and quickly: if Rinker were to shoot her now, at least all of Rinker's troubles would be over. She could walk away and not have to worry at all.

'You worry too much,' Rinker said.

'I anticipate,' Carmel said. She looked at Rinker. 'Let's get back to my place. Do you still have those address books?'

'Yeah.'

'And let's get his wallet and the phone book and whatever else that might have names in it . . . I've got to think about this.'

'You don't think it's in a safe-deposit box?'

'He's a drug dealer. He'd never have a safe-deposit box, not under his own name, anyway. We didn't find any fake IDs that he could use to get to a box under a different name, and we didn't find any keys . . . I suspect he did what drug dealers usually do: he left it with somebody he trusts.'

'Like who?'

'Like a lawyer. Except that I'm his lawyer. He could have another one, I suppose; I can find out. But he's a spic, so it's probably a relative. Anyway, we've got to do some research. In a hurry . . .'

'I'll cancel my plane ticket,' Rinker said. 'I guess we keep the guns.'

On the way back to Carmel's, Rinker glanced at her and asked, 'How much did you enjoy that? Back there?'

Carmel started to answer, then changed directions and asked a question of her own: 'Have you been to school? To college?'

'Well, yeah.'

'Really? I didn't think . . . you know.'

'Professional killer and all,' Rinker said.

'Yeah.' Carmel nodded. 'What'd you major in?'

'Psychology. Actually, I'm about eight credits away from my B.A. I should have it finished next spring.'

'Good school?'

'Okay school.'

'But you're not going to tell me which.'

'Well . . .'

'That's okay,' Carmel said. 'Anyway, I did sort of enjoy it, just a little bit, maybe. Whether I did or not, he had to go.'

'You enjoyed it just a little bit? Maybe?'

'Didn't you?' Carmel asked.

'No. I couldn't stand that sound he was making. That smell when he . . . you know. I didn't like it at all.'

Now Carmel took her eyes off the road for a moment, to look at Rinker. 'Don't worry, I'm just a sociopath. Like you. I'm not a psychopath or anything.'

'How do you know I'm not a psychopath?'

'From what Rolo told me — what he'd heard about you. Quiet, professional, clean. You do it because you can, and because you can make money at it, and because you're good at it; not because you have some slobbering lust to kill people.'

'Slobbering lust?'

'Listen, I've handled a couple of cases . . .'

Carmel had Rinker laughing by the time they got back to her place. And as they got out of the car, Rinker looked at her over the roof and said, 'Wichita State.'

'What?'

'That's where I go to school.'

Carmel had the sense that Rinker had told her something important. After a few moments, realized that she had. She'd told Carmel where she could be found.

Where home was.

Chapter Six

Three St. Paul cop cars and a crime-scene van were parked outside the Frogtown house when Lucas arrived. Up and down the street, people sat on their short wooden stoops, looking down at Rolo's house, watching the cops come and go. Lucas parked, climbed out of the Porsche, and started toward the house. A St. Paul uniformed cop saw him coming and squared off to stop him, but a plainclothes cop stuck his head out the door and yelled, 'Hey, Dick. Let that guy in.'

'You're in,' Dick said, and Lucas nodded and went up the steps. Sherrill was standing just inside the door. She was a dark-haired, dark-eyed madonna in a crisp yellow blouse, with a grey skirt in place of her usual slacks, and a black silk jacket to cover the .357 she carried under her arm.

'All dressed up,' Lucas said.

'A girl's gotta do what she can, if she wants to catch a guy,' Sherrill said, batting her eyes at him.

'Too early in the morning for bullshit,' Lucas muttered. He looked past her into the house, which had been ransacked. 'What's going on?'

'Come look. You'll like it.'

'Too early,' Lucas said again. But he went to look.

A St. Paul homicide cop named LeMaster showed him the body on the bed, chain around the neck, ankles and hands, pants pulled down around the thighs: 'One of the neighborhood junkies found him. About two hours ago – he came by looking for a wake-me-up. The dead guy used to be a big-time dealer.'

'No more?'

'LeMaster shook his head: 'He got his nose in it. Lately, he's been down to selling eight-balls.'

'Ain't that the way of the world,' Lucas said. 'One day it's kilos, the next day, it's one toot at a time.' He kept his hands in his pockets as he squatted next to the bed: 'Bunch of .22s in the head.'

'Yup. Could be your Barbara Allen killer. Or could be somebody who read about it in the paper and liked the sound of it.'

'Lucas nodded and stood up, scratched his nose and looked at the still-damp pools of blood around the body's feet and knees. 'What's all the blood from? And what's his name?'

'Rolando D'Aquila was his name; everybody called him Rolo. And the blood comes from some drill holes in his kneecaps and his heels. And his leg was bleeding from what might be a gunshot wound . . .'

'Drill holes in his heels?'

'Yeah – look at this.' The drill was lying on the floor at the end of the bed, three inches of stainless-steel drill bit sticking out of the chuck. Dried blood mottled the steel bit.

'Jesus Christ,' Lucas said. He looked back at the body. 'They drilled him?'

'Looks like. Gotta get his pants and socks off to know for sure, and the ME's guy hasn't been here yet . . . but that's what it looks like.'

'Bet that hurt,' Lucas said, looking at Rolo's face. His face looked compressed, leathery, like a shrunken head Lucas had seen on television. He looked hurt.

'See the pieces of duct tape on the floor? You can still see what look like chew marks on some of it. They probably taped up his mouth while they drilled him.'

'And the house was all torn up, so they were probably looking for something,' Lucas said. 'Like cocaine.'

'Yeah, but, boy – the gunshots in the head, all together like that, just like in the Allen case. None of the neighbors heard anything – and there are a lot of windows open these hot nights. Just like nobody heard anything with Allen. And the way they tortured him, it all looks professional. They had the tape and the chains and the padlocks and the drill – they knew what they were gonna do before they got here. It looks professional; like Allen.'

'You keep saying *they*,' Lucas said.

'I can't figure out how one guy could get him on the bed and get him all locked up like that. Had to be awkward. The way I see it, there had to be one to hold a gun on him, and at least one more to do the chains.'

'Get the slugs to the lab – they need to do a metallurgical analysis. If they're like the slugs in the Allen shooting, they'll be so bent up that they're just about useless for trying to match by the land marks.'

'We'll push it through,' LeMaster cop said. 'If they're the same . . .'

'Gonna be trouble,' Lucas said.

* * *

Sherrill was thumbing through a mens' magazine when Lucas picked his way through the trashed living room. 'What do you think?' he asked.

'I think this magazine is gay,' she said. 'It's basically a gear catalog, overlaid with pictures of guys who are gay.'

'You can tell from a picture?'

'Sure. Look at this guy.' She showed him a photo of a slender, shirtless, sweat-covered biker with a shock of dark hair falling carefully over his moody black eyes. 'He's either gay, or he wants you to think he is. They're all like that. Mountain climbers, canoeists . . . and look at the clothes. You see a guy walking along the street dressed like this and you say . . .'

'I coulda looked like that when I was a kid,' Lucas said.

She made a face, rolled her eyes up: 'Lucas, believe me, you did *not* look like this. He looks like he's been hurt by somebody. They all look like they've been hurt by somebody. Look at the bruised lips. You, on the other hand, always look like you just got back from hurting somebody else. Like a woman.'

'Thanks,' he said.

'No charge.'

'I just don't think you can make that judgment based on a picture . . .'

She looked at him closely, then smiled and said, 'Ah. I get it. You've been reading the Wholeness Report, or the Wellness Thing, or whatever it is. The Otherness Report. You gotta stop reading that shit, it's putting holes in your brain.'

'Yeah, it's . . . I don't know. But listen, what do you think about this?' He gestured over his shoulder with his thumb. 'Copycat? Coincidence? I haven't been that much on top of it.'

'Not a copycat, I don't think. We didn't give the details to the papers – we didn't tell them it was a .22, we didn't tell them that the shots were all grouped like that, we didn't tell them how close it was. You see the same tattooing on the scalp. And it was cold.'

'Nobody colder'n a wholesaler who's trying to make a point,' Lucas said. 'Maybe he held out on somebody, was trying to get back into the big deals.'

'Sure, but it's not *just* the coldness. It's all the other stuff that goes with it. It just doesn't seem like a copycat.'

'Could be a coincidence,' Lucas said, then admitted, 'But it'd be a pretty amazing coincidence.'

'You know the rule on coincidences.'

'Yeah: *It's probably a coincidence unless it can't be.*'

'You gonna jump in, now?' She grinned at him. 'Come on. We haven't worked together since old Audrey McDonald tried to take us off.'

'We have spoken a few times, though.'

'Is that what you call it?' She was teasing him.

'I'm thinking of getting in, if you and Black don't mind,' Lucas said. 'The Otherness Commission is driving me nuts. This would give me an excuse . . .'

'Glad to have you,' Sherrill said. 'That's why I invited you over.'

'The first thing we gotta do,' Lucas said, 'Is we gotta get that lawyer in – Allen – and bust his balls a little. Does he know Rolando whatever-his-name is? Does he use cocaine? Has he ever?'

'His attorney'll be on us like a chicken on a June bug.'

'Like a what?'

'A chicken on a June bug,' Sherrill said.

'Jesus, I'd almost forgotten about talking to you,' Lucas said. 'Anyway, don't worry about Carmel. I can handle Carmel.'

'The question,' Carmel said, as Rinker bent over a display case at Neiman Marcus, and peered at the Hermes scarves, 'Is whether whoever has it will look at it, and if he looks at it, if he'll come to me, or go to the cops.'

A sales clerk was drifting toward them and Rinker said, 'Whoever it is, I'll bet the name is in his address book.'

'Unless he knew him so well that he didn't have to write down a number,' Carmel said.

The clerk asked, 'Can I help you, ladies?' Rinker tapped the case: 'Let me look at the gold-and-black one, please. With the eggs.'

They spent five minutes looking at scarves, and then Rinker took the gold-and-black one, and paid with a Neiman credit card. 'You shop at Neiman's often enough to have a credit card?' Carmel asked, while the clerk went to wrap the scarf.

'I hit one of the stores once or twice a year, spend a few hundred,' Rinker said. 'The name on the card's not really mine, but I have all the rest of the ID to back it up, and I keep the card active and always pay it on time. Just in case. I've got a couple of Visas and Mastercards the same way. Just in case.'

'Just in case?'

'In case I ever have to run for it.'

'I never thought of doing that,' Carmel said. 'Running.'

'I'd run before I'd stand and fight. If a cop ever got close enough to look at me, I'd be screwed anyway.'

'Do you think *I* could run?'

Rinker looked at her carefully, and after a minute, nodded: 'Physically, it wouldn't be a problem. The question is whether you could handle it psychologically.'

The clerk came back with the wrapped scarf and the credit card: 'Thanks very much, Mrs. Blake.'

'Thank *you*,' Rinker said. She tucked the card away in her purse.

'Physically, I'd be okay? But psychologically . . .' Carmel was interested.

'Sure. You've got a hot image. Bright clothes, blonde hair, good makeup and perfume, great shoes.' Rinker took a step back and took a long look. 'If you dressed way down – got some stuff from a second-hand shop, you know, stuff that didn't go together that well, some kind of scuzzy dark plaid, drab. And if you grew out your hair, and colored it some middle-brown color, and slumped your shoulders and shuffled, maybe got some breast prosthetics so you'd have big floopy boobs . . .'

'My God,' Carmel said, starting to laugh.

But Rinker was serious. 'If you did that, your best friends wouldn't recognize you from two feet. You could get a cleaning lady job at your law firm, and nobody would know you. But I don't know if *you* could stand it. I think you like attention; you need it.'

'Maybe,' Carmel said. 'Maybe everybody does.'

'I don't. I don't *want* people to look at me. That's one reason why I'm good at what I do.'

'I really don't understand that,' Carmel said.

'I was a nude dancer for three-and-a-half years, from the time I was sixteen until I was twenty. You get pretty goddamned tired of people staring at you. You want privacy.'

Carmel was fascinated now. 'You were a . . .' Her beeper went off, a discreet low Japanese tone from her purse. 'Uh-oh.'

She glanced at the beeper, dropped it back in her purse, took out a cell phone and dialed. 'Maybe a problem,' she said. 'My secretary only uses the beeper if there's some pressure.' And to the phone: 'Marcia – you beeped me? Uh-huh. Uh-huh. Okay. Give me the number. Okay.'

She clicked off and said, 'Cop called. He wants to talk to one of my clients.'

'Doesn't it make you nervous, talking to cops all the time?'

'Why should it?' Carmel asked. 'I'm not guilty of anything, I'm just doing my job.'

'We've gotta spend some time looking for the tape, we can't go running around . . .'

'Actually, my client's name is Hale Allen,' Carmel said.

Rinker frowned: 'Any relation to Barbara Allen?'

'Her husband.'

'Jesus.' Rinker was impressed. 'How'd that happen?'

'He's a friend of mine and I'm a good attorney. Actually, I'm one of the best criminal attorneys in the state. The cops think he might've done it.'

'So you're on the inside,' Rinker said.

'Somewhat.' Carmel smiled down at Rinker. 'Makes it kind of interesting.'

'Certainly could be useful,' Rinker said. 'Is that why you took the job?'

'Not exactly,' Carmel said. Then her smile disappeared: 'But this cop who's calling – he wasn't working the case before. He's a deputy chief of police, Lucas Davenport. A political appointee. He used to be a regular cop, but he was canned for brutality or something. They brought him back because he's smart. He's a mean bastard, but really smart.'

'Well, hell, as long as he thinks her husband did it . . .'

'But it means we've got to get that goddamn tape,' Carmel said. 'If Davenport ever got a whiff of that . . . I'll tell you what, Carla, he's the one guy in the world who could run you down. The one guy.'

'As long as you're on the inside, he shouldn't be a problem,' Rinker shrugged. 'And if he gets to be a problem, we take him.'

Carmel gave her a long look, and Rinker asked, 'What?'

'You don't know him,' Carmel said.

'Look, if a guy doesn't know it's coming, and if you spend some time watching him, and thinking about it – you can take him. You *can*.'

Carmel came swinging down the hall to Homicide, spotted Lucas coming from the other direction, carrying a large clip-bound report. 'Davenport, goddamn it, have you been stepping on my client's rights again?'

'How are you, Carmel?' Lucas asked.

'What's the big book?'

'Ah, the Perfection Commission.'

'Oh, my God. I tried to read about it in the *Star-Tribune*. I felt like I'd been anesthetized.' Carmel presented a cheek, and Lucas pecked it. He took one of her hands, lifted it and stepped back so he could look her over, and said, 'You look absolutely . . . wonderful.'

'Thanks. How come we've never slept together? You've chased every other woman in town.'

'I only chase . . . no, that's not right.'

'What?'

'I was gonna say I only chase women who don't scare me,' Lucas said. 'But they all wind up scaring me.'

'I heard you were dating Little Miss Titsy, the cop, but you broke up.'

'That would be Sgt. Sherrill?'

'What happened? She have a bigger gun?'

'Carmel, Carmel . . .' Lucas held the door for her. Carmel stepped through, and saw Hale Allen at the far end of the room, leaning against a green filing-cabinet, deep in conversation with Marcy Sherrill. Marcy was standing a couple of inches too close to him, and was looking up into his eyes with rapt attention.

'Uh-oh,' Carmel said.

'By the way,' Lucas said, in a tone low enough that Carmel had to turn to catch what he said. 'I'm told your client is dumber'n a barrel of hair.'

'But, God, he's gorgeous,' she said. She ostentatiously bit her lower lip, sighed, and started toward Allen and Sherrill. Moving like a leopard, Lucas thought.

They needed to cover some old ground, Lucas told Allen, because he was new to the case. He hoped it wouldn't be inconvenient. 'I understand your wife has been released by the county . . .'

'Yes, finally,' Allen said.

'*That* took way too long,' Carmel added. 'I don't understand why they had to do twenty different kinds of chemistry when the woman's been shot seven times in the brain.'

'Routine,' Lucas said.

'Bullshit routine,' Carmel said, now in attorney mode. 'You should give a little thought to what it does to the grieving survivors. You're revictimizing the victims.'

'All right, all right,' Lucas said. 'This will only take a couple of minutes.'

'Where's the other guy? Black?' Carmel asked.

'Doing something else,' Lucas said. He looked at Allen. 'Tell me about your relationship with your wife . . .'

'Ah, Jesus,' Carmel said.

Ten minutes later, Lucas leaned toward Allen and asked, 'How well did you know Rolando D' Aquila?'

Allen looked puzzled. 'Rolando who?'

'D'Aquila. Also known as Rolo, I understand.'

'I don't know anybody by that name,' Allen said.

'Never bought a little toot from him?' Lucas asked.

'No, I never.' He shook his head. 'Toot?'

When Lucas mentioned D'Aquila's name, Carmel slipped back a step, and ran the numbers. They'd found the body, obviously. If they looked up D'Aquila's history – and they would get around to that, if they hadn't already – they'd find her name. They might wonder why she hadn't mentioned it.

'Why are you interested in this Rolando D'Aquila?' she asked Lucas.

'He was murdered last night,' Lucas said. 'He was killed the same way Mrs. Allen was – the method was identical.' He looked back at Allen: 'So you never represented him, or one of his friends, either in a criminal court or in a civil legal matter?'

'No, no, not that I remember. I've represented thousands of people in real-estate closings, so maybe, but I don't remember any Rolando . . .'

'Get off his case,' Carmel snapped. 'He's never represented Rolando D'Aquila in anything.'

'How do you know?' Lucas asked.

'Because Rolo only had one attorney.' Everybody was looking at her now, and she nodded. 'Me.'

After the interview with Allen, as they got coffee from the coffee machine, Lucas said, 'You were strangely quiet. That always makes me a nervous.'

'I was gonna be the good cop, if you were gonna be the bad,' Sherrill said.

'I agree; he is *very* good-looking,' Lucas said.

Sherrill laughed and then said, 'He's got these really amazing brown eyes. They're like perfect little puppy eyes.'

'He's about as bright as a perfect little puppy, too,' 'Lucas said. 'And he's sleeping with his secretary.'

'*A* secretary, not *his* secretary. Besides, he had a cold marriage, as I understand it,' Sherrill said. 'And I think his intelligence might lie in other areas than . . .'

'Than what?'

'Than like in, uh, being smart.'

Lucas choked on the coffee and said, 'Goddamnit, you almost made hot coffee go up my nose.'

'Good,' Sherrill said.

Chapter Seven

When Carmel got back to her apartment, Rinker was lying on the couch, a pillow behind her head, reading the *NBC Handbook of Pronunciation*. 'Did you know that the French nudie bar is called the foh-LEE-bair-ZHAIR?'

Carmel shrugged: 'Yeah, I guess.'

'See, that's what people get when they study French,' Rinker said, tossing the book on an end table. 'They learn how to pronounce neat stuff. I had to take Spanish for my BA, but there's nothing neat in the pronunciation. Like in French – I always thought it was foh-LEE beer-zhair-AY.'

'I don't know, I took Spanish, too,' Carmel said.

Rinker sat up, dropped her feet to the floor and asked, 'What happened with the cops?'

'They asked Hale about Rolo. They found his body this morning – some junkie dropped by, looking for coke.'

'Did you tell them that you'd represented Rolo?' Rinker asked.

For a split second, a lie hovered on Carmel's tongue. She rejected it and said, 'Yeah, I pretty much had to. They would've found out.'

'All right. So now they can tie you to Rolo, but they can't tie you to the crime, because nobody knows that you're . . . involved with Hale. Not even Hale knows it. Have I got that right?'

'That's right.' She wandered to a window and looked out over the city; it was a hot day, and a thin haze hung over the Midway area to the east. 'If it weren't for that fuckin' tape, we'd be in the clear. I'm thinking maybe we should have *strangled* Rolo, instead of shooting him – then then there wouldn't be *any* tie. That was a mistake.'

'Didn't think of it,' Rinker said. 'The gun was just the natural thing to do, since we had it right there.'

'Yeah, well, they're waiting for an analysis of the slugs. They can tell whether the bullets that killed Barbara Allen and the ones that killed Rolo came from the same batch of lead.'

'All right . . . gonna have to get rid of the guns pretty soon. Or buy a new batch of shells.'

'Did you come up with any ideas about the tape?' Carmel asked.

'Yes, I have,' Rinker said. She stood up, walked to a corner table, and picked up Rolo's address book. 'For one thing, do you remember when he said he gave the tape to somebody named Mary?'

'Yeah – but there aren't any names in the book, only . . .'

'Initials,' Rinker said. 'But I had a little time, so I started going through it. There are four sets of initials starting with M. So I walked down to your library, and looked in the cross-reference directories . . . and then I found out he was using a stupid little code on his phone numbers. He put the last number at the beginning. Like he'd have a number, say, that was 123 dash 4567 and he'd write it down as 712 dash 3456.'

Carmel was impressed. 'How'd you figure that out?'

'Because some of the prefixes didn't exist, and the ones that did were all over the place. One was for a dog-grooming service. I mean, why would he even bother to write it in his book? So anyway, the assholes I used to work for did some jail time, and they told me how guys would use these simple codes. So I juggled numbers until I found one that gave me all good prefixes. And then, everything else worked out – all the codes were residential, and two of the names that began with M were women. Or probably women. One was Martha Koch, but the other was just initial M – M. Blanca. Where's there's just an initial, it usually means a woman living alone. Younger woman.'

'Mary?

'No, it's something else – I called, and a woman answered, and I asked for Mary Blanca and she said I had the wrong number. She had a little accent, maybe Mex. But I was thinking about how scared Rolo was, and how he came up with the name Mary. I bet when you asked him for the name, and you said, *Quick*, I bet her name popped into his head, and it almost got out, but he switched at the last minute. Could be Martha, or it could be this other M.'

Carmel was skeptical: 'That's a long chain of could-be's,' she said. 'It could be some other M, or not an M at all.'

'Yeah, but we don't have anything else.'

'Rolo's name's gonna be in the paper tomorrow,' Carmel said. 'If this M doesn't know he's dead, she will tomorrow morning. Then she's gonna look at the tape, if she hasn't already. *Then* she's gonna give it to the cops.'

'So let's go talk to M. Blanco. And Martha Koch.'

'After dark.'

'Yup.'
'We're hanging by a goddamn thread,' Carmel said.

Martha Koch's life was saved by a baby shower; she never knew it.

'Lotta cars around,' Carmel muttered as she and Rinker started up the
Kochs' driveway; a dozen cars were parked along the street. The house
was a neat, modest, tuck-under ranch across the street from a golf course.
A curving line of flagstone steps led across a rising lawn to the front door.
The porch light was on, and the living-room curtains were open. At the
top of the steps, Carmen said, 'Uh-oh,' and stopped. Two women were
hopping around the front room, laughing, and one of them was looking
back and obviously talking to yet a third one, or more.

'Forget it,' Rinker said. 'We'll have to come back.'

They retreated down the steps, walked up the street to Carmel's Volvo,
and left.

M. Blanca's house was a long step down in affluence, one of a row of
old asbestos-shingled houses just north of a University of Minnesota
neighborhood called Dinkytown. Four mailboxes hung next to a single
door.

'It's an apartment,' Rinker said, her voice low.

'Lot of them are,' Carmel said.

'We gotta take care – there'll be other people around. You got the
money?'

'Yeah.' A few more steps and Carmel asked, 'What do I look like?'
Rinker was wearing her red wig; they'd both wrapped dark silk scarves
around their heads.

'You look like one of those religious ladies who always wear scarves,'
Rinker said.

'All right,' Carmel said. She added, 'So do you.'

At the front door, Carmel pointed a pocket flash it at the mailboxes.
The box on the left said *Howell*; the next one showed a strip of paper,
which had been peeled off. The third said in pink ink, *Jan and Howard
Davis*, with a green ink addition, in a child's hand, *And Heather*. The
fourth said Apartment A. She opened the left one, *Howell*, and found it
empty. The box with the strip of paper contained a phone bill addressed to
David Pence, Apartment C. She skipped the Davis box, and checked the
box on the far right. Empty.

'I think, but I'm not sure, that we want apartment A,' she whispered to

Rinker. Rinker nodded and they pushed through the outer door into a short hallway. Stairs led away to the right, and a high-tech Schwinn bicycle was chained to the banister. 'Not like my old Schwinn,' Rinker muttered.

Down the hall, on the left wall, was a pale yellow door. Another door, this one a pale Paris green, was at the end of the hall. The first door had a large metal B on it; the Paris-green door had an A. Rinker put her hand in her pocket, where the gun was, and Carmel stepped forward and knocked on the door.

The knock was answered by deep silence; Carmel knocked again, louder. This time, there was an answering thump, like somebody getting up, off a couch or a bed. A moment later, the door opened a crack, and a sleepy Latino man peered out through the crack and said, 'What?'

'We need to talk to Ms. Blanca,' Carmel said quietly.

'She's sleeping,' he said, and the crack narrowed.

'We've got some money for her,' Carmel said quickly. The crack stopped narrowing, and the man's eyes were back at the crack. He didn't argue. He simply said, 'I'll take it.'

'No. Rolo said we were only to give it to Ms. Blanca, if anything happened to him.'

'Oh.' He thought it over for a minute, as if this somehow made sense; and Carmel's heart did a quick extra beat. 'What happened to Rolo?'

'Quite a bit of money,' Carmel said. She wanted to sound nervous, and she did.

'Just a minute,' the Latino man said. The door closed and they heard him call, 'Hey, Marta.'

'Marta Blanca,' Rinker muttered. 'She bakes right.'

'What?' Carmel looked at Rinker as though Rinker were slipping away.

'Better biscuits, cakes and pies with Marta Blanca . . .'

Carmel shook her head, bewildered, then the man was back, and the door opened. He looked them over for a second, made a judgment, and said, 'Yeah. Come in.'

Carmel led the way into the apartment, which seemed to be decorated in brown; one lamp with a nicotine-yellow shade was turned on, the shade at a tipsy angle over a stack of *Hustler* magazines. The odor of marijuana hung around the curtains.

'How much money?' the man asked.

'We need to ask . . .' Carmel started, but then a woman came through the kitchen, apparently from a bedroom in the back. She was tucking her blouse into the back of her jeans. 'Are you Marta?'

'Yeah.' The woman still looked sleepy. 'What happened to Rolando?'

'He's dead,' Carmel said flatly. 'Somebody shot him.'

The woman stopped in her tracks, the blood draining from her face: 'Dead? He can't be dead. I just talked to him yesterday.'

'The cops found him this morning,' Rinker said, stepping out of Carmel's shadow. 'Was he a good friend?'

'He was he was he was . . .' she said, shakily.

'Her brother,' the man finished. Rinker flicked a look at Carmel, who nodded almost imperceptibly. Her hand moved in her pocket.

'Half-brother,' the woman said. She dropped on a chair. 'Ah, Jesus,' she said.

'It was on TV,' Rinker said.

'He said he gave you a tape to hold, and that if anything happened to him, we were supposed to come and get it, because if you keep it, somebody's gonna show up here and hurt you,' Carmel said, squatting to look the woman straight in the face. 'He gave us an envelope to give you. Money.'

The man said, 'We don't got no tape,' but the woman said, reflexively, 'How much?'

They had the tape, Carmel thought, and she felt a wire, tight in her spine, suddenly relax.

'Five thousand dollars,' Carmel said, speaking to the woman. The woman looked up at the man, who said, 'I dunno.'

Carmel took the envelope out of her pocket. 'If we could get the tape?'

The woman stood up, but the man put a hand out to her. 'I think we should look at the tape first,' he said.

'Rolando said not to,' the woman said, nervously dry-washing her hands.

'We need to get that tape . . .'

The woman flipped her hands up, explaining to Carmel, 'It's one of those funny little tapes, you need to get a special holder-thing to run it . . .'

'We're gonna look at the tape,' the man said, decisively. 'If you show up here to give us five thousand . . .' He smiled brightly and said, 'Then, I bet it's worth a lot more.'

'We really need the tape. Rolando wasn't supposed to get it, and the people it belongs to, you really don't want to mess with,' Rinker said. Her voice was flat, and sounded dangerous to Carmel's ear. The vibration apparently went past the Latino.

He sneered at her. 'What, the fuckin' Mafia? Or the Colombianos? Fuck those people.' He turned to the woman. 'We look at the tape.' And back to Carmel and Rinker, hitching up his pants. 'You bitches can leave the envelope here. If it's enough, we'll give you the tape. If not, we'll figure out a price.'

'Goddamnit, this isn't necessary,' Carmel said, stepping in front of Rinker. Out at the very edge of her vision she could see Rinker's gun hand sliding out of her pocket.

'Yeah, it's fuckin' necessary,' the Latino man said, his voice rising. 'What I fuckin' say is necessary, that's what's fuckin' necessary, right?' He looked at Marta. 'Is that right?'

She looked away and Carmel shrugged. 'If you say so.' She took another sideways step, and felt Rinker's arm come up with the gun.

The man stepped back, a little surprised, but still smiling slightly. 'What, that's supposed to scare me?'

That was the last thing he said: Rinker shot him in the center of the forehead, and he dropped in his tracks. The woman, Marta, clapped both hands to her face in disbelief, and before she could scream or make any other sound, Rinker panned the gun barrel across to her face and snapped: 'If you scream, I'll kill you.'

'Give us the tape, you get the money,' Carmel said.

'Oh my god oh my god oh my god . . .'

'The fuckin' tape,' Rinker snarled. The woman put a hand out toward the muzzle, as though she could fend off bullets, and slowly backed away, still looking down at the man.

The tape was in the kitchen, in a cupboard, inside a Dutch oven. She handed it to Rinker, who handed it to Carmel, who looked at it and nodded. 'You didn't make any copies?'

'No, no, no, no . . .' The woman was staring fixedly at Rinker now. Then the man in the frontroom groaned and Rinker turned and walked toward him.

'He's alive?' Marta Blanca asked. Rinker said, 'Yeah, it happens. Sometimes the bullet doesn't even make it through the skull bone.' She casually leaned forward, bringing the muzzle to within an inch or two of the man's head, and fired three quick shots into his skull. His feet bounced once, and he laid still.

Marta crossed herself, her eyes now fixed on Rinker. 'You're going to kill me, aren't you?' she said, with the sound of certainty in her voice.

'No, I'm not,' Rinker said. She showed a tiny smile.

Carmel, who had been carrying the second gun, shot Marta Blanca in the back of the head. As she fell, Carmel stepped forward and fired five more times. Then she smiled at Rinker, her eyes bright with excitement, and said, 'We got the goddamn tape. We got the *goddamn* tape.'

Rinker put the gun back in her jacket pocket and said, 'Let's get a drink somewhere.'

'Let's check the tape to make sure it's right, erase it, and *then* get a drink somewhere,' Carmel said.

Going out into the hall, they closed the door behind themselves; they took three steps and suddenly a shaft of light fell across their faces. They both looked right, standing in the hall, and then down. A small girl stood there, looking up at them. Their faces were illuminated by the light from the interior. Then behind the girl, a crabby mommy called, 'Heather! Shut that door!'

Carmel was fumbling at the pistol in her pocket, but then another door opened above them, and a male voice said a few unintelligible words; they both looked up, and the little girl closed the door.

'Gotta go,' Rinker said urgently.

'She saw us,' Carmel said.

But there were footsteps on the landing above and Rinker thrust Carmel toward the door. She went, hurrying, Rinker a step behind, out the door, down the sidewalk, the apartment door closing behind them.

'She was just a kid,' Rinker said. 'She won't remember. They might not find the bodies for a week.'

'Why can't this be easy?' Carmel asked. They hurried down the dark side walk toward the lights of Dinkytown, and she added, 'This is just like a dream I had when I was a teenager. A school dream, where I couldn't find my locker and the bell was about to ring, and every time I was about to find it, something else happened to keep me away from it . . .'

'Everybody has that dream,' Rinker said. 'We're in the clear.'

'Maybe,' Carmel said. She turned to look back; the dark figure of a man was climbing on a bike, and then headed away from them, out on the street. 'But I *am* on the inside; if anything comes out of that kid, we're gonna have to go back and clean up.'

'Let's get that drink,' Rinker said.

They had several drinks, and two midnight steaks, at Carmel's apartment. Carmel had a rarely used grill on her balcony, and Rinker did the honors, moving the meat and sauce like a professional. 'I once worked in a bar where we had an outdoor grill. Place was full of cowboys, wanted their steaks *burned*,' she told Carmel.

'Make mine not-quite-rare,' Carmel said. 'No blood.' Carmel was in the media room, looking at the tape: the whole episode with Rolo was on the tape, while the other tapes had only the final sequence. 'So this is the original,' she told Rinker with satisfaction. 'Even if there's a copy someplace, they could get me into court, but I'd prove it was a copy and could have been altered and I'd be gone.'

'Still be best if there weren't any copies,' Rinker said.

'You about done out there?'

'All done. Dinner is served.'

'Good. One more thing before we eat.' Carmel stripped the tape out of the cassette by hand, tossed the cassette pack into a waste basket, squeezed the jumbled tangle of tape into a wad the size of a softball, and dropped it onto the hot charcoal in the grill.

'That won't be coming back,' she said as she watched it burn.

'Three people dead because of that tape,' Rinker said, shaking her head.

'Ah, they were nothing, a bunch of druggies,' Carmel said. 'Nobody'll miss them.'

'Even druggies have families, sometimes,' Rinker said. 'I hated my step-dad and my older brother, I don't like my mom anymore, but I've got a little brother, he's out in L.A. and he does drugs, sometimes he lives on the beach . . . I'd do anything I could for him. I *do* everything I can for him.'

'Really,' Carmel said, impressed. They'd moved the steaks onto a seldom-used dining table. 'I've never been like that with anybody. I mean, I give to charity and all, but I have to. I've never really been where . . . I do *anything* for somebody.'

'Not even for Hale?'

Carmel shook her head: 'Not even for Hale.'

'You killed for him,' Rinker said.

'No, I didn't,' Carmel said. 'I killed for me – for something *I* want. Which is Hale. If he'd had his choice, who knows? He might've decided to stay with Barbara.'

'Mmm,' Rinker said, chewing. She swallowed, watched for a moment as Carmel worked her way into the steak and then asked, 'Would you have killed the little girl?'

Carmel said, 'You make me sound like a monster.'

'No, no. I'm just interested,' Rinker said. 'I'd do it, if it was *absolutely* necessary. But I'd hate doing it.'

'Why?'

'Because she's a kid.'

'So what? None of this means anything, this . . .' Carmel looked around. '. . . this life. We're just a bunch of meat. When we *think* something, it's just chemicals. When we love something, it's *more* chemicals. When we die, all the chemicals go back in the ground, and that's it. There's nothing left. You don't go anywhere, except in the ground. No heaven, no hell, no God, no nothing. Just . . . nothing.'

'That's pretty grim,' Rinker said. She pointed a fork at Carmel. 'I've seen people like you – philosophical nihilists. People who really believe all that . . . eventually, they can't stand it. Most of them commit suicide.'

Carmel nodded. 'I can see that. That's probably what I'll do, when I get older. If I live to get older.'

'Why not do it now?' Rinker asked. 'If nothing means anything, why wait?'

'No reason, except curiosity. I want to see how things come out. I mean, killing yourself is as meaningless as not killing yourself. Makes no difference if you do or you don't. So as long as you're not bored, as long as you're feeling good . . . why do it?'

'But you'd do it if you had to. Kill yourself.'

'Hell, I might kill myself if I *don't* have to,' Carmel said.

'Really?'

'Sure. For the same reason that I'm staying now. Curiosity. I can't be absolutely one-million percent sure that there's nothing on the other side; so as long as it's one-millionth of a percent possible, why not check?'

'Man, that's almost enough to bum me out,' Rinker said.

'It does bum me out from time to time,' Carmel said. 'But I get over it pretty quickly. I'm just an upper sort of person.'

'Chemically.'

'Absolutely,' Carmel said. After a couple more bites, she asked, 'How about you? How do you justify all this stuff.'

'I'm kind of religious, I guess,' Rinker said.

'Really?'

'Yeah. I don't think anything really happens in this world that isn't part of God's plan. And if God wants somebody to die, now, if that's that person's fate, I can't say no.'

'So you're just what . . . the finger of God?'

'I wouldn't put it exactly that way. It sounds too . . . vain, I guess. Too important. But what I do is God's will.'

'Jesus,' Carmel said. Then quickly: 'Sorry, if that offends you, I'll . . .'

'No, no, jeez, I hang around with Italians, for Christ's sake. Catholics, man. Nobody talks the talk like Catholics. I'm not exactly religious that way – I mean, I used to work in a nudie bar. It's just that I believe in . . . some kind of God. Not in heaven or hell, just in God. We're all part of it.'

'What about stuff like guns? Where'd you learn about that?'

'We always had guns in our house when I was a kid, my step-dad was a hunter. Poacher, really. So I knew about rifles and shotguns. Then the Mafia guys taught me the basic stuff about handguns, though most of them don't know a lot,' Rinker said. 'I figured that if I was gonna do this – be a hit man – I'd better learn about them. You can get most of what you need from books. There's an ocean of gun stuff out there.'

'So you know all about the bullets and how fast they go . . .'

'Pretty much. I don't reload – make my own ammunition – because that would be too much of a trademark,' Rinker said. 'Sooner or later they could get me on it. But factory ammo is as good as anything I could make up for my kind of work, anyway.'

'Are the guns really special? I mean . . .'

'Nah. Most of them are stolen, and they get passed around. I got a friend who picks them up for me, cuts the threads for the silencers. He checks them mechanically, and I fire them a few times to double-check, but basically, all my work is within ten feet or so. Up close. So I use fairly small calibers and fire several times.'

'You carry the silencers separately?'

'Yeah. A little plastic box with a couple of crescent wrenches and a couple pairs of pliers – if you saw them on an X-ray, it'd look like a tool kit. There's no way to hide guns, though. Not conventional guns, anyway.'

They talked for a long time, nihilism and religion, guns and ammo, and that night, very late, as Carmel was dozing off, she smiled sleepily as she replayed the conversation. She'd gone to college with a lot of finance and law students. They'd stayed up nights studying, not talking.

This night, she thought, was like what a lot of people did in college, a few beers with friends, talk about God and death.

She drifted peacefully away, and may have had a dream about a coil of videotape going up in smoke. And about guns.

Chapter Eight

Lucas and Black followed the Ramsey County medical examiner into the work room, where the body of Rolando D'Aquila was stretched out on a stainless-steel tray.

'They really fucked this boy over,' Black said, with a low whistle of disbelief. He'd heard about it, but hadn't seen the body. 'Look at his kneecaps.'

'Look at his heels, if you want to see something that must've hurt,' the ME said. He was a dark, hairy man with a beard. A Rasputin, with a Boston accent.

'So what are these letters?' Lucas asked.

'I've got a photograph for you, but I thought you might want to see it in person,' the ME said. He picked up one of the dead man's hands, and turned it over. On the back of the hand were a series of bloody scrapes that looked like:

Lucas and Black squatted, got down close: 'What is it?' Black asked.

'I don't know,' the ME said. 'But he did it himself, because we found the skin under his fingernails. He did it not long before he died – he had blood on his fingertips, which would have been worn away if his hands had been free, and he used them for anything. So: we think he might have known he was going to be killed, and tried to leave something behind.'

'Like the name of the killer,' Black said. 'Which is probably Dew.'

'Really?' The ME bent over the hand and said, 'I never saw Dew. I was looking at it the other way – I saw Mop.'

Black looked at Lucas: 'What do you think? M-o-p or D-e-w?'

'Beats the shit out of me,' Lucas said, standing up. 'Maybe we can actually see it better in a photo . . .' To the ME: 'What are the chances he cut himself up just thrashing around? I mean, they were drilling holes in his kneecaps . . .'

'Who knows, if a guy's being tortured? The scratches look deliberate –

the skin looks almost *ploughed* off the back of his hands. And the shapes look deliberate, not like thrashing or involuntary contraction . . . I think he did it on purpose.'

'Yeah.' Lucas scratched his head. 'Took some balls.'

'You don't see d-e-w?' Black asked.

'Yeah, and I see m-o-p, and I see something else, too, and I don't know what they hell that might mean,' Lucas said.

'What?' Black and the ME turned their heads, trying the scratches at different angles.

'I can see c-l-e-w – like the British spelling of clue,' Lucas said. 'But there's no clue. Unless it was something back at the house, near his hands.'

'Aw, man, that's too weird,' Black said. 'C-l-e-w equals clue?'

'Don't you see it?' Lucas asked.

'I see it, but I don't think that's it. I think it's initials, I think . . . Hey.'

'What?'

Now Black was scratching his head. 'I was talking to the St. Paul guys. They're looking for Rolando's sister – she lives over by the University, but they haven't been able to catch her at home. Her name is Marta Blanca. If you read the scratches backwards it could be an M instead of a W, and a B instead of a D . . .'

'Then what's all that shit in the middle?' the ME asked, pointing at the scratches.

'I don't know, this is just a theory,' Black said. 'But his hands were chained up . . . how were his hands?'

'Like this,' Lucas said, demonstrating. 'Over his head.'

'Then he couldn't see what he was doing, he was in all kinds of pain, he's panicked because he knows what's coming. I wonder if he was trying to get us to his sister?'

'Or that his sister had something to do with it,' Lucas said.

'Hey,' Black said, 'It's a clew, with an e-w. Let's go knock on her door.'

A little girl was playing with a plastic dump truck in the hallway of Marta Blanca's apartment house, in front of an open apartment door.

'Hello,' Lucas said. A mommy's voice called, 'Who's that?'

Lucas leaned over the little girl and knocked once on the door jamb: 'Minneapolis police, ma'am. We're looking for a Marta Blanca?'

'Down the hall. Apartment A.'

Black stepped down the hall and knocked on the Paris-green door at the end. A young woman appeared from the back of the open apartment, carrying a dish towel and a pan that she was in the process of drying. 'Is there some kind of trouble?'

Lucas nodded: 'Yes. Her brother was killed. We need to interview her; just a routine thing.'

The woman's eyebrows were up: 'I haven't heard them out this morning – Heather usually has the door open so she can play in the hall, and Marta usually stops to talk to her.' She looked at Black and then back to Lucas and asked, 'Do you have some kind of ID?'

'Yes, I do.' Lucas smiled, tried to look pleasant, took out his ID case, handed it over.

She looked at it, then back up at Lucas: 'I've heard of you. You only do murders.'

'What's that, mom?' Heather asked.

'Talk to you later,' the mother said to the girl, handing Lucas's ID case back. 'This is a policeman. He catches bad men.'

'I didn't see any men at Marta's,' the girl said.

'Okay,' Lucas said.

Black, at the end of the hall, said, 'Nobody home.'

'They were having a party last night,' Heather said.

Her mother frowned: 'I didn't hear a party – I didn't see anybody coming or going.'

'I heard them popping the balloons. Like at a birthday party,' the girl said.

Lucas looked down the hall at Black, whose face had gone tight. Black said, 'That's enough for an entry.'

'Right,' Lucas said. To the mother: 'You better take Heather back inside.'

'What? Why?' She turned her eyes down to the other door. Black had slipped his pistol out of his holster, and was holding it by his side, where the little girl couldn't see it. The woman looked back at Lucas, suddenly understanding, and said, 'Oh, no, no . . . Heather, c'mon. C'mon inside with mom.'

When they'd gone inside, Lucas nodded at Black, who lined up on the Paris-green door, then kicked it below the knob. The old door punched open, and Lucas, .45 in his hand, stepped past Black. One step and he saw the Latino man on the floor. Another step, and he saw the woman just beyond. They were both face down.

'Okay,' Black said, from behind. 'Watch me, man . . .'

The two of them edged through the apartment, looking for anyone else; but the place was empty except for the bodies. Lucas walked back to the living room. No signs of a struggle, nor had the little girl apparently heard any – but she had heard the balloons popping. These were executions, then, with silencers. He'd seen enough bodies in his career that two more shouldn't have affected him, but these did. The cool efficiency of the killer, swatting human beings as though they were so many gnats.

He shook his head asked Black, 'Got your phone?'

'Yeah, I'll call,' Black said. He was standing over the man: 'Goddamn, look at this guy's head. Same deal: half-dozen rounds.'

Lucas, slipping his gun away, squatted next to the woman's body. Her face was older than its years, he thought: careworn, but with smile-lines, too. The rims of her nostrils were slightly rough, reddened. Cocaine, he thought. 'Same here,' he said. And he added: 'This takes it away from Hale Allen. He might've been willing to kill his old lady for her money, but this isn't that. This is something else.'

'Yeah,' Black said. 'He was too fuckin' dumb, anyway.' He was holding the cell phone to his ear and said, 'Marcy? This is me . . . yeah, yeah, shut up for a minute, will you? Lucas and I are looking at a couple of more dead ones in an apartment in Dinkytown . . . No, I'm not. No, I'm *not*. I need you to get all the shit rolling over here, huh? Yeah . . .'

While he was telling her about it, Lucas moved quickly through the apartment. He was going through a scatter of paper on the kitchen counter when he heard a quiet, single knock on the door. He looked up just in time to see the mommy take two steps through the door. She said, 'Did you . . .' and then saw the bodies. 'Oh, God.'

Lucas stepped toward her: 'Please don't come in.'

She stepped back into the doorway, her right hand at her mouth, the other hand feeling for the door jamb. 'Don't touch anything, please, don't touch the door,' Lucas said urgently. 'Don't touch.'

She backed into the hallway. Lucas followed and said, 'We haven't processed the room yet, we need to bring in crime-scene specialists.' She nodded, dumbly, and Lucas added, 'I'd like to talk to you. I've got to wait here for a few minutes, until we get this going, but I'd like to see you and your daughter.'

'Heather?' Now she looked frightened.

'Just for a couple of minutes,' Lucas said. 'Maybe your place would be better . . .'

'Why do you want to talk to Heather?'

'She said she heard balloons popping. Those were probably guns. Between the two of you, maybe we can figure out a time that this . . . happened.'

The woman's name was Jan Davis. She was a small, slender woman with dishwater-blonde hair and high cheekbones. Her apartment was pleasantly cluttered with books, scientific reprints and a few music CDs, all classical. She scurried nervously around, picking up magazines, straightening chairs, making lemonade when Lucas went over. Heather bounced in a worn, oversized easy chair, watching Lucas, smiling when he looked at her. Outside, in the hallway, cops were setting up crime-scene lines.

'I have a daughter about your age,' Lucas told Heather. 'Have you started school yet?'

'Yes,' she said. 'I was promoted. I'm in first, now. When school comes back.'

'So you won't be the littlest kids anymore . . . there'll be kindergarteners who are smaller than you.'

'Yup.' But she hadn't thought of that before, and she slipped off the chair and ran into the kitchen: 'Hey Mom, Mr. Davenport says there'll be kids littler than me at school . . .'

A minute later, Davis came out of the kitchen with two glasses of lemonade – 'There's plenty more if the other gentleman wants some.'

Lucas nodded, and took the glass. 'I noticed on your mailbox on the way in, your husband, Howard . . .'

'Howard's not living here now,' she said firmly.

'Not for a while?' Lucas asked.

'About seven weeks. I just haven't taken his name off the mailbox.'

'So . . . what? You're going to get divorced?'

'Yes. I'm just finishing my thesis at the U,' she said. 'I've got a post-doc offer from Johns Hopkins, and Heather and I'll be moving to Baltimore in December. Howard won't be coming.'

'Well, I'm sorry,' Lucas said. And he was. After a moment's silence, he turned to look at Heather and asked, 'What were you doing last night when you heard the party at Marta's? Were you in the hall?'

Heather looked guiltily at her mother and then said, 'Just for a minute. I left my truck out there.'

'She's not supposed to go out in the hall at night, after it gets dark,' Davis said. 'But sometimes she does.'

'Do you know what time it was?'

'We were talking about that, before you came over,' Davis said. 'She was out there with her blocks and her bulldozer when I told her to come in. But she left her truck, and a few minutes later I heard her messing around out there, and I went out and got her. It was between eight and nine.'

'Eight and nine. You wouldn't have been watching television, or anything, so you'd know what show was on?'

Davis was shaking her head. 'No, I'm rewriting my thesis, the final edit, and I'd just shut down . . .' She cocked her head to the side, then said, 'Hey: I think the word processor has a time thing on it, that shows when the file was closed.' She hopped off the couch and headed for a back room. Lucas and Heather followed.

Davis' study was a converted bedroom, with a single bed still in it: 'Howard slept here the last few weeks he lived with us,' she said, offhandedly. She was bringing the computer up, cycling through the Windows 98 display, then bringing up the word processor.

'Yup.' She tapped the screen, and bounced in her seat a little, the way her daughter had. 'The file was stored at eight twenty-two. I stored it and got up and heard Heather in the hall, and told her to come back inside.'

'All right, that's something,' Lucas said. 'Eight twenty-two.' He looked at Heather. 'Did you see anybody when you were in the hallway?'

She shook her head. 'No.' Then added, 'I peeked when Mom was gone, and I saw two ladies.'

'Two ladies? This was after you heard the party balloons?'

She nodded, solemn in the face of Lucas's interest. 'How did you see them?' Lucas asked.

'When I heard them, I opened the door just to peek,' she said. 'I thought it was Marta.'

'But it wasn't Marta?'

She shook her head again.

'Did you know the ladies?'

'No.'

'Never saw them before?'

She shook her head.

'Do you remember what they looked like?' Lucas asked.

She cocked her head in a perfect rendition of her mother's thinking-mannerism, and after two or three seconds said, 'Maybe I do.'

Chapter Nine

Carmel Loan learned that the bodies had been found from TV3. She and Rinker were walking through the Skyway toward Loan's office, eating frozen yogurt, when Carmel spotted a printed headline under a talking head in a deli-window TV: Two Bodies Found Near University. She nudged Rinker with her elbow.

'That was quick,' Rinker said, looking up at the TV.

'So was the other one – we could have gotten a couple days on either of them, but we didn't.'

'I wonder about that kid,' Rinker said. 'I hope nothing comes out of that.'

Carmel nodded and said, 'Let me find out when these bodies were found. If the cops have released any information, I can go over there and ask how it affects the case against Hale . . . and maybe find out what they've got.'

'Too much curiosity might be dangerous,' Rinker said.

'I can walk that line,' Carmel said confidently.

Carmel went straight to Lucas:

'I understand you found them,' she said. 'I mean, you personally.'

'Yeah. Not one of the brighter moments in my day,' Lucas said. He was tipped back in his new office chair, his feet up, reading the Modality Report. He'd bought the chair himself, a grey steel-and-fabric contraption that felt so good that he was thinking of marrying it.

'I'll tell you what,' Carmel said. 'We got one upper-class woman and three spics dead, and I would suggest to you that there's something going on besides some guy trying to kill his wife for her money. I'm reasonably sure that you're smart enough to have figured it out.'

'I figured it out, all right,' Lucas said. 'Your goddamn client's a snake. He was financing the local cocaine cartel with his old lady's money – and she found out. After he killed her, he rolled up the rest of the group before they could talk about it.'

'You can't . . .' Carmel started. Then she stopped herself. She ticked her finger at Lucas and said, 'You're teasing me.'

'Maybe,' Lucas said.

'I just don't know *why* we haven't slept together,' Carmel said. 'Except that my heart belongs to another.'

'So does mine,' Lucas said. 'I just wish I'd meet her.'

Carmel laughed. Let herself laugh a little too long, even indelicately. Then, 'So I can tell my client that he can stop the heavy drugs, and try to get some normal sleep.'

'He's had a problem?' Lucas asked. He yawned and looked at his watch.

'He sees himself involved in traumatic rectal enlargement, at the hands – well, not the hands – of biker gangs at Stillwater.'

'Yeah, well . . .' Lucas said dismissively. 'Don't tell him he's clear, because we're still looking at everybody. But between you and me . . .'

'Yeah?'

'. . . he seems unlikely. And if we get him into court on a murder charge, and you ask me if I said that, I'll perjure myself and say "No, of course not."'

'That'd be a big fuckin' change, a cop committing perjury,' Carmel said. 'All right. I'll tell him you'll be easing up.'

'That'd probably be right,' Lucas said.

Carmel turned, as though to leave, then asked, ingenuously, 'You got anything on the new killings? Like potential clients I can chase?'

'Well, we got this, out of a kid,' Lucas said. He dropped his feet off the new chair, pulled open a desk drawer and took out a computer-generated photo. 'We're putting it in the paper.'

He passed it to Carmel, who looked at it for a minute and then asked, 'What is this?'

'What the kid saw.'

'This is shit,' Carmel said. 'This is nothing.'

'I know. But it's what we got.'

'It looks like two aliens, a tall one and a short one.'

'I thought they looked like grim reapers, the head things they have on.'

The silk scarves had helped. Carmel would've spent a moment giving thanks, if she'd had any idea who she might give thanks to. In the picture, the scarves gave their heads a tall, slender profile. The kid must have seen them as silhouettes. The faces within the silhouettes were generic enough to be meaningless.

'What are the head things?' Carmel asked.

'The kid didn't know. Maybe some kind of hat. Maybe they were nuns.'

'Good thought,' Carmel said.

'They're women, anyway,' Lucas said. 'At least the kid says they are.'

'The shooter in the stairwell was a woman,' Carmel said.

'The triumph of feminism,' Lucas said. 'We got equal-opportunity hitters.'

'Well . . .' Carmel flipped the photo back on the desk. 'On second thought, if you find her, call somebody else. She might be a little dangerous to know.'

'Especially if you lose the case.'

Carmel snorted as she went through the door. 'As if that might happen,' she said.

When Carmel got back to the apartment, she found Rinker's suitcase in the front hall, and Rinker just getting out of the bathroom, freshly showered, scrubbing her hair dry.

'So what happened?'

'We're clear,' Carmel said. She gave Rinker a short account of her talk with Lucas. Rinker was pleased with the outcome. 'I'm outa here,' she said. 'I've got to get back to my business.'

'Do you have a reservation?'

'Yeah, for four o'clock,' Rinker said.

'I'll drive you out to the airport,' Carmel said. 'Listen, what do you do in the winter?'

'Mostly work,' Rinker said, fluffing her hair. 'Where I live, there's not a hell of a lot to do outside.'

'Same here . . . You ever go to Cancun? Or Cozumel?'

'Cozumel. Acapulco. A couple of times. Practice my Spanish.'

'I try to get out of here for at least three weeks after it gets cold – a week in November, a week in January and a week in March,' Carmel said. 'We ought to go together. I've got connections, in the hotels and so on. It's a good time.'

'Jeez,' Rinker said. She seemed oddly pleased, and Carmel got the impression she wasn't often invited places. 'That's sounds nice.'

'So call me in October, and if you can get away, I'll set up the hotels and everything, and you can set up your own plane reservations, and we'll meet down there.'

'I'd like that,' Rinker said. 'What do you do? Lay on the beach? Shop? I kinda like to boogie . . .'

'Listen, I know some guys there, and there are always guys around . . . we'd be going around.'

Rinker held up a finger: 'Hold that thought, but this just popped into my mind, before I forget. The guns are in the closet. You gotta take them down and throw them in the river, or bury them somewhere. Also the box of shells – the shells are with the gun. They're the only things left that can hang us.'

'I sorta like them,' Carmel said.

'Fine. Spend a few hundred bucks and get a nice clean gun of your own. I can make a call, and have one sent to you: brand new, cold, no registration to worry about. If you want a silencer, I can handle that, too. But the guns in the closet have gotta go. I'm nervous having them here, even hidden. You gotta do it; I'll call you every ten minutes until it's done.'

'We can dump them in the river by the airport,' Carmel said. 'I know a place – then you won't have to worry.'

'Excellent,' Rinker said. She cocked her head. 'Listen, if we go to Cancun, what about my hair? I've always had the feeling that it's a pretty small-town cut, you know, like I'm already middle-aged or something. I thought . . .'

Carmel did cartoon breath-intake, and held her fingers to her breast: 'There's this woman down there, I've had my hair done every time I've gone down, she's a genius . . .'

Talking about Mexico, they almost forgot the guns. With the door open, and Rinker's suitcase in the hall, Carmel snapped her finger and whispered, 'The guns.'

She went back to get them, and fumbled the box of shells. There were still thirty-odd shells in the box, and they flew everywhere. Carmel hastily scooped them up, pushed them back in the box, and hurried to the door.

Before going to the airport, Carmel took Rinker to the flats below Fort Snelling on the Minnesota River. 'The fort's just a relic,' Carmel said, as they looked up the bluff at the revetments. 'The first thing ever built here, that's still around, anyway. The Army had a death camp for Indians right where we're standing. This was after the big revolt . . . they hanged thirty-eight Indians in a single drop, down in Mankato. This area, this is where they kept the survivors, especially the woman. Half of them died during the winter; most of the women were raped by soldiers.'

'Happy story,' Rinker said.

'I don't know what I'd do if I got raped, but it'd be something unpleasant, if I got my hands on the guy,' Carmel said.

'I bet,' Rinker said. She didn't mention the guy named Dale-Something. They found a quiet path along the river, checked to make sure there was nobody watching, and pitched the guns into a deep spot.

'That's it,' Rinker said. 'We're all done.'

On the way back from the airport, Carmel called Hale Allen.

Allen said, 'God, I was trying to get you earlier in the afternoon. Are you coming to the funeral tomorrow?'

'I was trying to get you, but all I got was your machine,' Carmel said. 'We've got some things to talk about. I spoke to Lucas Davenport this afternoon . . .'

'What? What'd he say?' Allen was anxious.

'I'm in my car, and I hate to talk on this cell phone. Why don't I just stop by? I could be there in twenty minutes.'

'Twenty minutes,' he said, with an uncertain note in his voice. 'Okay. See you in twenty.'

Not the most eager lover she'd ever had, Carmel thought as she ended the phone call. On the other hand, he didn't know they were lovers. Not yet.

In a couple of hours, he would. A certain kind of man, sharks-in-the-water, attorneys more often than not, alone with Carmel, would produce a pass. Sometimes, depending on her mood and the man, Carmel would receive the pass, and things would proceed. Carmel was far from a virgin, but had never had a long-term sexual relationship. One woman, who was almost a friend, had once confided to Carmel that one of her ex-suitors had said, to a number of people at a party, that Carmel frightened him. He felt like the fly, and she was the spider.

Carmel pretended to be puzzled by the comment, but wasn't entirely displeased: fear wasn't the worst thing to instill in a man, especially the man who made the comment, who was something of a thug himself. Still, after that, she tried to soften her bedroom image, tried to slow down a little. But she really didn't much care for the weight of a man pressing her down, the trapped feeling gasping over his shoulder, staring at the ceiling while he flailed around on top. And she was a little picky. She didn't like hairy shoulders – even less, hairy backs. She didn't like chest hair that connected with pubic hair. She didn't care for bald men or the untidiness of uncircumcised men; she didn't care for men who burped, or whose breath smelled of anything cooked, or who peed with the bathroom door open, or farted.

Orgasms didn't often happen, not with men; her best orgasms came alone, in the bathtub. Hale would change that, she thought. If not right away, she could train him.

Hale Allen lived on a quiet, upperclass street off one of the lakes, far enough from the crowds to have a certain peace in the evening, without the constant to-ing and fro-ing of thin young women with earphones and blades; but at the same time, close enough that residents could walk down and enjoy the mix when they wished to. The house was long and white, with lake-green shutters and a yellow bug light over the central door, and a long driveway that curved up a slope past fifty-year-old burr oaks. A small white sign at the edge of the driveway warned burglars that the house was protected by Insula Armed Response.

Carmel left the Jag under the spreading arms of an oak and rang the doorbell. A moment later, she heard the muffled pounding of stocking feet on a stairs, and then Hale opened the door, a white terry cloth towel in his hand. He smiled and backed up and said, 'Come on in,' and rubbed his damp hair with the towel. He looked like something off the perfume pages of *Esquire*.

She had never been inside his house – Barbara Allen's house, it turned out, was decorated with a cool and discerning eye, a mix of pieces new and old. But nothing *fabulous:* Carmel felt the instant chill of class inferiority. She moved into the living room, turned and said, 'I talked to Davenport.'

'Yeah?' He was eager.

'It's pretty much over with. They've got three more shootings by the same person – probably the same person – and you're an obvious non-candidate in all three of them.'

'So they're gonna do what? Talk to the press, tell them . . .'

'Doesn't work that way,' Carmel said. She took a slow turn past a small watercolor: no name that she recognized, but she did feel a vibration coming from the work – a simple street scene, probably New

York – and understood that it was good. She looked away from the painting: 'The way it works is, they don't say anything to anybody. They just go away. Then, if it turns out that you were involved, they don't look like dumbshits.'

'That's not fair,' Allen protested. Once again, she had to strain to think of him as a lawyer.

'Of course it's not fair. But they have the choice of, one: being fair to Hale Allen, or two: taking the chance that they're going to look like dumbshits. Which choice do you think a bunch of city hall bureaucrats is gonna choose?'

'By golly, that really makes me mad.' He hurled the terrycloth towel at a couch.

'Hey. Unless something new comes up, it's over,' she said. 'About Barbara – the funeral is at two?'

'Yes, at Morganthau's.'

'I won't be able to make the service; I'll be at the cemetery, though.'

'Thanks. I . . .' He plopped on the couch, picked up the damp towel, turned it in his large hands. 'I have some questions that I want to ask Barbara, and I've got some things I want to talk over, but I can't, cause she's dead. I can't get around that.'

'Like what do you want to tell her?' Real curiosity.

'Like, I want to tell her about Louise.'

Now Carmel was puzzled. 'Why? You'd only hurt her.'

'I wouldn't *only* hurt her; I think it's more complicated than that, don't you?'

'All right,' Carmel said. She sat on the couch next to him. 'Tell me about it. Tell me about Louise.'

Louise liked sex, and so did Hale. Barbara liked it better than, say, a fried egg sandwich, but not as much as a good soft back rub. 'When we were having sex, I always had the feeling that she was taking care of me, not making love with me. She was always waiting for me to finish. She always wanted it to be good for me, but then she always wanted to round out the night with a book . . .'

'Uh-huh, I know the feeling,' Carmel said.

The room was closing around them, getting tighter, the walls moving in, until there was nothing in the house but the two of them. He talked about Barbara, about Louise; laughed a little about some of Louise's excesses; cried a little about Barbara's idiosyncracies. Carmel patted him on the shoulder blades, then rubbed his back a little. He held one of her hands, turned it over, fondled it.

The room closed in and Carmel tipped back and there he was: a perfect little spread of hair on his chest; a tidy circumcision.

Unfortunately, she thought afterward, he didn't have the best of bathroom habits.

She sighed. So much to do.

Chapter Ten

Sloan was wearing khaki shorts, a black faux-leather fanny pack pulled around to his stomach, and a pink golf shirt. His legs were the color of skim milk, and so bony they might have been attached to a short ostrich. 'My wife made me wear them,' he said, looking down at the shorts. 'She said I was gonna get heat stroke, and there's no point in getting heat stroke on a vacation day.'

Lucas was peering over the top of his desk. 'You got your gun in the fanny pack?'

'Yeah. I got the pack from Brinkhoff. It's all Velcro, it's not really zipped up. See?' He stood up, pulled on the front of the fanny pack, and the entire cover came away. The revolver inside was attached by a single tab over the barrel, which tore away when Sloan pulled the gun out.

'Pretty slick,' Lucas said. He settled back. 'But it looks stupid.'

'My wife says . . .'

'Your wife has the fashion sense of a cockroach.'

'I'll tell her you said so.'

'If you do, I'll have to kill you.'

There was a tentative knock at the door. Lucas called, 'Come in.'

The door opened and Hale Allen stepped halfway inside, stopping when he saw Sloan with his khaki shorts, pink shirt and the pistol in his hand. 'You need to talk to Lucas?' Sloan asked.

'If he's not busy,' Allen said.

'I was just about to shoot him,' Sloan said. 'Could it wait until after that?'

'Well . . . Do you think he'd be better by lunchtime?'

'Go away,' Lucas told Sloan. To Allen, politely, with curiosity, 'Come in, sit down.'

'Is there anything new with the case?' Allen asked. He looked uneasily around the office as he asked the question; crossed and recrossed his legs.

'We're still working on it, but we're kind of stuck,' Lucas said.

A week had gone by since Lucas had spoken to Carmel Loan. All the crime-scene evidence had been exhaustively reviewed, but nothing was coming out. In the meantime, a Ferris wheel at a neighborhood carnival had collapsed, two children had been killed and seven more badly hurt. The execution killings had disappeared from the media, as reporters and state safety inspectors chased down every carnival in the state. The lack of both progress and outside attention had taken pressure off the investigation. Lucas had the feeling that the whole thing was headed for the dead-letter file.

'You heard about Barbara's parents?' Allen asked.

'Just rumors . . .'

'They were going to sue me – for wrongful death, claiming I was involved in killing Barbara, like that O.J. lawsuit,' Allen said indignantly. 'They were gonna try to keep me from inheriting, so *they'd* get her money. Then it turned out that ninety percent of the money goes to the foundation, not to me. If they sued me, and won, a hundred percent would go to the foundation. They wouldn't get a dime.'

'Ho,' Lucas said.

'Yeah. They said screw that, we aren't suing if there isn't any payoff. They dropped the whole thing.'

'Hum,' said Lucas.

'Exactly . . .'

Allen was indignant, but his eyes kept wandering away from Lucas. Lucas had seen it before in somebody who felt guilty about something, and was about to confess. Allen, Lucas thought, wasn't here to talk about his in-laws.

'So what else is going on?' Lucas asked, leaning back, trying to sound kindly. He wished Sloan were back. Sloan was a master at this. 'How are you doing? Are you okay? We were pretty rough on you for a while.'

'Well . . .' Allen smiled, and Lucas thought, here it comes. 'I came to see you because you know about the case, and you seemed like a pretty good guy, and everybody says you're pretty smart and you've been around . . .'

'Okay . . .' Keep him rolling.

'I've been feeling kind of weird about something. About the case.'

'You mean, psychologically troubled? I . . .'

'Not exactly,' Allen said. He leaned forward, intent now. 'You know, I really did love Barbara. She was fun, in a quiet way. But we were different, and this affair – you know that I had an affair?'

'Yes,' Lucas said. He gestured with one hand, as to say, *So what? Haven't we all?*

The tentative smile flickered over Allen's face again. 'When Barbara got killed, I felt terrible about it. Your guys found out about the affair, and I hadn't told Carmel. When she found out, she hit the roof. She went and talked to Louise, and now everybody's in an uproar . . .'

Lucas nodded: 'I can see why Carmel would be unhappy. Facing the possibility of defending you in court.'

'Yeah, yeah,' Allen said, brushing the comment away. So that wasn't where he was going, Lucas thought. 'The day you told her that you weren't so interested in me any more . . .'

Lucas glanced at a wall calendar, 'A week ago today . . .'

'Exactly a week ago,' Allen said, 'Carmel came over to my house to give me the news. And we had a drink, yadayadayada, and then she comes on to me.'

'Yeah?' Lucas' eyebrows went up.

'Yeah. Really hard. *Really hard*. And you know Carmel. She gets what she wants.'

Lucas allowed a faint man-to-man smile to slip onto his face: 'The next thing you knew, you were working closely with your attorney.'

'What she did was fuck my brains loose. And she's been back three more times since then. Does that sound bad? Does that sound crazy? I can't sleep thinking about it, but I really can't talk to any of my friends, either. They'd go batshit if I told them. Most of them are Barbara's friends, too, out at the club.'

Lucas shook his head: 'I wouldn't worry about it too much. I've seen all kinds of reactions to spousal deaths, and believe me, you're not the first guy to fall in bed with another woman after his wife's been killed. Maybe there's a drive for intimacy.'

'You think so?' Allen said. He seemed to brighten, momentarily. Relief? Lucas wasn't sure.

'It's something like that,' Lucas said. 'Listen, as long as you've told me all this . . . why Carmel? She doesn't seem like your type. Detective Sherrill told me that you were a pretty relaxed guy. Carmel, on the other hand . . .'

'Detective Sherrill, she's the one . . .' He made a figure with his hands. 'Yeah.'

'She seemed nice.' His eyes wandered away again, and he hunched forward in his chair: 'Carmel . . . pillow talks. She told me that she's been in love with me for two years, and hid it, because she thought it was hopeless, because I was married to a rich woman. She told me that Louise – that's the woman I was having an affair with – was a miserable gold-digger and a loser. She gets really violent about it.'

'Really?' Keep him rolling.

'I'm serious, once she grabbed me by the dick and said she'd cut it off if I ever put it back in Louise.'

'Whoa . . . And she said she was in love with you for two years?'

'Yeah, ever since a little thing in a restaurant. I couldn't even remember it.'

'Do you believe her? That she's been in love?'

'I know it sounds vain, but I do. You'd have to hear her talk. She remembered me saying things, doing things, places she'd bumped into me, times we'd just had a word or two.'

Lucas thought for a moment, and then said, 'Are you seeing her tonight?'

'Of course. Every night. She says we're gonna get married in a couple of years . . .'

'Huh.' Lucas turned in his chair to face his window, his fingers steepled at his mouth, and looked out at the street. He hoped he looked like Sherlock Holmes. Then he swivelled back to face Allen. 'Do you think if you suggested that you go out to Penelope's, that she'd go?'

'Penelope's? Oh, heck yes, she loves that kind of scene, Minnetonka, the lake, all that. Trendy, expensive . . .'

'Call her. She lives downtown, right? She's got some kind of fabulous apartment that was in the *Star-Tribune*?' Lucas knew exactly where she lived. He'd joked about it with a banker friend who lived in the same building.

'Right. And it is fabulous,' Allen said.

'Call her, suggest Penelope's, and when she gets to your place, suggest that she drive. Make up some kind of excuse. Sprained your gas pedal ankle or something. Nothing serious, so you have to limp. Just get her to drive.'

'She drives most of the time anyway,' Allen said. 'She doesn't like my car. I gotta brown-and-creme Lexus, she calls it a Jap car. She's got this red Jag.'

'Good. Don't tell her any of this, by the way,' Lucas said. 'Don't tell her you talked to me. Just get her out there and have a nice long meal.'

'I will. What are you going to do?'

'Observe,' Lucas said. 'Not me, another guy.'

'Observe what?' Allen asked.

'This whole thing sounds a little bit off to me. Remember, whether you think like this or not: you *are* a rich guy. And you're good-looking. Women are going to come after you, and it's hard to tell who's sincere and who isn't. So I got a guy on the staff who specializes in . . . mmm . . . what would you call it? Emotional readings, I guess. I'll have him take a look at the two of you, and tell me what he thinks. He'll look at her body language, stuff like that. I'll pass it along to you.'

'He's gonna eat with us?' Allen asked dimly.

'No, no. He'll just be there,' Lucas said. 'Don't go looking around for him or anything – just enjoy yourself and make sure that you stay long enough that my guy can get a reading.'

'An emotional reading?'

Lucas spread his hands: 'Hey, it's what I got.'

When Allen had gone, Lucas leaned back in his chair and stared at the ceiling for a few moments, thinking about Carmel Loan. He ran through everything she'd said to him since the Allen killing, and in running through the various conversations they'd had, he stumbled over one small gemstone.

When he'd last talked to her, she'd made a deliberately crude comment about three dead spics and an upper class woman. Anyway, he remembered it that way; and he remembered that they'd had difficulty finding anyone to claim the bodies, or anyone who would even admit to knowing who they were.

Had they released the names by the time he'd seen Carmel? He didn't think so. But who knows, maybe the television people had talked to the cops outside the house, and somebody made a comment. Or maybe a reporter had talked to a neighbor, and the names had gotten out. Maybe. That *could* explain how she knew the two Dinkytown dead were Latinos . . .

Carmel Loan. He scribbled her name on a legal pad, looked at it, then drew an arrow and scribbled another name: *Rolando D'Aquila*. Another arrow, at ninety degrees from the first, from Carmel to the next name, *Hale Allen.* He looked at that for a moment, drew another arrow from Carmel to *Barbara Allen*; and another from Carmel to *Dead Spics.* Of course, her connection to Marta Blanca and her dead boyfriend was purely part of his memory, nothing that could be proven . . .

A cold wind was already blowing through Lucas' chest. He knew what he was going to do – he even knew how he was going to do it, to the smallest detail – but the idea chilled him. He felt like a wealthy man about to shoplift something expensive. And fooling with Carmel Loan was not like messing with a doper or a player or a stick-up guy. If he screwed up, *he* could go to jail.

After a few minutes, he roused himself from the chair and walked down the hall to the Homicide office. Sloan was just leaving: 'The goddamned air conditioning is giving me goose bumps.'

'What are you doing tonight?' Lucas asked.

'Maybe taking the old lady out for a movie.'

'If you take her to Penelope's, on Lake Minnetonka, I'll pay for the meal and sign off on the overtime.'

'Ya got me,' Sloan said quickly. 'For one thing, if I said no, the old lady'd murder me.' Sloan had a daughter in college and tuition to pay, and luxury was hard to come by. 'What do I have to do?'

When Sloan had gone, Lucas called Jim Bone, president of Polaris bank: 'Jim, are you gonna be home between eight and nine tonight?'

'Yeah; you need something?'

'I need to talk. Ten minutes, maybe. I've been running around like a mad dog, and I can't spring any time, during the day, and besides, you're busy . . .'

'Come on over. Kerin would love to see you.'

'How's she doing?' Bone's wife was pregnant.

'Just starting to show . . .'

'You guys didn't waste any time.'

'Yeah, well, we're old people.'

Myron Bunnson told everybody that his mother was a stone freak hippie and that his *real* given name was Bullet Blue, and that his father had been an Oakland Hell's Angel, before the Angels got old. None of that was true. His parents were really named Myron (Senior) and Adele Bunnson, and they ran a dairy farm near Eau Claire, Wisconsin.

Bullet was working one of the three valet slots at Penelope's. He saw the red Jag swing into the lot and said to the other two, 'This is it. This is mine.'

'Three-way split, man,' said his friend, Richard Schmid, who was trying to convince his friends to call him Crank. The third valet nodded: 'Three ways.'

'No problem,' Bullet Blue said. 'I'm just workin' the chick.'

'Right.' Crank recognized the Jag. Bullet's chances of nailing this particular chick, especially dressed as he was, like an organ-grinder monkey, were slim and none, and slim was outa town. Still, Bullet Blue wanted the car, and they all had their favorites . . .

Blue took the Jag and ten bucks from Carmel, who flashed a smile at him. 'Thank you, ma'am,' Blue said, giving her his best look. The look apparently missed over her bare shoulder, and she was into the restaurant with her friend, a guy who Blue thought looked *way* too straight. Whatever. He hopped into the Jag, and rolled it into the valet parking area on the side of the restaurant. Lucas was leaning against a Chevy van, talking to the man who sat in the driver's seat.

'You got the money?' he asked Lucas.

'Keys?'

Bullet dropped the keys into Lucas' hand. Lucas passed them through the window to the man in the driver's seat, who took them and clambered into the back. Lucas handed Bullet Blue a small fold of currency. 'I'll talk to McKinley.'

'If we could just get her off this one time . . .' Bullet slipped the bills into his pants pocket. The three-way split only involved the ten bucks from Carmel.

'I didn't say I could do that,' Lucas said bluntly. From the van, they could hear the grinding buzz of the key-cutter. 'The best we could do is maybe drop the charge to something less heavy. But she's gonna do some time.'

'She's already done time,' Blue protested. He was talking about his sister, who came off the farm two years after Bullet, and started calling herself Baby Blue. 'She's been sittin' in jail for a month, waiting for the trial. Can't we get her time served?'

'Not with this one,' Lucas said. 'If she hadn't had the gun . . .'

'It wasn't her gun; it was Eddie's,' Bullet said heatedly.

'But she had it. I'll see if McKinley and the guys'll go for two or three months. As it is, she's looking at a year, and maybe more.'

'Anything you can do, man.'

'And you stay the fuck outa trouble, dickweed,' Lucas said. 'Go back home if you gotta.'

'Right. Spend my life pulling cow tits.'

'Then get your ass back in Dunwoody – how much time you got to go there?' Lucas asked.

'One semester.'

'One semester. You get out, you start making some good money, and you make it wherever you go.'

'Yeah, yeah,' Bullet said.

You don't want to hear my Dunwoody speech?'

'I just ain't made to fix cars, no more'n I'm made to pull cow tits; I'm made to rock n' roll.'

'You're made to . . .'

The man in the van spoke over Lucas shoulder: 'All done.' He handed Carmel's key ring to Lucas, and Lucas handed it to Blue.

'Dunwoody,' Lucas said.

'Rock n' roll,' said Blue, as he walked away.

Lucas, wearing his dark blue lawyer suit and carrying a black-leather briefcase, said, 'Jim Bone,' to the doorman at the desk, who looked at a list and said, 'And your name, sir?'

'Lucas Davenport.'

'Go right on up, Mr. Davenport,' the doorman said, making a tick next to Lucas' name.

Lucas had made a medium-sized fortune when he sold his simulations company; Bone's bank managed it. '. . . really risky,' Bone said. 'The economy could drop like a rock and who's going to pay a hundred dollars a round after that?'

Lucas nodded: 'Yeah, but I wouldn't have to make a hundred dollars a round – I could break even at sixty.'

'You don't know anything about running a golf course,' Bone said.

'Of course not; I wouldn't even try to. I don't even like golf. That's why they're talking about professional management.'

'It's not completely crazy,' Bone admitted finally.

'The whole point,' Lucas said, 'is that I could give my daughter that big chunk right now, take a mortgage on the rest, put all the excess into course maintenance, building value. By the time she's twenty-five or thirty, she owns the whole limited-partnership share, ninety-nine percent, while I own the general-partner's share, one percent, and we sell it and she's fixed. She picks up four or five million, minimum, and who knows? Maybe five or ten.'

'The concept's okay, but to tell you the truth, you might do better in the long run just to pay the government's bite . . .'

When they were done, Lucas said good-bye to Kerin, who seemed much softer than when he'd first met her; slower, happier, pleased with herself. Bone, at the door, said, 'I'll have the guys work it up for you. We'll have something in a week.'

'Thanks, Jim.'

There were five doors on Bone's floor. Three apartments in addition to Bone's, and the fire-stair door. No security camera. Lucas let the elevator doors close behind him, and pushed twenty-seven. As the elevator started up, he took a nylon sock out of his pants pocket, spread it apart, and slipped it over the top of his head, like a watch cap. If there were somebody in the hallway, he could slip it back off – maybe without it being seen.

But the hallway of the twenty-seventh floor was dead quiet. Still in the elevator, blocking the door with his foot, he pulled the nylon down over his face, turned up his coat collar, so it looked almost clerical, and did a quick peek out in the hall. No video cameras. He walked quickly down to Carmel's apartment, slipped the first key in. The key turned – the other, he thought, must be for her office.

There was one light on, somewhere at the back of the apartment.

'Hello?' he called. No answer. 'Hello?'

He did a quick tour, checking, his nerves starting to jangle. He'd done this before, but he'd make a poor burglar, he thought.

He started with her home Rolodex. There were dozens of names, most attached to the name of a law firm or a corporation – business acquaintances. There were a few names with a first and last, followed by a number, but usually, by two numbers. An office and a home phone, Lucas thought. Probably not a killer's number. There were ten numbers that involved simply a name and a number, and he copied those into a notebook.

Then, in the kitchen, he found another address book, this one, apparently, purely personal. He took a small Nikon camera from his briefcase, made sixteen shots, stopped to reload the camera, made eight more, and dropped it back in his briefcase.

Then he started through the apartment:

He found a Dell computer in her study, with a built-in Zip drive. He'd brought Zip, Jaz and Superdisks; he brought the computer up, clicked on the *Computer* icon, and dragged all of her documents to the Zip icon. As the computer began dumping to the Zip drive, he began looking through the array of filing cabinets on the other side of the room. He pulled the

101

drawers one at a time, and in the last drawer, found a mass of paid bills –
nothing big, just the usual once-a-month routine. He riffled through them
quickly, separated out the phone bills for the last four months, and used
the camera again. But the last phone bill was almost exactly a month
old . . .

He went into the kitchen, where he'd seen a neat stack of envelopes,
flipped through them, found the US West bill. With another little jangle of
nerves, he picked up a teakettle on the stove, tipped it to make sure there
was enough water, and turned it on.

He looked in the bedroom while he waited for the teakettle to heat.
Nothing obvious. He very carefully went through her drawers, afraid that
he would disturb them in a way she could detect. He found nothing. He
checked the closets quickly, and was closing the door when a brassy
sparkle on the floor caught his eye. The sparkle had a certain *quality* that
he unconsciously recognized. He stooped, scraped his hand along the rug,
felt it, picked it: an unfired .22 shell. He took a penlight out of his pocket,
searched the closet floor, but found only the one cartridge.

He thought about it for a second, then put it in his pocket. He was
closing the closet door when the teakettle began to hum. He hurried
back to the kitchen, let the raw steam play down the back of the envelope,
pried up the seal, took out the bill, shot a quick photo of the long-
distance calls, and resealed the envelope before the adhesive could dry.
He put the kettle back and sniffed: the smell of the adhesive hung in the
air, only faintly, but it was there, he thought. He hoped Carmel would
take her time.

In the office, the computer was sitting quietly; he paged quickly through
a few other folders, dragged a couple of them to the Zip icon, waited a few
seconds until the files had been dumped, then shut the computer down.

All right. What else? He was ready to leave; before he went, he took a
last look around.

The apartment *was* fabulous. But aside from the stuff in the filing
cabinets, and stuck away in drawers, it hardly seemed to have been lived
in: obsessively neat, everything in its place, like a stage set.

The phone in his pocket rang: Sloan.

'They're leaving,' he said. 'I just got my shrimp cocktail. I hope I'm not
supposed to follow them.'

'Nah, let them go. But what do you think?'

'They're tight, all right. It was kissy-smoochy all night. But I think the guy was expecting somebody else to show. He kept cruising the place, looking around.'

'Huh. Wonder what that's about?' Lucas asked, feeling just slightly guilty. Then: 'How come you're eating a shrimp cocktail and they're already leaving? You having it for dessert?'

'Well . . . yeah,' Sloan said. His voice went a little hoarse: 'I love these things.'

When Carmel got home, a little after eleven – she had to work the next day – she stopped at the threshold of the apartment and wrinkled her nose. Something, she thought, was not quite right. She couldn't put her finger on it: the air was wrong, or something. The apartment's chemicals had been disturbed. She walked through, leaving the hallway door open, so she'd have a place to run if she needed it, but found nothing at all.

'Huh,' she said, as she closed the hallway door.

By the next morning, she'd forgotten it.

Chapter Eleven

When Lucas got home, he took the CompactFlash card out of his pocket, dropped another one out of the Nikon, and read them into his home computer. After transferring the files to Photoshop, he sharpened the photos as much as he could and dumped them to his photo printer. That done, he called Davenport Simulations and let the phone ring until a man answered, his voice grumpy at the interruption.

'Steve? Lucas Davenport.'

'Hey, Lucas! Where've you been, man?' Steve smoked a little weed, from time to time; dropped a little acid on weekends, and let his beard grow. When the acid was on him, he could program in three dimensions. 'You don't come around any more.'

'I'd be like the ghost of bad news, the former owner hanging around,' Lucas said. 'But I needed somebody who could help me out with a computer problem. I thought about you . . . from your phreaking days.'

'I don't do that shit anymore, hardly ever,' Steve said. 'Uh, what do you need?'

'Is there anyone on the Net who could track down anonymous telephone numbers?' Lucas asked. 'If there is, do you know how you could get in touch with him?'

Steve dropped his voice, though he probably was alone: 'Depends on what the numbers are and how much trouble you want to go to. And whether you want to pay for it.'

'How much would it cost?'

'If you want *all* the numbers and don't ask any questions . . . I know a guy who does that kind of work. He could e-mail them to you for a couple of bucks a name. How many do you have?'

'Maybe fifty,' Lucas said.

'Oh, Jesus, I thought you were talking about hundreds. Or thousands. I don't know if he'd be interested in a little job like that.'

'I'd pay him more,' Lucas said.

'I can ask,' Steve said. 'Say five hundred bucks?'

'That's good,' Lucas said.

'I'm putting my name behind this, man. I'll be stuck for the five hundred if you don't come through.'

'Steve . . .'

'All right, all right.'

'I could use any other information they can find on the people who belong to the phone numbers – I mean, if they can do that.'

'That'd cost you more.'

'Go up to a thousand.'

'You got it: send me an e-mail with the numbers. I'll pass it on. You'll get it back by e-mail.'

Lucas copied odd, unusual or unidentified numbers from the photos and asked for names and addresses. He dumped the e-mail to Steve, then checked his own e-mail account, and found two letters, one advertising pornographic photographs of pre-teens, which he deleted, and another from his daughter.

Sarah was in the first grade, starting to read and write: but her mother, a TV-news producer, had shown her how to use a voice-writing software program. Using the voice-writer, Sarah now wrote Lucas a couple of times a week.

Lucas took fifteen minutes to interpret the voice-written text, and he wrote back, struggling to use words that Sarah could sound out, while at the same time trying to avoid the Dick-and-Jane syndrome. He was just finishing when a perky little female voice from the computer said, 'You have mail.'

He sent the e-mail note to Sarah, then clicked on his in-box. The sole piece of mail was a list of names and addresses attached to the phone numbers he'd sent out. All but two of the names had personal information attached. Lucas scanned it: the information appeared to come from credit bureaus, although some might have come from state motor-vehicle departments. At the end of it all was a price tag: 'Send $1000.'

'Quick,' he muttered. He looked at his watch. Just under half an hour.

He printed the numbers out, and turned to the documents he'd pulled from Carmel's computer. Though he spent less than five seconds with most of them – virtually all were work-related – it was after three in the morning before he wiped the disk, shut down the computer and went to bed.

The next day, he chopped the disk to pieces with a butcher knife, and dropped the pieces in two separate trash cans in the Skyway: he had an almost superstitious dread of computer files turning up when they weren't supposed to.

Then, while he was still in the Skyway, between the Pillsbury building and the government center, he noticed a woman in a shapeless black dress, wearing a white scarf on her head, babushka-style. He turned to watch her walking away; some religious or ethnic group, he thought, but he didn't know which. He went on to police headquarters, whistling, where he called Sherrill.

'Can either you or Black come by for a minute?'

'Which would you prefer? Me or Tom?'

'Stop,' he said. 'I just want to hear about the Allen case. And mention a couple of things to you.'

Sherrill came down a few minutes later and dropped into his visitor's chair. 'We're running out of stuff to look at,' she said.

'Let me tell you what Hale Allen told me yesterday,' Lucas said. He laid it out quickly, then told her about the ethnic woman in the Skyway. 'She looked like the aliens the kid described, when she was putting together that composite photo. So we need to get a low-angle photograph of somebody in a dark dress, wearing a scarf over her head; then we need to plug in a bunch of faces, including Carmel's.'

'Carmel Loan,' Sherrill said. 'That could get rough, if we went public and didn't have the goods.'

'Which is why I don't want her to know that we're looking at her. Not unless we get something solid.'

'All right,' Sherrill said. She pushed herself up. 'I can probably get a picture of Carmel from your lady at the *Star-Tribune* library, if she still works there.'

'She does,' Lucas said.

'And I'll have the ID guys put together a photo spread. We can base it on the composite the kid gave us. When do you want to talk to the kid?'

'The sooner the better,' Lucas said. 'I don't know how long memories last with little kids.'

'I'll try to set it up this afternoon.'

'Something else,' Lucas said. He dug in his pocket. 'Could you have the lab do an analysis on the slug?' He tossed the .22 shell to her. She caught it one-handed, looked at it, and then asked, 'What's going on, Lucas?'

'Nothing; it's one of my .22s. I just want to look at the difference between a random analysis and what we're getting from the slugs we took out of the dead guys. Do we really have a case based on a metals analysis?'

She looked at him, suspicious, turned the cartridge in her hand. 'Then, if I lost this particular shell,' she said, 'You wouldn't mind if I just sent in one of my own.'

Lucas said, 'Send *that* one in, huh? Just send it in.'

'This one.'

'That one.'

'Lucas . . .'

'Off my case, Marcy,' he said.

She grinned at him and said, 'Marcy, my ass. We're operating, aren't we?'

'Send the fuckin' thing in,' he said.

Lucas spent the morning running through the numbers he'd taken from Carmel's address books and phone bills: he'd marked fifty-five of them to be checked. In three hours, he'd half-filled a yellow legal pad with notes, but nothing promising.

A few minutes before noon, he got to the final long-distance call on the last of the long-distance bills: a call made two weeks earlier, he noticed, a couple of days after Barbara Allen's death. The note from the hacker said only, 'Small business phone listed to Tennex Messenger Service.' Lucas dialed the number and a woman answered on the first ring: 'Tennex Messenger Service.'

'Yes, could I speak to the Tennex manager? Or whoever runs the place?'

'I'm sorry, sir, Mr. Wilson is out. I can give you his voice-mail.'

'Well, I was just wondering how I could set up an account with Tennex.'

'I'm sorry, sir; we're answering service. All I can do is give you his voice-mail.'

'Okay, thanks, if you could do that . . .'

He was switched, and got a voice-mail introduction, a slightly vague voice that might have come from a drugged-out teenager: 'You have reached Tennex Messenger Service, your, uh, fastest messenger service in the DeeCee area. We are either, uh, on the phone or out on a call. We check back for messages, so, like, leave your name and, uh, phone number. Thanks.'

Not interested in talking to a strung-out bicycle-messenger, Lucas hung up, yawned, stood up and stretched, and walked down to Homicide. Black was at his desk, shuffling through papers; Sloan had his feet up, reading a *Pioneer Press*.

'Lunch?' Lucas asked.

'Yeah, I could see my way clear to a lunch,' Sloan said.

Sherrill pushed through the office door, spotted Lucas and said, 'I sent that slug in, and we're all set for four o'clock this afternoon.'

Sloan's eyebrows went up. *'Really? Where at?'* he asked.

Sherrill correctly interpreted his tone and implication: 'Shut up,' she said. To Lucas: 'Mama is not happy with the fact that we're coming back to see the kid. There was all the loose talk in the newspapers about hit men.'

'So I'll let you warm her up when we get there,' Lucas said. 'Woman talk, bonding, chit-chat, that kind of shit.'

'Sexism,' Sloan said, shaking his head sadly. 'And from a member of the Difference Commission.'

Lucas's hand went to his forehead: 'Ah, Jesus, I forgot. There's a meeting tonight.'

They looked at him with sympathy, and Sherrill patted his shoulder. 'It could be worse.'

'How?'

'I don't know. You could be shot.'

'He's *been* shot,' Sloan said. 'It'd have to be a lot worse than that.'

Lunch with Sloan was a long hour of gossip, with brief side-trips into current styles of crime. Murder was down, even with Allen and the two dead in Dinkytown – the fourth, Rolo, was on the St. Paul books. Rape was down, ag assault was down, coke was down, speed was up and so was heroin. 'Guiterrez told me that the day heroin started coming back, was a happy day in his life,' Sloan said, speaking of one of the dope detectives. 'He says Target's gonna get ripped off, and K-Mart and Wal-Mart, but at least they're not gonna have a bunch of robot-crazy coke freaks running around with guns, thinkin' that nothing can hurt them.'

Lucas nodded: 'Give a guy a little heroin, he goes to sleep. Give him a little more, he dies. No problem.'

'Shoplift like crazy, though,' Sloan said.

'A cultural skill,' Lucas said, lifting up the top of his cheeseburger to inspect the solitary, suspiciously pale pickle. 'Passed on by heroin gurus.

109

Somebody oughta look into it. An anthropologist.'

'Or a proctologist,' Sloan said. 'Say, with that commission meeting tonight, you won't be shooting.'

'I'm thinking of giving it up, anyway,' Lucas said. 'That goddamn Iowa kid shot my eyes out last time.'

'He's a freak,' Sloan said. 'He's shooting Olympic, now. He's got a target on his locker, ten bulls, every shot in the X ring. In the middle of the X-ring – you can see black all around the edges.'

'He's good,' Lucas said. 'At my age, you can't be that good. Can't do it. Your fine muscle control isn't fine enough.'

'Yeah, yeah. He's sort of a dumb fuck,' Sloan said.

'I heard he was actually a smart fuck.'

'Yeah, well – he's a dumb smart fuck.' Sloan looked at his watch. 'I gotta get going. I gotta talk to a guy.'

On the walk back to City Hall, Lucas realized that a mental penny had dropped during the lunch. Something was packed into the back of his head, now, but he didn't know what it was.

But it was, he thought, something important: he dug at it, and realized it involved the Iowa kid. The kid was still a uniformed cop, but he volunteered for everything hard, and he had a thing about guns. All kinds of guns: he dreamt about them, used them, fixed them, compared them, bought and sold them. A throwback to an old western gunfighter, Lucas thought.

He tried to think about the coming interview with Jan and Heather Davis, the photo-spread that Sherrill was putting together. A photo-spread involved some risks: if the child identified Carmel as one of the killers, and they went to court, then a witness-stand identification could be challenged on grounds that the police had contaminated the witnesses' memory with the photographs . . . So the whole thing had to be done just right.

As much as he tried to think about the upcoming interview, the shooter from Iowa always came back. Something that Sloan said about him. Something small. He just couldn't nail it down.

This, he thought after a while, *is what it's like be senile*. He had something in his head, but he couldn't get it out. Finally, he walked down to the locker room, wandered through, looking for the Iowa kid's locker: found it, with the target on it, just like Sloan said.

'Checking out the competition?' a tall blond cop asked. Another shooter, and Lucas nodded at him.

'I heard about the perfect score,' Lucas said. He leaned forward to look at it: the bullseye on the target was called the ten-ring, but inside the bull was another, much smaller circle: the X-ring, not much bigger around than a .22 slug. There were ten small target faces on the target sheet: and in the middle of each X-ring, a slightly soft-edged hole. Around each of the holes, the full X-ring line could be seen. Lucas whistled.

'Guy's abnormal,' the cop asked. He was pulling on a bullet-proof vest, slapping the Velcro fastening tabs in place. 'My eyes are supposed to be 20–20, but I can't even *see* the X-ring on them .22 faces. Keeping them inside the ten-ring is one thing; keeping them inside the X, man . . . that's abnormal.'

'It's tough,' Lucas agreed. 'I've never done it.' He took a last look, shook his head, and started back to the office. Keeping them inside the ten-ring was one thing, but inside the X . . .

He went back to his office, scrolled through the list of phone numbers he'd sent off on the Internet. And there it was, the last one.

Tennex Messenger Service.

'Sonofabitch,' he said. That had to be a coincidence.

He was still thinking about it when Sherrill and Black showed up with a file of full-length color photos of women, silhouetted, wearing head scarves with dark raincoats. A dozen different faces had been grafted into the folds of the scarf, as if the faces had suddenly been hit by light from a doorway.

'Not bad,' Lucas said, looking through them. 'This one is Carmel?'

'Yeah – it's weird how context makes a difference; I wouldn't recognize her in a thousand years in that get-up,' Sherrill said.

Black and Sherrill drove over together, Lucas followed. Davis met them at the door: 'I hope we can do this without a lot of trauma,' she said, her voice tight.

'There's no reason to be any trauma at all,' Lucas said. 'If she can't pick out a photograph, we're done.'

'What if she does? What if this killer hears about it?'

'The killer won't hear about it from the police,' Lucas said. 'We'd do a videotape deposition, and keep her name confidential until a defense attorney did his discovery motion – by that time we'd have somebody in jail for first-degree murder, and there'd be nobody to come after her.'

'The whole thing just scares the heck out of me,' Davis said, hugging herself as though she were cold.

Heather was playing with a fleet of trucks in a back bedroom: 'You know what you need?' Sherrill asked. 'You need a farm tractor. Maybe a cultivator to pull behind it.'

'I had a tractor, a John Deere, but it got lost,' Heather said. Her eyes narrowed. 'The tractor was good, but you know what I really need?'

'What?'

'When we bought the tractor, we bought a combine to go with it, but I didn't have anything to put the corn in. I could use a grain truck.'

'Yeah . . . well.' Sherrill was out of her depth. 'Let's look at these pictures, and we'll get you back to the trucks.'

'Mom said you could probably get me a ride in a police car,' Heather said.

'Mmm, if you ask Uncle Lucas here, he could probably fix it.'

'He's not my uncle,' Heather said.

'I can probably fix it anyway,' Lucas said. 'Come on and look at the pictures.'

She did: she looked at them all, carefully, and when she was done she said, 'Nope.'

'Nope?'

She looked at her mother. 'They don't look right.'

'If they don't look right,' Davis said, 'then, they don't look right.'

'You're sure none of them look right . . .' Lucas said.

'Well, they all look *sorta* right, but not *really* right.'

'If that's what you say, that's what you say,' Black said. They all stood up.

'Can Uncle Lucas still get me a ride in a police car?'

Out on the sidewalk, Sherrill said, 'Well, gosh-darn.'

'That's a big gosh-darn from me, too,' Black said. 'Though I don't know if I'd want to put a kid on a witness stand with Carmel Loan ready to cut her up.'

'I'd take anything right now,' Lucas said moodily. 'I'd take a chimp if it was ready to pick her out.'

'So what're you going to do?' Sherrill asked.

'Gonna go home,' Lucas said. 'Have a beer. Think about it. Cry myself to sleep.'

Chapter Twelve

Lucas arrived at City Hall at little after ten o'clock in the morning – early for him – closed the door on his office, typed a memo, heading it 'Confidential,' and recorded his interview with Hale Allen. He hand-carried it to Rose Marie Roux, the chief of police.

'How was your trip?' he asked.

'A Las Vegas convention in the middle of the summer – it was so hot that I was afraid to go outside.'

'Dry heat,' Lucas said.

'So's an oven,' she said. 'I was so bored I almost started smoking again . . . whatcha got?'

He handed her the memo and she read it and said, 'Goddamnit, Lucas, this is awful. Why don't you ever come up with easy stuff?'

'I do,' Lucas said. 'I don't bother you with it. And this, I don't want anybody to see but you and me, Sherrill and Black, and maybe one judge. File it and forget it, until we need it.'

'Covering your ass,' Roux said.

'Covering everybody's ass,' Lucas said. 'I need to get her phone records for the last few months, and I need this to back up a subpoena.'

'Talk to Ross Benton,' Roux said. 'He'll give you the subpoena *and* keep his mouth shut. He'd love to see Carmel get nailed. She makes a game out of fucking with him in court. He had trouble with some decisions in that Prolle case, and she called him Schizo the Clown and it got in the *Star-Tribune*.'

'All right. I'll carry a copy over to him, get the subpoena.'

'I hope you know what we're doing,' Roux said. 'I'm too old and tired to get burned at the stake by Carmel Loan.'

Lucas talked to Benton, the judge, and got his subpoena. 'Let me know how it comes out,' Ross said, a light in his eye.

'Probably nothing,' Lucas said. 'I'm beggin' you not to leak it.'

'Don't worry. If it's nothing, and she finds out about this subpoena, I'll stick a gun in my mouth.'

* * *

Lucas walked the subpoena over to the phone company, presented it to the correct vice-president, emphasized the need for confidentiality and the criminal penalties for any breaches of it. The vice-president responded with the correct pieties, and they both walked down to a technical center where the information was printed out. Lucas asked the vice-president to note the date and time on the printout and sign it.

'Hope this doesn't get me into trouble,' the vice-president said.

'We're trying to nail a Mafia hit-man,' Lucas said.

'Pretty funny,' the VP said, as he signed.

Back at City Hall, Lucas thought about the pros and cons of asking a favor from the FBI. His stomach growled once, then again, and he answered: he walked down to the cafeteria and got a sandwich, ate it and read the paper, then walked back to his office and dug Mallard's card out of his desk drawer.

One problem with the FBI was that once they signed on to a case, its agents tended to get a little over-enthusiastic: laser-sighted submachine guns, helicopters, computerized psychological profiles. A further problem was that they also tended to be under-experienced. A guy who came out of college, went into the FBI, and then spent twenty years working as an agent had about as much experience with actual criminals as a patrol cop a year out of tech-school. So you'd look at a slightly greying forty-five-year-old – somebody about Lucas' age – and you might think, hmm, not too bad. Then you'd find out that in cop years, he was about twenty-five.

On the other hand, the experience that they *had* tended to be with heavy hitters . . .

After another moment's hesitation, he thought about Mallard's attitude during their meeting: Mallard was one of the brighter ones, Lucas thought.

Mallard picked up his phone on the first ring. 'Yes.'

'I have an intuition,' Lucas said, after he identified himself.

'I'd be inclined to listen to an intuition,' Mallard said. 'Our Minneapolis guys are strangely impressed by you. Or scared, or something.'

'Thank them for me, the next time you see them.'

'I didn't say they *liked* you,' Mallard said. 'They say you refer to us as the Feebs.'

'Well, that's, uh, the old rivalry.'

116

'Sure,' Mallard said. 'So what's your intuition?'

'We have a possible suspect. Not for the shooter, but for the woman who hired her. To be honest with you, I'm not going to identify her because she's a hot potato, and if I'm wrong, she'd nail me to the wall. I could be looking for a job somewhere *way* out-state.'

'So much for the preface,' Mallard said, 'What's the intuition?'

'We, uh, acquired a number of telephone contacts our suspect made about the time of the killing. One of them was in Washington – right where you are . . .'

'Not the state.'

'. . . and when I checked it, I got Tennex Messenger Service. Nobody home. It's an answering service. And I was pretty much told that there's never anybody home . . . And just yesterday I was talking to a friend about target-shooting, and he told me about this young Iowa guy we've got, who just shot a round where he not only kept everything in the ten ring, but also inside the X-ring.'

'Ten-X Messenger Service,' Mallard said. 'That's a pretty far-out intuition.'

'That's what I thought.'

'The odds are about twenty-to-one against it being anything.'

'I was thinking fifty-to-one,' Lucas said.

'That's the best odds I've ever had on this woman,' Mallard said. 'I'd jump at a thousand to one.'

'You gotta go easy with this,' Lucas said. 'None of that laser-sighted submachine gun shit. Or black helicopters.'

'Nobody'll ever know,' Mallard said, 'Until we want them to. Where can I call you direct?'

Lucas gave him a number and Mallard said, 'Call you tomorrow morning.'

Lucas hung up, leaned back and looked at the phone. Mallard, the dust-dry but thick-necked economics professor, had shown a glimmer of genuine excitement. As though he shared the intuition . . .

Sherrill walked in without knocking, sat down without asking, and said, morosely, 'My problem is, I'm a cop.'

'Good-looking cop,' Lucas said, rolling with it. 'And ya gotta big gun.'

'I'm not being playful, here,' Sherrill said. 'It's suddenly become a problem.'

Lucas frowned, recognizing the serious set to her face: 'What happened?'

'The slug you gave me,' she said. 'It came back from the lab.'

'Yeah?'

'Yeah. Lucas, the analysis is identical to the analysis on the D'Aquila and Blanca killings. Not the Allen, though.'

'Huh,' he said, but he felt a tight kick of pleasure.

Sherrill continued: 'So me being a cop and all, I gotta ask you – where'd you get it?'

'I could tell you I found it on the floor at the Blanca killing, and forgot about it,' he said.

'That'd be utter bullshit,' she said.

'Such things have happened, even to the best of us,' Lucas said.

'Not to you. Not to me, either,' she answered.

'I'll tell you, if you want to know. If you tell anybody else, they might put me in jail. But if you want to know . . .'

'You'd tell me?'

'Yup.'

She balanced it for ten seconds, then said, 'I gotta know.'

Lucas nodded. 'I broke into Carmel Loan's apartment, searched it, found the shell in the closet. There was only one. I thought about leaving it, and trying to get a search warrant, then finding it – and if it came back confirmed, we'd have something heavy. But I couldn't think of any way we'd ever get a search warrant. And I could think of about a million ways Carmel or any good defense attorney could impeach that kind of evidence. You know, we just happened to find only one shell, in her closet, and it just happens to match, and we are the only people who handled the other slugs . . . it'd be strong, but it wouldn't be definitive.'

'So you took it.'

'That and some other stuff,' Lucas said. 'Computer records, phone records.'

'Anything she can trace?'

'No. Don't think so.'

'Well, goddamnit, Lucas . . .'

He leaned across the desk, intent: 'Listen: we *know* about her now. With this shell. That's the most important thing that could happen in a case like this. We've got a fix on who did it. Now we can start putting things together. We were stuck, now we've got a focus.'

'I wish you'd told me before you went in there,' Sherrill said.

'I couldn't. It was really best that you didn't know. It's still best. If anybody asks me, I didn't tell you, even now.'

'I suppose . . .' She stood up, sighed, and said, 'All right. I just forgot what you said.'

'Of course you didn't,' Lucas said.

'Goddamnit, Lucas . . .' She flared for a minute, then settled back. 'So what next?'

'I just got a subpoena for Carmel's phone records, and walked over to the phone company and got them,' he said. 'I'd already checked them, from what I got in her apartment, but this gives us some legal support . . .'

'Something weird?'

'Yeah. One odd call. And she made that phone call just before the D'Aquila killings.' He filled her in on the Tennex Messenger Service, and his call to the FBI.

'Tennex – sounds like a rock band,' she said, her voice moody.

'You're thinking of the Quicksilver Messenger Service.'

'Never heard of it,' she said. She slumped in the chair, scanning the computer list of phone calls: 'There's nothing before the Allen hit.'

'No . . .'

'You hear what I just said?' She asked. 'I actually said, *hit*. Jesus, I'm a TV movie.'

'You know what I'm wondering?' Lucas asked. 'What if Rolando D'Aquila was her contact with the killer? From what you guys dug up, he had some heavy Mafia connections once, and this shooter – she's supposed to do a lot of Mafia contracts.'

'But you know what?' Sherrill asked, sitting up. 'Rolo's contacts, his drug supply, mostly came out of St. Louis, which was unusual. At the time, most of our traffic came out of L.A.; it was just shifting over to Chicago, back then. St. Louis was nothing – never had been, and never was again after Rolo went down.'

'And this shooter . . .'

'Has contacts in the St. Louis mob. That's what the Feebs say.'

'That's something,' Lucas said. 'Maybe we can work with that.'

Carmel Loan was sitting in her office; she could feel Hale Allen's touch from the night before, the balls of his thumbs on either side of her spine . . . She was trying to read a deposition, but her eyes defocused and she suddenly giggled. The man was unnaturally sexual; a memory popped into her head, she thought it was from a movie, somewhere back in time, a woman telling a man, 'Women don't want sex. Women want love.'

What complete drivel, she thought. Women want sex; they just also want love. And this must be it, she thought, giggling in the middle of the day. She remembered exactly how he'd taken her by the . . .

Her phone rang, a private outside line, and she started, found herself, took a breath and pulled herself back to the day. 'Carmel,' she said. Not many people had this number.

'You remember me?' the voice asked.

'Sure.'

'Why don't you send me a few bucks?'

'Whatever you say, pal. At twenty percent?'

'Carmel Loan-Shark, hey?' He laughed at his own pun. 'But I'm selling, not borrowing.'

'I don't think I'm in the market for anything right now. But whattaya got?'

'First of all, ya gotta agree not to do anything about it for a day or two. Not many people know about this, and if you come charging over here, they could figure me out as your source.'

'Okay, so what it it?

'Lucas Davenport, Tommy Black and Marcy Sherrill put together a photo spread for some witness to look at, in those killings over in Dinkytown.'

'Okay . . .' She was casual, but she felt a chill.

'Guess whose face was in the spread?'

'Uh, the Virgin Mary's.'

'Very close, but no cigar. Actually, your face was in the spread.'

'Mine?' She was shocked, and let it show through. The guy on the other end of the line was a cop.

'Yup. I don't know why. Maybe because they had a picture, because there were a bunch of other faces in there. The weather girl on Channel Three was in there . . . they were looking for tall blondes.'

'Maybe that's it,' Carmel said. 'But it pisses me off.'

'Thought you'd like to know.'

'Watch your mailbox,' she said.

'I will,' he said, with a purr of pleasure.

Some people, Carmel thought when she hung up, get hot at the prospect of cash. Not because of what it can buy, or what it may represent, but just with the pure, smooth, slightly greasy feel of currency. The cop was one of those. She didn't understand it; but then, she'd never tried very hard. She was grateful the need existed, and that she could fill it. A couple of cops had been useful over the years.

After she thought about it for a while, she took a walk out to a pay phone, punched in Rinker's number, and left a message.

Chapter Thirteen

Bright and early the next morning – a cool morning that promised heat in the afternoon; with pale blue skies that went on forever – Mallard called Lucas from Washington. The call came in an hour before Lucas had planned to get out of bed; he took it in the kitchen.

'We have some news on the Tennex connection,' he said, as Lucas yawned and scratched. 'I've also got a question. Two questions.'

'What's the news?'

'There is no Tennex Messenger Service, as far as we can tell, and never has been.'

'That's nice,' Lucas said.

'That's what I thought. The phone number goes into a suite of short-term offices. There're a couple of receptionists out front from eight o'clock in the morning until seven at night. In the back, there're a couple more women running a high-tech switchboard. The switchboard works around-the-clock. The offices are rented by the week or the month, mostly by businessmen here to lobby the government. They're about two-thirds full at any given time. Each of the offices has an individual number, which the switchboard women answer with the name of whoever is renting it at the moment. The answering-service calls come in on separate numbers, which the switchboard women answer with a specific name, depending on which number rings. Tennex only has the answering service. No office.'

'So who pays the bills? Where do the checks come from?'

'We don't know, yet. We want to listen on the Tennex line for a couple of more days before we talk to the people who run the place. But I'll tell you what – and this is my question . . . Did one of your people, a woman, call Tennex from a payphone yesterday evening?'

'No.'

'Somebody from Minneapolis did,' Mallard said. 'The only phone call that came in all day.'

'Huh . . . what time?'

'Around five-thirty, our time.'

'Huh. We took a photo-spread over to a little girl who actually saw the shooters . . . you probably read about her, in the files.'

'Yes.'

'We had a photo spread with the face of our suspect inserted in it. We got nothing, but that would have been about an hour-and-a-half before your call. And I'll tell you what: this woman's got some contacts inside our department. Probably inside yours, as far as that goes.'

'Ours didn't know about the photo spread.'

'All right – if there was a leak, it was us. *If there was a leak* . . . but damn it, I would have leaked to her myself, if I'd known she might call. Do you have a recording of the voice?'

There was a brief pause, as if Mallard were contemplating the stupidity of the question. 'Of course,' he said.

'I want to hear it,' Lucas said. 'I know the suspect personally, I've spoken to her in the past week. Maybe I could nail it down.'

'Which leads to my second question,' Mallard said. 'What's her name?'

'Jesus . . .'

'I've got to have it. This is turning into something. As long as your case was nothing more than an intuition, it was one thing. Now it's another.'

'She's a well-connected defense attorney here in town. A millionaire, probably. And I *know* she gives money to the politicians – U.S. senators, congressmen, you name it. If you fuck this up, they could find us both buried in the back yard.'

'Three people here will have the name. That's all. If we're buried in the back yard, the other two guys'll be buried under us, I guarantee it.'

Lucas sighed, hesitated, and said, 'All right. Her name is Carmel Loan. I can't tell you how nervous this makes me.'

'The woman who called yesterday identified herself as Patricia Case.'

'I'll check around, but I've never heard of her,' Lucas said. He picked up the St. Paul phone book, thumbed through it to Case.

'Could be some kind of code,' Mallard said. 'Although that's pretty far-fetched.'

'*Tennex Messenger Service* is far-fetched . . . did you get a location on the pay phone?'

'Yeah, just a minute. Uh, it's at 505 Nicollet Mall.'

'Five-Oh-Five,' Lucas muttered, as he ran his finger down the Case listing in the phone book. He said, half to himself, 'There aren't any Patricia Cases listed in the St. Paul phone book. I don't have the Minneapolis book here at the house.'

'We already checked, and there aren't any Patricia Cases. We also checked the 505 number, and got some department stores. There's a Nieman Marcus.'

'That's an easy two-minute walk from Carmel Loan's office,' Lucas said. 'I can check, but it might be the *closest* pay phone to Carmel's office.'

'Interesting,' Mallard said.

'Please don't let anything out about Carmel,' Lucas said urgently. 'Not yet.'

'Nothing will come out of this end. I swear to God.'

'One more thing,' Lucas said. 'When are you going to hit this place? The office suite? Go in and talk to the people?'

'We'll give it another day, anyway.'

'Call me the night before. I'm three hours away: I'd like to be there when you do it.'

'No problem. Anything else?'

'One other thing . . . one of the victims, Rolando D'Aquila, used to be a heavy drug-dealer. The word from our drug people is that he bought his coke out of St. Louis, a Mafia connection down there. Not Colombian or Mexican, but old-line Mafia. And this shooter, his woman, she seems to tie in down there.'

'Damn,' Mallard said, 'I'm letting something happen here that I've never let happen before.'

'What's that?'

'I'm getting my hopes up.'

Then for two days, nothing happened. Carmel didn't get a call-back. She stayed close to the magic phone, but she never heard from Rinker. Was there a problem with the contact phone? Was it tapped?

The FBI was equally frustrated. There were no more calls to Tennex: nothing. At the end of the second day, Mallard called Lucas back. 'We're going in tomorrow, if nothing happens to slow us down. We want to get in before the end of the week.'

'I'll get a flight out tonight.'

'We can cover that, if you want,' Mallard offered.

'No thanks, I'll do it from here.'

'All right. Anything new?'

'I sent one of my people, Marcy Sherrill, down to St. Louis to schmooze their organized crime people. There's nothing going on up here.'

'If Sherrill's the one I remember from the meeting, she oughta schmooze pretty well.'

'One of her many talents,' Lucas said. 'See you tomorrow.'

Lucas called his travel agent, got a business-class ticket on the nine o'clock Northwest flight into National and made a reservation at the Hay-Adams. He liked the Hay-Adams because, the half-dozen times he'd stayed there – even the first time – the doorman said, 'Nice to see you again, sir.'

Then he called Donnal O'Brien at D.C. Homicide and said, 'Hey, Irish.'

'Jesus Christ, the outer precincts are heard from,' O'Brien said. 'How'n the hell are you, Lucas?'

'Good. I'm coming to town tonight. I'd like to get together tomorrow, if you've got the time.'

'Want me to get you at the airport?'

'I'll be really late,' Lucas said. O'Brien had four kids to take care of. 'I'll get a cab down to the Hay-Adams. I'll do my thing with the Feebs tomorrow morning, and make it over to your shop by when? Three o'clock?'

'I'll plan on three. Maybe go out for a couple beers, huh?'

'See you then,' Lucas said.

The flight to Washington was a nightmare: nothing wrong with the plane, the flying conditions were perfect, and the trip was on schedule, but airplanes – winged planes, not helicopters – were the only really phobia that Lucas was aware that he had. He dreaded getting on one, sat rigidly braced for impact from the time the plane backed away from the departure gate until it nosed into the destination gate, and was never really convinced that he'd survived until he was walking through the terminal at the other end.

As they came into Washington, he had a postcard view of the Washington Monument. He ignored it. There was no point in looking at the view when you were only seconds away from flaming death. Somehow, the plane got down, and the stewardesses suppressed their panic well enough to smile at him and thank him for flying Northwest.

The Hay-Adams was excellent, as usual. The White House, framed in the window over the desk, looked like an expensive 3-D photo reproduction, of the kind found in commercial aquariums – until you understood that it was real.

He slept very well, having been properly welcomed back.

Mallard arrived at ten o'clock in the morning in a blue Chevy, followed by another blue Chevy carrying three more agents. Lucas was waiting just inside the door, and when he saw Mallard step out of the car, pushed through to the sidewalk: 'Nice hotel,' Mallard said, looking up at the Hay-Adams facade. 'I once got to stay in a Holiday Inn with suites. I didn't get a suite, but I walked past the door to one.'

'If you guys treat me right, I'll let you stand in the lobby while I have dinner tonight,' Lucas said.

'You're all heart,' Mallard said. He was wearing a blue suit with a dark blue necktie with tiny red dots on it. He had a stainless-steel cup full of coffee in the Chevy's cupholder. He took a sip and said, 'If you want some, we can stop at a Starbuck's.'

'I'm fine,' Lucas said. 'Why all the troops?'

'There are five of them – the two receptionists, the two women on the switchboard, and the manager – so I thought there ought to be five of us.'

'Yeah? Well, if they charge, go for the lead one,' Lucas said, as he got comfortable in the lumpy front seat. 'If you can turn the lead one, the rest of them usually follow.'

'You'd be dead in an hour, in Washington,' Mallard said. 'In Washington, the leaders are at the back of the stampede.'

The office suite was off Dupont Circle, a nondescript granite building that might, on close inspection, pass as ordinary. Lucas, Mallard and the other three agents went into the building like a mild-mannered rugby scrum – a tight little group of conservatively dressed, short-haired men, all reasonably large and athletic, who, if they were mistaken for anybody at all, would be mistaken for the Secret Service.

Lucas had seen FBI scrums before, but had never been part of one.

Mallard held up his ID to the receptionists, one bottle redhead and one real blonde, and said, 'We're from the FBI. We'd like to speak to Mrs. Marker.' Two of the agents had peeled off from the group as Mallard stopped at the desk, and gone through a door into the back. Covering the switchboard, Lucas thought.

The blonde receptionist was a carefully coiffed middle-aged woman whose glasses had blue-plastic frames with silver sparkles embedded in the plastic. When she saw Mallard's credentials, her hand went to her throat: 'Well, yes,' she said. 'I'm not positive that she's in.'

'She's in,' Mallard said. 'Dial 0600 and ask her to come out.'

The receptionist asked no more questions: She picked up her phone, punched in the numbers and said into the mouthpiece, 'There are some gentlemen from the FBI here to see you.'

'Thank you,' Mallard said.

Louise Marker was a chunky young woman with only one eyebrow, a long furry brown stripe that sat on her brow ridge above both eyes. She had exaggerated cupid's-bow lips, colored deep red, beneath a fleshy, wobbly nose. In *Alice in Wonderland*, she would have been the Red Queen.

Tennex had been a customer for seventy-two months, she said, and paid the rent and phone bill each month with a cashier's check or a money order. She kept the recipient's receipt for all seventy-two checks in a green hanging file. Most of the checks and money orders came from different banks in each of the cities of St. Louis, Tulsa, Oklahoma, and Kansas City, Missouri. Four checks came from Dallas-Fort Worth and three from Denver. Two checks came from Chicago and from Miami, one each from San Francisco, New Orleans, and New York.

'How does she find out how much she owes?' Lucas asked. 'The phone bills are always different?'

Marker shrugged: 'We add them up and put a message on the voice mail, on the twenty-ninth of each month. A few days later, the check comes in. End of story.'

'And the voice mail goes through the phone company, so you wouldn't even handle that call.'

'That's right.'

'Why would you bother with your service at all? With a receptionist?'

'Well, you gotta have a phone – the phone company won't let you in on the service if you don't have a phone,' Marker said. 'We're the phone.'

'That's nuts,' one of the FBI agents said. 'They pay you all this money for a phone?'

'It is *not* nuts,' Marker insisted. 'We don't explore the backgrounds of our clients, because we don't have the resources, but we know what they are, most of them. They're mostly trade associations who can't afford a full-time office in Washington, but want people to think they can. People like politicians. So if a politician calls here, a receptionist answers, we tell them that nobody's in, and switch them to voice mail. Then somebody at the real office out in Walla Walla or wherever, calls here a couple of times a day, gets the message and returns the call. And if they have to actually come here, to Washington, we can rent them a suite and all the business machines, the whole works. We're not the only people who do this, you know; there're a half-dozen others . . .'

Lucas prowled the office and found an airline magazine, and opened it to the map of the national airline routes. The Midwestern and Mid-South cities that were the sources of most of the checks – Kansas City, St. Louis and Tulsa – lay in a neat circle with Springfield, Missouri, at its center. On the other hand, if the sender of the checks came from Springfield, or close by, and mailed the checks from neighboring large cities to avoid pinpointing herself, why hadn't she ever gone to Little Rock? It was hardly further than the others, at least on the airline map.

And the other checks were so scattered that they probably indicated that the killer either traveled a lot, or arranged for different people to send the checks. Though it was unlikely that she would ask other people – that'd be too much exposure. So she traveled.

'. . . never talked to her,' Marker was saying. 'I don't even know if it's really a *her*, I always thought it was a *him*.'

'Why'd you think that?' Mallard asked.

'I don't know. Because he ran a messenger service, I guess. You kind of think that's like a guy job.'

Mallard and his three agents began in-depth interviews with all five women, taking them one at a time. Lucas stood outside of Marker's office for a while, watching her talk with Mallard; her eyes would flick out to Lucas, then back to Mallard, and then out through the door to Lucas again. After ten minutes, Lucas stuck his head in the door: 'Thanks for letting me ride along. I'll give you a call this afternoon.'

Mallard said, 'Hold on a second.'

Out in the hall, away from the five women, he said, 'Not too exciting.'

'I gotta think about it,' Lucas said.

'The problem is, we don't have an edge, a crack, anything we can get a hold of. We'll have our local agents run down these checks: maybe somebody'll remember her.'

'The most checks she got from one bank is six, and those were months apart,' Lucas said. 'I'd bet she went to a different teller every time, paid cash.'

'Maybe we can run down the actual paper checks, and get fingerprints. We're gonna process all the paper we got here. And when the next check comes in . . .'

'Do everything,' Lucas said.

He turned back to look at the building as he walked away, and saw Mallard looking after him. The call-in arrangement was clever: it was also not quite right.

Donnal O'Brien was a husky black man with a small brush mustache and five kids at home: his wife had gone out for a loaf of bread one night, and never came back, he said, 'Just too quiet in that convenience store, I guess, with none of the kids around.'

She was now living in North Miami Beach with a retired DC cop named Manners: 'The drug guys called him Bad Manners. I think he retired with a little more than the regular pension, seeing as how he didn't bust anybody for the last three years he was on the force.'

Lucas had met O'Brien at a computer training conference when Lucas was still hawking his police-simulation software. They'd had a few beers, shared information a couple of times. When O'Brien was still married, he and his wife had once spent a week at Lucas's Wisconsin cabin.

O'Brien was sitting in a small grey-walled cubicle reading a *People* magazine story about a lesbian golfer when Lucas leaned in the doorway: 'Did you know that Kitty Veit is a lesbo?'

'I don't know who Kitty Veit is.'

'She shot a sixty-three in the final round of the women's grand-am last weekend, at Merion, and won three hundred and twenty thousand dollars. She's the only woman who ever shot a sixty-three there.'

'You mean golf?'

O'Brien sighed. 'Never mind. Anyway, she's a lesbo.'

'And that offends your golfer's sense of propriety?'

'No, it makes me wonder if I got an operation, I could shoot a sixty-three.'

'You'd probably just sit home all day and play with your tits.'

'Mmm. Hadn't thought of that.'

'How ya been?' Lucas asked.

'Tired. Let's go get a Coke.'

They found an empty booth at a small, moderately greasy diner with Formica table-tops and cracked red plastic booth seats. The counterman drifted toward them and O'Brien called, 'Big Coke and Big Diet Coke.' Lucas told O'Brien that he was thinking of buying a golf course, and O'Brien didn't believe him. Five minutes later, when he did believe him, O'Brien started fishing for a job as a greens keeper.

Lucas laughed: 'I haven't bought it, yet.'

'Keep me in mind, I'd be great at it,' O'Brien said. 'I'm two years from retirement if some asshole doesn't shoot me first. Work in Minnesota? Hell, yes.' Then, his voice pitched down, he asked, 'What's going on. You're working, right?'

'Yeah. We had some people executed in the Cities . . .' Lucas gave him a quick rundown, left Carmel Loan's name out of it, and concluded with the FBI entry at the answering service.

'Never heard of the place. Louise Marker?'

'Yeah. Just like it sounds, like Magic Marker, M-A-R-K-E-R.'

'Four dead. Never heard of a pro going in for something like that . . . You might get three or four dead all at once, but not in a series, like they're hunting them down.'

'There's something going on,' Lucas said. 'It could be something really simple – a money thing. The hit goes sour, somebody gets a name or a connection, and then this killer chick has to come back and clean up.'

'Impossible to prove, though,' O'Brien said. 'I get pretty goddamned depressed about it sometimes. Crooks are getting too smart, they move too fast. Hit here, gone tomorrow.'

'Be nice to pull this chick down, though,' Lucas said. 'I'd like to see if you've got anything local on this Marker, or any of the people who work there. Even word-of-mouth. The Feebs don't have anything that's not on paper . . .'

'I'll check around,' O'Brien said. 'And I'll tell you what: I know this guy named George Hutton, he works in fraud . . .'

They caught Hutton standing at a bus stop where a desk sergeant said he might still be, if they hurried.

'George,' O'Brien called across the street. A bus was rolling down the block. 'Wait.'

They crossed at the corner and Hutton looked at his watch and said, 'Two minutes and I'm out of here, gone for the week. Then the local Black

Irish shows up with some guy in an expensive suit and I get this really bad feeling . . .'

'All we need is a name,' O'Brien said. 'Let me tell you a name.'

'One name,' said Hutton. He looked at his watch.

'Louise . . . Marker.' O'Brien had moved to one side of Hutton so he could speak directly into the other man's ear. Hutton closed his eyes and tipped his head back, so that he'd have been looking at the sky, except that his eyes were closed. He stood like that for a moment, then opened his eyes and looked at Lucas and spoke to O'Brien.

'Who's the guy?'

'Lucas Davenport, a deputy chief from Minneapolis. Davenport Simulations.'

'I know that,' Hutton said. Then: 'Look up Maurice Marker, formerly Marx, of Marker Dry Cleaners, Inc. New Jersey. He had a daughter named Louise. How old is your Louise?'

Lucas said, 'I'd say early middle age – forty, maybe. A little chunky.'

Hutton nodded: 'That'd be about right. What's she doing?'

'Running an answering service.'

Hutton nodded. 'Yeah. Look up Maurice Marker.' He peered down the street: 'That's my bus.'

Lucas said good-bye to O'Brien, caught a cab to the FBI building and called Mallard, who came down to get him.

'We need to look up a dry cleaner named Maurice Marker or Maurice Marx,' Lucas said.

'Where'd you get the name?'

'From a cop here in DC – some kind of savant guy, he knows names.'

'Huh. Well, let's go punch it in.'

Maurice Marker, now retired to south Florida, had a short FBI biography. He had once owned a chain of dry cleaners in New Jersey, with a sales staff consisting of a dozen men with severely bent noses. The bent noses were not around much, but they made nice salaries, with excellent benefits, including full dental and medical, as well as life insurance and retirement plans.

'These guys would bring in a chunk of cash from dope or broads or gambling or whatever, give it to Maurice, he'd run it through the cash register, write off their salaries against taxes, take a chunk for himself, and everybody was happy,' Mallard said. 'He had thirty-three dry cleaners when he retired. He sold the stores to another guy, who did the same thing until he went away.'

'Where'd he go?'

Mallard peered at the computer: 'About four miles east of Atlantic City.'

'Is Louise in there?' Lucas nodded at the computer.

Mallard ran his finger down the monitor screen: 'Yep. Not necessarily the same one, of course. Just a minute.' He opened a spiral notebook, flipped through to the back, ran his finger down a page of chicken-scratch handwriting, then looked at the screen. 'I'll be damned. Same birth date. That's our girl.'

Lucas turned away, paced a few steps, paced back, turned away again. 'So. She's connected. Could be a coincidence, but probably not.'

'Probably not.' Now Mallard got to his feet, and started following Lucas in the pacing. 'Goddamn it, Davenport, I'm getting a hard-on.'

'You haven't gotten any more calls since the one from Patricia Case?'

'No . . .'

'Then it's possible that was some kind of a warning call. A code . . .'

'It's possible that Tennex only gets one call a month . . .'

Lucas was shaking his head: 'No. You know what it is? The answering service is a blind. Or partially a blind. That's why it's not just a phone ringing in an empty apartment somewhere. I mean, why not that? It'd be easier.'

'So what are you saying?'

'That one of those women there is a cutout, somebody the killer can go to for more information. One of the women is really an alarm, and we probably rang it.'

'It'd have to be Marker,' Mallard said. 'There are ten different women who work on those switchboards, either full or part time, and they rotate shifts . . . There wouldn't be any way to know which operator would be answering which call, so they'd have to have some special instructions from Marker if anything unusual came up on Tennex.'

'So let's bring her in,' Lucas said.

'On what?'

'Nothing. Scare the shit out of her.'

'That's, uh, sort of not our operating procedure,' Mallard said.

'Fuck your operating procedure. Bring her in, let me talk to her.'

'Let me make a call,' Mallard said.

* * *

Marker demanded an attorney, and Mallard was happy to give her all the time she needed.

'If we're not out of here by seven, I'm gonna miss my plane,' Lucas said.

'I'll have my secretary see if there's another flight out,' Mallard said. 'Gimme the ticket.'

Marker's attorney, who showed up two hours after they'd taken her in, was a cheery blond named Cliff Bell. He wanted to know what the hell was going on.

'Your client is a front for a professional killer we're tracking,' Lucas said.

'I don't think . . .' Bell started, but Lucas stopped him.

'Wait, wait,' Lucas said. 'Let me make my little speech, here. This woman, the killer, has murdered almost thirty people in more than a dozen states. A lot of them are those nasty southern states with those strange ways of executing people – like Florida, where the guy's eyeballs went up in a puff of smoke when they pulled the switch on Ol' Sparky . . .'

'That's unnecessary,' Bell said.

'No, it's not,' Lucas said. He leaned toward Marker. 'That's what we're talking about here, Miss Marker. The electric chair. The gas chamber. Lethal injection. When we nail this woman, we have the complete option of taking you with her. You connected the people who were contracting the killings, to the killer – and you knew about it.'

'I didn't know it was a killer,' Marker sputtered, but Bell snapped, 'Shut up, Louise.'

Louise didn't: 'I thought it was some kind of political or real-estate scam, for Christ's sakes . . .'

'Shut up, Louise,' Bell said. To Lucas: 'What's the deal?'

'The deal is, we don't have to take her. We can, we don't have to. She can go home right now, if she wants. But we won't make this offer again. Right now, if she tells us everything she knows about Tennex, we're willing to assume the best: that she may have guessed that she was facilitating some kind of criminal enterprise, but thought it was a minor political deal. I can't see her doing any hard time for that. If she doesn't take the deal, right now, while the trail is hot, then tough shit. We'll get this woman some other way, and we'll take Louise with her.'

'We need some time in private,' Bell said. Mallard found them a private room. When he came back, Lucas noticed that he seemed to be sweating.

'I'm not used to this kind of stuff. Police stuff. We usually have four specialists and three lawyers doing the talking. Spend a couple of weeks prepping for the thing.'

'Sometimes, if you keep the momentum going, keep people talking, you get something you'd never get when everything's a formal tit-for-tat,' Lucas said.

'I know the theory,' Mallard said. 'We usually operate on a different one . . . and I'm just hoping we don't get our tit-for-tat in a wringer.'

Bell brought Marker back fifteen minutes later: 'We want a letter from Mr. Mallard, outlining the deal as laid out by Agent Davenport. Then we'll give you a statement.'

The letter took another half-hour: Bell turned a little sour when he learned that Lucas worked for the City of Minneapolis, but Mallard smoothed him over.

'So tell us,' Lucas said. He had his feet up on Mallard's desk, a tape recorder running in the middle of Mallard's blotter-calendar. Marker and Bell sat in wooden visitors' chairs, while Mallard sat back on a couch with his legs crossed, drinking from his endless mug of coffee.

The connection, Marker said, had been set up by a man named – so he said – Bob Tennex, although he sounded like East Coast Italian.

'Sounded? You didn't see him?'

'No. It was all done by telephone . . .'

'You set up the account without seeing the guy?'

'That happens, from time to time. If we get a check, and the check is good, we offer that service . . .'

Since the connection was set up, Marker said, she'd spoken to a Tennex representative several times, and it was always a woman. Marker had Caller ID on her phones, purely as a matter of course, and had noticed that the calls came in from all over the Midwest, and sometimes from other parts of the country. Kansas City was prominent: four or five calls had come from there. Another name that stuck in her head was Wichita, because, while only two calls had come from there, the woman had been angry both times about problems with the phone company's answering service.

'She wanted us to get on them – they had a couple of breakdowns,' Marker said.

'But that's not the only thing she asked about, is it?' Lucas asked. 'You had some other agreement with her. About people making inquiries about the messenger service, about the police coming in.'

'She really just thought it was some kind of minor political hustle – those things go on all the time here,' Bell said.

'So what was it?' Lucas asked.

'Uh, well, if somebody came snooping around, I wasn't supposed to do anything, except . . . wait.'

'Until what?'

'Until she called me,' Marker said, her voice barely audible.

'You're gonna have to speak up,' Mallard said.

'Until she called me,' Marker said.

'And then what?'

'She'd call and ask, 'Is Mr. Warren in?' And if nobody had been around, if I didn't know anything, I'd say, 'You've got the wrong number: this is Marker Answering.' But if somebody had been around, I'd say, 'No, but Mr. White's here. Would you like me to put your call through?'' '

'How many times did you do this?' Mallard asked.

'Two different times. About three or four years go, something must've happened, and she called me every day for two weeks.' Mallard said, her voice dropping again.

'Ah, shit,' Lucas said. 'Then she called you yesterday or today, didn't she? This afternoon?'

'She's been calling for a week, every day. And today, about an hour after you left the first time. Before you came and got me again,' Marker said. 'She was calling from Des Moines, a pay phone, I think. I could hear the cars.'

'And you gave her the Mr. White line.'

'Yes,' she squeaked.

'Did you get the job because of your father?'

'Maybe. Tennex said he knew Dad.'

'Where's your father living now?' Lucas asked.

'Well, he's not,' Marker said. 'He died of colon cancer last year.'

'I'm sorry,' Mallard said.

'They said it was all the chemicals from the dry-cleaning,' Marker said. 'I'll probably go that way myself. A lot of us do.'

There was more, but nothing significant. They released Marker, and

Mallard drove Lucas to the Hay-Adams, retrieved his bag from the luggage room, and took him to the airport.

'So you think she's gone,' Mallard said.

'Yeah. And I think I'm the guy who tipped her off by calling into Tennex.'

'Nothing to do about that,' Mallard said. 'You were just running checks on a list of phone numbers. It was a long shot.'

'Yeah, but Jesus. That close.'

'We've still got a lot to work with – all those checks, all the phone calls. We've got something, now. I'll bet we have some kind of description of her in a week. I'll bet we unravel some kind of connection.'

'How much?'

'What?'

'How much will you bet?'

Mallard sucked on his teeth for a moment, then said, 'About a dime, I guess.'

Lucas nodded. 'Get me to the plane on time.'

The plane, as it happened, was going to Minneapolis – with a stop in Detroit.

'Aw, no, I gotta fly direct,' Lucas told the check-in attendant.

'Nothing tonight, except through Detroit,' the clerk said, punching up her computer. 'We could get you on a flight tomorrow morning that goes straight through . . .'

'Aw, man . . .'

He went through Detroit, miserably suffering through two take-offs and landings. He was surprised at the safe landing in Detroit, but quickly convinced himself that it would be the second half of the flight, the unnecessary half, that would kill him, so achingly close to home . . .

As miserable as he was, two things occurred to him:

Wichita, Kansas, was a large enough city that it might attract the eye of somebody who traveled out-of-town to make her calls; but Marker had said the killer was *angry* when she called from Wichita. Was it possible that she lived close to Wichita, and made spur-of-the-moment calls out of anger when something went wrong with the answering service? He got the airline flight magazine out of the seat pocket in front of him, and looked at the flight map again. Wichita, he thought, would be as viable a home town as Springfield. Something to think about . . .

The second thing came to him as they were landing in Minneapolis: he was looking down at one of the lakes where he'd expected the impact to occur – he could see himself struggling to get out of the flooding cabin, but his legs and arms were broken and he couldn't unfasten the seatbelt – and the name *Des Moines* popped into his head.

If the killer came from either Springfield or Wichita or virtually anyplace around those cities, and if she were driving to Minneapolis, she'd go through Des Moines.

If she had done that, he thought, she'd be here now.

He looked down at the broad multi-colored grid of lights that made up the Cities and thought, '*Somewhere.*'

Chapter Fourteen

Carmel didn't understand the silence: days had passed since she'd left the message for Pamela – if Pamela was her name, which Carmel doubted. Still, she should have gotten back.

Had something happened to her? Had Carmel's name come up through Pamela – had Pamela been caught? Was she in one of those stainless-steel federal pens somewhere, sweating through the sensory-deprivation stage of a multi-level interrogation? Was the phone connection corrupt, or discontinued, or worse, tapped? What was going on?

She'd worked through her defense two hundred times, and all two hundred times, she'd walked. The cops didn't have a case, couldn't have a case. There was nothing to build a case on – unless that little girl had identified her.

Her contact with the cops said that nothing had come of the photo spread, but *Davenport* was running this routine, and he was worse than tricky, he was *bad*. If he was sure that she was involved, he might be sticking together a morality play, to frame her. With nothing more than a sliver of evidence, a woman could go to prison for life, if a jury didn't approve of her life-style.

She shouldn't have fucked Hale, that was the truth of the matter. Just shouldn't have. Should have waited. Even if there were no proof, if a jury found out she'd fucked Hale the night before his dead wife's funeral, she was history. And where in the hell was Pamela?

She was in her apartment, trying to work, when the phone rang. She glanced at her watch: probably Hale, but she said, 'Be Pamela.'

And Rinker said, 'You got time for a drink?'

Casually: 'Sure, where are you? I'd hoped you'd call.'

'Remember that place we went, the bar where we saw the guy with the cowboy scarf? Let's go there.'

'Oh, sure. An hour from now?'

'Be careful, though; it's dark around there. You'll get eaten by a stalker.'

'I'll bring my switchblade,' Carmel said, laughing. 'See you in an hour.'

* * *

Stalker? Pamela thought Carmel was being followed? Is that what that meant? And the place where they saw the guy with the red silk cowboy scarf wasn't a bar, but the lobby of her hotel. Was that where she wanted to meet?

Before she left her apartment, Carmel changed into a loose long-sleeved silk blouse, jet black, with black slacks and a small gold necklace. Ten minutes after she hung up the phone, she was on the street in the Volvo. She took a twisting route out of the downtown area, eased along a one-way lane on the edge of the Kenwood area, past homes of the rich and the strange, and checked her back trail: nothing.

But if what she'd read about complicated tags was right, the cops might have three or four cars following her, changing off, some in front, some behind. She pulled over to the side of the lane, waited two minutes: nothing went by. What if the car were wired, and they were following her from a distance?

No way she could tell that.

Besides, she was beginning to feel that she might be a little delusional. She'd read hundreds of criminal files in her lifetime, and the heavy surveillance never started until the case was made. Before that, they were simply too expensive. The cops might go for a phone tap, or loose surveillance, but there wouldn't be a multi-car track across town.

She looked at her watch. She still had a half hour before she was supposed to meet Pamela. She headed south, on and off I-35, round and round quiet city blocks, looking for anything that might be a follower. At the south end of the loop, a heavy jet roared five hundred feet overhead, and she turned, heading north, moving fast now. She took the car straight into the hotel parking garage, got a ticket, left it, and took the stairs down to the lobby.

Rinker was sitting in a corner. She saw Carmel step out of the stairway, smiled, stood up and walked back to the elevators. She was just getting in the elevator car when Carmel caught up with her.

'Did you understand what I saw saying on the phone?' Rinker asked, as the elevator car started up.

'I think so. I'm not being followed, unless they've done something electronic, and I'd be willing to bet they haven't – if they really think I'm involved, it's way too early in the investigation to have twenty-four-hour surveillance. But right now, there's nobody with me.'

'I sort of bet myself you'd be coming out of that stairwell,' Rinker said. 'It's what I would have done. Zip into the garage, take the stairs, they can't stick too close behind or you'll spot them . . . and by the time they sneak in, you're in one of five hundred rooms.'

'They'll go through five hundred rooms if they have to, if it gives them a professional killer,' Carmel said.

'Which is why I'm trying not to touch anything hard, except the TV remote control, the on-and-off faucets in the bathroom, and a few things like that. I'll wipe them before I leave.'

'What about the credit card?'

'Good card, fake name,' Rinker said.

'So what's going on? I was worried when you didn't call back, I thought they'd picked you up.'

'You tell *me* what's going on. Why'd you call?' Rinker asked.

'This Davenport guy, the cop. Remember?'

Rinker nodded.

'He took some pictures over to show the little girl who saw us. I was in the photo spread.'

'Ah, jeez. Why?

'I don't know. I've got a contact in the police department, and nobody knows what's going on. But apparently, the kid failed to identify me. Nothing came out of it.'

'But why would they take your picture over in the first place?'

'That's the question,' Carmel said.

Rinker had a room on the seventh floor. Inside, Rinker opened the mini-bar, took out two cans of Special Export. 'I got glasses,' she said.

'Can's fine,' Carmel said, popping the top. 'I really didn't expect you to come all the way back from . . . wherever. I just wanted to talk.'

'Yeah, well, I got a little problem of my own,' Rinker said. She sat on the bed and Carmel pulled the chair out from the tiny desk and sat down. 'The day before you called me, I got another call, at the answering service. A guy who was supposedly trying to get in touch with Tennex. But when the receptionist asked if he wanted to leave a message, he said no. Then two days later, the cops showed up. That's all I know – cops were asking questions. I don't have any easy way to find out more.'

'Huh.' Carmel thought about it for a minute, then took a cell phone out of her purse, and her address book. She checked a number, as Rinker watched, and punched it in. 'Calling my guy,' Carmel said to Rinker. Then, into the phone: 'This is Carmel. Anything else happen?' She listened for a moment, then said, 'I stopped by to see Davenport a couple of times. He's never in . . . Uh-huh. Uh-huh. Well, I'll probably stop and see him tomorrow, then. Okay. And listen, I'll send along another envelope. Keep your eyes and ears open; this thing is starting to scare me. I'm afraid they're setting me up on something. Uh-huh. Well, you know Davenport. Uh-huh. Talk to you tomorrow.'

'What'd he say?' Rinker asked.

'He said Davenport was out of town, and the rumor was, he was at the FBI headquarters. In Washington.'

'Shit.' Rinker said it sharply, expelling breath. 'What's going on? They're on to you *and* me? How could that happen?'

'I called you once from my apartment,' Carmel said. 'This last time, I called from a pay phone, but I did call Tennex that one time, the first time, about Rolo, from my apartment. If they're looking at my long-distance billing, if they're checking everything . . .'

'Even if they were, how did they pick out Tennex? It's a goddamn messenger service.'

'Maybe they picked on it because they couldn't find anything behind it. Maybe just luck. What does Tennex mean? Would that mean something to somebody?'

'No. When we were setting this up, we were talking in the kitchen of this guy's restaurant down in St. Louis, and we were wondering what to call the company, and I saw this name on this air-filter thing he had there. Tennex. It sounded like something, so I said, "How about Tennex?"'

'So that's not it.'

'I don't see how,' Rinker said.

'All right. So we've got to do some prospecting.'

'Very carefully.'

'Very. And there's something else,' Carmel said. 'If it looks like I'm in trouble, why wouldn't you just shoot me and walk away? I mean, that's something we ought to talk about.'

'Well, I sorta think of you like . . . well, almost a friend,' Rinker said. 'I mean, we've done some stuff together, and we get along, and we're probably going to Mexico together, pick up some guys. So . . . I could ask you the same thing.'

'I don't know how to find you,' Carmel said. 'So I couldn't, even if I wanted to. Which I don't.'

'If you need some other reason, I can give you one,' Rinker said, swallowing beer. 'I gotta find out why I'm in trouble. These guys I work with – if the feds start snooping around, or your pal Davenport, all they've got to do is dump me, and *they're* safe. They have a couple more people like me out there, and I'd walk out the front of my apartment someday and boom, that'd be it. So I gotta find out. If the feds start bugging my guys, I gotta know, and take some precautions.'

'These guys are . . . Mafia?'

Rinker shrugged. She looked like a slightly over-aged cheerleader, bouncing softly on the hotel bed. 'Yeah, I guess. If you're gonna put a label on them. I mean, they're Italian, most of them. Except Freddy, he's Irish, or his grandfather was. And I guess Dave is like a Polack, they're always giving him shit about it. They're sorta the Mafia, but they're more like a bunch of guys who watch NFL *Monday Night Football* and pick up stuff that falls off trucks. Some of them are pretty mean, though. Like Italian bikers.'

'Huh.' Carmel showed a small grin. 'I thought it'd be more dignified than that.'

'Maybe back East. Not in St. Louis,' Rinker said.

'So are you gonna be around?'

'In and out of town, until we figure out what's going on,' Rinker said. 'I'm going to Washington tomorrow. I want to talk to this woman who runs the answering service.'

'What if they're watching her?'

'Then I won't talk to her,' Rinker said.

'I'm gonna try to get in touch with Davenport tomorrow, if he's back. I'll see what he has to say for himself.'

'Be careful.'

'Always.'

Rinker gave Carmel the name she was using at the hotel, and as Carmel was leaving, said, 'Hey – this Davenport. Do you know where I could get a picture of him?'

Carmel shook her head. 'No. I mean he's probably been in the paper any number of times, but I don't . . . wait a minute. I bet I do know. He also ran a company called Davenport Simulations, computer simulation-things for cops. If you check the library, the business section, the local business magazines, I bet you'd find something.'

'Cut the page out with a razor . . .'

'Don't get caught,' Carmel said. 'The library people can be mean pricks when it comes to people cutting up their magazines.'

Chapter Fifteen

Lucas was sitting in his office, pushing deeper into the Equality Report. Reading the perfect, politically correct prose had become a Zen-like exercise. The words flowed softly and without meaning through his brain, an unending stream of nonsense syllables that eventually metamorphosed into a cosmic hum, and allowed other ideas to bubble up.

He was on page ninety-four when Carmel knocked. He thought it was Sloan: 'Yeah, for Christ's sakes, come in.'

Carmel opened the door and stuck her head in. Surprised, Lucas stood up. 'Sorry about that,' he said. 'I thought it was somebody else.'

'A little mistake like that is nothing compared to what you're *gonna* get into,' Carmel said, stepping into the office, pushing the door closed. She put one fist on her hip and said, 'A little birdie told me you stuck my face into a photo spread on that Dinkytown murder. The Blanca chick and the other guy. I want to know why.'

'We were looking for photographs of long-legged blondes, and you were available,' Lucas said, his voice flat.

'Bullshit,' she said. Her mouth was like a short stretch of barbed-wire. She dropped into the visitor's chair opposite him, and stretched her legs out, but didn't really settle in: she was like a spring, all squeezed down and about to explode. 'So *why*? You *are* fucking with me, and if I don't get a good reason, I'll see you in court and let the judge ask you why.'

Lucas nodded: 'It'd be an interesting lawsuit. I don't know what you could possibly sue us for . . .'

'Some of the best civil lawyers in the U.S. fuckin' A. sit down the hall from me, and I don't doubt that they could find ten reasons that a judge would like,' she said, her voice glassy-edged. 'For one thing, I represented Rolando D'Aquila and several of his associates in the past, and now you're hauling my picture around and showing it to people around this crime. Are you trying to discredit me as an attorney? It might seem so . . .'

'All right, you're smarter than I am, Carmel,' Lucas said. 'You want the real reason? The reason is that a witness who probably saw the killers described one of the women in a way that you resemble. And you admitted to several people that you knew and represented Rolando D'Aquila, and not only that, that you were representing a man suspected of hiring somebody to kill his wife – a murder committed by the same person or persons who committed the D'Aquila killing. So far, you are the *only* connection we can find between the killing of Barbara Allen and the killing of the other three. And that's why we took the photos around; and if you don't like it . . .'

'What?'

'Tough shit.'

They sat staring at each other for a few seconds, then Carmel smiled quickly and said, 'All right. I wanted to know.' She stood up to leave. 'I didn't have anything to do with any of these killings. I've been trying to work out in my head how they could have happened, and I can't come up with anything.'

'I can't ask you what connection Hale Allen has with D'Aquila, because you're his attorney . . .'

'And it would be absolutely unethical for me to tell you, if there were any. I'll tell you this, just between you and me and the door jamb – there isn't any connection. My theory is, Barbara Allen was killed by accident, or mistake, when she got in the way of something else. Something involving drugs and these latinos. Then the cop came along by accident and the whole affair went up in smoke. But my theory is, Barbara Allen had nothing to do with it – and what you really ought to be doing is looking for the other guy who ran from the Barbara Allen scene. The guy that Barbara Allen got killed for seeing, and the cop got there too late to see.'

Lucas thought about it for a few seconds, then said 'We've gone over all of that.'

'And?'

'It worries us.'

'It should worry you, and you ought to go over it some more,' Carmel said. 'And stop showing those fuckin' pictures around.'

'There was only one witness, Carmel,' Lucas said. 'She gave you a clean slate. She didn't even say, "Maybe."'

'Good.' And she was gone.

Lucas leaned back in his chair, fighting back the little trickle of adrenalin. Carmel was a challenge. He picked up the Equality Report, and the zen-hum began again, while his head worked through Carmel's visit. If she hadn't killed anyone, would she have made the visit when she heard about the photo spread? Absolutely. Would she have made it if she was guilty? He thought about it for three seconds. Absolutely, she would have. She had a fine, discriminating taste in the mannerisms of innocence. So he'd learned nothing.

But the cartridge: the .22 he'd picked up in her apartment was a fact. Couldn't use it in court, couldn't even admit that it existed. But the slug in that .22 said Carmel was guilty. Guilty of *something*, anyway. Just for argument's sake, say the bullet *was* usable in court. How would she defend against it? He turned it over in his mind: she'd say the bullet came from D'Aquila. That he'd stored a bag in her closet, or that he'd planted it for some reason . . .

D'Aquila. Another image popped into the back of his brain. He leaned forward, let his chin drop on his chest, closed his eyes, concentrated. After a minute, he pushed himself out of his chair and half-jogged down the hall to homicide. Neither Sherrill nor Black was in, but the D'Aquila file was in Sherrill's work tray. He flipped through it, and found the coroner's photo of the fingernail gouges that D'Aquila had scratched into the back of his hand before he was executed. Lucas looked at it, turned it over, and thought, if you simply separated out some of the lines . . . if you realized that D'Aquila, panicked, tortured, facing execution, was not exactly writing in a notebook, and couldn't see what he was doing, then

might resolve itself out this way:

C loan.

Begin with a C. The next letter was an L, just a straight up-and-down line without the bottom line. The next letter, he thought, was intended to be an O, but was confused by the bar across it. If the bar were moved over one place, it would make an A – leaving the final letter as an N. C Loan.

'Goddamnit, Carmel,' he said.

The door opened behind him, and he turned to see Sherrill. 'Looking through my desk?'

'Looking through the D'Aquila photos,' Lucas said. 'Look at this.'

Sherrill was looking at *him*. 'Jeez, you're really pumped. What've you got?'

He laid it out for her. In ten seconds, Sherrill was convinced. Black, who arrived two minutes after she did, was not.

'The problem is, you could make anything out of those scratches, once you start disassembling them,' he said. 'I can see five or six different words in there.'

'Yeah, but none of them are words that are relevant to the investigation, except this one: C Loan,' Lucas said.

'Maybe that's because we haven't figured out all the possibilities,' Black said.

Sloan came in during the argument, looked at the photos and shook his head: 'I could take some recreational drugs and maybe believe it, but if you've got an unstoned jury, you got a problem,' he said.

'Well, it's a piece,' Lucas said finally. 'We get a few pieces and pretty soon we've got a case.'

Black and Sloan started talking to somebody else, and Sherrill said quietly, 'Is it possible that we can only see it because we already *know*? Because of the slug?'

'Nah, it's there,' Lucas said, shuffling through the pictures again. 'Goddamnit, it's *there*.'

Rinker flew into Washington on a Saturday afternoon, fifteen hours after Lucas had flown out of the same airport. She stopped at a magazine store and bought the best map she could find, picked up her rental car, and checked into the downtown Holiday Inn. From there, she called her bar in Wichita and talked to the assistant manager, a shy cowboy named Art Durrell, and was assured that nothing had burned down, that the customers were happy, that the fat in the deep frier was hot enough, and the refrigerators were cold enough.

'When that asshole from the health department comes back, we want a hundred-percent clean bill, Art,' Rinker said. 'You can never tell when those reports'll wind up in the local newspapers.'

'We're the cleanest place in town, Clara, and everybody down at the health department knows it,' Durrell said. 'Stop worrying. Enjoy yourself.'

At two o'clock, a rat-faced man with too-long, stringy black hair, wearing a denim jacket, jeans and cowboy boots – a man who looked the part of a movie drifter – knocked at her door and, when she answered, handed her a package wrapped in brown paper that had been cut from a grocery sack.

'From Jim. The phone's probably good until Sunday,' he said, and left. She opened the bag and took out a Colt Woodsman, a silencer, a sealed box of .22 shells and one freshly stolen cellular phone. The package had cost her eleven hundred dollars. She screwed a silencer on the barrel of the pistol, loaded the magazine, opened a window and fired a shot through the curtain. The gun made a loud 'whuff' and the action cycled. She stepped over and looked at the curtain, and after a second found the small hole made by the .22 slug as it passed through. Everything worked.

Louise Marker lived in an apartment complex in Bethesda, an expensive place of three-story yellow-brick buildings arranged around a series of swimming pools set in grassy lawns. If government employees lived there, Rinker thought, they were generals. There were, however, no uniforms in sight. Perhaps a hundred residents, almost all of them young to middle-aged women, lay scattered around the pools in conservative one-piece bathing suits. None of them was Marker. Marker had never seen Rinker, but Rinker had seen Marker, a couple of times. She'd made a point of it, for just this occasion. Wandering casually through the people around the pools, Rinker punched Marker's number into her cell phone and a woman answered on the third ring. 'Hello?'

And Rinker said, 'Jean?'

'No . . . You must have the wrong number.'

'Ah, sorry.'

Getting into Marker's building was not a problem: she timed her step to a couple of women in bathing suits who were headed for a side door. She followed them through the outer door, just far enough back that one of them had time to use her key on the inner door. Rinker had her own keys in her hand, jingling, but caught the door, nodded, said thanks and kept going and the other two women thought nothing of it.

Marker was on two: Rinker took the stairs, did a quick peek at the door to make sure there was nobody in the hallway, then punched Marker's phone number back into the cell phone as she walked down to Marker's door. There was interference, but at least the phone should ring on the other end.

Again, the woman's voice. 'Hello?' A little asperity this time; expecting another wrong number?

Rinker said, 'Could I speak to Mrs. Marker?' And at the same moment, she rang the bell at Marker's door.

Marker said, 'Who is this?'

'This is Mary downstairs at the office . . . did I hear your doorbell ring?'

'Yeah, just a minute.' Rinker heard her put the phone down. The hall was still empty, and she took the pistol out from her shirt just as the door popped open. Marker opened her mouth to ask a question and Rinker brought the gun up to her forehead and said, 'Step back.'

Marker, the good Mafia kid, said, 'Oh, no,' and stepped back. Rinker stepped inside, then whispered, 'I am going to speak very softly: I am going to put my gun in my shirt, and we are going for a walk outside. But first, finish your phone call.'

'What?'

'Finish the phone call.'

Marker nodded, mystified, went back to the phone.

'Hello?'

'This is Mary,' Rinker said into the cell phone. 'You left your car keys down here this morning, they're at the main desk.'

'Oh, thanks,' Marker said, shakily. 'Uh, I'll be right down.'

'See you,' Rinker said, and she punched off the phone. Then she pointed her index finger at Marker, crooked it, and stepped back into the hallway. Marker followed like an automaton.

'You're going to kill me,' Marker said, when they were in the hall, the door closed behind them. 'I should scream.'

'If you scream, I'll kill you. Otherwise, I've got good reasons not to. But I've got to ask you some questions.'

'What was that about the telephone?'

'The feds may be listening in.'

'Probably are,' Marker said. Then: 'You're Tennex.'

Rinker nodded. 'Walk down the hall.'

'I did just like you told me . . .'

Rinker started her rap: 'I don't want to hurt you, because if I do, then they'll know for sure that Tennex is what they're after. Do you understand that? Right now, they don't know for sure.'

'Uh, yes.'

'But I'll kill you if I have to. If I ever have any hint that you talked to them about this visit, that you're looking at photographs, then I'll come

150

back for you. And if I'm caught, the people who run me will worry that other connections would be made, and they'll come looking for both of us. In other words, if you talk to anybody about this visit, you're dead. Do you understand?'

Marker swallowed hard and nodded.

'So who came to see you?' Rinker asked.

Marker told her all of it: starting with the first phone call, the call that seemed uncertain about Tennex – a guy's voice, baritone, educated, cool – to the raid by the FBI.

'Not a cop? The guy who called?'

'High-class cop, maybe.' She told Rinker about the FBI, about Mallard, about going down to the FBI building.

'Was one of the guys named Lucas Davenport?'

'I don't think so, but they didn't introduce everybody. There was one guy who kept wandering away. Big guy, tough guy. Didn't look FBI, he had this really nice suit. Didn't look government. Looked like, you know, a hoodlum.'

Rinker dipped in her pocket and came up with the folded page she'd taken from *BizWiz*, a computer magazine that covered Twin Cities business. 'Is this the guy?'

Marker took it, looked at it for a half-second and said, 'That's him. Yeah. He looks better in real life, though.'

'Did you hear his voice? Could he have been the guy who called that first time, the confused call?'

Marker thought about it for a second. 'Yeah, you know, he could have been,' she said slowly. 'Yeah, you know . . .'

After a few more questions, Rinker said, 'I just want to reiterate: I was very careful coming here, very careful about wire taps and even bugs in your apartment. So nobody knows. If anybody *ever* knows, you're dead.'

Marker nodded rapidly. 'Okay. Good. That's good.'

'I learned a trick in a previous business of mine, when I was much younger,' Rinker said. 'And that was, how to forget. You'd just say, "Okay, that never happened. I just dreamed it." And pretty soon, whatever happened becomes like a dream, and you start to forget it.'

'You're forgot,' Marker said fervently. 'Honest to God, you're forgot.'

Before she left town, Rinker stopped at a bank and rented a safe-deposit box. She paid a year in advance, wiped the gun, and left it in the box. Next time she was through the area in her car, she'd pick it up.

* * *

From the airport, Rinker dialed Carmel's magic cell phone, and Carmel answered on the second buzz: 'Yes.'

'You know that guy we saw on TV?' Rinker asked.

'Yes.'

'He was here. For sure.'

'Shit. I wonder how he knew?'

'Don't know,' Rinker said. 'I'll be back tonight at ten-fifteen on Northwest.'

'I'll pick you up. I think we're cool for this very moment, but we can talk when you get back.'

On the plane, eyes covered with a black sleeping mask, Rinker dozed, and between small patches of sleep she thought about Carmel. She could solve quite a few problems by simply killing the other woman. But there were problems with that. Carmel wasn't stupid, and she might already have taken out some kind of insurance: a note written in a check book, or left in a safe deposit box, with what she knew about Rinker. A note that would be found only after she was dead. Another problem: this Davenport guy was as close to Rinker as he was to Carmel. How had he gotten there? Did he know even more? Was he digging around the bar in Wichita? Carmel was a source of information about Davenport, which could be important . . .

A final reason not to kill Carmel: Rinker actually liked her. Like some kind of sister, something Rinker had never had. Rinker smiled when she thought of Carmel's invitation to do Mexico. She'd been planning to go, by God, and if they got out of this, she would. Get a couple of thong bikinis and a nice close bikini wax, some of those drinks with little paper umbrellas and lots of pineapple, and maybe do a couple of those Mexican dudes.

As to Davenport himself, Rinker had read the *BizWiz* report, and Davenport sounded like a smart guy. And mean: he was a stone killer, no doubt about it. He was like one of those Mafia guys she'd known, a guy running a big coin-op company or garbage-hauler, a businessman who kept a gun in his pocket.

Of course, she'd killed three or four of those. Not even geniuses were bulletproof.

* * *

In Minneapolis, sitting in front of a muted television, Carmel considered the possibilities. Maybe, if she had a chance, she should kill Pamela, or whatever her name was. It would only make sense, from a criminal-defense point of view. There really was only one perfect witness against Carmel, and if Pamela were gone, then Davenport could go shit in his hat.

She sighed, got up and wandered into the kitchen, got a glass of orange juice. She'd really hate to kill the other woman: she actually liked her. Pamela could become a friend, for God's sakes, the first real one Carmel would ever have had.

She sipped the juice and wandered back past all of her perfect black-and-white photos, barely seeing them. If she was thinking about killing Pamela, then it was probable that the other woman was thinking about killing *her*. And maybe was equally reluctant to do it, for some of the same reasons.

If things should change, Carmel thought, if it became really necessary to get rid of Pamela, she damn well better move first and fast. She wouldn't have a second chance. She glanced at her watch. Time to go get her at the airport.

Rinker tossed her light bag in the back seat of the Volvo, and Carmel said, 'I can think of three possibilities.'

'Which are?'

'We do nothing. I sat down with a legal pad tonight and tried to work out the worst possible scenario. I can't see how they could ever, ever have come up with enough against us to arrest either one of us. If they did, I don't see how they could convict either one of us, unless you've left fingerprints behind or dropped your billfold or something.

'Nothing like that,' Rinker said. 'What are the other two possibilities?'

'Our major problem is Davenport. Forget the FBI, forget these other cops who are digging around. If we get rid of Davenport, they'll never figure out who we are. On the other hand, getting rid of him would be more than risky, it'd be dangerous. He's not only violent, he's lucky. One time he was shot in the throat and would have died, except a surgeon was standing right there with a jackknife and did an emergency tracheotomy and they made it to the hospital . . .'

'Are you joking?'

'No.'

'Ah, man, that's the most scary thing you've said about him: that he's lucky.'

'The third possibility is that we set up and run a little play – a little pageant – that would somehow make all these killings make sense. The alternative theory: it's one way you can beat what seems like an open-and-shut case against a client. Give the jury something that makes more sense, or seems to . . . If we created exactly the right pageant, even if Davenport knew there was something wrong with it, they couldn't get out of it.'

'What are you recommending?' Rinker asked.

'Number one. Do nothing. Sit and wait. I don't think anything more will happen. We know the cops are on the phone in Washington, so we never use it again. I'd love to see their file on the case, but that won't happen unless they make a move on Hale . . .'

'All right. So we sit.'

They rode in silence for a while, then Rinker asked, 'What if this car is bugged?'

'They're not *that* smart,' Carmel said. 'This is Mom's car. She even uses it, when I don't need it, and she wants to haul something – bulbs or plants or something. But I need a car that nobody really knows about, especially when I've got a hot case. Sometimes, you don't want people looking at you.'

'Your folks get divorced?'

'No, my dad killed himself,' Carmel said. 'He was an endodontist, did root canals all day. He got tired of it, sat down in his chair one afternoon when he'd finished with a patient, wrote a short note to the world and strapped on a nitrous oxide mask.'

'Jesus.'

'Yup. A good way to go, I guess, but he had to work at it, a little. Had to override some safety things, pinch off an oxygen tank and so on. When I go, I don't want to have to think about it. I just wanna *go*.'

'I don't wanna go. Not for a while,' Rinker said.

'What about your folks?' Carmel asked.

'My dad took off when I was a baby,' Rinker said. 'And my good old step-dad used to fuck me once or twice a week until *I* took off.'

'Your step-dad still around?'

'No.' Rinker looked out the window. 'He went away one day. He hasn't been seen since.'

'Like your dad,' Carmel said.

'Not exactly, no,' said Rinker.

Chapter Sixteen

Sherrill came back from St. Louis with blue circles under her eyes. 'Didn't get any sleep?' Lucas asked. He tried to keep his voice flat, but there might have been a *tone* to it, he thought.

'I had to fuck all the guys on their organized crime squad. That kept me up nights,' Sherrill said. They were alone in his office.

'Hey . . .' He was offended.

'Hey, yourself . . . the way you asked the question,' she said.

'I was just trying to . . .'

'Forget it. Anyway, I didn't get any sleep. Every night I'd roll around in the bed and the blankets were too heavy and the pillow was too thick and the room smelled bad. And I'd think about you and me.'

'Uh-oh.'

'I tried not to,' she said. 'I just couldn't help myself. I was wondering if we did the right thing. I was wondering if I ought to get you someplace and screw you blind, just one more time. Or two or three more times, but not forever. Just sort of good-bye.'

'I had the feeling you'd already done that,' Lucas said.

'Yeah, I did,' Sherrill said. 'Besides, sex wasn't really our problem, was it?'

'Nah. The sex was pretty wonderful. At least, from my point of view.'

'So what was it?'

'I think, uh, you might be a natural upper, and I'm a natural downer . . .'

'Yeah . . .'

'That's what you concluded?'

'I concluded that I oughta get a new boyfriend, and you oughta get a girlfriend, then we'd be done with it.'

'I'm too tired to look,' Lucas said. 'You get one.'

'Yeah.' Sherrill said. She nibbled on her bottom lip. 'Maybe.'

Lucas said, 'We're dead in the water, here. The feds are still sitting on their wire tap, on Tennex, but nobody's calling.'

'Are they tapping Carmel?'

'Maybe. They say they're not – yet – but they could be lying about it.'

'The FBI? Lying?'

'Yeah, yeah . . . you get anything?'

'I got about twenty names,' Sherrill said.

'Lot of names.'

'Yeah. But if there's a Mafia-connected guy in St. Louis who can order these hits, his name is almost for-sure on the list.'

'So what?'

'I'm getting to that,' she said. 'You know how you guys were looking at where all those checks came from? And you figured the person sending them must come from southwest Missouri or eastern Kansas or those other places?'

'Northern Arkansas or northern Oklahoma . . .'

'So if we do an analysis of these Mafia guys, who are all like these uptown dudes wearing loafers with no socks and driving Cadillacs . . . and if we find one of them has a lot of calls going out to some farm in East Jesus, Oklahoma . . .'

Lucas looked at her for a second and said, 'That's good.'

'You like it?'

'First decent idea anybody's had in a week.' He pulled open his desk drawer and found Mallard's card. 'Even better, it involves dealing with bureaucrats from the phone company: I mean, this is Mallard's *life*.'

Mallard liked it: he had three agents working on it overnight, and called Lucas back in the middle of the afternoon, the next day. He was, Lucas thought, a teeny bit breathless.

'Have you ever heard of Allen Kent?'

'No . . .'

'He's this Italian guy – his father's name was Kent, he was nobody, but his mother's family was tied right to the top of the St. Louis *and* the Chicago Mafia families, back when Sam Giancana was running the world.'

'Who's he been calling?'

'Well, he calls all over the place, he's a booze distributor. He calls every little goddamn bar in the Midwest. But he's got an AT&T calling card which he uses when he's out-of-town, and we analyzed all those calls for the past ten years and guess what?'

'He's actually Lee Harvey Oswald and he's holding JFK in a cave.'

'No. But you know we have all these Mafia-related hits attributed to this woman. In each case, Kent was making calls from Wichita, Kansas, between twenty-four and thirty days before each hit. He'd spend two days there, each time, every time. Now, you figure he goes out to Wichita to meet the shooter and give her the assignment, and maybe talk about information she needs. Then she needs time to do some recon – we know she's careful, we know she's watching the target for a while before she moves. And maybe she needs some time to get oriented in each new city . . . and time to drive there, if she drives like we think she does.'

'You think she's from Wichita,' Lucas said.

'We think it's a possibility. We even think we might have a name.'

'Yeah? What is it?'

'John Lopez.'

Lucas grappled with the name for a moment. 'John?'

'Yeah. A guy, disguised as a woman, which makes a lot of sense, when you think about it. A woman hitman for the Mafia? Come on. Never happen. We found him in our data base: he's Puerto Rican, five-five, one hundred and thirty pounds, so he could be a woman. He's a mean little bastard, too. Back a few years ago, there was a massive amount of cocaine coming in through the south coast of Puerto Rico, and then it was transhipped by plane to the states, because there's no customs on Puerto Rican flights – it's an internal flight. He was one of the mules, hauling it up to Chicago, taking the money back. When he was busted, he gave up all the Puerto Rican links in return for immunity and protection, but claimed he didn't know who he was dealing with in Chicago . . . We now think it might have been the Mafia, and that's where he hooked up with Allen Kent.'

'How'd he get to Wichita?'

'Witness protection. God help us, but we might have been protecting the biggest professional killer in the states.'

Lucas felt slightly deflated: the Feebs were gonna make the bust. 'Are you going out there?'

'Absolutely. I'm taking everything I got with me. Lopez supposedly runs a flower shop out there, like a longtime hood is gonna run a flower shop.' Mallard laughed, and Lucas looked at the phone: Mallard seemed to be running a little hot.

'Mind if I watch?'

'Hell, no. I'm going out this afternoon, I'm leaving here in five minutes. We're staying at the Holiday Inn, uh, the Holiday Inn East. We got a warrant going on a wire tap, and we're getting all of his phone records now . . . Listen, I gotta run.'

'All right,' Lucas said. 'I'll see you down there, probably tonight, if nothing comes up. I'm driving down.'

'You could fly in a couple of hours . . .'

'Yeah, yeah, I'm driving,' Lucas said.

Lucas was a longtime Porsche driver. He enjoyed driving the car up to a couple of hundred miles, but it was not a long-distance cruiser. Six hundred and fifty miles would leave him both shaken and stirred. Besides, the Porsche needed servicing.

'Look,' he told his Porsche dealer on the telephone, 'You're gonna charge me an arm and a leg, so I oughta get something decent for a loaner. I know damn well that you've got that BMW on the lot, because I saw Larry showing it to a guy . . . yeah, yeah, I don't want a Volkswagen Passat. How about this: I'll pay mileage. I'll pay you fifteen cents a mile, and I buy all the gas. I'm driving to Wichita, which is six hundred and fifty miles, more or less, so that's thirteen hundred miles, you'll get a couple of hundred bucks for three or four days, and then I won't be hassling you about your slow work on the Porsche . . . Come on, goddamnit. Whattaya mean, fifty cents? The government doesn't pay fifty cents, and that's supposed to cover gasoline . . .'

He got the 740IL, a long black four-door with a cockpit like an F-16's, grey leather seats, a CD-player in the trunk and sixty-one thousand miles on the clock, for twenty-five cents a mile. He was two miles out of the dealership when he tripped the ill-placed hood-cover latch with his left foot, without knowing what he'd done, and the hood began rattling up and down. Fearing that the hood was about to blow back his face, he swerved to the edge of the highway and risked his neck to re-latch it. He tripped the hood lever again, five minutes later, and again took the car to the shoulder. This time, he called the Porsche dealer, who said, 'You're tripping the hood with your left foot. Stop doing that.'

Lucas found the hood latch and said, 'That's a good place for it.'

Thirty miles out of town, a yellow light popped on the left dash that said, *Check Engine*, and he took it to the side again, fearing that he was about to blow a rod. He was still within cell phone distance, and he called the dealer again, who said the light meant that the emission system wasn't working quite right. 'Don't worry about it; it doesn't mean anything.'

'On any other car, "check engine" means all your oil just ran out on the road,' Lucas said.

'That's not any car,' the Porsche guy said. 'When the oil runs out on the road, that one says STOP! In big red letters.'

'So the light's gonna be on all trip?'

'That's right, pal. You wanted it, you got it,' the dealer said, without a shred of sympathy.

'There's this whistling noise . . .'

'The windshield's not quite right. We're gonna try to reseal it when you get back.'

'I'm beginning to think this thing's a piece of shit,' Lucas grumbled.

'What do you want for sixty-five thousand?' the Porsche guy asked. 'You shoulda took the Volkswagen.'

But the car was comfortable, and certainly looked good. He made the six hundred and fifty miles to Wichita in nine hours, whipping through Des Moines and Kansas City, pausing only for gas and a sack of hard-shell Taco Supremes at a Taco Bell. He got a room at a Best Western, called Mallard's office in Washington, where an after-hours secretary said she'd relay his number to Mallard. Mallard called five minutes later: 'We're downtown at a place called Joseph's. Let me read the menu to you . . .'

Lucas ordered a steak, medium, baked potato without sour cream, and a Diet Coke. He found Joseph's fifteen minutes later, just as the waiter was delivering the food to Mallard and an angular grey-haired woman named Malone. She was just about his age, Lucas thought, somewhere in the murky forties.

'Malone is our legal specialist,' Mallard said, as he went to work on the steak. 'She keeps track of the taps and the warrants and all that, and talks to the judge when we need to talk to him.'

'Are you an agent?' Lucas asked.

Malone had just pushed a tiny square of beef into her mouth, and instead of answering, opened the left side of her pin-stripe jacket so Lucas could see the butt of a black automatic pistol.

'Nice accessories,' Lucas said. Trying a little bit.

'Cop charm works really well on me,' Malone said, after she swallowed. 'I get all a-twitter.'

'You wanna stop that?' Mallard asked. 'I hate middle-aged courtship rituals.'

'What's his problem?' Lucas asked Malone.

'Recently divorced,' Malone said, tipping her head at Mallard. 'Still loves her.'

'Sorry,' Lucas said.

'Not true, anyway. I'm all done with that,' Mallard said, and for one small second he looked so miserable that Lucas wanted to pat him on the back and tell him it'd be okay; but Lucas didn't believe it would be, and Mallard wouldn't either. 'Besides,' Mallard added, 'I'm not all alone in that condition.'

'If you're talking to me, you're talking to the wrong person,' Malone said. 'I don't like any of them.'

'Them?' Lucas asked.

'Four-time loser,' Mallard said, jabbing his fork at Malone.

'Jesus,' Lucas said. 'In the FBI?'

'If it hadn't been for the second one, I'd be a deputy director by now,' Malone said.

'What'd he do?' Lucas asked.

'He was an actor.'

'Bad actor,' Mallard said.

'No, he was a good actor; he just couldn't stay away from the nude scenes,' Malone said. 'The killer was when the *Washington Post* interviewed him, nude, and he mentioned he was married to an FBI agent.'

'Not the best career move,' Mallard said. 'We were all still wearing white shirts.'

'You got number five figured out yet?' Lucas asked.

'Not yet,' Malone said. 'But I'm looking around.'

'This is what it is,' Mallard said, breaking into the dialogue, 'Is that we've got nine guys here, and we're watching Lopez twenty-four hours a day. He's got three phones, we're listening to all of them, and we've already gotten a couple of ambiguous calls. I mean, people talking in circles about something besides flowers. Nothing that would implicate him, but something's going on . . .'

'Could I hear them? Your tapes?'

'Sure. I've got an edited tape you can listen to tonight. Tomorrow, when he moves, we'll hook you up with him.'

'Good enough,' Lucas said. 'I don't want him to see me, though, not if he's been in and out of the Cities. I've been on TV a couple of times with this stuff . . . he might've caught it.'

'You must be sort of a celebrity, then,' Malone said. 'A local hero.'

'Come on, guys,' Mallard said. 'Please? Malone?'

Mallard sprawled on the bed in his motel room while Lucas sat in the single easy chair and Malone perched against a credenza. They listened while voices said, 'I thought I'd stop by today . . . Not much point . . . Really? Then when do you think would be a good time? . . . Gotta be by tomorrow, unless something happened on the way down. I haven't heard anything – I could give you a ring if you want . . . That'd be good, I'm getting, you know . . .'

Lucas said, 'He's peddling dope.'

'I already suggested that,' Malone said. 'It sorta made people unhappy.'

'Can't be sure that it's dope,' Mallard said defensively.

'Sure it is,' Lucas said. 'I can even tell you what kind.'

'Heroin?' suggested Malone.

'Yup.' Lucas nodded.

'Maybe that's the old Chicago system working,' Mallard said.

'I don't see a murder contractor trusting a junkie to kill people,' Lucas said.

'Maybe *he's* not a junkie . . .'

'That was a small retail sale you were listening to,' Lucas said. 'If he's a small retail dealer, chances are, he's a junkie.'

'On the other hand, since he had somebody coming in from a long way off . . . maybe not,' Malone said. 'He seems to be buying wholesale.'

Lucas shrugged. 'Could be – but it's strange behavior for a guy who's supposed to be a paranoid superkiller. I could see a killer buying cocaine or maybe speed from a good, tight retail connection, but I can't see one actually *selling* the stuff. That means he's dealing with all kind of craphead junkies who'd sell him out for a dime.'

When they finished with the tapes, they all sat around for a minute and then Mallard said, 'The Yankees are on cable.'

'I gotta get outside,' Lucas said. 'I've been sitting in a car all day.'

'Where're you going?' asked Malone.

'Maybe find a bar,' Lucas said. 'Have a couple beers.'

'I could do that,' Malone said. 'I'd like to change into something a little more relaxed.'

Mallard sighed and said, 'All right. I guess it's better than staring at a TV.'

Malone glanced at him, a thin line forming between her eyes; it disappeared in a half-second, and she said, 'So why don't we meet back here in a half hour?'

Lucas got back to Mallard's room a few minutes before Malone; when she got back she was wearing black slacks and a soft black jacket over a sheer blouse. Beneath the blouse, Lucas thought, she was wearing a frilly black bra; and to the left, under the jacket, he could still pick out the slightly lumpy form of the semi-auto. Going out the door, Malone went first, and Lucas got the finest possible whiff of something exotic; something cool and icy.

Malone got to the front passenger door first; Mallard got in the back. Malone looked at all the lights on the dashboard and doors and steering wheel and asked, 'How come small-town cops get cars like these, and we get Tauruses?'

'Because we fight government corruption at every turn,' Mallard said.

'Minneapolis is bigger than D.C.,' Lucas said.

Malone made a rude noise, and Mallard said, 'Stop it.' On the way downtown, Lucas spotted a Wichita cop car sitting at a corner and pulled in ahead of it. Mallard asked, 'What're you doing?' and Lucas answered, 'Research.'

He got out of the car carrying his badge case and when the cop in the driver's seat rolled down the window, Lucas flipped open the case and said, 'Hey guys – I'm a cop from up in Minneapolis going through with a couple of friends. We're looking for a bar or cocktail lounge, you know, something decent?'

The driver took Lucas' badge case and studied the ID for a minute, grunted, 'Deputy chief, huh?' then handed it back and looked at his partner. 'Really aren't many places to talk . . . What do you think? The Rink?'

'Be about the best,' the partner said. 'Four blocks straight ahead to the second light, take a right, about four or five more blocks down. The Rink.'

'Great,' Lucas said, straightening up. 'Buy you guys one, if we're still there when you get off.'

'Thanks, but we're working the overnight,' the driver said. 'Say, let me ask you this. What's your base pay up there, in Minneapolis?'

They talked about salary, vacation and sick-leave policy for a couple of minutes, then Lucas walked back to the 740, climbed inside, tripped the hood latch, got out, slammed the hood, got back in and they drove to the Rink.

Rinker was standing behind the bar, reading a register tape, when Lucas walked in. She was so utterly astonished that she showed nothing at all, as though she'd been hit in the forehead with a hammer. When she recovered, after a full five seconds, she noticed that he was with a woman who looked like a lawyer and a dry-faced, thick-necked man who might be an academic; or maybe a college wrestling coach.

She turned away from them and walked down the bar and into the back, where she could stand behind a pane of one-way glass.

'Something going on?' one of the kitchen boys asked, picking up her rapt attention.

'Guy walked in, I thought he might be an old boyfriend from a very long time ago,' Rinker said.

'Which guy?'

'Finish the freezer,' she said.

'Just askin'.'

She watched Lucas for ten minutes, and finally decided that he wasn't interested in the bar: if he'd come here for her – and what other reason could he have for being here? – he certainly wasn't looking for her. He was putting a little light bullshit on the lawyer woman, Rinker decided, and the lawyer liked it.

Rinker wondered what would happen if she simply walked out into the bar. Would he jump up and bust her? Were there other cops closing in on the bar, or stationed outside? If he was here on business, why was he drinking beer and bullshitting the woman? Was he that good?

She broke away from the glass and walked rapidly back through the kitchen to the flight of stairs that went up to her small office. The office had been built under the roof of what had originally been a one-story building, so the ceiling slanted and it had windows going out only one end of the building. Looking out, she couldn't see anything unusual – nobody in the streets, no cars with men lurking inside.

But it wouldn't be that way, anyway, she thought. If they were coming for her, they'd probably wait until they could get her on the sidewalk, alone, or at her home. They wouldn't walk into a bar and risk a shootout in a place full of bystanders . . .

Rinker had a long couch at the end of the office, and she sometimes napped on it. Now she lay down, closed her eyes, and tried to work it out. She could only find one answer: that somebody had given her up. Somebody who knew where she lived. She'd told Carmel that she went to Wichita State, so Carmel knew where she lived, but not her name, or about the bar. But if Carmel had given her up, then they'd know almost everything, and they would have come in hard.

She had to call Carmel, she thought. But not from here . . .

And right now, maybe she'd walk out on the floor, talk to some people. If they were planning to jump her, she was dead meat anyway. And if they weren't, maybe she could learn something.

Rinker's bar had two major rooms, one for drinking and talking, and the second for drinking and dancing. The dance floor was polished maple, taken from a bankrupt karate studio, and probably the best dance floor in any bar in Wichita; all surrounded by deep-backed booths upholstered in naugahyde. When Davenport and his friends arrived, the band – live music on weekends – had been taking a break. They were setting up for their third and final set when Rinker cruised through.

She worked all the booths around the dance floor, talking with people she knew or had often seen in the bar, mostly under-40s white-collar; the band played soft rock and cross over country. She bought a beer for a guy who'd walked away from a car wreck earlier in the day, and for a couple who were out for the first time since a kid was born. She listened to a guy-walks-into-a-bar joke:

Guy walks into a bar, and the bartender says, 'Boy, I didn't expect to see you today, after last night – you were really bummed out.' And the guy says, 'I was so bummed out that I went home and looked in my medicine cabinet. I had a big bottle of a thousand aspirins in there, and I decided to kill myself by taking them all at once.' The bartender says, 'So what happened?' And the guy says, 'Well, after the first two, I didn't feel so bad.'

She laughed and tracked Davenport between the heads of the dancers, who were just moving out on the dance floor again as the band cranked into a country dance piece. Davenport was in a front-room booth, facing her through the smoky atmosphere. He was paying no attention to her at all, or to anybody else in the bar, as far as she could tell. He was a good-looking guy, in a hard way, just starting to get a little grey around the temples. She drifted toward him.

* * *

Lucas was laying a very mild hustle on Malone, while Mallard tried to steer the conversation back to police work. Malone didn't want to know about police work, but when Lucas suggested that they dance, she said, 'I don't dance like that.'

'Is that a philosophical position?'

'I just don't dance to rock or country. I never learned. I can foxtrot; I can waltz. I can't do that kind of boppity . . . you know.'

'Too self-conscious,' Lucas said. He was about to go on when a woman stopped at the table and said, 'You all doing all right here?'

'All right,' Lucas said, looking up at her. She wasn't a waitress. 'Who're you?'

'I'm the owner, Clara. Making sure that everybody's being treated right.'

'Good bar,' Lucas said. 'You oughta open another one like it, up in Minneapolis.'

'You're from Minneapolis?'

'I am,' Lucas said. 'These folks are from back east.'

'Glad to have you in Wichita,' Rinker said. She started to step away, but Malone, who'd perhaps had one more beer than she was accustomed to, said, 'Your band doesn't play waltzes, does it?'

Rinker grinned and said, 'Why, no, I don't believe they do, honey. You wanna waltz?'

'This guy's got the urge to dance,' Malone said, pointing at Lucas with her long-neck, 'And I can't dance to rock. Never learned.'

'Well, you oughta,' Rinker said. She looked quickly around the bar and then said to Lucas, 'I'm not doing anything at the minute, and I *like* dancing. You want to?'

They were dancing for five seconds and Lucas realized he was out of his depth.

'You're a dancer, a professional,' he said, and Rinker laughed and said, 'I used to be, kinda.'

'Well, slow down, you're making me look bad. And I'm a lot older than you are.'

'Ah, you dance fine,' Rinker said, 'For a Minneapolis white guy.'

Lucas laughed and turned her around; she was good-looking, he thought, one of those tough-cookie smart blondes who'd been around a bit, liked a good time, and could run a spreadsheet like an accountant. Maybe was an accountant.

'Are you an accountant?' he asked.

'An accountant?' They were shouting at each other over the music. 'Why would you think that?'

'I don't. Just making up a story in my head.'

'A story? You're not a reporter, are you?'

'Nah, I'm a cop. Just going through. I stopped to talk to some friends.'

'You don't look like a cop. You look like a . . . movie guy, or something.'

'Flattery will get you everywhere,' Lucas shouted back.

She laughed, and they danced.

But late that night, an hour after the bar closed, Rinker climbed in her car and headed for Kansas City. She would *not* break the routine: she would *not* make a business call from Wichita. She arrived in KC in the early morning hours, pulled into a convenience store and started dropping coins in a pay phone. When she had enough, she dialed Carmel; and Carmel, sleep in her voice, answered on the second ring. The cell phone, Rinker thought, must have been on the bed stand.

'We've got another problem,' Rinker said.

'What's that?'

'I just gaily danced the night away with your friend and mine . . .' She let it hang.

'Who?'

'Lucas Davenport. Right here in River City.'

'Goddamnit,' Carmel said. She ripped off a piece of thumbnail, snapped at it; she could hear her own teeth grinding in the telephone earpiece. 'He's working on some kind of information. I don't know enough about you or your friends to know where it might be coming from . . .'

'It's more complicated than that,' Rinker said. 'He had no idea who I was. He must be there for something – I mean, what are the chances of a coincidence? Zero? Less than zero, I'd say . . .'

'So would I.'

'He had no idea who I was,' Rinker repeated. 'I was hoping you might get something from your sources in the police department.'

'Not much chance,' Carmel said. 'My guy thinks of himself as a kind of harmless leaker of information that's gonna get out anyway. He really wouldn't tell me anything that he thought might get somebody hurt . . .'

'So maybe we need to put some pressure on him.'

'Listen to this: he did tell me that they keep coming back to me. Even my source is getting a little strange with me. He thinks Davenport's got something, and I think it has to do with that kid.'

'Damnit. Even if the kid told him something . . . oh, shit.'

'What?'

'Just had a thought. If the kid for some reason got the tag number on that rental car . . . I told you that I use fake credit cards and IDs to rent them. I told you about that?'

'Yeah. You keep the cards good by using them . . .'

'I've paid them from Wichita. I've been careful, but I've gotten bank drafts here to pay those bills.'

'You think?'

'I don't see how the kid could have gotten the number. It was dark, and she was back inside when we left, and we were way down the block.'

'Maybe it wasn't the kid. Maybe . . . wasn't there a guy on a bike?'

'From upstairs? Why would he take our tag number?' Rinker asked.

'I don't know. But that would explain a few things. Can you come up here?'

'Yeah. I'm in KC now. I'll be up there tomorrow.'

'Bring your . . . tools,' Carmel said. 'We may have to talk to somebody. And I gotta think about this. Maybe by the time you get here, I'll have some ideas.'

Chapter Seventeen

Lucas stayed in Wichita for two days, tracking Lopez and listening to the FBI taps. The longer he listened, the more convinced he became that Lopez was a small-time dealer, supplementing the flower shop take with a little side money. The side money, Lucas decided, was going straight into his arm.

A woman named Nancy Holme, carried on Lopez' state tax forms as an employee, did virtually all the work, showing up early to take deliveries of fresh-cut flowers, staying late over a hot computer. Lopez would arrive sleepy, nod off at midday, and leave sleepy. The Feebs couldn't decide whether Holme was in on the game or not. She never took delivery of drugs. Lucas suggested that they look at *her* as the killer. They did, and rapidly concluded that she wasn't.

The night before he left for Minneapolis, Lucas, Malone and Mallard went back to the Rink. The woman he'd danced with, the owner, wasn't working, he was told. 'She's got to travel on business a couple of times a year, and this is one of those times. Too bad, she liked you,' a waitress told them, her over-active eyebrows semaphoring a tale of two ships passing in the night.

'A tragedy,' Malone said, when the waitress left with their orders. 'Davenport leaves another broken heart in a dusty western town.'

Rinker was in the Twin Cities. Carmel met her at the hotel, and at Rinker's direction, had ridden up three extra floors on the elevator, and had taken the stairs down to Rinker's floor. Rinker, when she let Carmel in, was wearing a black wig.

'How do I look? Mexican?' Rinker asked as she closed the door.

'You're too pale,' Carmel said. 'You could maybe make Italian.'

'I'll go back to the redhead, then,' Rinker said.

Carmel had been thinking about Davenport: 'Somehow, they're tracking you. And for some reason, they're pushing on me. I thought about your car, and the possibility that they're tracking it, but that doesn't seem

169

likely. That would mean that they had to have two pieces of luck: to get onto Tennex, and to get the tag number. I don't believe it. What I'm wondering is, could they have found a connection with your St. Louis friends? Could they be squeezing somebody?'

'Only one guy in St. Louis knows exactly who I am and what I do, and there are maybe two more who suspect – a couple brothers who run a bar down there. And the brothers wouldn't know who you are. The one guy would . . . he knows your name. He's the guy Rolo called.'

'My contact in the PD says that another detective, a woman named Sherrill, went down to St. Louis for a couple of days last week, and the word around the department is that she was talking to the St. Louis organized-crime guys,' Carmel said.

'I don't know why my guy would be dealing me,' Rinker said, thinking about it for a moment. 'He takes a lot of power off me: you know, he's the guy who knows the finger of God, as you put it. The guy who can hook you up. And if I go down, he goes down.'

Carmel took a short turn around the hotel room, checked herself in a bureau mirror, turned back and said, 'Let me tell you something I learned as a lawyer: everybody will deal. Everybody. Have you ever heard of this new federal lockup in the Rockies?'

'No . . .'

'You gotta cement cell about half the size of this hotel room. It has a concrete bed platform and stainless steel sink and toilet fixtures in concrete stands. No bars, just a steel door and an unbreakable window that shows nothing but a rectangle of sky – you can't even see the sun. There's a black-and-white TV bolted in a corner. That's it. You're in there twenty-two to twenty-three hours a day, and you're monitored every minute. I've had a couple of clients try to commit suicide in there, and neither one made it – although one made it when they put him in a hospital after his second try. He tried to kill himself by standing against one wall and running full speed into the wall across the room, with his head down. He cracked his skull. He finally managed to kill himself in the hospital – this was his third try – rather than go back. You hear what I'm saying?'

'I'm not sure,' Rinker said.

'What I'm saying is, torture is alive and well in the United States of America,' Carmel said. 'It just doesn't involve physical pain. It involves isolation, year after year of solitary . . . They could take your Mafia friend out there, show him through the place, let him talk to a couple of inmates, and he'd give you up.'

'But he hasn't,' Rinker said. 'Because if he had, they'd be on me like a hot sweat. But they're not. I swear to God, Davenport didn't have any idea who I was, and neither did the other cops. We *danced*, for God's sake.'

'That wasn't too great a move,' Carmel said.

'I had to find out if they were there for me – I couldn't stand it,' Rinker said. 'To tell you the truth . . .'

'What?'

'What if he's *fated* to find me? That's what scares me. I've got this guy I can't shake because it's *my* time.'

'Jesus, Pam, you gotta take a couple aspirins or something,' Carmel said. 'Lay down for a while. 'Cause, believe me, it's nothing like that.'

Rinker sighed, and let her shoulders slump. Carmel actually *did* make her feel better. She was so *sure* of herself. 'Okay.'

'So we still have the question, What do we do?' Carmel said. 'Davenport knows something. He's working off something. What could they have given him at Tennex that put him in Wichita? Why is he pushing on me?'

'I don't know how he got to Wichita. I was a fanatic about being careful.'

'What about your Mafia friend? Even if he's not deliberately giving you up, is there any way he could have pointed them at Wichita?'

'Hmph.' Rinker had to think about it for a minute. 'I didn't let him call me there. He always came out to deliver the messages. But he's always on the telephone. If somehow they managed to sort out his calls while he was there . . . I don't know. It sounds weak. I mean, he goes everywhere. Why would they focus on Wichita?'

'They've got all kinds of ways of doing those things – statistics,' Carmel said. 'I'd be willing to bet it's something like that, especially if Davenport didn't know who you were.'

'He didn't. I'm sure of that.'

They went over it several times, and finally Carmel said, 'You know, we're coming to the crunch, here. If Davenport's mining some kind of line of information, it might lead to you, or it might lead to me, or it might not. It's hard to put a case together. I'd say it's about fifty-fifty whether we should sit tight, or move somehow.'

'What move?'

'One possibility is, we could go talk to the kid, and the kid's mother. We could find out what they told the cops. Then we'd know about that angle.'

'What if it's a trap?'

'I don't think it is. I don't think any cop would put a kid in play, not when you're talking about professional killers,' Carmel said. 'If any cop would, it'd be Davenport – but I don't think even he would.'

'And you're saying that after we talk to them, we kill them? The kid and her mom?'

Carmel shrugged: 'If we have to.'

'We'd have to find some other way to do it. I'm not going to kill the kid – I've been thinking about it,' Rinker said. For the first time since they started meeting face-to-face, Carmel picked up the warning edge in Rinker's voice that she'd heard when they talked on the phone, when the problems began developing.

'Okay. But if you really think you're the finger of God . . . what's the problem?'

'I'm just not gonna kill that kid. Fuck the finger,' Rinker said.

'So we find a way not to kill them – not unless we absolutely have to,' Carmel said. 'You didn't kill that Marker woman in Washington. We should be able to figure something out.'

'You said going after the kid was one possibility. What's the other?'

'We could do something that would make it impossible for them to prosecute us, even if they figured out who we are,' Carmel said.

'How would we do that?' Rinker asked.

'I've been thinking about it, ever since you called,' Carmel said. 'I call it Plan B.'

Plan B took a while to explain; Rinker was not so much appalled as amazed.

Lucas got back to Minneapolis late the next afternoon, dropped the BMW at the Porsche dealership, sank into his own car with a sigh of relief, and headed downtown. He'd told Sherrill and Black when to expect him, and they were waiting in the Homicide office.

'Not so good?' Sherrill asked.

Lucas shook his head: 'He's not the guy. He's a small-time dope dealer.'

'But they still think he's the guy?'

'Mallard still thinks there's a chance. He's got an smart assistant named Malone, and Malone was ready to go back to Washington and start over,' Lucas said.

'Goddamnit,' Black said. 'Did you hear about the sniper?'

Lucas shook his head: 'What sniper?'

'Car got hit by rifle fire last night during rush hour. One car, one windshield, nobody hurt. Couldn't find a shooter, and we thought maybe it was an accident. Then this afternoon, right at the start of the rush hour, a little after three, the guy came back. Two cars hit, a woman hit in the neck, she's in surgery. Some guy coming down the road behind her stuffed a wad of newspaper in the hole in her neck, probably saved her life. But the media's going batshit – the radio stations, all the drive-time guys. I mean, this is *their audience* being shot at . . .'

'So everybody's out?'

'Well, you know Sloan's working the Hmong thing and Swanson is still chasing down stuff on the Parker case; so people are making noises like taking us off Allen. They say just a few days, but you know what that might mean . . .'

'I'll talk to Rose Marie,' Lucas said. 'But the question is, what've we got to do? What's left that we haven't done?'

They all looked at each other, and finally, Sherrill shrugged. 'We were waiting for you to tell us.'

Lucas said, 'What're you doing tonight?'

'Nothing,' Sherrill said.

'Why don't you hang around and see if Carmel's going anywhere?' Lucas suggested.

'If we're gonna start tailing her, we're gonna need more than two guys,' Black said. 'They're gonna be hard to come by. Given the sniper and all that.'

'So we don't have a fulltime tail – just somebody hanging around. Maybe we get lucky.'

'Ah, Christ,' Sherrill said. 'I'll do it, but I have a feeling I'm gonna be pulling my weenie.'

Rinker brought a wig with her: she'd have *big* hair, Texas hair, when she went in. She'd wear jeans, gym shoes, rubber kitchen gloves, two pistols under a black sport jacket, a handkerchief and a nylon rolled up tight as a watch cap.

173

Carmel would be wearing a slinky bloody-red dress with spangles, matching red shoes and lipstick. 'How do I look?' she asked.

'You look terrific,' Rinker said, admiration riding in her voice. 'God, if I could look like that . . .'

'You're beautiful,' Carmel said.

'No, I'm not,' Rinker said. 'I'm cute. I look like I should be in the *Playboy* college issue, Duke University's Miss Perky Nipples.'

'Does Miss Perky Nipples carry .22 Colt Woodsmans . . . would it be Woodsmans, or Woodsmen?'

'No, she probably wouldn't. I don't know the correct grammar, but I got two of them, and they were stolen fourteen years ago from a gunstore in Butte, Montana, and haven't seen the light of day since. I'm cool.'

Carmel nodded, 'You *are* cool.' She took a last look at herself in a full-length mirror, twirled and said, 'When I get that boy home tonight, I am going to fuck him rudely. Rudely.'

'Good luck,' Rinker said. 'I sorta wish I was . . . involved with somebody. It's been a while.'

'Is it hard to meet guys in Wichita?' Carmel asked, screwing on an earring clasp.

'It's hard for *me*,' Rinker said. 'You know, a gal who runs a bar? What kind of guys am I going to attract?' She answered her own question: 'Most of them have got a bottle of Jim Beam in the trunk . . .'

'Too bad you couldn't hook up with Davenport,' Carmel said, jokingly.

'He'd be a possibility,' Rinker admitted. 'He could be fun, in a big-galoot way.'

'Mean big-galoot,' said Carmel.

'I could see that,' Rinker said. 'I could *feel* it.' After a second, 'But he sorta . . . handles you. Moves you around. Touches you. Not feeling you up, or anything, but he's just . . . I don't know. All over the place.'

'If he sees you here, we're fucked,' Carmel said.

'Unlike when I saw him in Wichita,' Rinker said. Then: 'I thought about coming on to him a little, but that would've been . . . too much. Anyway, I don't expect to see him again the rest of my life.'

She picked up the first of the pistols, jacked a shell into the chamber, set the safety and slipped it into her gun girdle, under the jacket. Rinker looked at Carmel. 'You ready?'

Chapter Eighteen

Black canceled a date and climbed into the back of Sherrill's Mazda with a pepperoni pizza and a bag of hot nacho cheese crackers.

Sherrill said, 'You're a cruel fuck. If I ate any of that stuff, it'd go right straight to my thighs.'

'So don't eat it. Concentrate on other things. Flowers. Small children,' Black said.

'I'm having a hard time concentrating. With my future husband on his way up to . . .'

'. . . slip a little English bacon to Carmel Loan.'

'You're so crude. And whatever he's got in there, I doubt that it resembles bacon.'

'You mean, in stripes, or in flatness?'

She giggled: 'God, I love talking dirty with you. It's so jock-like, so . . .'

She couldn't think of a word; through the plate glass doors of Carmel Loan's building, they could see Hale Allen's back as he signed into the building. Then a short redhead came around the corner from the elevators, into the lobby, and Sherrill said, 'Here comes . . . nope.'

The redhead walked past Allen, giving him the once-over, pushed through the glass doors, looked left and right, put her hands deep in the pockets of her black sport coat, and headed down the block. Inside, Allen walked away from the security desk and around the corner to the elevators.

As they watched them, a patrol car pulled in behind the Mazda and the red lights began to flash. 'Ah, man,' Sherrill said, looking in her rear-view mirror. The loudspeaker on the cop car blared, 'Drop your car keys out the passenger window. Now.'

Instead of dropping her keys out of the window, Sherrill held her badge case out. After a minute, the flashing lights stopped, and the driver of the cop car approached from the back, shining a flashlight on the badge case. Sherrill pushed the door open, dropped her feet to the street, looked at the cop and said, 'What the fuck are you doing?'

'What are *you* doing?'

'I'm on a goddamn stakeout. I *was* on a goddamn stakeout,' Sherrill said. 'Now I'm in a goddamn comedy routine.' People had stopped up and down the street, to watch.

'Well, jeez, we're sorry.' The cop looked around at the audience and flapped his arms helplessly. 'You shoulda told somebody, instead of just lurking around here. The doorman called. He said you'd been here for hours.'

Sherrill could see the doorman in Carmel's building peering at them through the lobby window. 'Yeah, well: now I'm gonna drive around the block and park again,' she said. 'And I'm telling you. Stay away from me or I swear to Christ, I'll shoot you.'

The cop peered in the back window and said, 'Hi, Tom.'

'Hi. Want some nachos?'

'Nah. Give me heartburn . . . so you're gonna go around the block?'

'Yeah.'

'Well. Be cool.'

Sherrill started the car, and they rolled away, Black laughing in the back. Then Sherrill started: 'God, I love police work.'

Two minutes later, they were back on watch, Black still relaxed in the back and even deeper into the nachos. 'How you been?' he asked through a mouthful of chips and cheese. 'Since you and Davenport?'

'I miss him. A lot,' she said.

'He's an asshole. Sorta.'

'I miss him anyway,' she said. 'Besides, while I agree he's an asshole, he's not an asshole like you think he is.'

'Oh, I think I know.'

'Just 'cause you're queer doesn't mean you know. You're still a guy.'

Black contemplated the statement, formulated a reply, ate the chips as he worked at it: carefully formulated replies were necessary in the stakeout business. You could sit for hours, and you didn't want to run out of stuff to talk about – or piss off your partner – too soon.

'Let me tell you my theory of queerness as relates to the straight male,' Black said. And he did, and after a while – ten minutes – Sherrill said, 'I never would have thought of any of that.'

'You're not gay.'

'It's not that. It's just that I couldn't have come up with such an utter crock of shit.'

Black put a final three nachos in his mouth and settled back to formulate another reply. Before he got a good paragraph together, Sherrill said, 'Here they come – and Jesus Christ. Look at that dress.'

Black peered over the sill of the back window. Allen and Carmel stepped out through the glass doors, Allen wore a dark jacket that Black suspected was lightweight cashmere; tan, expensive-looking slacks; and loafers. Carmel was in a shocking, low-cut red party dress and red shoes.

'Nice dress,' Black said.

'Nice? A little gaudy, don't you think? And her tits are about coming out.'

'I don't know,' he said. 'Color is always good in clothing. And skin display is nice, in the summer.'

'Don't give me the fag act. Look at her. She's like a billboard.'

'All right. She's obviously a tart,' Black said.

'Thank you. Not nearly fine enough to aspire after the lovely Hale.'

'And she certainly doesn't have your tits.'

'You don't think?'

'Marcy, you've probably got the third-best tits in Minneapolis. Davenport says sixth best, and of course, he would know from first-hand observation, while Sloan says second best – I don't know about Sloan's qualifications . . .'

'He has none, and shut up, we're going.'

'Let me get my Big Gulp off the floor . . . Ah, shit.'

Rinker missed the foul-up with the squad car; she'd already turned the corner, and was headed back to her hotel to pick up her car. She felt heavy as she went. She might have to kill the two of them, the mother and daughter. Might *have* to. And that felt wrong. These were people who'd never had a chance; they weren't people who'd screwed up somehow, had gotten too stubbornly close to something that was bad for them . . . It was like all that gang-banger talk years ago, of *mushrooms* popping up in the line-of-fire. This mother and daughter were essentially mushrooms, and Rinker had always thought of herself more as a surgeon than as a gang-banger . . .

She'd have to do this right.

Carmel and Hale Allen went to a club called The Swan, which had a twelve-piece orchestra and a blonde chick singer with a voice like

177

buttermilk, and danced. Old-style dances, cheek to cheek, hand in the middle of the back. Carmel could reach Hale's earlobe with her tongue, which she did every few minutes, and which had a profound effect on him. After the third dance, he growled, 'Let's get out of here.'

'*No*,' she said, in her best cat voice. 'You've got to be *patient*.'

Sherrill and Black watched from a balcony seat as Allen and Carmel moved around the dance floor, stopping now and then to talk with friends; all of the friends, Sherrill decided, had a certain slickness that she disliked. She mentioned it to Black.

'I think they teach you that in law school,' Black said.

'Hey, I know some pretty nice lawyers.'

'So now we're gonna be sincere?'

'No, I was just wondering. There's this subset of people who look *slick*. See? Look at the guy in the white coat, and the woman he's with. Slick.'

'They spend too much time looking at themselves, without being professionals,' Black said. 'Professionals – actors – can look perfect, and look right at the same time. These guys try to look perfect, and they just look slick.'

'Much more of this surveillance chit-chat and I'll throw up.'

Rinker scouted the Davis' neighborhood, saw nothing at all. Of course, if it were a trap of some kind, the cops might be in an apartment across the street or up the stairs and she'd never know until they were kicking down the doors.

But it didn't feel that way; it didn't have the creepy close feeling of movies, when a guy was in hiding. And somehow, she thought, it would feel that way. There'd be that peculiar stillness of the moment when you hide in somebody else's house, and they walk in . . . and they *know*. She didn't feel that here.

Rinker had taken two FedEx boxes from a FedEx stand, and taped them together. She left the car a block from the Davis apartment – she noted the lights under the window shades, so somebody was home – and walked back, carrying the box. A guy was following his dog down the other side of the street, paying no attention to her.

Rinker turned in at the house, jogged up the stoop, and stepped inside the entry and stopped. She could hear a stereo from up the stairs, nothing from the back, from the Davis apartment. She moved closer to the Davis door, listened. The rhythm of voices – or one voice, a woman's voice. She glanced around, took the pistol out of her belt and stuck it under her left arm, pinned to her side. She knocked once.

The rhythm of the voices stopped, and she heard footsteps. The door opened on a chain, and a woman peeked out. 'Yes?'

'We got a FedEx upstairs for you, the guys did. They forgot to bring it down, so I did.' Rinker said cheerfully. She bounced the box in her hand. The woman didn't hesitate, said, 'Oh, thanks. Just the minute,' and pushed the door shut and began to work the chain. Rinker quickly stooped and put the box on the floor, then reached up and pulled the nylon down over her face, pulling it down like a condom.

The woman opened the door and the pistol was there, pointing at her head, and Rinker whispered, harshly, 'Step back or I'll kill you.'

Jan Davis, stricken, hand at her face, eyes wide, stepped back. 'Please don't hurt us.'

Rinker kicked the box into the apartment, pushed the door shut, and rasped, 'If a cop comes in now, I'll start shooting and we'll all be dead. Are the cops watching this place?'

Davis's head was wagging back and forth, a *no*, and a little girl called out, 'Mom? Who's that?'

'Get her out here,' Rinker said, flicking the tip of the pistol toward the bedroom door.

'You're the . . .'

'Yeah. I've never killed a kid in my life, and I hope I never have to. But you gotta get her out here. Then I'm gonna ask you two questions, and I'm gonna tell you something – if you answer the questions right – and then I'm gonna leave.'

'You're going to kill us . . .'

'Mom?'

'If I were gonna kill you, I wouldn't be wearing a mask,' Rinker said. 'Now get her out here.'

Davis stared for another moment, then said, 'Heather, honey? C'mere, honey.'

The girl stuck her head out of a bedroom a minute later. She was wearing yellow underpants and a yellow shirt, and was carrying a Curious George monkey doll. 'Mom?'

'C'mere, honey.' Davis backed toward her daughter, groping for her hand. The girl looked at Rinker and said, 'Did you kill those people?' Her eyes were as wide as her mother's had been.

179

Her mother said, 'Shhh,' and Rinker said, 'Here's the first question. What did you tell the police about the people you saw in the hallway?'

Davis glanced down at the girl and then back at Rinker: 'They had pictures. We didn't tell them anything, because Heather didn't see anything. She couldn't even make one of those drawing pictures.'

'Did the police talk to anybody upstairs?'

'They talked to everybody in the house, but nobody saw anything. Everybody's been talking to everybody, but nobody even saw you and . . . the other person . . . leaving. Nobody saw . . .'

'Nobody.'

'No.' Davis shook her head, and Rinker was struck with the straight-forwardness of it. She looked at the little girl.

'And what did you do, little girl?'

Heather told her: how she went to the police station, how she tried to make a drawing, but she didn't know any faces. They showed her pictures, but she didn't know them. As she spoke, she stood up tall, with her feet together, as if she were a Marine standing at attention. And Rinker suddenly knew that the child understood what was happening. That she was talking for her *life*. Rinker suddenly teared up, and said to Davis, 'Send her back to the bedroom.'

'Go, honey.'

'You come too, Mom,' Heather said, pulling at her mother's hand.

'I've got to talk to this lady,' Davis said, and the fear lay right on the surface of her eyes. Heather saw it as clearly as did Rinker.

'Don't worry, kid, I'm not going to hurt anybody,' Rinker said. 'We've just got to have some grownup talk.'

'I've heard grownup talk before,' the girl said.

Rinker looked down at her. All right; she probably had. She looked back at the mother: 'You don't tell anybody I was here. You could actually provide them with a little more information about me – how tall I am, what my voice sounds like. I couldn't tolerate that. If you do that, if you tell anyone I was here, I'll come back and kill you. And if they kill me first, then one of my associates will come here and kill you, because they'll feel like they've got to make the point. And they won't let you go. They don't give a *shit* about people like you. Do you understand?'

The vulgarity, the *shit*, hung in the air between them, and lent Rinker's speech authority – a killer's authority – and Mom nodded dumbly. 'We'll never tell. Honest to god, we'll *never* tell,' Jan Davis said.

'Go sit on the couch,' Rinker said. 'Don't get up for five minutes, no matter how much you want to. I'm going to walk out of the house, and I don't want you to see my car.'

Mom nodded again, and pulled the child across the living room to the couch, and they sat down.

Rinker stepped back to the door, stopped, brought the pistol up, and fired a single shot. A photograph of Davis, in earlier years, with two other women, fell off the wall, a perfect pencil thick hole punched through the glass and Davis' eyeball, in the photo.

'Absolute and complete silence,' Rinker whispered.

And she was gone.

Out the door, down the stoop, up the street, in the car. And she breathed out.

'Let's go home,' Black said. 'They're gonna be here all night.'

'Best time to pull something is about five o'clock in the morning,' Sherrill said, but she yawned.

'Yeah, and if we really think that, we should put a twenty-four-hour watch on them. But we can't do twenty-four hours ourselves. I'm so fuckin' bored, I can't think, and the back of my boxer shorts is about five inches up my ass because I've been sitting here too long.'

'Take a walk,' Sherrill said.

'I'd get mugged.'

'Not in this neighborhood . . .'

'By the goddamn security patrol. You see those guys? Would you give those guys a gun?'

'All right.' Sherrill sighed and turned the key, cranked the car. 'There's gotta be something else we can do. I can't believe we sat in this car for eight hours and never came up with a decent idea.'

'There's nothing left. If Carmel did it, and I'm not giving you that . . . she's gonna walk.'

Jan Davis lay in bed, all night, barely closing her eyes. She fought down an impulse to flee to her parents' home in Missouri – she wouldn't be completely welcome, since the divorce. Her parents had liked Howard better than they liked her, she thought, feeling alone and isolated. Besides, she'd seen the *Godfather* movies, and she knew about these people, the

Mafia. Running wouldn't help: they'd get you anywhere. She decided to stick to routine.

Heather had been going to day school all summer, getting a head start on first grade. Davis had hoped against hope that somehow, in the morning, Heather would have forgotten what happened the night before. But she hadn't – she looked like she'd gotten as little sleep as her mother.

'Should I go to school?' she asked, first thing.

'Yes. We are going to forget what happened last night. That was a bad dream.' Davis tried to be cheery; but it wasn't working.

'Is she going to come back and hurt us?'

'No, no, no, nothing is going to happen. Let's just pretend that nothing happened, nobody came.'

'But the lady came.'

Davis wanted to shake her. Wanted to scream at her, wanted to impress her with the danger, but didn't know how. 'Heather, listen: that was a very bad lady. Very bad. We have to pretend that she wasn't here. We have to pretend that she was a bad dream. Remember the bad dream you had about Mrs. Gartin chasing you? We have to forget it, just like we forgot the dream about Mrs. Gartin.'

'I didn't forget that dream,' Heather said solemnly. 'I just told you I did.'

'But you don't have it any more.'

'No . . .' She ate cornflakes.

And before she could bring the subject back to the Rinker, Davis said, 'I'm supposed to see your father this afternoon.'

Heather looked up from the cornflakes. 'Is he going to come to see me?'

'Not this afternoon, I don't think. This is business. But I'll tell him you'd like it if he came over.'

'Okay. Do you think he'll come . . .'

And the talk went that way. All the way to school, Davis looked for trailing cars, looked for short women with red hair, looked for those small competent hands, but she didn't see anybody exactly like that. And Heather never mentioned the bad lady, not once, all the way to school.

Mrs. Gartin's School took children from three to six, and taught them letters and numbers and shapes and colors, music, and phonics for the older children. Mrs. Gartin and her two associates tried to keep the little boys from beating each other and victimizing the little girls, and encourage the little girls to socialize.

At the back of the big kids' room – Mrs. Gartin never even saw it any more, just another blob in the background – was Officer Friendly's full-size, standup cut-out, sponsored by Logan's Rendering Co. Officer Friendly's telephone number was on the front of the poster. Officer Friendly had visited the school, and talked to them about being careful, about bad men and women, and how the police were there to help children. He left behind the cutout.

Heather saw his picture every day, and this day, summoning all her intentness of purpose, she went into Mrs. Roman's cubbyhole when the rest of the class followed Mrs. Roman out to recess, and called the number. She'd called her Mom several times, and knew about dialing nine.

Officer Friendly, whose real name was Dick Ennis, was something of a drunk ('Not an alcoholic,' he said. 'Alcoholics go to meetings.'), and was late to work more than half the time; not that anybody cared. And mostly, when he was sober, he was a pretty good Officer Friendly. For one thing, he liked kids, and had several of his own by two ex-wives. For another, he'd been a decent street cop. In any case, he'd just arrived at his office, put his sack lunch in his desk drawer, and had turned to go for coffee when the phone rang. He dropped into his chair and picked it up.

Heather said, 'Is this Officer Friendly?'

And Ennis said, 'Yes, it is. Can I help you?' He thought the little girl on the other end of the line might be five years old.

'Yes. A bad lady came to my house and scared my Mom and me.'

'Uh-huh. Who is this? What is your name?'

'This is Heather Davis. My phone number is . . .'

Smart kid, Ennis thought, as he scribbled down the number. 'Okay, Heather, how did the bad lady scare your Mom and you?'

'She had a gun and she had a mask that she pulled down over her face, and she said if we told anybody, she would come and kill us. And she shooted a picture of my mom. And now my Mom is scared to tell anybody.'

Ennis sat up, his forehead wrinkled. 'When did this happen?'

'Last night when it was dark.'

'Nobody called a policeman?'

'No. Some policeman came to see us, but they went away. Then this lady came and told us not to talk to any more policeman. Ever.'

'Some policemen came to see you? Do you remember who they were?'

'One was a man and one was a woman,' the girl said.

'Do you remember their names? Either one?'

'Yes.'

'Could you tell me what they were?' His own small children had taught him patience.

'One was named Mr. Davenport, and one was named Miss Sherrill.'

'Jesus Christ,' Officer Friendly said.

Chapter Nineteen

Sherrill was still asleep when Lucas called. 'We maybe got a break,' he said.

She picked up the intensity in his voice, heard the traffic in the background. He was on a cell phone. She sat up, rubbing sleep from her eyes with the heel of her hand. 'What happened?'

'That little kid called in, Heather Davis – she called Officer Friendly, you know the guy, what's-his-name . . .'

'Ennis.'

'Yeah. She says the shooter was at their apartment last night, and warned her mother not to talk to us. She told them if they did talk to us, she'd come back and kill them both.'

Sherrill hopped out of bed and started for the bathroom, trailed by a twenty-foot coil of white phone wire. 'What time was that?'

'Nine, or a little after. Just dark.'

'Then it wasn't Carmel,' Sherrill said. 'We got her coming out of her building around eight-thirty, followed her to the Swan, and watched her dance the night away.'

'You did that? Tracked her?'

'Yeah, me and Tom. You sound surprised . . .' She lifted the toilet seat and sat down.

'I wasn't sure you were going to, the way we left it yesterday,' Lucas said. 'Seemed like a long shot . . .'

Sherrill lost the rest of what Lucas was saying, suddenly falling off into a mental movie of the previous night. She came back when Lucas asked, 'Marcy? Are you still there?'

'Lucas . . . Goddamnit, I think we might have seen the shooter. Last night. Coming out of Carmel's building.'

'What?' He didn't believe it.

'Honest to God.' She told him about the redhead who'd left as Hale Allen was going in. In her mind's eye, she could see the woman brushing past Hale, giving him the once-over, then stepping outside on the walk and looking up and down the street.

'Could you identify her?'

She thought about it for less than a second: 'I don't think so. I wasn't paying attention to her. I mean, there's a good chance it's not even her . . . but still, she was a shorter woman, a small woman, but in pretty good shape, like a gymnast; like Baily said. And she had big red hair.'

'That was her – I'd bet you a hundred bucks it was her,' Lucas said. 'We've gotta throw a net around the building. And we've got to get something on Carmel's phones. Find somebody who'll sign a warrant to tap them.'

'Where are you? Are you at Davis's house?'

'No, I'm in my car, heading for the kid's school. She's still there – I'll be there in five.'

'I'll get dressed and head out . . .'

The inside cop, the tipster, called Carmel just as Lucas and Sherrill were breaking off their conversation:

'You're in the clear,' he said. He didn't bother to identify himself.

'What happened?'

'I'm not sure exactly, but the rumor is, this little kid called in, and said that the shooter was back at her house last night and her mother was afraid to talk about it. And the rumor is, you were being tracked, and they know it can't be you because you were out dancing at some fancy place. I'll tell you what, Davenport went running out of here like a fullback. I mean, he was *runnin'*.'

'Jesus, they were following me?' She was shocked. She hadn't felt it. She'd always thought she'd be able to feel it. Maybe because of Hale, his closeness . . .

'All over you, I guess,' the cop said. 'A good thing, because you're in the clear.'

'Why didn't you call me before? When you heard they were putting the tail on me?'

After a pause, the cop said, 'You know I can't do that.'

Carmel promised another payment, rang off and dialed Rinker.

'And it was the kid who called the cops,' Carmel said, as she finished relating the cop's tip.

'Jesus, I never thought about that,' Rinker said. 'She's so small.'

'But it works out,' Carmel said, excitedly. 'You found out that there really was nothing coming out of them, and even if the cops force the

mother to talk this time, what can she give them? And now, the cops know
I *wasn't* there. They just stepped all over their own case. All you have to
do is disappear, and we're cool.'

'Bout time,' Rinker said.

'Although,' Carmel said pensively, 'we still don't know why they were
messing with me to begin with.'

'Let it go,' Rinker said. 'I'm getting out of here. If I move now, I can be
through KC before the rush hour.'

'Don't go yet,' Carmel said. 'Hang around for a day or two. If they're
following me, you can't come around here, but . . . just hang around.'

'You think?'

'Yeah. Just overnight, to see what happens – to see if we need to settle
anything else. See if the kid and her mom keep their mouths shut. See if
anything comes of that.'

'All right,' Rinker said reluctantly. Minneapolis seemed more and more
like a tar-baby. She was anxious to get out. 'One more night.'

Lucas arrived at Mrs. Gartin's School a little after ten o'clock in the
morning. He parked on the street down the block, and walked back under
low-hanging maple trees. A light summer breeze had popped up, and a
patch of yellow coneflowers bobbed their bright heads and brown eyes at
him from the school garden. Behind the garden, and behind a low wooden
fence, he could see a playground for small kids, with tractor-tire sandboxes
and a gentle tube-slide.

Mrs. Gartin was a heavy woman in a print dress, with small jowls and
smile lines. She was surprised to see him.

'Heather called you?'

'Yes. It's important that I talk to her right away.'

'I should call her mother . . .'

'Her mother may be in some danger, which is why I have to talk to her
right away.' He let a little cop show through his polite smile. 'If you
should take me to her?'

'Well, I . . .' She spasmodically shuffled some papers on her desk,
cleared her throat and said, 'She's down in Mrs. Roman's room.'

Heather sat in Mrs. Roman's office with Lucas, and told the story: Lucas
took her over it twice, and when they finished, had no doubt that she was
telling precisely the truth. Sherrill arrived just before they finished with

the second runthrough, and Davis arrived two minutes later. She was panic-stricken.

'What are you doing?' she screamed. 'What are you doing with my daughter? You have no right to talk to my daughter . . .'

'Yes, we do,' Lucas said, as gently as he could. But it didn't come off well, and Davis grabbed Heather's arm and would have been out the door if Sherrill hadn't been blocking it.

'You can't leave,' Sherrill said.

Heather began to cry, and said, 'I only told them . . .'

'I'll call a lawyer,' Davis shrilled.

'You can call anyone you want to, but life would be simpler for all of us, including you, if we talked about this for a few minutes,' Lucas said.

'She's going to kill us, she said she would kill us . . .'

'She's not going to hurt anyone,' Lucas said.

'You weren't there,' Davis snapped. 'She said she was going to kill us, and she meant it. Frankly, I'm not nearly as impressed with you and your cops as I am with her.'

'We will put you where she can't find you . . .'

'She's with the *Mafia*,' Davis screamed. 'They can find *anybody*.'

Lucas shook his head and Sherrill said, 'Listen, quiet down. Whatever's happened, has already happened. We need to ask you a few questions, and then we need to arrange things so you're absolutely safe.'

'That's impossible now,' Davis said. The anger was still closer to the surface than the fear, but now the fear was bubbling up, too.

'No, it's not, not at all. We have experts in it,' Sherrill said. 'You know why you don't hear about the Mafia killing cops? Because they're afraid to. Just think about that . . .'

When Davis had calmed down – not before a few nasty moments with Mrs. Gartin, who made an ill-timed appearance with a box of ginger snaps – they took her through Rinker's assault. Heather sat on her mother's knee during the talk, and Davis even showed a small tremulous smile when told about how her daughter called Officer Friendly.

One solid piece of information came out: 'I could see the ends of her hair, and I'd swear that it was a wig. There was just something un-hair-like about it. And I could see her hands, and I saw her face when she first came to the door, and she just wasn't that real fair complexion that redheads have.'

'But you couldn't describe her face?'

'No, you know, she had this box, and I looked at the box . . .'

'Do you still have the box?'

'No, I . . . threw it away,' she said. 'It's in the dumpster behind the apartment. It's a FedEx box.'

'Was she wearing gloves?'

'Oh, yeah. I can remember that. They were disposable plastic gloves, like dentists use. Oh, yeah.' The gloves impressed her: a professional killer, after all.

When they were finished, Lucas said, 'I can't see you being called as a witness. Your information helps us a lot, in some ways, but it's not something that we'd use in court.'

'I won't testify,' Davis said. 'I mean, I *won't*.'

'So let's talk about what you want to do now,' Sherrill said.

What Davis wanted to do was to pretend that nothing had happened. 'Could she know about this? That we talked to you?'

'Uh, word leaks out of police stations from time to time,' Lucas said carefully, thinking about Carmel's sources. 'Is there any possibility that you could take off for a couple of weeks, or a month?'

'I've got a job I've got to go to at the U,' she said. 'I gotta eat . . .'

'I can fix that,' Lucas said. 'I can probably fix a paid leave, and if I can't, we can find some money in city funds to make up what you lose. Do you have some folks . . .?'

Davis shook her head. 'I don't want to go there. You know what? If you can do it? I've got a laptop, I could do a lot of work on my thesis if I could get somewhere quiet, just Heather and me. When I was still with Howard, we stayed at these townhouses up on the North Shore, they were really nice . . .'

'We can do that,' said Lucas. He turned to Sherrill: 'Call Bretano down in Sex. Get her going on this.' He turned back to Davis. 'We'll hook you up with Alice Bretano. She works with abused mothers and kids and knows about hiding them and getting money and so on . . . she'll take care of the whole thing.'

'And you're sure they won't find us?' Davis asked doubtfully.

'They won't even bother to look,' Lucas said. 'There's just no percentage in it.'

When she didn't appear convinced, Lucas said, 'Let me tell you about the Mafia. They're a bunch of guys who are willing to hurt people for money, and they hustle dope and prostitutes and they loan-shark and all of that. But they're just a bunch of guys. They don't have any big intelligence service and they don't back each other up like they say they do . . . they're just sort of aaa . . .' His eyes went to Heather, who was looking up at him with big eyes. '. . . jerks. But I won't lie to you: this one woman, the one you saw last night, *is* somebody to be afraid of. But we're gonna get her. And we're not going to give her any reason to hurt you. If she didn't hurt you last night, she's not going to.'

Sherrill called Bretano in Sex, explained the problem, and Bretano said she'd handle the whole thing; she could be at the school in ten minutes.

Outside, while they waited, leaning against Lucas' Porsche, Sherrill asked, 'Now what?'

'We got two things out of that, for sure: we know she's a redhead, or at least wearing a red wig, and that she's a small woman in good shape, which means that you probably saw her last night. So now we crank everything up. We put a twenty-four-hour watch on Carmel's building, and if we get her inside, we take her – this woman.'

'On what?'

'On nothing. On bullshit. On assaulting a police officer, resisting arrest, anything. But I want her picked up and identified. Nailed down. I want to know where she comes from. I want mug shots of her, so we can paper the country with them if she gets out, and then runs. That means you're gonna be living outside Carmel's building. We maybe see if we can find a place, an apartment or an empty office, where you can watch from.'

'I'm out of the investigation?' Sherrill asked.

'A little bit out – but if we nail this woman quick, you're gonna be the one to do it.'

'What're you gonna do?'

'First thing, I'm gonna get some guys and I'm gonna knock on every door for two blocks around Davis' apartment. There are people on the streets there at night. Somebody must've seen this woman, whoever she is.'

Lucas got a half-dozen uniformed cops walking the neighborhood. He hated the job himself, and wasn't good at it. The good ones had open Irish or Scandinavian faces, young guys who looked like they might slap you on the back, women who might enjoy the odd bit of gossip. Empathizers.

190

Lucas and Bretano had brought Davis and her daughter back to the apartment, and waited while they packed. When they left, Davis gave the keys to Lucas: 'Use the phone or the toilet, if you have to. I'll pick them up when we get back.' Having the cops around had restored some confidence – but she still wanted to get out of town, and in a hurry.

Lucas used the apartment as a temporary headquarters, while the uniformed cops worked the neighborhood, moving back and forth, visiting and revisiting homes, waiting for people to get home from work, sorting bullshit from egg cremes. A little after three o'clock, a cop named Lane wandered into the apartment, carrying a Pepsi, and sat down in a kitchen chair. Lucas was at the kitchen table, just getting off the phone.

'What?' he asked.

Lane leaned back, took a hit on the Pepsi: 'I've been trying to get a break into plainclothes for more'n a fucking year now, and I can't get it done.'

'I thought I saw you in plainclothes . . .'

'Yeah, yeah, that was just the drug guys looking for a fresh face. After a few weeks, my face wasn't fresh, and I was back sitting in a squad. What I'm saying is, you gotta help get me outa this fuckin' uniform.'

Lucas shrugged: 'I don't know you very well, you know? I don't know what you'd bring to the job especially . . .'

'I was the guy who found that .380 in the McDonald case last fall, you remember? I mean, there was luck involved, but I'm a lucky guy. I pushed it, and we rang the bell.'

Lucas nodded. 'I remember. And being a lucky guy is pretty critical . . .'

'I know. But I keep getting this bullshit about being good on the streets, and all that. How they don't want to lose me off patrol. But I don't want to *be* on patrol, and they're gonna lose me anyway, if they don't move me. I'll go someplace else . . .'

'This is the only place to work in the state,' Lucas said. Then he tried to put him off. 'Anyway, you know, let me ask around . . .'

Lane cracked a grin. 'I really didn't come in here to make a speech about getting off patrol, but I thought I'd take the opportunity, especially since I look so good right now.'

Lucas' eyebrows went up. 'Oh, yeah?'

'Yeah. I was down the street, at 1414, there's a Mrs. Rann, Gloria Rann. She got home at about nine-fifteen last night. She knows because she caught the bus at University and Cretin when she got off work at nine, and it takes ten minutes to get home, and she was hurrying because she had a show she wanted to watch at nine-thirty. She just had time to put the garbage out before the show started. She sees a small athletic woman getting into what she thinks might have been a green car parked on the street, right on the curb at her house. She couldn't see the woman's face, but she thought she might be a college kid, because she looked athletic and because the neighborhood has a lot of college kids around. And . . . she had big hair.'

Lucas leaned forward: 'That'd be right.'

Lane said, 'Yeah. She fits the profile you gave us. Anyway, I ask Mrs. Rann if she'd ever seen the car before, and she said, 'No, it wasn't from around here.' And I say, 'How do you know that?' And she says, because when she was walking home from the bus, it was still a little light, and she *looked* at the car because it was parked right in front of her house.'

He paused for dramatic effect and Lucas said, '*What?*'

'It had an Avis sticker on it. It was a rental car.'

'Sonofabitch,' Lucas said.

He took Lane with him to the airport, tracked down the Avis manager, who was out at the return area, and brought him back to the main office. The manager didn't need a search warrant. He said, 'Let me run a list for you. But I can tell you right now, it's gonna be eighty to ninety percent guys. Probably won't be more than ten or fifteen women.'

'Mid-sized green car, athletic-looking woman, small,' Lane said. 'Maybe a redhead.'

The manager's hands were hovering over the computer keyboard, but he stopped, turned to Lane and frowned. 'Small and athletic redhead? Nice, uh, figure?'

'That's what we understand,' Lucas said.

'Could it have been a champagne Dodge? Instead of green? Because I swear to God, a woman who looks like that returned a champagne Dodge up at the check-in, not more than fifteen minutes ago. She's gotta be in the airport.'

Lucas snapped: 'Where do I find the head guy for airport security?'

A fat young man named Herter had handled the return and remembered the woman well; Lucas and Lane spent two hours trolling Herter and the manager through the airport gates, looking for Rinker's face. Nothing. A lot of small athletic women, a few of them redheads, but no killer.

The check-in record showed the car in, without damage and a full tank of gas, twenty minutes before Lucas and Lane arrived at the Avis desk. Herter said the woman had headed for the main terminal, but had been carrying only a small bag, like an overnight case. There were no security cameras that might have recorded her face, at least, not on the immediate route into the terminal.

'She might still be here in town,' Lucas told Lane and Tom Black, who'd come out to the help with the hunt. 'The FBI thinks she drives to wherever she's going. It would make sense for her to drop her car in the airport garage, where there are thousands of cars going in and out all day, and then renting a car to do the hit with. Then, if there's any problem, she can ditch the car and there won't be any record attached to it.'

'We should know about the record any time,' Black said. 'The Nebraska cops are running down the address.'

'If it's her, they're not gonna find anything,' Lucas said. 'But I'll tell you what: we've got to get to the Mastercard acceptance people who clear charges, and they've got to tell us instantly if she makes any more charges . . .' He looked at Lane: 'You think you could set that up?'

'Yeah.'

'Then go do it; and get out of the uniform before you start talking to people.'

'All right.' He took off, running.

Black said, 'The crime-scene guys gotta be done by now . . .'

'If it's her, there won't be anything.'

And the crime-scene guy said, 'I wouldn't hold my breath on these prints. I mean, we got prints off the passenger side and outa the back seat, but we got nothing from the steering wheel, from the outside door handle, from the inside handle, from the radio knobs, from the seat . . . they'd all been wiped. Wiped clean, by somebody who worked at it.'

'Goddamnit,' Lucas said. Five minutes later, a detective from Lincoln, Nebraska, called and said, 'There's a street like that, and there's an address like that, and there's even a woman with that name, but she's forty-eight years old, she's got nine ferrets that she never leaves, she's got black hair and I'd say she goes about two-ten on the bathroom scales. She says she's never been to Minneapolis and never rented a car, and she's got a Visa and a Sears card and a gas card but no Mastercard.'

'The shooter's outa here,' Lucas said to Black, after he got off the line with the Nebraska cop. 'She might still be in the Cities, or on her way home, but we're wasting our time out here.'

'Except we got a decent picture of her,' Black said. 'We've got two guys who saw her close up, and not all that long ago. We'll have a composite photo of her in an hour.'

'There's that,' Lucas said. He held up his thumb and forefinger, a half-inch apart. 'But goddamn: we were this close. *This close*.'

'So now what?'

'So now we paper the town with her picture. If she's still here, maybe we can shake her out.'

Chapter Twenty

Carmel called Rinker at the hotel, and said, without preface or identification, 'Get out of there now. Your picture's on TV.'

'What?' Rinker's heart started thumping, and she looked wildly around the room, looking for clothes, looking for anything with prints, ready to sprint.

'Davenport's got a composite photograph of you, and it's on TV. They're going to show it again on Channel Three in about one minute.'

'Hang on'.

Rinker picked up the TV remote and brought up Channel Three. A talking head, a serious brunette who looked like a former Miss America, was saying, '. . . an Avis rental car at the airport. Two Avis personnel, whose identities are being withheld, provided police with a composite photograph, shown here. If you have seen this woman . . .'

Rinker looked at the picture for a moment, then told Carmel. 'That doesn't look like me.'

'To you it might not look like you, but to me it does – in a general way,' Carmel replied. 'And they'll be taking it around to hotels and motels and everything else, asking for *anybody* who fits the general description.'

Rinker nodded at the phone. 'All right, I'm outa here in fifteen minutes.'

'Go on down to Iowa,' Carmel said. 'Des Moines. They don't get the Cities TV stations there, and you can be back here in three hours, if you need to be. Give me a call on this phone when you get there, give me a number.'

'What're we going to do?'

'We have to go to Plan B. Somehow, he's onto us. I don't know how, but he's working something.'

'Ah, man, can you handle it?'

'I can handle it,' Carmel said grimly. 'Now get out of there.'

'I'm gone.'

Two detectives, Swanson and Franklin, responded to a tip from a bellhop at the Regency-White, and took the composite photograph to the manager, who shook his head. 'I don't know the lady, but I only see a fraction of the people who come through.'

'Could we find out how many single woman are in the hotel, and go from there?' Franklin suggested. 'Then maybe we could talk to the room maids.'

'Most've them have gone home already,' the manager said. He had a small mustache but otherwise, Franklin thought, looked a lot like PeeWee in *PeeWee's Big Adventure*. 'I can get the room service people, and the bellhops.'

Between the available desk people, they narrowed it to four women: two who more or less fit the composite, and two who nobody could remember seeing. The bellhop, who everybody called Louis, didn't know what room she was in, but swore she fit the picture. 'That's her,' he told Swanson. Swanson called Lucas and told him they had a possible ID.

'Wait for me,' Lucas said.

They waited, working through people on the restaurant staff: two of them had seen the woman, they thought, but then maybe not. The picture wasn't that good, was it?

Lucas arrived on the run, left the Porsche at the curb and said, 'If a cop comes along, tell him it belongs to Chief Davenport,' he told the doorman.

'Right, chief,' the doorman said, and saluted. Just like New York, or something.

Franklin met him in the lobby and said, 'We're ready to go up.'

'Any more IDs on her?' Lucas asked.

'Couple of possibles – but they say they can't quite tell from the photo.'

'Yeah, but it's the best we've got,' Lucas said. He studied the picture for a few seconds with the same strange feeling of *deja vu* that he'd experienced when he'd first seen it. He felt that he knew the woman, because, he thought, she was a perfect *type*: a cheerleader. Cute, busty, athletic. He knew a hundred women just like her: hell, there were twenty just like her on the police force. Sherrill was just like her, take away the black hair . . .

'Michelle Jones,' the manager muttered, tapping on a door.

'Just a minute,' a woman's voice called.

The three cops took a step back, leaving the manager looking quizzically at them. Then he realized that the woman might come out shooting, and started to take a step back. Then the door opened, just two inches, and Michelle Jones looked out: she was black.

'Sorry, wrong room,' Swanson said. 'We're checking a security problem.'

There was no answer at the next room. Lucas nodded at the manager, who used his key and stepped hastily away. Swanson turned the door knob and they went in.

'Christ, it looks like somebody was beaten to death,' Franklin said. Clothing was strewn around the room and across the bed; two pair of panty hose, apparently damp, hung from a door, and a wool sweater lay on the rug, drying on top of a bath towel. Two suitcases, both open on the floor, looked like they'd been rifled by a fast-moving thief.

'Nah, it just look like my wife's been here,' Swanson said. 'This is just a fuckin' woman.'

The manager crooked his head out from behind the protective bulk of Franklin: 'I think the gentleman is right,' he said. 'Single women . . . and you should see what they put in the toilets. Women'll put anything in a toilet. We once had a woman whose dog died, and she tried to flush it down the toilet . . .'

'Small dog?' Franklin asked.

'Well, yeah.' The manager's eyes seemed to cross. 'I mean, nobody'd try to flush a German shepherd.'

The third room was also empty: but very empty. No sign of a presence other then the disturbed covers on the bed.

'You're sure there's supposed to be somebody in here?' Lucas asked.

'Oh, yeah,' the manager said, looking around in disgust. 'She skipped. I know what that feels like. She's skipped.'

'Then this is her,' Lucas said. 'Let's get the crime scene guys in here.'

'Four hundred bucks,' the manager said.

'Yeah, well, don't touch anything,' Franklin growled.

Franklin and Swanson went to the last room on the list, while Lucas looked around the empty room, and a moment later, Franklin came back: 'Better have a look at this chick.'

This one fit, too: a cheerleader, with the blonde hair, blue eyes, good shape, a little busty. And again, Lucas had the sense of *deja vu*: 'Do I know you?' he asked.

'No,' the woman said, a little angry and a little more scared. 'Who are you?'

'I'm a deputy chief of police,' Lucas said. 'Where are you from?'

'From Seattle . . .'

Lucas spotted a wedding ring. 'And you're married?'

'Yes, and I'd like to know . . .'

'What are you doing here? Are you in town on business?'

'What's going on?' she demanded, the fear fading, and the anger growing.

'Just tell me,' Lucas said patiently. 'Are you here on business?'

'Yes, I'm here for the perio convention at the Radisson . . .'

'What's a perio?' Franklin asked. He was a very large black man in a yellow plaid sport coat, and he loomed in the doorway like a dark moon.

'A periodontist. I'm a dentist,' she said.

'Thanks,' Lucas said. He glanced at Franklin and shook his head and said to the woman, 'We've got a situation here, which Detective Franklin will explain to you . . .'

Outside in the hall, Swanson said to Lucas, 'A gum gardener.'

'A what?'

'A gum gardener. That's what periodontists are called by other dentists.'

'Yeah? I'll treasure that piece of information.'

Lucas went back to the empty room to wait for the crime-scene crew. He wanted only one piece of information: that the china handles on the bathroom fixtures had been wiped. If they'd been wiped, this was the room, and they were too late.

Franklin went off to check on the last room again. Then the two crime-scene guys arrived, and Lucas told them what he wanted to know. One of them stepped into the bathroom, looked at the china handles on the sink, took what looked like a perfume bottle out of his briefcase and sprayed a steel-colored dust on the handles. Then he stuck his head in the sink so he could get a closer look. When he emerged, he said, 'Wiped. Slick as a whistle.'

'Goddamn it, I knew it,' Lucas said.

Franklin returned. 'Last lady came in, from that room that was all torn up. She's fifty, and she'd got a dog. A small one. I offered to flush it for her, but she said no.'

'Okay,' Lucas said. To the crime-scene guys, 'She probably wiped the place down, but I want you to dust *everything*. Anything we get . .'

'Look at this,' the second crime scene guy said. He was emerging from the shower, and he was holding a small hotel-sized bar of soap.

'What?' Lucas asked.

'I think she forgot to wipe the soap.'

* * *

'She forgot to wipe the what?' Mallard asked

'The soap,' Lucas said. 'A bar of soap.'

'You can't leave prints on a bar of soap. Wet soap?'

'Well, you can one way,' Lucas said. 'If the soap squirts out of your hand and you leave it on the floor, and then get out and dry yourself and remember the soap, and pick it up and put it back in the soap dish, then you can leave prints. At least, that's what we think – one corner of the soap was squared off and cracked, like it'd been dropped. The hard part was getting the soap back to the office without screwing up the prints. That was a goddamned nightmare.'

'How're you processing it?'

'We put it in a refrigerator down in Identification.'

'You put it in what?'

Lucas was irritated: 'Do we have a bad connection or something? I can hear *you* perfectly.'

'Why'd you put it in the goddamn refrigerator?' Mallard asked. He was getting loud, for a guy who looked like an accountant, even *with* the thick neck.

'We figure if we can harden it up enough, we can dust it and pick up the prints,' Lucas said. 'I mean, we can see them, we're just scared to death of doing anything to them. If you blow on them, they could fade.'

'Ah, Jesus. I'm gonna call the fingerprint guys here and get them in touch with your guys,' Mallard said. 'Maybe we can help.'

'Did you get the composite?' Lucas asked

'Yeah. We're running it against all former suspects, anybody who's ever been around one of these cases.'

'What ever happened to the guy in Wichita? Is he still peddling dope?'

'Little asshole,' Mallard said. 'We've still got a watch on him, I still got Malone out there with the team, but she's bitching thirty-six hours a day about getting back. And if you know the suspect was in Minneapolis, and we know Lopez wasn't, then I'll call her off.'

'She was here, the shooter was,' Lucas said.

'Then I'll tell Malone to wrap it up. Still can't believe it's a woman. Anyway, I'm gonna drag the files over to witness protection and have a talk with them. We got enough on their boy out there to send him away for three hundred years.'

'Just because Lopez didn't pan out, doesn't mean that some kind of

Wichita connection isn't good,' Lucas said.

'I know that; and if you've got any suggestions, I'd be happy to have Malone look into them. It'll take her a couple of days to wrap things up.'

'I've got nothing, not at the moment,' Lucas said. 'And look, have your guys call our ID guys right now; I'm scared to death about what's gonna happen when we take that bar of soap out of the crisper.'

'The what?' Mallard asked.

'The crisper, you know, where you keep the lettuce and radishes and . . .'

'Don't tell me. Please, just don't tell me.'

A guy named Manual found Lucas in the Homicide office talking to Sloan, and said, 'We're gonna try to take the prints.'

'Ah.' Lucas and Sloan both got up and headed down to ID. In the Identification section, they found four people standing around a hippie with shoulder-length hair and a dangly silver earring. He appeared to be about sixteen, and was holding a Nikon F5 camera with a weird lens. The bar of soap sat on a Tupperware lid on the desk.

'What's going on?' Lucas asked, looking at the hippie.

'Don't touch me,' the kid said. 'If anything falls on the soap, spit or anything, it's all over.'

He was looking down at the soap through the camera, which he held no more than a foot above the bar. 'He's my kid,' a cop named Harry muttered to Lucas. 'Great photographer. That there's what you call your basic ring-light, there on the end of the lens. It's really a flash, and he's looking right down on the prints, with half the ring-light turned off so he'll get some shadow . . .'

'Shut up,' the kid said.

Everybody shut up and Lucas was about to open his mouth and ask if he knew what he was doing, when the flash went; then again. The kid shot twenty-four pictures in five minutes, using the ring-light, then no ring-light, and finally with reflected light from a sheet of tinfoil. When he was done, he looked at Lucas and said, 'I could see them, pretty good. Three prints, a little smudged, but coming right up at me.'

'You think you got them?'

'If I can see them I got them,' the kid said. 'I'm gonna run this over to a one-hour slide processor by Rosedale. It'd help if you could call them and tell them to put me at the front of the line.'

'You did slides?'

'Yeah; I get a lot better resolution that way, when I scan them . . .' Lucas must have looked puzzled. The kid added, 'I assumed you wanted a digital file. We can phone it to the FBI and they can start the search.'

Lucas turned to Sloan: 'Go find somebody to run this kid over to Rosedale in a squad, lights and sirens. Tell the picture people to start running the film as soon as he gets there. We want it.' He turned back to the kid. 'I'll sign you up for a consultant's fee. I'll give the forms to your dad. If the pictures come out.'

The kid left with Sloan, and Harriet Ashler, the chief fingerprint-specialist, said, 'All right; back in the fridge for a minute, just to firm things up.'

She put the soap back in the fridge, and they all stood around looking at the refrigerator for three minutes – it was a small brown office model from Sears, with two lunch sacks and an aging apple on one shelf, and a bottle of cran-apple juice in the door – and then she took it back out and touched an unmarked piece of it. 'Still nice and hard,' she said. 'Let's try it.'

The technique, which they agreed upon with the FBI, was to blow a light dry graphite dust across the prints, then try to softly pick up the dust with a piece of Magic Mending Tape. Ashler sprayed dust on the smallest, least-clear print, then squatted next to the bar of soap. 'Tape.'

Somebody handed her the roll of Magic Mending tape. She gently lowered a loop of the tape across the first print, let it rest on the carbon particles for a moment, then lifted it.

'Shoot,' she said, squinting at the tape. She picked up a magnifying glass and looked again.

'What happened?'

'No print,' she said. She looked back at the soap. 'It just sorta pulled little tiny pieces of the soap away . . . it's totally wrecked.'

'All right, stop,' Lucas said. 'Let's get it back in the fridge, and talk to the Feebs again. Maybe we ought to do some experiments on another bar of soap with our own fingerprints before we try again.'

Ashler nodded. 'That'd be best – but I thought we needed it in a hurry.'

'Maybe not, if Harry's genius kid came through.'

Harry's genius kid came through. Sloan had personally taken him to the Roseville store, because Sloan liked to drive fast in city cars with lights and sirens, and they were back in less than an hour. 'Four of them are pretty good,' the kid said. 'If Mr. Sloan can take me back to my place, I'll scan them in and we can ship them over to the FBI.'

Lucas was looking at the slides, holding them up to a fluorescent light. They didn't look like much, but they looked better than other prints he'd seen. They looked better than what he'd been able to see with the naked eye. 'Harry,' he said to the kid's father, 'Your kid is a fuckin' genius.'

Rinker got to Des Moines a little after five o'clock in the afternoon, checked into a Holiday Inn, and called Carmel on the cell phone.

'More bad news,' Carmel said. 'My guy in the police department says they've got your fingerprints.'

'I wiped everything,' Rinker said, but she could feel the uncertainty in her own voice.

'He says they took them off a bar of soap they found in a room at the Regency-White,' Carmel said. 'Davenport's guys.'

'A bar of soap?'

'Yeah. He said they were sending them to the FBI.'

'I'll call you back,' Rinker said. She remembered picking up the soap. She hadn't thought to wipe it. She rang off before Carmel could protest, and sat quietly on the bed, pulling herself together for a moment. Despite her self-control, a tear trickled down her cheek: that fuckin' Davenport. She took three deep breaths, exhaled, then punched nine numbers into the phone. 'This is Rinker,' she said, when the man answered. 'I gotta pull the plug.'

After a long silence, the man said, 'You're sure?'

'It's the Minneapolis deal. They've been to my place, even if they don't know it; but they're sniffing around Wichita. They've got a bad picture of me, but it's a picture, one of those computer deals. Now I think they might have my fingerprints.'

'How could this happen?' Disbelief in his voice.

'You wouldn't believe it. But you tell Wooden Head to get out to Wichita with the money. I'm gonna clean out the bank there, go to my bottom-line ID – I'm shredding everything else – and I'll leave him the papers. He can take the bar and find a new manager; but my prints'll be all over the place. He should try to wipe everything he can, but I don't think he'll get everything.'

'What about your apartment?'

'I'm gonna try to get in and out, quick,' she said. 'I'll check the place first.'

'I didn't think anybody had your prints.'

'They don't. I've never been printed. That's the good news. But they've been getting too close, and sooner or later, they just might put things together. I can't take the chance.'

'All right. Jeez, Clara . . .'

'Yeah, yeah, yeah. I'll get back in touch, when I can.'

'Where are you now?'

'Minneapolis. I'll be leaving here in a couple of hours, I've got some cleaning up to do. But if I drive straight through the night, I ought to be in Wichita by the time the banks open.'

When she finished, she called Carmel back: 'I'm closing down my life,' she said. 'I'll just be a figment of your imagination by this time tomorrow.'

'You mean you're . . . giving up the bar?'

'Everything,' Rinker said: 'Now listen: do you still think we go for Plan B?'

'Well, if you got caught, or if there's something more on me . . . I mean, that'd settle things.'

'All right. I've got to run to Wichita. I'll see you tomorrow night, probably.'

She made two calls to the airport, then called a cab. She left her car and luggage at the Holiday Inn, but took her guns. The cab dropped her at Shack Direct Air, where a laconic pilot who looked far too young to be allowed in airplanes was waiting in the pilot's lounge, reading the *Wall Street Journal*. 'You Miss Maxwell?'

'Yes.'

'I was supposed to get some money.'

She took two thousand dollars out of her purse and handed it to him. 'We're outa here,' he said.

She arrived in Wichita a few minutes before midnight, took a cab straight to the bar, said, 'Hey, Johnny,' to the bartender who said, 'You're back?' and she said, 'Yeah, but I'm running. See you tomorrow.'

'Heavy date?'

'Something like that. I'm taking the van, so don't worry about it.'

'Okay.'

From the back room she got a dozen liquor boxes and the keys for the bar's van, a big practical Dodge. On the way back to her apartment, she stopped at a convenience store, bought a package of plastic garbage bags, and hauled them with the liquor boxes back to her apartment. She lived on the second floor, and carried the boxes up in three trips, four at a time, and tossed them into the kitchen. After the third trip, she shut the door behind her, and started packing.

Tried not to think about it: just packed. She packed a sock bunny that her mother had made her, when her mother was still functioning as a human being, before her step-dad had beaten the liveliness out of her. She'd gotten the bunny for Christmas when she was six; it was the single oldest thing she possessed. She packed the photographs taken with other dancers at two or three bars around St. Louis, with people at the booze warehouse, where she'd worked after the dancing ended. She packed the first two-dollar bill that the bar had taken in – they'd saved the first two-dollar bill because they'd forgotten to save the first dollar.

She packed: she'd lived in the place for six years, and it had been as much a home to her as anything she'd ever had, and it took a while. She hummed while she packed. Hummed like an angry bumble bee. 'That fuckin' Davenport,' she said. 'That fuckin' Davenport.'

When she'd packed everything important to her, including her school books and papers, she realized that she couldn't pack *everything* that was important to her. She couldn't pack the *place*. She sat on the bed and smoothed the sheet, and went once more through the chest of drawers, where even the tired cotton underwear suddenly seemed important . . .

'That fuckin' Davenport . . .' And this time, she cried. Let it go, couldn't stop it.

Ten minutes later, eyes red, she was wiping the place with Lysol.

By three-thirty in the morning, she was finished. If the cops really took the place apart, they might find a print or two, but it'd take weeks. She took the last of the boxes down to the van, moved the van down the street, then went back to the apartment. Her apartment was at the end of a hall, and when she'd first moved in, she'd made a small change: she'd placed a wireless movement alarm, which she bought at Wards, just above the window at the end of the hall. The alarm, when tripped, set off a buzzer or a strobe on a small console next to her bed. She chose strobe, put the console next to her face, placed her guns on the floor next to her bed, and let herself slip into a fitful sleep.

She hadn't thought that the man in St. Louis would ever harm her; she had almost that much faith in him. But not quite that much. She'd told him she hoped to be in Wichita by the time the banks opened. If he were going to make a move against her, probably using one or the other muscle heads that always seemed to be around, the guy most likely would be waiting at her apartment, waiting for her to open the bank and then come back.

Coming from St. Louis, even by air, would put him in Wichita at least a few hours later than her. He'd have to be found, and an airplane would have to be rounded up, or he'd have to get in his car and drive . . . If he was coming, she really wouldn't expect him before six o'clock or so.

He was better than that. He arrived at five.

She thought she actually woke a minute before the alarm went. Whatever, she sat up with the strobe flashing in her face. She hit the *off* button, and looked at the clock. Five minutes after five. She got to her feet, picked up both guns, cocked them, and headed for the kitchen, moving slowly, careful not to bump anything, to set off a vibration, absolutely silent in her bare feet. She was still wearing the thin rubber gloves, hot and tacky on her hands. The gloves were ivory-colored, and she could see them better than she could see her arms, like two disembodied fists floating though the dark.

Whoever was in the hall had hesitated at the door. She moved past it and stepped into a closet with sliding doors. The left door was half open, and she moved behind it, where she could still see through the open panel. Then the man outside knocked, and called her voice, quietly. 'Clara? Clara?' Another soft knock, then a key.

He had a key, which meant the man in St. Louis must have copied hers. Stupid. She just left her keys laying around, the keys to everything. She worried that there were more security lapses that she'd never known about. Then she pushed the worry out of her head, and focused on the weight of her guns.

The door opened, a darkening shadow, then the man stepped inside; she was less than two feet away, and he stepped inside far enough that she could see that he was carrying something in his right hand. From the way he was carrying it, it had to be a gun. She lifted her own gun, ready to fire, when the man whispered – the softest breath – 'Easy . . .'

She thought he was talking to her and almost blurted something out, when she heard more soft movement – and the man she *could* see wasn't moving. There were two of them.

The first moved down the hall toward her bedroom, while the second moved quietly across the living room to the second bedroom, which Rinker used as a TV room and home office. After a long minute of silence, the man down the hall came back, stepped toward the second bedroom. And the second man stepped out of the second bedroom.

'Not here, yet,' he said quietly.

'Then we wait until Wooden Head calls,' said the first man.

'In the dark?'

'Yeah, in case she comes.'

'I'm dead on my ass,' the further man said. 'I get the couch, if that's a couch.'

The second man lay down on the couch, the first sat in an easy chair, lit a cigarette. Rinker never allowed cigarettes in her house. The second man said from the couch, 'What if she smells that smoke?'

The smoker said, 'Shit,' and dropped the cigarette butt on the hardwood floor and ground it out with his foot. She'd sanded the floors herself, and sealed them. The man's action almost moved Rinker, but not quite.

'You seen this chick?' one man asked.

'Once, I think. Gotta nice rack.'

'The Guy seemed kind of scared of her. You know, like he was all that, *Get her quick, don't give her a shot.*'

'Never seen a chick who could take me,' said the second man. 'In fact, if this is the same chick I'm thinking about, I wouldn't mind fuckin' her first.'

'Don't think that way. If the Guy's nervous, we don't want to be fuckin' around.'

'Yeah, yeah.'

'Now shut up; I'm gonna get some sleep.'

'Listen for the shots,' the second man said. 'Then you'll know she got here.'

Five minutes later, Rinker heard the first tentative snore from the man on the couch; the man on the chair sat unmoving, as far as she could tell. They were like that for another five minutes, the man on the couch breathing deeper, snoring more regularly; then the man on the couch stood up, lit a cigarette and started toward her. She withdrew just an inch into the deeper darkness of the closet. When he brushed by, a shoulder width away, she stepped sideways, then out of the closet in a dance-step, her left pistol arm coming up. He never heard her, saw her or suspected her. She fired a double-tap into the back of his head and took three quick steps to the couch. The man on the couch snorted when the first man hit the floor, and may have been about to wake up. Rinker fired two more shots into his forehead.

Lights.

She got the lights on. The man on the floor was bleeding, but the blood was running out on vinyl. She could get that. The other one wasn't bleeding much, just two small bubbles of blood over his brow ridges: slugs never exited.

She'd have to hurry, she thought. The sky outside seemed brighter: the summer dawn was not far away. She ran to the kitchen, got a roll of duct tape, and taped the wounds on the mens' heads. Stop the bleeding: leave no more traces than she had to. The back window, overlooking the communal dumpster, would open wide enough, she thought, and the screen would swing free. She dragged the man on the couch to the window, opened it, laboriously shoved him into the window hole, took a last look around, and pushed him out. He hit the tarmac below with a dull sloppy *whock.*

The second guy, the one on the vinyl, was smaller, and she moved him more easily, over the sill, out the window; the impact, broken by the man already on the ground, was softer.

With the two men outside, she hurried, quietly as she could, down to the van, backed it up to the dumpster, and dragged the two bodies into the back.

She was tired. The bigger of the two guys probably went two-ten, maybe two-twenty. He was a lot of work. She sat for a moment in the van, catching her breath, and then started out. Ten minutes later, she was in the countryside. Fifteen minutes after the dumpster, she was crawling down a one-lane track, next to a creek. She remembered the place from a country ramble earlier in the year; she remembered the unfenced cornfield that bordered on the track.

The dawn was coming as she dragged the men through a patch of weeds, ten rows back into the corn. With any luck, they wouldn't be found until October, when the corn was picked. Before she left, she took their wallets, pocketed the money – a little over a thousand, total – and their drivers licenses. On the way back to town, she fed the miscellaneous paper in the wallets out the window, little anonymous scraps every couple hundred yards or so. In town, she stopped at trash can and dumped the two empty wallets themselves.

Done.

Back to the apartment, up the stairs. A little after six o'clock in the morning: a little less than three hours before the banks opened. She'd spend it, she decided, wiping the place again. Every coat hanger, every Coke can, every can and bottle in the cupboards and refrigerator. At the end, she wrote two notes – the first, a note to the landlord:

Sorry to do this to you, Larry, to skip out on the lease, but you've got the last month's rent, and I'm sure you can move the place in a hurry. I've got bad personal problems with my ex – if the asshole does find me he's gonna kill me – and I gotta get out of here. You can have the furniture and everything else in the place, instead of the rent. Sorry again, and have a good life. – Clara.

The landlord was greedy enough that he'd be moving the furniture out ten minutes after he got the note. If he could move somebody else in, in a hurry, she'd have that much less to worry about, involving fingerprints.

The second note she put in an envelope, which she sealed. She scrawled the St. Louis' guy's name on it, and under that wrote, 'Private.'

The bank took five minutes, in a private booth. She spent most of the time wiping the box; much of the rest of the time putting one hundred and eighty thousand dollars in a brown paper bag. She also collected a brown cardboard folder that held her best, bottom-line, last-chance ID: credit cards, a Missouri driver's license, a passport and up-to-date plates and registration for her car.

And a deed: the deed sold The Rink to James Larimore – Wooden Head – for $175,000, a fair price six years ago when she'd bought the place, and then two months later sold it to Wooden Head. The sale had been a technical one, though witnessed by all the proper authorities. Until Wooden Head had the deed in his hands, Rinker was the owner. Now, he would get it; and he was getting a deal.

Wooden Head was waiting at the bar, in the back. He had a head the size of a regulation NBA basketball, but squared a bit, and small, delicate features and tight, dry eyes all squeezed into the middle of his face. He brought a briefcase with him.

'What we've got to do, is this,' Rinker told him. 'You gotta take a walk, so you don't see it. Then I'm gonna get a bottle of Lysol and wipe everything in the office, and up and down the stairs. I'll take everything out of the files that you need, and we'll run it through the Xerox machine. Probably no more than fifty or sixty pieces. I don't want any prints left behind.'

'When do you want me back?'

'Give me an hour. It'd be best if you just sat across the street in the doughnut place, read the papers for while. Then I could find you if I need you . . .'

'Okay.'

'You guys are getting a deal,' Rinker said. 'And here – you can read this while you're eatin' the doughnuts.' She handed him the deed. 'This place is worth four, if it's worth a dime. You might get four-and-a-half.'

'We're taking a risk,' he grunted. 'Covering for ya.'

'A lot less risk if you keep wiping the place after I'm gone,' Rinker said. 'When the cops show up, if they do, you don't want to have anything to do with me. I left a note for my landlord saying I was having trouble with my ex, so you might say I told you that.'

'It's weak,' Wooden Head said.

'So what? It's what I got, and it's better than nothing. Half the cops'll figure I'm buried in a cornfield somewhere.' Wooden Head's eyes slid away from hers. He knew about the two guys at the apartment, she thought.

'All right,' he said. 'I'll be back in an hour.'

The bar was a quick rerun of the apartment: she wiped everything, Xeroxed critical papers using plastic disposable gloves, dumped everything she didn't want in plastic garbage bags, and cried for a while. When Wooden Head came back, she was ready to go.

'By the way,' she said, 'Give this note to the Guy. It's private.' She handed him the sealed envelope, picked up her briefcase, took a last look around.

'You going back to the apartment?' he asked.

'Yeah I've gotta wipe that, too,' she said. 'But who knows? Maybe the cops'll never find it.' She looked at her watch: almost ten. The pilot would wait until noon. Plenty of time.

'The money's clean,' Wooden Head said, as his good-bye. 'Enjoy yourself.'

She stopped at that, peered at him: 'You know what I do? For a living?'

'I've got an idea.'

'Then you'll take me seriously when I tell you this: if this money's not clean, I'll come for you.'

And she was gone.

Wooden Head walked out to the main bar and watched through the windows as Rinker climbed into the beat-up van and drove away. Then he picked up a phone, called a number in Los Angeles, and was tripped through a switchboard to St. Louis.

'Yeah?'

'It's me. She's on her way to the apartment.'

'Okay. You give her the money?'

'Yeah. She says if it's not clean, she'll come for me.'

'Nothing to worry about, in five minutes,' the Guy said.

'It's clean anyway,' Wooden Head said. 'By the way, she gave me an envelope to give to you.'

'What's in it?'

'I don't know.' He held it up to a kitchen light. 'It's sealed up, and it says, *Private*.'

'Open the fuckin' thing.'

Wooden Head opened it, shook out the message and the two driver's licenses. The names on the licenses meant nothing to him.

'There's a note that says, 'I'll give you this one. Try again, and I'll come visit.' And there are two drivers' licenses. The names are . . .'

'I know the names, you don't have to say them,' the Guy said. After a long silence, Wooden Head said, 'You still there?'

'Yeah.' More silence. Then, 'Listen, you sure that money was clean?'

Wooden Head nodded at the phone. 'Yeah, it was clean. It came from the political fund.'

'Good thing,' the Guy said. He sounded a little shaky. 'Goddamn *good* thing.'

Chapter Twenty-One

Rinker hauled the van full of garbage bags to a trash-transfer station, dumped them, wiped the van and left it at the airport. The pilot, looking a little sleepy, was sitting in the charter lounge reading a old copy of *Fortune*. He spotted her, helped her carry her three oversized suitcases to the plane, and had Rinker back in Des Moines by mid-afternoon.

'Can I give you a ride anywhere?' he asked, when they were on the ground.

'Thanks, that'd be nice. I'm going to a Holiday Inn . . .'

He made a mild pass at her on the way; she was nice about saying no. He left her at the motel, where she checked out, picked up her car, and found a store that sold wigs.

'My mama is getting chemotherapy and her hair is starting to fall out. I need to get a wig for her,' she told the sole saleswoman. The saleswoman looked sad: 'I'm sorry about your mother,' she said in a kindly way, patting Rinker's arm. 'It would be better if she were here, though, for a fitting.'

'Well, she really can't be,' Rinker said. 'She's almost exactly like me, but her head is a little larger, maybe. We measured and it's about a quarter-inch bigger round, and also, she's still got a lot of hair, though it's starting to come out. She'd like to get something big enough to fit over what hair she's still got. She hopes she won't lose it all.'

'Does she have a color preference?'

'We talked about that, and she wants her natural color, which is grey,' Rinker said. 'It doesn't have to be a great wig, just to get her back and forth from the house to the hospital. And then if she loses all of it, we can come back and get another one.'

'Let me show you our Autumn Sparkle series . . .'

Rinker took an Autumn Sparkle, thanked the kindly saleswoman, moved on to a walk-in hair salon, and walked in. An hour later, with her hair in a skull-tight punk cut, and wearing plain-glass tortoise-shell glasses, she climbed back in her car and headed up I-35 toward Minneapolis.

* * *

Mallard called Lucas that afternoon and gave him the bad news. The fingerprint search was coming up dry.

'We're gonna change some things around on the computer search, but it doesn't look good,' Mallard said. 'Tell you the truth, I'd be willing to bet she was never printed.'

'Damnit,' Lucas said. 'We never quite get her. I swear to God, we didn't miss her by more than a half-hour at the airport, maybe fifteen minutes.'

'But we're knocking on the door,' Mallard said. 'We've got more on her than we ever hoped for. Now it's just a matter of time.'

Late that evening, Hale Allen sat naked on the edge of the bed, his damp hair still tousled from the lovemaking and the shower that came afterwards. He was examining his toes in the light from the nightstand, and clipping his toenails. He hummed as he did it, and every time the clippers snapped, Carmel flinched, and Allen would say something about the clipping, aloud, but mindlessly, to himself: 'Got that one,' he said, as a clipping fell on the magazine he was using to catch them. 'There's a good one.'

Carmel tried putting her fingers in her ears, but it was no use. She was about to roll out of bed when the magic cell phone went off in her purse. She crawled to the end of the bed, reached over the end-board for her purse, dug the phone out, lay back and punched the *talk* button.

'I'm back,' Rinker said.

'Where at?' Allen looked at her from his side of the bed, and she mouthed, *sorry-business* at him. He grinned and rolled over toward her, pushed her legs apart; she let him do it.

'Hotel down by the airport.'

'Dangerous,' Carmel said. Allen put his head down and nibbled.

'I look different. A lot different,' Rinker said. 'Not a problem. But the question is, do we do Plan B?'

'I've been thinking about that,' Carmel said. She ran her hands through Allen's hair. 'I guess it really wouldn't mean much to you, but it'd get me off the hook. For good.'

'But that's good for me,' Rinker said. 'The question is, how do I do this by myself? I don't know the details of . . .'

'You don't do it by yourself,' Carmel said. She pulled gently on Allen's ear, guiding him a little to the left. 'I'll help.'

'Can you get out?'

'Yeah. But I'm in the middle of something right now, I can't really get into the details . . . Call me tomorrow morning about ten o'clock.'

'You with somebody?'

'Yeah.'

'Hale Allen?'

'You got that right,' Carmel said.

'Talk to you tomorrow,' Rinker said.

Carmel said to Hale, 'Come up here, you.'

'I like it down here. It smells like bread.'

She whacked him on the side of the head and he said, 'Ow, what was that for?'

'Not very romantic, like a loaf of Wonder Bread, or something.'

'I was just joking.' He held his hand to his ear; she *had* hit him a little harder than she'd intended.

She smiled and said, 'Okay. I'm sorry. Come up here and I'll make it better.'

Sherrill was sitting in her own car, alone, a block from Allen's house. A radio beeped, and she picked it up: 'Yeah?'

'Another light just went on in the living room.'

'Thank God. There might be something left of Allen after all.'

The guy on the other end chuckled: 'We'll take her back home, if you want to join the parade.'

'I'll be two blocks back.'

She dropped the radio, picked up her cell phone and dialed Lucas' number from memory. He picked it up on the first ring.

'You up reading?' she asked, without identifying herself.

'Yeah.'

'I think we're about to take Carmel home,' Sherrill said. 'This is obscene.'

'Not a flicker out of her, huh? Not a move?'

'Nothing. Damnit, Lucas, we might have lost the chance.'

'I know, but we've got to hang on for a while,' Lucas said.

'And I'm getting kind of lonely.'

'So am I,' Lucas said. 'But I'm not going to invite you over.'

'I wouldn't come anyway,' Sherrill said.

'Good for both of us.'

After a pause, Sherrill said, 'Yeah, I guess. See you tomorrow.'

Ten minutes later, Carmel came out of the house and walked briskly to her car. A little too briskly, on a nice night like this, a little too head-down, Sherrill thought. Of course, everything Carmel did was slightly theatrical; there was no way she could know she was in the net . . .

The next day was brutal: Lucas talked to Mallard, who had nothing new, and checked on the Carmel net a half-dozen times, and got cranky with everyone.

Carmel talked with Rinker twice on the magic cell phone. 'See you at ten-fifteen,' she said.

Carmel went home at six, as she usually did; called Hale Allen at six-thirty, and told him that she'd have to work on the Al-Balah case that night: 'I've got to go back to the office. Jenkins ruled that the cops can have the tire as evidence, and I'm trying to put together an instant appeal.'

'Well, all right,' Allen said. She thought she might have detected just a hair of relief in his voice. 'See you when? Thursday?'

'Maybe we could catch lunch tomorrow . . . and I'll give you a call tonight.'

'Talk to you,' he said.

Carmel got out of her business dress, put on a short-sleeved white shirt, jeans and tennis shoes, and a light red jacket. She pushed a black sweatshirt into her briefcase. This was July, but it was also Minnesota. She didn't feel like eating, but she did, and carried the microwave chicken dinner to the window and looked out over the city. If they were actually watching her, from one of the nearby buildings, they should see her.

When she finished, she tossed the tray from the chicken dinner in the garbage, went back to her home office, disconnected the small digital answering machine from her private line, and stuck it in her briefcase with the sweater. A little after seven o'clock, she rode the elevator down and walked out of the front of the building, looking at her watch, carrying her briefcase. She wasn't absolutely sure the cops were there, but she thought they were: not looking around, trying to spot them, nearly killed her. She walked to her office building, enjoying the night, used her key to get in the front door, signed in with the security guard, and rode the elevators up to her office.

The entire suite was silent, with only a few security lights to cut the gloom. She turned the lights on in the library and in her office, turned on the computer, and went to work. Jenkins, the judge in the case she was working, *had* ruled the cops could have a spare tire owned by Rashid Al-Balah, and, unfortunately, there was blood on the tire. The only good aspect of it was that the cops had had the car and tire for almost a month before the blood was found, that they'd often taken it out for test drives – once to a strip joint – and, Carmel argued, the blood could have been anybody's, given the general unreliability of DNA tests. Or even if it did belong to Trick Bentoin, Bentoin could have cut himself before he disappeared, and simply was not available to testify to the fact . . .

She got caught up in the argument, moving back and forth from the library to her office, and nearly jumped out of her skin when the security guard said, 'Hi, Miz Loan.'

'Oh, Jesus, Phil, you almost gave me a heart attack,' she said.

'Just making the rounds . . . you gonna be late tonight?' She could already smell the booze: Phil was an old geezer, but he could drink with the youngest of them.

'Probably. Got a tough one tomorrow.'

'Well, good luck,' he said, and shuffled away toward the entry. She heard the door close, and the latch snap, and looked at her watch: twenty minutes. Time to start moving.

She got the answering machine out of her briefcase, carried it into the library and plugged it into the phone there. Back in her office, she pulled the black sweater over her head. She left the computer on, and turned on the small Optimus stereo system. The system played three disks in rotation, and would play them until she turned it off. She left the red jacket draped over her chair.

Ready.

The building had a five-story parking garage. Carmel stepped out of the suite, checked to make sure that the security guard had moved on, and then trotted briskly down to the stairwell at the far end of the hall, and down seven flights of steps. The cops might be watching every entrance and exit to the parking garage, but, she thought, they couldn't be watching all of it. Of course, if they were, she was screwed . . .

But it was a good bet, she thought. She poked her head through the door on the fourth floor, saw nobody. A single empty car, a red Pontiac, sat halfway down the ramp, but she'd seen it before. Not a cop. She glanced again at her watch: one minute. She waited it out, hearing nothing at all along the concrete corridors of the building, and then opened the door again.

Here was the only spot that she'd be in the open: she walked quickly across the top of the floor, and stepped into the corkscrew exit-ramp. She heard a car moving up the entrance ramp: had to be Pam, she thought. She listened, heard the car turn into the exit spiral, and nodded. The car started down, made the turn toward her . . . A grey-haired old lady was looking through the windshield. Carmel recoiled, then saw the hand waving her forward: 'Get in.'

'That's you?' The car stopped, just for a half second, and Carmel jerked open the back door and flopped on the seat, pulling the door shut without slamming it. 'Get under the blanket,' Rinker said.

Carmel was already doing that, rolling onto the floor, her head on the driver's side. She pulled the blanket over her legs and lower body, and lay quietly beneath it. The entrances and exits from the building were on opposites sides: and even at this time of night, there were always a few cars coming and going. With any luck at all, the cops on the entrance side – if there were any – wouldn't be calling out the cars coming and going, so the cops on the exit side wouldn't notice the odd fact that a grey-haired old lady in a Japanese car had gone in one side and come right back out the other . . .

She heard Rinker lower the driver's side window; heard the cashier mutter something, and a minute later, they were rolling out of the building.

'You can get up on the seat,' Rinker said a minute later, 'But I wouldn't sit up, yet. Let me take a few side streets, see if there's anybody back there.'

'If there are, there's nothing to do but run for it,' Carmel said cheerfully.

'Yeah, well, just stay down for a few minutes anyway.'

Rinker didn't know anything about throwing off a following car, but she'd watched enough cop shows on television to know that they might be both in front of, parallel to, and behind her. She took the car across the Washington Avenue bridge to eliminate the parallel cars, a block the wrong way down an empty one-way street to eliminate the forward cars, and then quickly along a one-way frontage road in the warehouse district, looking for followers. She didn't see anybody, and that was the best she could do.

'Best I can do,' she told Carmel.

'I can't think of anything else,' Carmel said. 'Pull over; let me get in the front.'

* * *

Max Butry came from a short line of mean cops; his father was one, and so was Max, the meanness beaten into him from a tender age. 'You don't stay alive long on the streets unless . . .' his father would say, following with a lecture about a specific point of manhood in which Max was faltering: 'You don't stay alive long on the streets if you hide behind your hands. What if some greaser's got a shiv, huh? He'll cut your hands right off. You gotta come down on those boys . . .'

And his father would come down on him, show you how you beat a guy right into the ground by getting in close and on top of him, and fuck all your cherry greaser knives.

Butry carried the attitude onto the force; and on this night carried it into the bus station. A desk clerk had called to say that two guys were smoking dope in the john, and the smog was getting so thick nobody could get in to take a leak. By the time Butry arrived, though, the smokers had gone, and he turned around and banged back through the door.

Outside, three skaters were practicing slides off a planter onto a curb. There was nothing illegal about this, but Butry considered skateboards one symptom of the decline of American civilization, and himself, by virtue of the badge in his pocket, one of the pillars of that civilization. 'They don't gotta respect the man – hell, they probably don't even know you – but they goddamn well gotta respect the badge,' his father said. 'If they don't respect the badge, the country starts caving in. Look what they got with the niggers down in Chicago. There are places in Chicago where you can't even show the badge or the niggers'll carve you up like the Christmas turkey. And you know how that started? It started when the first fuckin' nigger saw the badge and didn't show respect and nobody called him on it. And from there, the word got around, and the next thing you know, the world caves in. You got that? Huh?'

Niggers, skateboarders, trans-gender migrants, yuppie scum, all the same stuff. People without respect. Butry swerved out of line to cross with the skaters. One of them, the toughest-looking kid, maybe sixteen with the baggy pants and the chain billfold and a ball-point pen tattoo on his forearm, saw Butry coming and there was no respect at all in the way he looked at him.

'Hey, dickhead: get them boards outa here. This is a bus station, not a playground,' Butry said.

And the oldest kid said, 'Fuck you, asshole.'

Butry pulled his badge with one hand and his gun with the other; which would have gotten him fired if anybody else had been around to see how early it came out. 'I'm a fuckin' cop, wiseass. See the badge? Now sit on the fuckin' ground and put your hands over your heads, all three of you . . .'

The smallest of the kids, who looked like he might be fourteen, and had the bony look of a boy who hadn't eaten right for a month or maybe a few months, that lonely, hollow-cheeked glow of hunger like a personal portrait, said 'Fuck you, fat boy.' He pulled up his t-shirt to bare his belly, and to show off a half-dozen steel rings that pierced the skin around his belly button. 'Here: you want to shoot me? Here, shoot me, asshole.'

Butry was fast, faster than the kid, who may have been slowed by hunger: Butry's hand lashed out, open but heavy as a ham, a slap that knocked the boy off his feet.

'On your goddamn knees,' he screamed. 'On your goddamn . . .'

At the very last second, he began to realize that he was over his head, but that very last second was too late. The young kid had come back up, on the toes of his ragged black tennies, and in his hand that pointed toward Butry's nose was a piece-of-shit two-barrel Crow derringer; you couldn't, as one of the gun magazines noted, expect to hit your target at six feet. But the gun was only nine inches from Butry's face when the kid pulled the trigger, and the .45 slug went through the bridge of Butry's nose and out the back of his skull.

His father had forgotten to tell Butry that you don't fuck with people who have nothing to lose . . .

The three skaters froze in the impact of the blast, in the sight of the falling cop; then the oldest said, 'Run,' in the harsh semi-whisper of panic, and the three scooped their boards and were running across the street through the moving cars like a pack of starving terriers.

Sherrill and Black were slumped in her car, and Sherrill was talking to Lucas on her cell phone: 'I'm starting to feel like a country song,' she said. 'There's something wrong about not feeling right . . .'

Then their radio burped and and Black picked it up and Sherrill said to Lucas, 'Just a minute,' and then a dispatcher was screaming something about a cop down, shot at the bus station, three men running away, everybody available get to the bus station, looking for three youths possibly carrying skateboards and last seen running toward Loring Park . . .

'We got a call, there's a cop down, shot, we're going,' Sherrill said. And to Black, behind the wheel: 'Go-go-go . . .' and Black was already going.

Carmel said, 'Listen, Pam . . .'

'It's Clara,' Rinker said. 'My name is really Clara. Rinker.'

'Clara?' Carmel tasted the name for a second. 'I like that. Clara. Better than Pam.'

'Anyway, you were saying . . .'

'You are looking at this from the wrong point of view. People have always been allowed to kill in self-defense, and my dear, this is exactly what we're doing. We're trying to defend ourselves: Davenport has put us in this position, and we really don't have much option. So what I'm saying, is this: I don't understand how you could kill for money, and not feel bad about it, and now you can feel bad about killing in self defense.'

'I think it's because I know these people, or, anyway, I know about them,' Rinker said. 'They're not dirtbags who deserve it. They're just people who are in the way.'

'No, no, no, they're not in the way; they're simply essential to us. We could not kill them, but that would leave us exposed. I'll tell you what; if you want, I'll do all the shooting . . .'

'Who actually does the shooting is hardly the point, if we both cooperate in setting up the killing.'

They weren't exactly arguing: they were exploring, Carmel thought. Rinker – Clara – was feeling some qualms, while Carmel felt none at all. They were working together through the grey ethical areas of murder . . .

'This is the place – the brick house, with the white shutters,' Carmel said, pointing across the dashboard as they rolled past the house. 'We've gotta decide now: I don't want you coming in unless, you know, at some level you *believe*, that you *know*, that what we're doing is necessary. We're not doing it out of madness, we're doing it out of forced necessity.'

'I'm not objecting so much from any kind of definable, rational viewpoint; I'm saying that I feel a little different about this,' Rinker said. 'I even worry about the effect it will have on *you* . . .'

'Don't worry about that.' Carmel took the car to the curb, killed the engine. 'Are you in or out?'

'I'm in,' Rinker said.

Lucas arrived at Hennepin Medical Center to find Sherrill standing with a group of cops on the sidewalk by the emergency entrance. When she saw the Porsche, Sherrill broke away from the group and walked into the headlights just as Lucas shut them off. 'He's dead,' she said, as Lucas got out of the car.

'Damnit. I was afraid this would happen some day,' Lucas said in a low voice. 'Butry was an asshole and not too bright. It's a bad combination.'

'Yeah, well, he was a cop.'

'Yeah. They got a line on the shooters?'

'They're gone. Desk clerk said there were three skateboarders, kids, outside the station who might've seen something, but they took off right after the shooting. We're looking, but we ain't finding.'

'What about Carmel?'

'She's locked up in her building. I'll head back there as soon as I'm sure there's nothing I can do with this thing.'

'Probably no point,' Lucas said. 'It's so late now . . . What about Butry? Who's his next of kin?'

'Haven't found anybody yet,' Sherrill said. 'His folks are dead, no brothers or sisters, far as we know. Never married . . . hell, there might not *be* anybody.'

'Must be somebody.'

'I hope so,' Sherrill said. 'If there turned out to be nobody . . . That'd be the worst thing I ever heard of.'

Chapter Twenty-Two

Carmel and Rinker stood on the porch steps, each of them holding a phone book, and leaned sideways to peer at the curtained windows. The windows were dark, and nothing was moving. Nobody home. As stupid as it was, it was something they hadn't counted on. Plan B was going down.

'She's gotta be around,' Carmel complained. 'I called her office today, and she picked up the phone.'

'She's probably off visiting her mother or something,' Rinker said. They were both a little deflated, and wandered back down the dark sidewalk toward the car, carrying the phone books.

'Visiting.' Carmel stopped in her tracks. 'Yeah, I bet she's visiting . . . C'mon.'

'Where?' Rinker was puzzled.

'Up to Hale's place.'

'But I thought we were going to take Clark first. If we don't take her, there's no point in . . .'

'I think she's at Hale's place. I'll bet you a dollar.'

'Hale's?'

'Yeah. Hale's.'

At Hale's, Carmel cruised past, slowly. The back window, Hale's bedroom, showed just the faintest glow on the window shade. 'She's there. He's got this votive candle . . .'

'What an *asshole*,' Rinker said. 'I'm mean, you're talking about marrying him? And he's still sleeping with his ex-girlfriend?'

'Sneaking,' Carmel said. 'Can't say he's not sexually active.'

Carmel continued around the block, and pulled to the curb fifty yards up the street from Allen's house, where they could see the back window. She punched up her car phone, and on the second ring, a light came on in the bedroom. A moment later, Hale Allen picked up.

'I think I can get out of here, darling,' Carmel cooed. 'I've got to stop at my apartment for a minute, then I'll be over.'

'Maybe I should come to your place . . .' Hale said.

221

'No, no, I'm already in the car. See you.' And she hung up.

Five minutes later, Louise Clark squirted out of the house like a wet watermelon seed. She jogged down the sidewalk and climbed into a silver Toyota Corolla.

'Really makes me angry,' Carmel said. 'Really, really . . .'

'I can't believe it,' Rinker said. 'It's like a complete emotional betrayal. You're tough enough to take it, but other women? They could be totally emotionally crushed by something like this.'

In another ten minutes, they were back at Clark's house, walking up the sidewalk again, Carmel carrying the phone books. Clark had just gone inside, and the lights were coming on. Rinker caught Carmel's arm and whispered, 'Let me go first. If she sees you . . .'

At the door, Carmel stepped to the side and Rinker pulled open the storm door, propped it back with her foot, took a breath, dropped her gun hand to her side, and knocked urgently on the door with her other hand. They heard Clark walking toward the door, and a voice through the wood panel: 'Who is it?'

'Clara Rinker, from down the block,' Rinker said. 'I think you've got a little fire.'

'A fire?'

'A little fire, by the corner of your house, there's smoke . . .'

The door opened, tentatively; no chain. Rinker stiff-armed it, hard, and it banged open, past the startled, mouth-open face of Louise Clark. The gun was up and Rinker was inside, pushing her, followed by Carmel. Louise cried, 'Carmel, what are you doing? Carmel . . .'

Carmel said, 'You're fucking my boyfriend. That's gotta stop.' She caught the sleeve of Clark's blouse, and pulled her toward the back of the house. Rinker kept the gun in her eyes.

'Carmel, Carmel . . .'

'You're fucking my boyfriend,' Carmel said. They could see the bathroom down a short hall, a door open in the hall to one side. Carmel flipped a light: the bedroom. 'Lay down on the bed, and keep your mouth shut,' Carmel said. 'Just keep your mouth shut.'

'You're going to kill me,' Clark said, sinking on the mattress. 'You killed those other people.'

'Don't be ridiculous, we're just gonna talk to you about Hale,' Carmel said. 'We're gonna get a few things straight.'

They got her down on the bed, face-up; got her down on the pillow. Then Carmel walked around the bed and said, 'Look at me,' and when Clark looked at her, Rinker, who'd been kneeling on the floor with the gun, reached forward, put the barrel of the gun against Clark's temple, and pulled the trigger.

The bullet shattered Clark's skull, continuing through her head and into the wall on the other side. A red cone of blood, on the pillow, pointed back to Clark's head like a crimson arrow; the expelled shell landed next to her ear. The gun was a neat ladies' .380, with a neat ladies' silencer. As Rinker had explained to Carmel, a .22 didn't always kill with one shot, even from two inches, and a second shot would be awkward if the victim was supposed to be a suicide . . .

'Good,' Carmel said, looking down at the body. 'You can see exactly how it happened. The rest of it probably won't be necessary, because they *were* back there fucking, but let's do it anyway.'

Getting Clark out of her clothing without smearing anything was the hard part; she'd soiled her underpants, so they left them on, found a pink negligee in her chest of drawers, and pulled that over her head and let her drop back on the bed.

'Ah, God, we forgot the pubic hair,' Carmel said.

'Yuck.'

Rinker lifted Clark's negligee and Carmel slid one hand into her pants, gave a tug, and came back with a half-dozen pubic hairs, which she folded into a piece of notebook paper.

'The coke,' Rinker said. 'And the gun.'

'Yeah.' Carmel had had a bit of coke on hand, had rounded up a few more grams during the week. She put it all into a amber medicine bottle and dropped it into the bedstand drawer. Rinker took one of the silenced .22s out of her carry-girdle. They hid it in a winter boot, in the closet.

'That's it?' Rinker asked.

'I think so,' Carmel said. 'Except for the nitrites.'

'Okay,' Rinker said. 'Just set the phone books up over there.'

She fit Clark's hand to the gun, aimed it at the phone books, and pulled the trigger. The slug hit the front phone book with a *whack*!, and they fell over. The slug hadn't made it through the first one. 'Get the phone books, and let's go,' Rinker said, as she picked up the empty shell.

Ten minutes later, they were back at Allen's place.

'We can't go back now,' Rinker said. 'If we go back now, nothing will make any sense.'

'I don't have any intention of going back,' Carmel said.

'I sorta thought, when we got right down to it . . .'

'You sorta thought right. But you've got to have priorities,' Carmel said. 'That's one of the first things we were taught in law school: prioritize. Besides, he was getting on my nerves even before this Louise Clark thing. You ever been with a man who lays in bed at night and picks the calluses on his feet?'

'No . . . And tell you the truth, that seems kind of minor.'

'Not if you've got a ten o'clock appearance the next day and there's all kinds of pressure and you need sleep more than anything, and he's over there, pick, pick, pick . . . And he tries to sneak it in, so I won't hear it, so I wait . . . God!'

'How do you want to do it?'

'I'll just do it,' Carmel said. 'There's nothing else to do at this end. No arrangements of anything.'

'I'll go around the block,' Rinker said. 'Hurry.'

Carmel got out, walked down the block to Allen's. He met her in a bathrobe, at the door, with a big grin. 'God, you got off,' he said. 'That's great.'

'Gotta make a call,' she said. She called the office law library, the answering machine, dropped the receiver on the table, said, 'C'mere,' and walked around him back to the bedroom.

'What?' He looked at the phone, puzzled, then went after her.

He was six or seven steps behind her. At the bedroom door, she slowed, let him catch up, turned with the gun, bringing it up. His warm brown puppy-dog eyes had no chance to show fear or anything else. She pulled the trigger and the gun went *whack!* And Hale Allen, as dead as his former wife, started falling backward. Carmel fired three more times as he fell, and afterward stepped up beside him, pointed the gun down at his forehead and fired twice more: *whack, whack.* And again into his heart: *whack.*

'Goddamnit, Hale,' she said, as she walked back into the bedroom; 'You were my one true love.' Her photo smiled at her from the bedstand as she opened the folded piece of notebook paper, and let the odd strands of Clark's pubic hair fall on the sheet. On the way out, she hung up the phone, then looked back at Hale Allen's motionless body.

'You prick,' she snarled. 'Screw around on me . . .'

She kicked him in the chest, and then again, in the face, and then in the arm; and, breathing hard, went to the door. On the street, Rinker was coming around for the first time. Carmel stepped out and Rinker pulled over. 'That was quick,' Rinker said, as Carmel got in the car.

'No point in messing around,' Carmel said. 'Let's move.'

'Did you say good-bye?'

'I didn't say anything,' Carmel said. 'I did the phone thing, got him walking, and shot him in the head.'

'Huh.' Rinker continued on for a block, then said, 'You know something?'

'What?'

'We're good at this. If I'd met you ten years ago, I bet we could have set things up so that all of my outside jobs pointed somewhere else.'

'Not too late for that,' Carmel said. 'When you get to wherever you're going, you get established, set up a couple new IDs, cool off for a while . . . and then come talk.'

'It doesn't bother you? At all?'

'Actually, I kind of like it,' Carmel said. 'It's something different, you know? You get out of the office. You see lawyers on television, running around the courthouse, but ninety percent of my time is sitting in front of a computer. This is a little exercise, if nothing else.'

Back at Clark's, Rinker carefully pulled the clip, pressed an extra shell into the bottom of the clip, using a piece of toilet paper to keep her prints off of it, then reloaded the cartridges in the same order that they'd come out. They left the gun next to Clark's hand on the bed, but pointed away. 'I saw a suicide once, one of my clients,' Carmel said. 'The gun was like that.'

'Then that's good,' Rinker said. She took a last look around. 'We're done.'

On the sidewalk outside, Carmel looked up at the sky and said, 'I'm gonna miss you. Do you think you could get the *New York Times* wherever you're going?'

'I'm sure I could.'

'Okay. Then listen: I'll leave a message for Pamela Stone in the *New York Times* personal column on Halloween, and the days around there. It'll just say something like, "Pamela: Zihautanejo Hilton, November 24–30." Or wherever. That's where I'll be, if you feel safe and still want to do Mexico.'

'I'll look for it,' Rinker said.

'Listen, are you gonna need the other gun?'

'No, probably not. I've got a couple more stashed.'

'Could I have the one you've got?'

'Sure, but it could be dangerous. If you were caught with it.'

'I'll hide it out,' Carmel said. 'But if anything else comes up . . .'

'All right.' As they got back in the car, Rinker slipped the gun out of her girdle, pulled the clip, jacked the shell out of the chamber, pushed it back into the clip and handed the pistol to Carmel. 'There you go. Be careful.'

'I will be . . . Are you gone then?'

'Yeah. I gotta move: I'll be out of the country in a week. And I've got to make a few stops. I've got money stashed all over the place.'

Back at the parking ramp, Rinker and Carmel shook hands: good friends, who'd been through a lot together. 'If I don't see you again, I'll remember you,' Carmel said.

'See you in Mexico, Halloween,' Rinker said. 'Hey – and don't forget to check that phone tape, and erase it, if there's anything on it.'

'Top of my list,' Carmel said.

She walked back through the building, let herself into the office suite, unplugged the answering machine, and listened to her messages. The call from Hale's house had *something* on it, but she doubted that anyone could tell what it was. She was taking no chances, though. She replaced the phone tape with a new one, stripped the tape out of the cartridge, and burned it. The little fire left a nasty odor in the office and she opened an outside window, to air it.

She could see three or four cars parked up and down the street. At least a couple of them, she thought, were loaded with cops.

With the answered phone call, and the watching cops, she had the perfect alibi. She should wait a few minutes, cool out, and get back home, she thought.

And maybe have a good cry. Although she didn't feel much like crying; she was more excited than saddened.

Man, that was something else.

He was right there and Whack! Whack! Whack!

Alive, then dead. Something *else*.

Chapter Twenty-Three

Allen's body was found by his secretary, who first called Carmel to find out if she'd seen him.

'Well, no, I haven't,' Carmel said. She felt a crawling sensation on the back of her neck: this was it, the beginning of the end game. 'Not since day before yesterday – I had to work last night. I did talk to him last night, though. Sometime about 11 o'clock, I think.'

'Well, I don't know what to do,' the secretary said. 'He missed a closing this morning, and people are upset. He could miss another one if he's not here in the next twenty minutes. That's not like him.'

'How about his cell phone? That's permanently attached to him.'

'It rings, but there's no answer.'

'Huh. Well, maybe we ought to check with a neighbor or something,' Carmel said. 'I'd go, but I don't have a key, and I do have a court date.'

'I've got a key,' the secretary said, the concern right on the surface of her voice. 'He keeps an emergency key in his desk drawer. I can go over . . .'

'You don't think anything's *happened*, do you?' Carmel asked. She put concern in her own voice. 'I bet he just lost track of time somewhere, he was talking about buying a new sport coat . . .'

'He was supposed to be here at nine o'clock. That's a lot of time,' the secretary said.

'Now you've got me worried,' Carmel said. 'Keep me posted.'

As the secretary, whose name was Alice Miller, hung up, it occurred to her she'd just had her most congenial conversation with Carmel Loan, who tended to treat secretaries like unavoidable morons. Allen, she thought, was known for a certain mellowing effect he had on women . . .

When Allen didn't show up for the next closing, she apologized for him, told the participants that she was very concerned, that he hadn't been heard from; that she was going to his house to check on him. She felt increasing concern as she drove out to Allen's house. And once there, she called back to the firm to make sure he hadn't shown up in the meantime. He hadn't.

227

Miller got out of the car and looked up the driveway. Remembered what had happened to Allen's wife; started up the drive. The house felt occupied, but quiet: a bad vibration. She stopped in the driveway and said, 'Oh, God,' and crossed herself.

The front door was open an inch, and she called, 'Hale? It's Alice. Hale?'

No answer. She stepped inside, and some atavistic cell deep in Alice Miller's brain, a cell that had never before been called upon, triggered, and Alice Miller smelled human blood.

Knew what it was, somehow, deep in the brain. Clutched her purse to her breasts and took three more steps into the house, leaned sideways, looked into the hall . . .

At Hale Allen's shattered skull.

She may have screamed there, inside the house. Later, she couldn't remember. For sure, she turned and ran toward the front door, still clutching her purse, turned just before she got to the door to look back, to see that Hale Allen's corpse wasn't following her, and ran straight into the door jamb.

The blow nearly knocked her down. She dropped the purse, dazed, struck out, and pushed her hand through the glass window on the storm door. Now she did scream, a low wavering cry, and clutching her bleeding arm, she managed to get outside, where she ran down the driveway. A man was walking his dog along the curb, and she ran at him, whimpering, bleeding badly from the arm cuts.

'Help me,' she cried. 'Please please please . . .'

The responding cops thought Alice Miller probably had something to do with the shooting, as cut up as she was. But the patrol sergeant who was second at the scene took a moment to walk through the house, to note the drying blood on the floor and the fresh blood on the door. He listened to Alice as she sat on the grass next to the squad car, and finally said, 'Call Davenport. And somebody ride this lady into the hospital.'

Sherrill and Black got to Hale Allen's house five minutes before Lucas. Black looked at Allen's body and said, 'Totally awesome. Somebody shot the shit out of him.'

'Poor guy,' Sherrill said. Her lip trembled, and Black patted her on the back.

'How long was Carmel loose last night?' Black asked. 'You didn't go back, did you?'

'No, but John Hosta did. She came downstairs at one o'clock and went right home.'

'This is a little different than the other ones,' Black said, looking closer at the gunshot pattern. 'Not a .22 for one thing. Bigger caliber. Still not huge, but bigger. And whoever shot him, really unloaded . . .'

'Lover's quarrel,' Sherrill said.

'Jesus, if we hadn't been watching Carmel, she could be in trouble,' Black said.

'I don't know,' Sherrill said. 'To tell you the truth, they were still running pretty hot. I don't think they were at the shooting stage.'

'Maybe he blew her off, maybe . . .'

A cop at the door called in to them: 'Davenport's here.'

'All right,' Sherrill said. 'Let's talk.'

Lucas was in a cold rage: he should have thought of this. He should have understood that Hale Allen might be in trouble. Had Allen discovered something? Had Carmel told him something in pillow talk? Something that led to accusations?

Sherrill walked him through the house, watching him. 'Take it easy,' she said, once. 'You're gonna have a goddamned heart attack.'

'I'm not gonna have a goddamned heart attack,' Lucas grated.

'Your blood pressure is about two hundred over two hundred. I know the signs, remember?'

'Off my case,' he said. 'And tell me about Carmel.'

'She was loose for a while last night,' Sherrill said. 'More than an hour.'

'It'd take a hell of a coincidence,' Lucas said.

'It'd take more than that,' Sherrill said. 'She would have had to leave the minute we did, get over here, work herself into a rage, shoot him, get away without any neighbors hearing the shots . . . it's bullshit.'

'Maybe the other woman did it, the shooter,' Lucas said.

'Look at the wounds,' she said. 'That looks like somebody who was pissed off, not a cold-blooded professional killer.'

'But look at the group in the forehead . . . *that* looks like a pro.'

'Yeah, but . . .'

'This is ludicrous,' Lucas said. 'I don't even believe it. What happened to the woman who found the body? Alice . . .'

'Alice Miller. She's getting her arm sewn up. She saw the body and took off and ran right through the door, put her hand through the glass.'

'She's not . . .'

'No. She came here looking for him, because he'd missed a couple of serious appointments, and she couldn't get through to him,' Sherrill said. 'Besides, even if she was a put-up deal, did you ever hear of anybody slicing up their arm for verisimilitude?'

'Veri what?' Lucas eyes slipped over to her, and she caught the unspoken amusement, out-of-place as it might be.

'Fuck you,' she said. 'I know some multi-syllabic words.'

'I've just never heard that spoken before,' Lucas said. His minuscule grin slipped back into the cold stare. 'I need to talk to Carmel.'

A uniformed cop stuck his head in the door: 'The Miller woman is calling from the hospital. She wants to talk to whoever's in charge.'

'Probably you,' Lucas said to Sherrill.

Sherrill nodded and went to take it, and somebody laughed and yelled at somebody outside the door: crime-scene crew was coming in. Lucas met the crew chief at the door and said, 'About a million people have already trampled through, but nobody's been past his feet. I need every goddamned thread and hair and print and stain you can find.'

'Bad news?'

'This is very bad news,' Lucas said. 'The newspapers are gonna tear us a new asshole.'

Sherrill was back, moving fast: 'You remember Allen had a girlfriend, Louise Clark, had an affair with her, before his wife was killed? Before he started seeing Carmel?'

'Yeah?'

'Miller was calling to tell us that Louise Clark also didn't make it into work today. And as far as Miller knows, Clark didn't call in to tell people she wouldn't make it. Miller isn't her supervisor or anything, just heard she wasn't around, and didn't really put it together with Allen . . .'

'All right,' Lucas said. 'Let's get her address and get over there. Goddamnit, what is this? What is this?'

Louise Clark was a fine picture of a murder-suicide, stretched across her bed in her pretty pink negligee, the gun fallen away from her hand on the pillow. The gun had a silencer screwed onto the snout.

Lucas brought a kitchen chair into the bedroom and reversed it at the end of the bed and sat down, his arms on the back of the chair, his chin on his hands, and stared at her. Another cop came in and looked at him, and then at Sherrill: Sherrill shrugged and the cop made a screw-loose gesture at his temple, and backed out of the room.

After two minutes of staring at the body, Lucas said, 'It's perfect.'

'Perfect?'

'Someplace in this house, we're gonna find either a gun, or shells, or something else, that'll tie her to the earlier shootings. The only thing we won't find is, we'll do some swabs and there won't be any semen. Usually, there's semen, and there won't be any, because they couldn't do that. And we'll get the ME to check Allen, and he won't have had sex in the last twenty-four hours, because they couldn't do that, either.'

'By they, you mean . . .'

'Carmel and the shooter-chick.'

Sherrill looked at him for a moment, wordlessly, then turned and walked back out of the room, only to return three seconds later: 'Lucas, I could make a pretty good case that Louise Clark *is* the shooter-chick. She was sleeping with Allen; she's a low-level secretary, and if she gets rid of the old lady, and she marries Allen, she goes from being poor and single to rich and married. She's got the motive . . . she's got the gun.'

'Where'd a goddamn low-level secretary get a silencer like that?' Lucas snarled. 'You buy a silencer like that on the black market, it'd cost you a grand. And who did the tooling on the muzzle? Did you find a machine-shop in the basement?'

'No, but Lucas . . . what if she's the shooter, and she knows Carmel that way? What if Carmel's her lawyer?'

'And Carmel starts screwing her boyfriend, knowing that the woman she's kicking out of the saddle is a professional killer? Bullshit. Nope: this is a set-up. That's why there won't be any semen, and that's why we're gonna find a gun,' Lucas said. 'When you said you could make a pretty good case that Clark is a shooter, you're exactly right. You could. And a pro defense attorney like Carmel could make an even better one. She could make a perfect case. Trying to get anyone else for these murders is pointless: we'll never do it.'

'What're we gonna do?'

'I don't know what you're gonna do,' Lucas said, standing up. 'But I'm going up north. You can handle this fuckin' thing.'

Lucas arrived at his cabin a little after five o'clock, driving back roads most of the way to dodge the Wisconsin state patrol, the most rapacious gang of weasels in the North Woods. As he drove, the image of the dead Louise Clark hung before his eyes.

Then, just before the turnoff for his cabin, he saw a neighbor, Roland Marks, driving an orange Kubota tractor along the side of the road. The tractor had an oversized loader on one end, and a backhoe on the other. Lucas pulled off and climbed out of the car, and Marks rode the throttle back to idle.

'What the hell are you doing?' Lucas asked, walking around the tractor. Louise Clark began to fade.

'Gonna clear me off some snowmobile trails on the back,' Marks said. Marks had forty acres of brush, gullies and swamp across the road. He called it his huntin' property.

'You don't know how to drive a tractor,' Lucas said. 'You're a goddamn stockbroker.'

'Yeah? Watch this.' Marks drove the backhoe down a shallow slope into the roadside ditch; did something with the controls, set the brake, turned his seat around backwards, lowered hydraulic support pads on both sides of the tractor, and raised the bucket. With one slow chop, he took a couple of cubic feet of dirt out of the bottom on the ditch.

'How much did that thing cost?' Lucas asked, impressed despite himself.

'About seventeen, used,' Marks said, meaning seventeen thousand dollars. 'Got four hundred hours on her.'

'Jesus, you're starting to talk like a shitkicker.'

'What're you doing this evening?' Marks asked.

'Going out in the boat.'

'Why don't you come over? I'll check you out on this thing.' He carefully dumped the dirt back in the hole where he'd gotten it; only half of it slopped over the edge.

'Yeah? What time?'

'Half-hour?'

'See you in a half-hour.'

Lucas turned the pump and the water heater on, got a light spinning rod and carried it down the dock and flipped a Moss Boss out into a shallow area spotted with water lilies. The Moss Boss slid and skated frog-like through the lilies and reeds, back up to the dock. He threw it out again, then again, and on the third cast, a bass hit. He fought it in, unhooked it, dropped it back in the water. A twelve-incher, and fun; but he didn't eat bass.

He flipped the Moss Boss around the dock for twenty minutes, taking three small bass, tossing them all back, feeling his shoulders loosen up. Louise Clark was almost gone. After the last cast, he walked back up the sloping lawn to the cabin, got four cold Leinies out of the refrigerator, put them in a grocery sack, and had one foot out the door when the phone rang.

He stopped, thought about it, shook his head at his own foolishness, and went back.

'Yeah?'

'Sherrill. I'm down at the ME's. They're doing the autopsy on Louise Clark.'

'Anything, yet?'

'Yeah. She'd had sex shortly before she was killed. The semen hadn't been dissipated yet, and they got a pretty good sample. But to tell you the truth, I figure there's only one place it could have come from.'

'Man! I don't believe that,' Lucas said. He was shocked. 'What about Allen?'

'They haven't started on him, but I'll let you know. If you want to know.'

'Of course, I want to know . . .'

'Okay. And there's more stuff. We found the gun, just like you said. It's a Colt .22 with a silencer. Stuffed inside a boot in the closet. And we found a couple hundred bucks worth of cocaine in the bedside table. There's the connection to Rolo. Crime scene found some pubic hair in Allen's bed. In fact, they've got three different samples. Most of it comes from Allen, but some of it's blonde, and that'd be Carmel – but there's a third sample that's this mousy-brown color. We don't have the lab work yet, but I know it came from Clark. I *know* it.'

'All right. Call me back when they get to Allen. Keep pushing the ME, don't let them put anything off until tomorrow. We need it now . . .'

'You going fishing?'

'Actually, I was on my way out the door. A neighbor's gonna teach me to run a backhoe.'

'Speaking of backhoes . . .'

'What?'

'You never told me that special agent Malone of the FBI was a woman. And a woman with a sexy voice who wants to dance with you.'

'Didn't seem relevant,' Lucas grunted. 'Our relationship is purely professional.'

'She wants you to call her, in Wichita. I've got a number.'

Malone picked up the phone on the first ring. 'Hello, Lucas Davenport,' she said. 'I'm told you're off rusticating.'

'Fishing,' Lucas said.

'I wanted you to know that I'm moving up to Minneapolis with my group, and Mallard is coming in from Washington. We're very interested in this Louise Clark. Very interested.'

'There's something wrong with the whole thing. Did Sherrill tell you about the semen?'

'No, nothing . . .'

Lucas summarized his conversation with Sherrill and Malone said, 'If the semen checks out, if the DNA checks out . . . that's it.'

'Makes me feel weird,' Lucas said. 'It's not right. This Clark isn't a pro killer, not unless she was doing it for the fun of it. Because she didn't have any goddamn money.'

'Could have had it hidden away.'

'Bullshit,' Lucas said. 'She kills people, but hides it *all* away? The inside of her house looked like a cut-rate motel. She had a TV set that couldn't have been worth more than a couple hundred bucks, new. Everything in the place said she was a secretary, and struggling to keep her head above water.'

'All right. Well, I'm coming in tomorrow. Maybe, when you get back, you can take me out for a nice little foxtrot somewhere – some place where you won't spend all of your time dancing with the waitress.'

Lucas carried the sack of beer next door to the Marks' place. Lucy Marks was snipping the heads off played-out coneflowers as her husband maneuvered the Kubota in and out of a shed. The shed showed splintered wood at the side of one of the doors, evidence of a recent impact.

'Role tells me you're gonna learn how to run the tractor,' she said, shaking her head. 'I'm glad I bought the quart-size bottle of peroxide.'

'Hey . . .'

'Lucas, you gotta encourage him to be careful. I'm afraid he'll roll it over on himself. He's like a kid.'

'He'll be all right,' Lucas said.

'That wouldn't be beer in that sack, would it?'

'Couple Leinies,' he said, guiltily.

'Yeah, well, I'll take the Leinies, you go figure out the tractor. When you get back, we'll fry some crappies and we can have the beer then.'

'Well . . .' She gave him a look and he handed her the bag.

The Kubota was . . . different. Running wasn't a problem, but maneuvering the joystick for the backhoe took a little practice: 'I'll have you buttering your bread with this thing before we're finished,' Marks said, enthusiastically. 'I figure with a few hours practice, I could do all the driveways for this whole area, come winter.'

'Jesus Christ, Role, you make what, a half-million dollars a year selling stock? And now you're gonna pick up an extra two hundred dollars a month doing driveways?'

When Lucas was checked out, Marks showed him where he was going to hide the key in his shed: 'Anytime I'm not up here, you're welcome to use it.'

'Maybe I could help you brush out a couple of those trails,' Lucas said; he liked the backhoe.

'Terrific.' Then, as they walked back up toward the cabin, 'You gettin' any?'

Lucas could see Lucy Marks on the lake side of the house, cleaning up the grill.

'Overtime? I don't get overtime any more . . .'

'Pussy,' Marks said. 'Crumbcake. You know? It sorta looks like . . .'

'Yeah, yeah. As a matter of fact, I just took a call from a nice-looking forty-ish FBI lady who's coming to Minneapolis and wants me to take her out to foxtrot.'

'Foxtrot? Foxtrot, my ass. If it was me, I'd drop about nine inches of the old French-Canadian bratwurst on her,' said Marks, who talked big but was the most faithful man on earth. As they came around the corner of the house, he hollered at his wife: 'Lucas is gonna jump an FBI agent.'

'A female, I hope,' Lucy Marks said. She was spraying something on

235

the grill, turning her face away from the coals.

'She wants to foxtrot with him,' Marks said. 'She called him up.'

'Sounds promising,' Lucy Marks said. 'How'd this happen?'

'I was down in Wichita, and we were in this bar and she didn't dance to rock music, so I was dancing with the owner . . .'

He trailed off, and after a few seconds, Lucy Marks said. 'Lucas? You still in there?'

'Excuse me,' Lucas said, 'But I gotta go. I'm sorry.'

He jogged away, across the lawn toward his own place, leaving the Marks at the grill, looking puzzled. At the cabin, he fumbled out the number Sherrill had given him for Malone, and dialed it. One of the FBI agents, a man, picked it up and said, 'John Shaw.' Lucas said, 'Let me speak to Malone.'

'She just left . . . I could try to catch her.'

'Catch her, goddamnit . . .'

The phone on the other end clattered on a desk and Lucas hung onto the receiver, eyes closed, rubbing his forehead. Could this be right?

Two minutes later, Malone picked up the phone and said, 'Malone.'

'This is Lucas. Did you get the composite of the shooter?'

'Yes. Pretty good.'

'Close your eyes, and think about the woman I danced with at that club in Wichita, whatever it was. The Rink.'

'My eyes are closed. I . . . hmm. Gotta be a coincidence.'

'Hey, I'm a great-looking guy,' Lucas said, 'I know that, but just between you and me, Malone, not that many thirty-year-old women are coming onto me anymore. And with this one . . . I had the feeling she was more interested than she should have been, and maybe not in sex. I didn't know why . . .'

'. . . Or maybe you thought it was sex . . .'

'Maybe I did, whatever. But I tell you, from talking to the people up here who saw her, and looking at that picture, something kept knocking at the back of my head,' Lucas said. 'I finally figured it out: if she's not the same chick, she's her twin. And if she was up here, she could very well have seen me on television. And if she did, and I walked into her place in Wichita, and then just sat down for a cheeseburger and a beer . . .'

'All right,' Malone said, reluctantly. 'Sounds like a loser, but give me a couple of hours. I'll check it out. You'll be up at your cabin?'

'I don't know,' Lucas said. Out through the screen, he could see the

236

lake, flat, quiet, a perfect North Woods evening coming on. And he'd just gotten there. 'I think I'm gonna head back to the Cities. I'm telling you, I think she's the shooter.'

He was out on I-35, driving way too fast, and still a long way north of the Cities, when the cell phone burped. He picked it up, and heard the first two words, then lost the signal. He punched it off; three minutes later, it rang again, and he answered it: Sherrill, breaking up, but audible.

'Your FBI friend called; she's all cranked up. That woman you danced with has disappeared – cleaned out her apartment, quit her job at the bar . . .'

'. . . I thought she owned it.'

'. . . So did everybody, but she was really just the manager. It's really owned by a guy named James Larimore, who is also known as Wooden Head Larimore, who is *really* connected, really *connected*, in guess-where?'

'St. Louis.'

'Yup.' The cell connection was getting cleaner. 'So your FBI friend freaked, and got a crime-scene crew into the apartment, and guess-what again?'

'It'd been wiped.'

'Top to bottom.'

'Got her, goddamnit,' Lucas crowed. 'We got her. What's her name?'

'Clara Rinker.'

'Rinker. Fuck those FBI pussies, Marcy. We broke this fuckin' thing right over their heads.'

'Yeah, well . . . want to know where Wooden Head got the name Wooden Head?'

'Sure.' The adrenalin was pumping; he'd listen to anything.

'He was once in a bar when people started shooting, and he caught a ricochet, and the slug stuck in his skull bone, in his forehead above his nose. Made a dent, and stuck, but didn't go through. They say everybody was laughing so hard, the gunfight stopped. Even Wooden Head was laughing.'

'So he's a tough guy.'

'Very tough. And they ain't gonna get much out of him. He says he don't know nothin' about nothin."'

Chapter Twenty-Four

Malone met him at the airport: 'You look kinda green,' Malone said. 'Tough flight down?'

'Naw, it was all right,' Lucas mumbled. He looked back through the terminal window at the plane, and Malone caught the look and said, 'You can't be one of those . . . you're not afraid to fly?'

'It's not my preferred method of travel,' Lucas said, walking away. She scrambled to catch up, and he turned his head to ask, 'What'd you get from the bar? Prints? Photos. We need to get a photo out *now*.'

'Airplanes are about fifty times safer than cars,' Malone said. 'I thought everybody knew that. Not only that, most people are distracted when they're driving, because they fall into routines, while pilots are trained . . .'

'Yeah, yeah, enough,' Lucas said. 'I don't like to fly because I've got problems dealing with control issues because I've got an unconsciously macho self-image, okay? That make you happy? Now what about Rinker?'

'We can't find a photograph,' Malone said. 'And there's no reason for you to be defensive about a fear of flying . . .'

'There's gotta be a photograph . . .'

She gave up. 'There are no photographs in the apartment, and none in the bar. Either she didn't have any, or she took them with her. We checked with people who were more-or-less friends . . .'

'More-or-less?'

'She didn't have many real friends,' Malone said. 'She was friendly, without friends. Nobody who worked at the bar had ever seen the inside of her apartment.'

'A loner.'

'Psychologically, anyway.'

'Driver's license?'

'We checked her driver's license and she was wearing a red wig and glasses the size of dinner plates, and she had her head tilted down . . . what I'm saying, is, that composite you had was better. Wichita State also had a copy of her student ID, and that's as bad or worse than the driver's license. She was careful. What we are doing, though, is we're refining the composite. It'll be as good as a photograph by this evening.'

They walked out of the terminal into the already-warm Kansas air; the sun had still been low on the horizon when they landed, and Lucas had expected a little more cool. Malone led him to an unmarked Ford parked in a no-parking zone with a local cop watching over it. 'Thanks, Ted,' Malone said to the cop, who nodded and gave her his best front-line, band-of-brothers cop grin. Saved her parking place; next week, he might be saving her ass someplace, in a savage fire-fight out on the burning plains of Kansas.

Then again, maybe not . . .

'And there's another thing,' Malone said, as they pulled away from the curb.

'Uh-oh,' Lucas said.

'The crime-scene guys found a couple of small smears of fresh blood on the floor of her apartment. A man who lives down the street, was getting up early to go fishing . . .'

'In Kansas?'

'Yeah, I guess they do, somewhere. Anyway, he gets up and sees a couple of guys going into her apartment building. They looked out-of-place, he thought – they looked like football players, big guys, and they both wore suits. But they had a key and he just thought they were a couple of apartment people coming home after a night out. So he went fishing and didn't think about it until one of our guys went around knocking on doors.'

'Two guys in suits, middle of the night.'

'Just about dawn.'

'And blood on the floor.'

'There is no apartment in the building with two guys in it, and we can't find any two guys who were out late. It's not a big apartment. Eighteen units – we've talked to everybody.'

'There was no disturbance.'

'No. She had a motion detector in the hallway, which would have been invisible if you didn't know what you were looking for. If she was in there, she should have known they were coming. Of course, she might have expected them. There was no sign of a struggle . . .'

'So she shot them?'

'That's a possibility, other than the fact that there're no bodies in the place, and she'd have to carry two football-sized guys out the hall and down a flight of stairs to get rid of them. On the other hand, if they shot *her* . . . a couple of big guys could handle a small woman fairly easily. If you were big enough, you could hold her under your coat, and walk right out.'

'Were they wearing coats?'

'The fisher-guy says they weren't, but you get my point. They could handle her a heck of a lot easier than she could have handled them.'

'They could have walked away together,' Lucas said. 'They could have been helpers. She *could* have cut herself packing up her stuff.'

'Which is sort of my theory, right now,' Malone said. 'Although the other theory has some attractions. If we get this woman . . . We've got a half-dozen states where they've got the death penalty, and where they've got lots of evidence on one or another of her killings. The only thing they don't have is the shooter. If we wanted to release her to those states for trial, sooner or later she'd wind up in the electric chair or the gas chamber or strapped down to a gurney. With that kind of leverage, we could squeeze her pretty hard. We could put some pretty big holes in the St. Louis mob with her information.'

'And that's what you want.'

'Of course,' she said. 'If we get the top guy, the guy who probably ran her . . . he knows *everything*. If she was willing to pin the tail on him, we could show him the same set of electric chairs and gas chambers. If he talked, two years from now, St. Louis would be cleaner than . . . I don't know – Seattle.'

'Seattle has Microsoft.'

'Okay.' She showed the tiniest of smiles. 'Than Minneapolis.'

'Thanks.'

'Anyway, the mob guys in St. Louis know this as well as we do. It wouldn't be too far-fetched to think they might send a couple of shooters to fix the problem.'

'She might be too smart for that,' Lucas said. 'I got the impression of smartness from the lady. So we know the mob could send a couple of guys, and the mob knows it could send a couple of guys, and she knows it. And if everybody knows it, do they send a couple of guys?'

'I don't know,' Malone said. 'I do know one thing that's pretty unique.'

'Yeah?'

'You're the only guy I know who's literally danced with the devil.'

Lucas saw the big window the minute he walked in the apartment door.

He had an advantage over Malone and the other FBI agents – when they'd first arrived, they were looking for Rinker herself, and didn't know about the blood on the floor. One of the FBI crime-scene techs pointed him around the apartment, and finally he asked, 'Did you check the outside window ledge on that big window?'

The agent looked at the window, and thinking fast, said, 'Not yet,' as if it were next on the list.

'Would it be all right to lift it up?'

'Let me get one of the guys to do it,' the agent said.

'What're you thinking?' Malone asked.

'I think carrying *any* body out of this place would take a fruitcake,' Lucas said. 'But throwing them out the window, if it's night time . . .' He peered out: 'They'd land right behind the garbage dumpster. You could back a car right up to them.'

One of the technicians came over, looked skeptically at the window, and said, 'Let me get this.'

Lucas stepped back and the tech unlocked the inner window, and lifted it easily. The outer window was a convertible aluminum glass-and-screen affair; the glass had been pushed up, and the screen was in place. 'Screen's a little loose,' the tech said. He was working awkwardly through surgeon's gloves. 'Let me . . .'

He used a small pocket knife to slip the screen up an inch, which allowed him to pull it out of the frame. He leaned it against the wall, and they all looked at the bottom end of the screen, and the brick wall outside.

'Huh.' The tech grunted and got down close to the brick, leaning out through the window.

'What?' asked Malone, glancing quickly at Lucas.

'You know any reason why a brick would wear tweed?'

Wooden Head was being interrogated by a team of specialists from Washington. Lucas and Malone watched for a few minutes, then left. If the team missed anything, Lucas wasn't smart enough to figure out what it would be – the team was taking Wooden Head apart inch by inch, and they were good.

'I'd suggest we get a bite at the Rink, but somebody would probably spit in the hamburger,' Malone said.

'So let's get something someplace else. Then maybe I can rent a car and get back home.'

'Really? You'd drive back instead of fly?'

'Really,' Lucas said.

'We've got a car going up later today, a couple of guys from the crime-scene crew to review the work at the last two killing scenes . . . you could ride along. I think they're leaving around three, and plan to drive straight through.'

'Sign me up,' Lucas said.

They stopped at a downtown diner, got a tippy table, and Lucas looked at one of the legs and told Malone, sitting opposite, 'See that lever on the end of the leg? There's a lever sticking up.'

'Yeah?'

'Push the lever toward me, with your foot.'

'What's that for?'

'It levels the table,' Lucas said.

Malone pushed the lever with her foot, and the table stopped tipping. 'Where'd you learn that?' she asked.

'I used to be a waitress,' he said. 'Before the operation.'

Over coffee and grilled-cheese sandwiches, Malone filled Lucas in on everything the FBI had figured out about Clara Rinker – they had her biography from childhood, but still no good pictures. 'She was in trouble a few times when she was a teenager, but nothing serious. Never got mugshot or printed. She was a runaway, and she might have had reason to be. We think she was probably raped a few times by her stepfather, who disappeared, by the way. And maybe by one of her brothers.'

'Did he disappear, too?'

'No, he's still around, but he doesn't talk much about her. He claimed he couldn't remember her.'

'That's helpful.'

'The picture sort of fills out, though. She's a sociopath, I think, but not a psychopath. She never showed that much enthusiasm for her work, she just did it very effectively. She had to take SAT tests to get into Wichita State, and she did okay: quite well on verbal skills, less good on math. About 700–550, which is pretty exceptional when you understand that she ran away from home in the ninth grade.'

'I knew she was smart,' Lucas said. 'She got out of here so cleanly that

I expect she's got a hidey-hole somewhere. Digging her out could be tough, especially with those horseshit photos we've got so far. Say: I think I know from somewhere that the SAT people require photo IDs for their tests.'

'I don't know,' Malone said. 'But we'll check.'

'If that's blood you found on the ground behind the dumpster, and it comes from more than one person, then she's still out there. Otherwise, I don't know. It's hard to think that she's dead and gone. Outa reach.'

'Worse things have happened,' Malone said. 'At least the killing would stop, until they find somebody else. But I know what you mean; it'd be good to have her.'

'She got any foreign languages?' Lucas asked.

'Spanish,' Malone confirmed. 'She's in her fourth year of college Spanish, got A's all the way through. One of our guys talked to her Spanish instructor, who said that if she goes South, across the border, she'll be speaking it like a native in six months. Said she was already pretty good, and had a good ear for the accent.'

'I wouldn't be surprised if she's already down there,' Lucas said. 'Goddamnit: we were an inch short about five times in a row.'

'What about the woman in Minneapolis – Carmel Loan?' Malone asked. She ate her cheese sandwich in small, tidy bites, pausing every second or third bite to dab her mouth with a napkin; she looked like a history professor, Lucas thought, but an oddly sexy one. Maybe that somehow explained how she'd been married four times, but none of the marriages lasted. Maybe her husbands-to-be expected a nice, reserved history professor, and got an animal instead; or, maybe, it was the other way around.

'I need to lay in my bed and think about Carmel,' Lucas said. 'Maybe I could z-out in the back of the car this evening, going back home. But let me ask you this: given what we have right now, how convincing a case could you make against Clara Rinker?'

Malone rolled her eyes up, and to one side, thinking. After a moment, still silent, she scratched the back of her neck, and wiggled in her seat. Finally, she said "We could probably get her. Sooner or later; give us enough trials, we could get her.'

'But it sure isn't open-and-shut.'

'Not quite,' Malone said. 'We'll probably get some prints, sooner or later. Find something she forgot about. But even if we put them with the prints you got off that bar of soap, all we'd do was prove that she was in Minneapolis. We have a mountain of evidence, we just don't have any direct tie. But I think the mountain would get her. Given the right jury.'

'So the same evidence could be applied to somebody else – it's not impossible that Clara's the wrong person,' Lucas said.

'Well, it's pretty improbable.'

'But . . .'

'. . . not impossible,' she agreed.

'You've got a lawyer with your group, don't you? Besides you?'

'Couple of them,' Malone said.

'Would it be possible to send one up to Minneapolis – the smartest one – with the whole Rinker file, and get with one of our assistant country attorneys and make a case against Louise Clark? That she was the shooter? I mean, we found the gun, we found all kinds of evidence that she committed at least one murder; I'd like to see what other evidence we could put together from other cases. If there is any.'

Malone was puzzled: 'But you said that was a put-up job. Why would you want to make *that* case?'

'Because, just between you, me, and the doorpost, I know damn well that Carmel Loan helped set up these killings. I don't know exactly why, although sex might have had something to do with it – or it might not have. Maybe it was money, or just for fun. But she's in it, up to her neck. And I can tie Carmel to Clark. If I can make a case that Clark is the shooter, and I can tie Carmel to her, maybe I could talk a jury into sending Carmel away.'

'Oh, man, I don't know – that doesn't sound overly ethical.'

'I ain't a fuckin' lawyer I'm just a humble cop,' Lucas said. 'So I don't know about ethics. But could you send a lawyer up? We can work out the details – the ethics – later.'

She was peering at him over the diner table, and said, 'I'm not sure I want to know the details.'

'But you'll send somebody up?'

'I guess.' She had one small crumb of toast sitting on the left corner of her mouth, and Lucas picked up her napkin and dabbed it off for her.

'You had a crumb,' he said.

She shrugged and met his eyes. 'The story of my life . . .'

Chapter Twenty-Five

Sherrill agreed with Malone. 'That is the goofiest thing I've ever heard.'

Black disagreed: 'How about the Tracy Triplets and the thing with the gourd? You said *that* was the goofiest thing you'd ever heard. That you'd *never* see that peak again.'

Sherrill's eyes stayed with Lucas, but she spoke to Black. 'Okay, this is the second goofiest thing I've ever heard. The Tracy Triplets are still first, but only because of the midget. If it wasn't for the midget, this would be goofier.'

Lucas wasn't smiling. 'This is *not* goofy. You're starting to piss me off.'

Sherrill was waving her arms. 'Lucas, how'n the hell can you convict an innocent dead woman of something she didn't do?'

'Shouldn't be too tough,' Lucas said. 'We do it a few times a year with innocent *live* people. How hard could it be to do it with a dead one? *She* certainly won't care. And we *will* get Carmel.'

'Jesus, man, I don't know,' Black said. 'This ain't a game.'

'I know. But maybe we'll break something loose. So what I want, is I want everybody out working on connections between Louise Clark and Carmel. They were about the same age – did they ever go to the same school? Did they ever hang out at the same place? They must've known each other, so let's make them into friends. Let's put together some ideas that'll tighten up the story on Clark, something we could take her to court on . . .'

'If she were alive,' Black said.

'Yeah. If she was alive.'

'This won't work if Carmel doesn't hear about it. We want her to react,' Lucas said. A half-dozen detectives were crowded into Lucas' office: Sherrill, Black, Sloan, a guy from drugs, two from sex. Lucas wanted people he'd worked with and could trust. 'We know she's got at least a couple of sources inside the department, so we want you to blab. Gossip. Homicide is tying Carmel Loan to Louise Clark, and through her, to the killings.'

'Why don't you call some of your pals at TV3?' Black asked.

'I'd rather have them ask *me* about it,' Lucas said. 'I don't want it to be an obvious plant. Rumors are better than actual stories. In fact, if the newsies hear about it, I'll probably deny it.'

'Refuse to comment,' Sherrill said. 'That always makes their little weenies hard.'

Carmel heard about it almost immediately. 'They're what?'

'They're tying you to Louise Clark. If they can tie you to her, you could be in trouble.'

'But I didn't do anything,' she said with asperity.

'Yeah, well, whatever. Listen, things are getting a little warm around here. I'm getting out of the information business for a while, okay?'

'You mean, 'Don't call,'' Carmel said.

'I'm not trying to be an asshole, but they're pulling out all the stops. They've got a half-dozen guys working on it. Davenport told somebody that they'll have you inside by the end of the week.'

'That's absurd.'

'I thought you'd want to know . . . so I'm signing off, okay? This last one's a freebie.'

'Fuck your freebie,' Carmel snarled.

Black found an invitation to a lawyer's Halloween Ball organized by members of several downtown firms. A photo of four of the women who organized the ball, including Carmel, was on the back of the program, and Louise Clark's name was in the list of people who'd volunteered to help out.

'What you should do,' Lucas told Black, after he'd seen the photo, 'Is get in touch with these other women, and ask them about the relationship between Carmel and Clark. How closely did they work together? That kind of thing.'

'I think Clark was probably a flunky – Xeroxed the invitations, or something.'

'That's fine, but ask anyway,' Lucas said. 'One of the people you ask will call Carmel, and tell her you're asking . . .'

Then Sherrill came up with a strong tie, one that surprised everybody: Louise Clark's phone records showed two calls to Carmel Loan's unlisted home phone in the week before Clark was killed. Both calls were late at night.

'I can't think why they would be talking – why Clark would be calling her. But it's an amazing tie,' Sherrill said.

'It's almost enough by itself,' Lucas said. 'You know what? I want you to go over and brace Carmel about this, face-to-face. Tell her it's part of the Clark investigation, and we just want the question answered . . . no big deal.'

Carmel's face was the color of her fabulous bloody-red silk scarf: 'She never called,' Carmel shouted. 'She never called.'

'Ms. Loan, somebody called – from her house to yours. This isn't bullshit – this is the list straight from the phone company. I brought a Xerox copy for you.' Sherrill was sitting in front of Carmel's desk, and she unfolded the Xerox and pushed across the leather desk pad. '. . . and you can call the phone company yourself, if you don't think this is accurate.'

Carmel snatched the Xerox copy from the desk, looked at the two underlined phone calls. She shook her head angrily, said, 'No. This is . . .' But then she trailed off, and her head swung sideways and down, a pensive look crossing her face.

'You know what this is?' she asked finally, looking up at Sherrill. 'That sonofabitch was calling me from her house. He was sleeping with me three nights a week, and when we weren't together, he was sneaking over to her place.'

Sherrill looked doubtful: 'Well . . .' She stood up. 'If you say so.'

'That's what it is,' Carmel shouted, shaking the Xerox copy in Sherrill's face.

Lucas was not amused by the story. He shook his head, fiddled with a sport-coat button. 'I'm starting to feel sorry for her,' he said. 'Almost.'

'My question is, where are you going with this? I mean, *exactly* where?' Sherrill asked.

They were alone in Lucas' office, streetlights coming on outside the single window; a soft glow lingered in the sky. A perfect summer night, a night for walking around the lakes, Sherrill thought. Lucas said, 'You're the only one who knows about the shell I found in her bedroom closet.'

'Unless you told somebody else,' Sherrill said.

'No. It's just you and me,' Lucas said. He pulled out the typewriter tray on the top corner of his desk, leaned back in his chair and put his feet up. 'But something happened to get that shell in there. Somebody dropped a box of shells, somebody ejected a shell and didn't pick it up, or somebody was punching a bunch of shells into a clip and fumbled them . . . If Carmel sees me find a shell there, and if I find it in just the right circumstances, I think she'd come after it. Either her, or the shooter.'

'You mean like . . . any shell.'

'Sure. Any shell. Any .22. Whatever happened to get that shell in the closet, Carmel will know about. If I find a shell in the closet, she'll know she's fucked. Especially if she hears about the scratches on the back of Rolo's hand and our other corroborating evidence, whatever it might be.'

'What'll she do?'

'Suppose I find the shell on a Friday night. Suppose everybody has left her apartment, except me, and I find the shell while I'm taking a last look around. I know where I found the original, so I'll find this one in exactly the same place. I show it to her, and she claims I planted it, or whatever. And I say, "The only shells I have to plant are already fired. If we get a metallurgical match on these slugs and some of the killer slugs, Carmel, you're all done." And then I tell her I know she's involved . . . from the phone messages, or something.'

'And . . .'

'And I say, "We'll let you know first thing Monday morning." Then I put the shell in a baggie, and I leave. I go home. Drive slow, give her a chance to catch me. And we put a net around the house, and I hang around . . .'

Sherrill frowned. 'You think she'd come after it?'

'If she knows that it'll match. And she probably knows that. If we give her the whole weekend to stew about it.'

'Boy. The whole thing smells a little like entrapment.'

'Look, you and I know she's involved,' Lucas said. 'If she comes after me, then we've got her. If you try to entrap somebody, and their response is to shoot you . . . I mean, you can't defend yourself against entrapment with attempted murder. And, in fact, we can outline some of this to the other guys – tell them that we're trying to lure the killer in. That we'd never use the fake shell. That way, we avoid the entrapment charge.'

'But we won't tell them that there once was a real shell.'

'No . . .'

'It's getting trickier by the minute.'

'Mmmm. Be nice if we could find a few more things to tie Clark to Carmel . . .'

'Well, hell, we're inventing the shell, and the whole relationship, we could invent a few ties, too,' Sherrill said. 'Like . . . suppose we find out where she took a vacation, and we leak the word that Clark took a vacation there at the same time. There's no way for Carmel to know that she didn't.'

'I hope this is getting through to her,' Lucas said. 'I hope her leak in the department's still good.'

'We need to write a script,' Sherrill suggested. 'When we get the warrant for her apartment, we could drop all of these little nuggets. You could say something, I could drop something, Sloan . . .'

Lucas nodded, looked at his watch. 'Good idea – think of some stuff. And I'll think of some. But right now, I've got to go to the Reality Commission, we're talking about non-certifiable minorities tonight.' He thumped the Report which sat on one side of his desk. He was on page four hundred and thirty.

'Non-certifiable . . . what is that?'

'Well, you know: minorities that don't fit into racial, handicapped, sexual-determinant, age-determinant, religious, ethnic, or national-origin groups.'

'Jeez, I would have thought that covered everything.'

'Oh, no. There was a case in Wisconsin of a white, Episcopalian male in his early thirties, non-handicapped, heterosexual, English heritage . . .'

'A perfect WASP . . .'

'Wouldn't even pee in the shower,' Lucas said. 'Anyway, he was a member of one of the animal-protection groups, and his co-workers tormented him by displaying photographs of pork chops and link sausages in the workplace, and they'd talk about going to McDonald's for cheeseburgers. He got $750,000 from the city of Madison for emotional imperialism.'

'Well – Madison.'

'That explains a lot of it, of course,' Lucas said, nodding. 'But apparently we need a policy. You know, covering non-religious ethical minorities.' Then he closed his eyes, rubbed them with a thumb and forefinger. 'Jesus Christ, what'd I just say?'

Carmel could feel the rage building. She knew what the cops were doing. They were building a 'just in case' case – hoping to build a good enough story that a jury would put her away, *just in case* she was the killer.

Somehow, she thought, Davenport had fastened on her as the killer. And, she had to admit, it had never occurred to her that in eliminating any possibility that she could be tied to Rinker, she'd thoughtlessly incriminated somebody to whom she *could* be tied. And there was no way for her to explain that Clark wasn't the killer. How could she know?

Carmel had tried forty-four murder cases in her career, winning twenty-one of them. That was considered an excellent average, since most involved a man found standing over his dead wife with a handgun, and when asked why he did it, had told the cops, 'She was gettin' on my ass, you know?'

Three of the cases she'd lost still haunted her, because she shouldn't, in her opinion, have lost them. She'd broken the state's case, she'd thought, and after-verdict interviews with the jurors had suggested that she'd lost only because the jurors *wanted* to believe the cops. They hadn't had the evidence, but they'd convicted because the cops suggested they should.

That could happen to her . . .

Fuckin' Davenport . . .

Worse, the word was getting out. She might be going psycho, she thought, going paranoid, but she thought she could see it in the eyes of her colleagues. The questions: did you do it? Did you help? Did you drill those little holes in Rolando D'Aquila's kneecaps?

An interview with one of Carmel's friends produced the casual information that she'd been in Zihuatanejo the November before last. 'Save that,' Lucas told Sherrill. 'When we shake her apartment down, we'll drop the information that Clark was there at the same time – we'll jump her about it.'

'All right.'

'What else you got?'

'Not much – it's really thin. Clark took a course in legal writing at the U, at the same time Carmel was at the law school . . .'

'So they were at law school together.'

'Not exactly.'

'Close enough for government work,' Lucas said. 'Get more.'

John McCallum, managing partner of the firm, stopped at Carmel's office and asked, 'What the hell is going on, Carmel? We hear the police are looking at you in connection with all these murders.' He was using the same whiny voice that had caused him to lose half of the consumer liability cases he'd once tried, Carmel thought.

'It's all crap, John,' Carmel said. But she could feel the blood rising in her face, and the impulse to rip McCallum's larynx out of his throat. 'The cops are trying to put pressure on me – I don't know why.'

'Yeah, well, make them stop,' McCallum said.

'I'm working on it.'

'You know the firm will stand behind you . . .'

'Bullshit. You'd drop me like a hot potato, if you could,' Carmel said. 'Of course, I can beat any charge they bring against me, and then I'd make a hobby out of suing you for damaging my career. You might get out of it with your oldest car and a pair of shoes.'

'That sounded almost like a threat,' McCallum said.

'Excuse me, if I wasn't direct enough,' Carmel said. 'That *was* a threat. If the firm doesn't back me up on this, I'll personally take you to court and pull your testicles off.'

'I don't have to listen to this,' he said. His eyes flinched away from her wolverine's gaze, and he turned to go.

'You don't have to listen,' Carmel said, her voice as deadly as a razor. 'But you better think about it. 'Cause I'm serious, John. You've seen me at work: you don't want to piss me off.'

Sherrill typed all the ties into a memo, and dropped it on Lucas' desk. 'Enough for a warrant?'

Lucas looked down the list, and nodded. 'We'll need a photo of the cuts on the back of Rolo's hand, and the phone records.'

'Both office and apartment?

'Both. But we'll do the office first. Seal her apartment, so that she can't get in to destroy anything, then brace her at the law firm. We'll need a dozen guys, a crowd, to make it really inconvenient . . . look through all her paper files, and we'll need a computer guy to copy her computer records. We'll need to subpoena the firm's phone records, too.'

'Might be some court problems with that.'

'Yeah, but we can nail them down, anyway. Let the county's attorney's guys argue about what we should get.'

'When?'

'Write up the warrant now, we'll walk it over to the county, let them know what's coming,' Lucas said.

'What if they're shaky?'

'Fuck 'em. Besides, they don't mind seeing us fall on our asses from time to time – and this'll all be on our heads.'

'So we go in . . .?'

'Tomorrow. Friday.'

Sherrill looked down at her memo: 'This is gonna be somethin'.'

Chapter Twenty-Six

All the paperwork was done by noon Friday. Lucas took Sherrill, Sloan and Franklin to lunch, after leaving word for the rest of the search team to meet at his office at three o'clock. Sherrill, Sloan and Franklin knew about the warrant, as did Black, who'd gone to St. Paul to get photos of Rolando D'Aquila's self-inflicted scratches.

'Why don't we just go?' Sherrill asked, as they settled into a booth at the Grey Kitten. A waitress hustled over, dropped four menus on the red-checkered vinyl table-cloth, and moved on.

'Because I want it later in the day,' Lucas said, when the waitress was gone. 'I want people starting to go home. I want the process harder for her to stop. And maybe she'll be a little more tired this way. She went to work when? Seven this morning?'

Another cop drifted by, a uniform guy on his day off. He was wearing grass-stained shorts and a t-shirt with a moose on the front. He smiled at Sherrill: 'Hey, Marcy.'

'Hey, Tobe,' Marcy said. 'You look a little scuffed up.'

He looked down at his shorts, nodded and said, 'Softball.'

'Good, good,' she said, and her eyes drifted back to Franklin. After a moment, Tobe said, 'Well, see ya,' and drifted away. Lucas glanced at Sherrill, who smiled, well-pleased.

'She got there at seven o'clock,' said Franklin, who'd been working with the surveillance crew. 'First light in her apartment was five-forty-five.'

'So we go into the office at three o'clock, and put a man on her apartment door at the same time,' Lucas said. 'We stay at her office until about five, and then we move the act over to the apartment. I want both the office and the apartment taken apart. Everything in the computers, all records showing phone calls, money spent, safe-deposit numbers, everything.'

'We'll need a new warrant to get into the safe-deposit boxes,' Sloan said.

'By that time – Monday – we'll either be done with her, or completely fucked,' Lucas said. 'Although we ought to get the warrant anyway. If there's something in one of those boxes, it'll put a little more pressure on her.'

'You really think she'll come after you?' Franklin asked. He didn't know about the cartridge that Lucas had found; he knew only that Lucas would drop one, and pretend to find it.

Lucas shrugged. 'I think she'll do *something*. If we do this right, she oughta feel pretty cornered by the time we're done – and the only way out of the corner will be to get that shell back.'

The waitress came back and they ordered. And when the waitress was gone, Franklin asked, 'Has anybody here ever been on one of these things, when everything went just like you thought it would?'

They all thought about it for a few seconds, then Lucas shook his head, and Sherrill said, 'Never happen.'

At three, the surveillance team put Carmel at her office. Lucas sent two men to camp out at her apartment door – 'Nobody goes in without my say-so. And if there's anybody inside when you get there, they don't leave until I see them' – and led the rest of the group in a ragged line three blocks across downtown to Carmel's office. Another two drove over, in a van, to carry any items seized as part of the search.

Carmel was in the office of another partner when Lucas presented the search warrant to the secretary, and started feeding men into Carmel's office. Lawyers started coming out of adjoining offices and one of them yelled, 'Hey, what are you assholes doing?'

'A search,' Sherrill said, facing off.

'You got a warrant?'

'We've served it,' Sherrill said.

'You're assholes,' the lawyer shouted, and then another one started to boo, and five seconds later, the office was a raucous cacophony of boos, catcalls and hisses. A few seconds later, Carmel pushed her way through the crowd and faced off with Sherrill.

'Out of the fuckin' way,' she said.

'I'll let you in, but you are not to touch anything or interfere in any way,' Sherrill said. 'If you do, I'll throw you out.'

'Yeah?' Carmel pushed closer to her. They were chest-to-chest, not quite touching.

'Yeah,' Sherrill said. She didn't budge. 'And if you touch me, I'll knock you on your ass, and haul you downtown on an assault charge.'

Carmel almost faltered. 'Never stick,' she said.

'Tell that to your teeth when you're digging them out of the back of your throat,' Sherrill said. She waited another beat, then stepped aside. 'Don't touch, don't interfere.'

Carmel stepped past her, and a few of the lawyers in the hall started cheering, 'Go, Carmel.' Inside her office, Carmel spotted Lucas, who was standing, hands in pocket, watching a computer technician slip copy software into the floppy slot on Carmel's computer.

'What is this?' she hissed.

'We're searching your office, looking for any information or physical articles concerning your involvement in the murders of Hale Allen and others. When things are under control here, we're moving over to your apartment.'

'My apartment?' Her hand went to her throat.

'Your apartment. Right now, it's sealed. You can be present when we enter it, if you wish.'

After a long moment of astonished silence, Carmel said, 'You're nuts.'

'No, but I'm afraid you are,' Lucas said. 'We've got quite a bit of the picture with you and Louise Clark.'

'I have nothing to do with Louise Clark. Nothing. You can ask . . .'

'You just went to Zihuatanejo, at the same time by accident?'

'What?' Carmel sputtered. 'I never saw her in Zihuatanejo. I'd never go there with a . . . a . . . *secretary*. I went there by myself.'

Lucas now took a long moment to look her over. Then, half-turning away, he said, 'Sure.'

One of the vice guys found Louise Clark's name in Carmel's Rolodex, lifted it out, put it in an evidence bag. Another found a long paper record of the D'Aquila drug trial, and bagged that, too. The lawyers in the hallway began chanting 'Fuck you, fuck you, fuck you,' and one of the senior partners came down and tried to quiet them. They didn't quiet. The chanting got louder, and the partner grinned slightly, shrugged and went upstairs; the approval as explicit as they'd ever get from that particular partner. Two minutes later, another group of lawyers arrived, from another firm in the building, and joined the chanting.

Carmel was shouting over the noise. 'You think I killed Hale? We were gonna get married. I was here the night he was killed. Look in our phone records, asshole, you'll find that he called me, we talked for ten minutes . . . Hey asshole, I'm talking to you . . .'

And outside, the lawyers began chanting, 'Asshole, asshole, asshole . . .'

Sherrill was getting angry, but Lucas touched her shoulder and grinned: 'Haven't had this much fun since we beat up that shitkicker in Oxford.'

And Carmel screamed, 'What are you laughing about, asshole?'

And Lucas let it out, a long, rolling laugh. Outside, the lawyers were chanting, scratching at the glass windows to Carmel's outer office, watching him laugh and laugh . . .

At five o'clock, leaving three detectives at the office to look through the last of the records, Lucas moved the act to Carmel's apartment. Carmel followed in her bloody-red Jag, which had been searched while it was parked in the office ramp. Lucas and four others were in the elevator when it arrived at the fifth floor, where Carmel's parking space was.

Carmel got on with a man who she'd introduced at the office as Dane Carlton, her personal attorney. Lucas knew him to nod to, a tall, slender, grey-haired man with a cool demeanor and icy blue eyes behind plain gold-rimmed glasses. He was wearing a blue suit with a white shirt and wine-colored tie.

To Lucas, Carmel said, 'Fuck you.'

Lucas sighed, looked at Carlton. 'You should tell your client to watch her mouth.'

'I'm her attorney, not her guardian,' Carlton said bluntly.

'And he's gonna rip you a new asshole when we're done with this,' Carmel said.

Lucas looked at Carlton. 'That right?'

Carlton, with the tiniest movement of his head, said, 'Yes.'

When Carlton and Carmel got out at Carmel's floor, Sherrill, looking after him, put her mouth close to Lucas' ear and whispered, 'I get the feeling he could do it.'

Lucas said, 'I know him. He could.'

The search team was methodical and undiscriminating. They were looking for guns, cartridges, records, notes, letters – anything that would tie Carmel to any of the people who were murdered. They found a half-dozen notes and e-mails written to Hale Allen, most of them simply setting up dates.

Franklin, wearing white plastic gloves, gave one of them to Lucas:

'Fuck around on me, and I'll kill you,' Lucas read aloud.

Carlton glanced at Carmel, who rolled her eyes. But she was angry, and getting angrier, Lucas thought. He dropped the D'Aquila scratches on her the first time he got an opening, which came when Carmel started screaming again.

'You're messing up my goddamn clothes, those clothes are worth more fucking money than the city can pay . . . Dane, we gotta recover for this, they're wrecking that suit.'

Carlton said, 'We will, Carmel.' He turned to Lucas: 'Chief Davenport, why don't we end this charade? There's no evidence that Carmel had anything to do with any of these killings. You're simply fishing – and we will eventually find out why. It appears to be a personal crusade against one of the most highly regarded criminal attorneys in the state. Have you lost a case to Carmel? What is there in *your* past . . .?'

'I don't have anything against Carmel,' Lucas said, injecting a little steel into his voice, 'I always kind of admired her. She's a tough attorney. I stopped admiring her when Rolando D'Aquila used his fingernails to carve Carmel's name into the back of his hand while he was being tortured and then executed.'

Carlton showed a thin smile: 'That is . . . one of the more amazing things I've ever heard.'

'You'll be even more amazed when you see the scratches. Or gouges – doing it had to be almost as painful as getting the holes drilled in his knees. And he didn't just carve her initials. He carved her name: C. Loan. Quarter-inch grooves in the back of his hand . . .'

Carlton glanced at Carmel, who'd frozen in place when she heard D'Aquila's name. 'I just don't believe it,' Carlton said finally.

'Well, we've got D'Aquila's body on ice in St. Paul, along with the blood that dried on his hands and arms while he was carving her name out. So you all can go over and look at it. I'm sure you'll find your own pathologist to examine the body . . .'

Carmel started to interject something, but Carlton waved her down, and turned to Lucas with a slightly warmer tone of voice. Lucas knew what he was doing: he was looking for information, anything that might someday help a defense. 'We *will* challenge it, of course; because whatever might be carved on Mr. D'Aquila's hand, it isn't Carmel's name.'

'You can say that without seeing it?' Lucas' eyebrows went up.

'Of course. Because it can't be Carmel's name.'
'Okay,' Lucas said, mildly. 'If that's your story.'
'It is, and we're sticking to it,' Carlton said.

The search continued. Sloan, one of the more mild-mannered of the homicide cops, mentioned to Carmel, in passing, that they knew about her connection with Clark at law school. Lucas, outside the bedroom when Sloan and Carmel were talking, heard Carmel spluttering, 'She was a secretary, for Christ's sake.'

And Sloan answered, 'C'mon, Carmel, we know she took that legal writing course the same time you did.'

'If she did, I didn't know about it.'

'Ah, c'mon,' Sloan said. 'You guys go way back. You even did that Halloween Ball together. It's right on the program.'

'Jesus . . . you guys.' But she was scared, now. More angry than scared, but scared nevertheless.

At six o'clock, with Carlton glancing at his watch every two minutes, the search team began breaking up. A crime-scene crew had been brought in to take samples from Carmel's bed, the guestroom bed, and to dust the guestroom for fingerprints. They began packing their gear, and Sloan told Lucas he was heading home. Then two more detectives checked out, and Carlton asked Lucas, 'I assume you're not planning anything else dramatic? No new papers to serve . . .'

Lucas shook his head: 'No. We're about done. I'm gonna take one last cruise through the place . . .'

Carlton went to Carmel and said, 'I'm chairing a bar meeting at seven o'clock. Will you be all right here?'

'Sure. It's all over.'

And Sherrill, her voice low, asked Lucas, 'Got the shell?'

'Yeah. Take off as soon as Carlton's out of here.'

'I'll be across the street with Sloan. Franklin and Del are headed for your house.'

Carlton left, Sherrill looked at her watch: 'You want me to stay?' she asked Lucas. 'I'm kind of in a rush.'

'Take off,' Lucas said. 'I'll say good-bye to Carmel, make sure nobody left anything behind.'

260

Carmel shouted at Sherrill, as she left, 'Good riddance to all of ya. Fuck ya. Fuck ya . . .'

Sherrill flashed her the finger, over her shoulder, and Carmel's eyes widened and she took a step after Sherrill, and Lucas stepped between them and said, 'Hey, hey . . .' Then, to Sherrill, 'Knock it off, okay?' At the same time, he winked at her.

'Yeah, yeah . . .' And she was gone, too, and Lucas and Carmel were left alone in the fabulous apartment.

Chapter Twenty-Seven

Carmel asked, "Are you wearing a wire?' They were still standing in the living room, by the open door to the hallway.

'No. Should I be?' Lucas stepped over to the door and pushed it shut.

'When I think about it, I don't really care,' Carmel said. "I'm gonna get you for this, Davenport, I swear to God. I'm gonna dedicate my life to it.'

'Gonna take a lot of dedication, if you're out at the women's prison for thirty years,' Lucas said.

She flushed, and he could see her eye-teeth, bared, as she spoke: "There's not gonna be any prison. Not for me. Could be for you, when we're done with you. You've got nothing.'

Lucas shook his head and said, 'They're arguing about that over at the courthouse. Some of the guys think we've got enough, some of them don't. Gonna be close.' He drifted across the living room as he talked, poked his head into the guestroom, then continued to her bedroom, Carmel following him down the hall. 'What do you want in here?' she demanded.

'I'm just closing the place down, making sure nobody left anything behind,' he said. The shell was between two shoes in the open part of the closet. 'I'll tell you something, Carmel. Just between you and me – and I don't care if *you're* wearing a wire. I know you were involved in these killings. I know it. I know you were involved in the first one, Barbara Allen, and I think you did it because you wanted Hale. You were screwing him before the body was in the ground.'

'You don't know that.'

'I do know that. Hale told me that.'

'Hale?' Her hand went to her throat.

'Yeah. We had a long talk about you. I know all about you, about your sexual preferences, about what you like to talk about in bed. And you know what? You scared the shit out of Hale. He didn't have the courage to stop you, but he did have the courage to come in and talk to me, and I taped it. Hale telling me about how you hated Barbara, about how she was holding him back, about how he was lucky to be rid of her.' Lucas was adding that last bit on, but he bet it was true.

'That sonofabitch,' she said.

'Naw. He was just a dummy. Worked hard, liked women, not too much upstairs. Not a lot of guts, either – but he was just trying to get through life. He felt guilty about Louise Clark, but a lot of guys who love their wives have affairs. And Louise was something else in bed. He couldn't stop talking about her. He said she could suck the chrome off a trailer hitch: that's the way he put it. He said that compared to Clark, you were like the Roman Army, just grinding him down.'

'He never said that,' Carmel shouted. But there were tears streaking her face now, and she hated it, and screamed louder, 'Hale never said that.'

'Yeah, he did, and I think you know it, because it rings right,' Lucas said. He felt odd, standing in the cool, professionally-feminine bedroom, alone with this tear-streaked woman, hands in his pants pocket, almost abashed: he felt cruel. He pushed on. 'He said you were like some kind of machine, marching all over him. But he was afraid to dump you, because he was . . . *afraid*. Because he thought you may have killed his wife.'

'Louise Clark killed her . . . and him.'

'Oh, *please*,' Lucas said, sounding in his own ears like a character in a New York TV comedy. 'Louise Clark *had* him. He was going to marry her, as soon as he could get rid of you. And Louise Clark, to tell you the truth, was a good match for him. Smart enough, but not exactly the wizard of the western world. But a nice woman. And good in bed. And as far as we can tell from talking to all of her friends, Louise Clark had never fired a gun in her life, right up to the day when we found her in the middle of that phony suicide tableau in her bedroom.'

'Fuck you, Davenport,' Carmel said, crossing her arms over her chest. 'Get out of my house.'

Lucas said, 'Yeah, I'm going: I'll scout the . . .' It seemed a little faked, he didn't do it quite right, the frown, the near double-take, but Carmel was tired, stretched out of shape. 'What is that?'

'What?' Carmel was confused.

'Here,' Lucas said. He brushed past her, pushed the sliding door back so he could get a better look at the shoe. 'Goddamnit.'

He stood up, took Carmel by the arm and said, 'Come out here,' tugging her toward the living room.

'Let go of me . . .' She tried to pull away.

'I just want you out in the living room with me . . .' And in the living room he shouted, 'Hello? Hey, anybody here? Goddamnit . . .'

Carmel took a step back toward the bedroom and Lucas said, 'No.' And he said it with bite, and she stopped. He looked around, stepped into the kitchen, got a roll of Saran Wrap from the kitchen counter and carried it back toward the bedroom. She followed behind him and he knelt by the closet door and pushed the shoe away and, wrapping his thumb and forefinger with Saran Wrap, picked up the cartridge.

'A .22,' he said. He looked at her. 'A fuckin' .22'

'You put that there,' she said.

'Bullshit. You know I didn't put it there. And I'll tell you what – I bet it's got your fingerprints on it. I bet it'll check out when they do the metallurgy, won't it? What'd you do, drop a box of .22s in the closet? Shuck out a clip or something? How'd the cartridge get into your closet, Carmel?'

Davenport seemed to recede from her. He loomed over her in real space, but the pressure on her was so great that he seemed to squeeze down, until he looked like a little man seen through the glass peephole on an apartment door. Carmel's brain stopped: she couldn't bear this. She said something to him, but she didn't know what, and walked stiff-legged out of the bedroom. He was talking to her, at her, reached out to her, but she batted his arm away.

She was screaming back at him, but a broken, isolated part of her brain seemed to be in control, now. She walked straight across the living room, picked up a fistful of car keys from the entry table, and went out the door, leaving the door open, Davenport staring after her, saying something incomprehensible at her back . . .

Out the door, down the hall, into the elevator, pushing blindly at the buttons, out the door at Five, into the parking ramp, down the ramp to the blue Volvo, into the trunk, into the gym bag, out with the gun.

Because this is where she'd put the gun she got from Rinker: the car, with her mother's registration under her mother's new married name, nobody to know, nobody even to look at such an out-of-character non-Carmel-like motor vehicle.

She marched back through the door, propelled by the rage, got the elevator where it waited, the gun solid in her hand.

Lucas watched her go out the bedroom door, thought, '*Whoa.*' He followed after her, holding the shell. He had to tell her that he was taking the shell with him: she had to see the shell go in his pocket. But something about the way she was walking, robotlike, across the front room. And suddenly he feared she'd had some kind of a stroke, and he said, 'Carmel? Carmel? Are you all right?'

Then she was gone down the hall. He stood uncertainly in the bedroom door for a moment, expecting her to come back, then flipped out his cell phone, punched a speed dial button and said, when Sherrill answered, 'This is me. I think something's happened to Carmel. She just went out of here, acting weird.'

'Want us to come back up?'

'No. I'll . . . Well, maybe. Yeah. Come on back. Think of some reason to come back, I'm gonna check on her.'

Lucas walked across the living room, out into the hall – and she was gone. Either through the door into the stairway, or the elevators. Lucas walked down to the elevators and pushed the button. He bounced on his toes for a moment, thought about going down to look at the stairway door, then thought about the apartment door and hurried back, checked that it wasn't locked and started to pull it shut. At that precise moment, an elevator *dinged*, and Lucas stepped toward it. 'Carmel?'

She stepped out of the elevator: Lucas didn't see it as it was coming up, didn't instantly recognize it in the context, but then . . .

Carmel fired at him as the sights crossed the line of his face and saw the surprise and the gun jumped and Davenport was moving sideways and down and she felt the rush of a kill and tracked him with the barrel and fired again and again and then . . .

Lucas felt the first shot sting his neck and then he was moving, diving back into the apartment, felt another shot across his shoulders, and then, back in the living room he was rolling across the fabulous carpet, as a hornet's nest of bullet fragments ricocheted off the door a few feet away. As he fought to get upright and oriented, his cheek stung, then something hit him in the thigh, and his own gun was coming out and Carmel was in the doorway . . .

Lucas fired one shot and Carmel felt as though she'd been hit by a baseball bat. The .45 took away a fist-sized chunk of skin just below her rib cage, and she staggered back. Hurt. Bad hurt. Hospital. She still had the keys to the cars in her left hand, and she turned and lurched down toward the elevators. The doors were just closing, and she slapped at the button and they started to open and she looked back and saw Lucas peek from behind her doors and she fired again, and let herself fall into the elevator.

Lucas fired twice more, but had a bad angle at the closing doors; one slug hit the doors, the other might have slipped inside . . . He crawled toward them and pushed the down button.

'Fuckin' gun,' Sherrill said to Sloan, in the lobby, their guns coming out. 'That was a fuckin' gun. A big fuckin' gun.'

'Wait for the elevator, it's coming down,' Sloan said, 'I'm taking the stairs.'

'Too far, too far,' Sherrill said, but Sloan was moving: 'Gotta block them, gotta block the parking ramp.'

'Careful,' she shouted after him.

'Call in,' he shouted back, and Sherrill got her cell phone out and pushed the speed-dial for dispatch and began shouting into it as the numbers came down to five. Then it stopped, and Sherrill ran to the stairway and yelled up, 'Elevator stopped at five, watch the ramp.'

'Got it,' Sloan called.

The other elevator was going up again and Sherrill, without thinking, punched the Up button, trying to get Up. The first one, the elevator that stopped at five, started down. But the other rose inexorably to twenty-seven before it stopped. She ran back to the stairway access and shouted after Sloan, 'The elevator's on twenty-seven . . .'

At that moment, the second elevator dinged in the lobby. She shouted at the frightened security guard, 'Turn off that elevator, Stop it. Can you stop it on this floor? Stop it!'

He ran to the elevator as the door opened, but then almost slumped, stopping outside of it: 'My, God, there's blood . . .'

Sherrill pushed him aside, saw a puddle of blood in the middle of the carpet. 'How do you stop it?' she asked.

'Pull the red emergency-stop button.'

She saw it, a red knob the size of her thumb, and pulled it out. 'That'll do it?'

'Yeah, that . . .' The security guard looked up at the numbers above the elevator doors. 'The other one's coming down.'

'Oh, fuck. Get out of the way.' She stood back from the elevator doors, her pistol level at gut level: remember the chant, *two in the belly and one in the head, knocks a man down and kills him dead . . .*

Then the elevator doors opened and she saw Lucas on the floor with his gun pointing at her chest and blood streaming into his eyes and Sherrill screamed, 'Lucas, Lucas, Jesus . . .'

The elevator seemed to move at a deliberate and insolent crawl; Carmel pushed herself up, realized that her arm was burning; looked, and saw more blood. Her body was on fire. She staggered into the hallway at five, out to the parking ramp. The stairwell came up just inside the parking ramp door, and somebody was on the stairs, coming up. 'Fuck you,' Carmel screamed down at the man. She could see his arm, still three flights down. He stopped and looked up at her, and she fired the gun, once, twice.

Sloan braced himself. He was only on three-and a-half, confused. Carmel? Two shots sailed past, and he aimed blindly up, and fired once.

Carmel, fearless now, the pain tightening her, fired another shot, then another, and then got a click. She'd used up the clip. 'Fuck you,' she screamed again, and lurched out into the ramp. A dozen steps, and she was at the bloody-murder-red Jag, which was right there. Fumbling with her keys. On fire, she was on fire.

She backed out, aimed the Jag down the ramp, and stepped on it.

Sloan heard the parking-ramp door bang shut. He took another quick peek, then another, then ran up to the next landing. He heard the Jag start, screech away. He was on four-and-a-half now. He ran back down, through the fourth-floor door, heard her coming all the way. Lifted the .38, and as she turned the corner, fired a shot at the windshield. No effect, and the car's back end twitched out as Carmel gunned it again, and he fired another shot at the driver's side window as she passed him; but he was slow and the shot smashed through the back window and then she was down the ramp and around the corner.

Sloan ran back through the door and down to three, but at three, Carmel was already going by, and he ran down to two, and she was coming and he knew he was too late, so he kept going, and at one he burst into the lobby and screamed at Sherrill, 'She's coming down the ramp . . .'

As he ran toward the front door, he registered Lucas on his knees, the blood, Sherrill with the gun, and then the red Jag blasting through the wooden guard arms at the exit and out into the street, wheels screaming, car sliding, going away from him and Sloan ran out into a street full of people and couldn't fire his gun . . .

Lucas had done an inventory and was shouting 'Not bad, not bad,' and was trying to get up, while Sherrill screamed, 'Lay down, you're hurt, lay down,' and Lucas finally pushed her roughly out of the way and hobbled toward the front of the building and saw Sloan running away down the street and Carmel's Jag just turning the corner at the far end . . .

'Didn't think of this,' he said, trying to grin at Sherrill. Blood trickled down at the corner of his mouth. 'That she'd do this. She cracked.'

'Lucas, ya gotta sit down, the ambulance . . .'

'Fuck a bunch of ambulances . . .' And they saw people at the other end of the block, turning to stare, and Sherrill shouted, 'She's coming back, she went around the block.'

Lucas started to run, half-hobbled, toward the end of the block, Sherrill finally leaving him to run on ahead, her pistol out, shouting at people, 'Police, get away, police . . .'

Lucas saw her stop at the curb, then raise her gun . . . and the Jag came from behind the building and Sherrill pointed her pistol at the sky as the Jag hurtled by and Lucas came up and said 'Jesus Christ, she's doing a hundred and twenty . . .'

Carmel wasn't feeling much: a kind of mute stubbornness, a will to do what she pleased. She turned the last corner, realized that she was going the wrong way on a one-way street: and the wrong way in any case – the hospital was behind her. Instead of trying to turn, she focused her eyes on the Target Center, the auditorium where the Minnesota Timberwolves played basketball. Focused on the building and pressed the gas pedal to the floor.

She was going seventy at the end of the first block, a hundred when Davenport saw her, at the end of the second. The car topped out at the end of the fifth block, at about a hundred and thirty. She drove straight down the white line between two lanes, cars dodging away from her, white faces going by like faces on postage stamps, half-seen, half-realized, frozen in expression. She hit a stout black man carrying a grocery sack, in which he had milk and cookies and a dozen oranges. He never saw her as he crossed at a crosswalk, looking into the grocery bag, thinking about opening the cookies. He was too heavy, he shouldn't have bought them, his wife would kill him . . . He never saw Carmel coming and she hit him with the very center of the Jag and he flew over the car as though lifted by angels.

At a hundred and thirty miles an hour, Carmel hit the curb outside the Target Center and the Jag went airborne, turning, tumbling . . .

Lucas and Sherrill watched, appalled, as the car hit first the black man and then the concrete wall.

The black man was dead in a tenth of a second; he'd felt nothing but a sudden apprehension. As for Carmel, the transition from life to death was so sudden that she never felt it.

In the silence following the shattering impact, an even dozen oranges bounced and rolled in the dirt along the street, bright and promising like the best parts of a broken life.

Chapter Twenty-Eight

Charlie Ross and his yuppie flip-fone pals at the Merchants Bank in Portland, Oregon, had invented a new classification system for women. One that went down, not up. One duckling was a woman who bordered on the acceptable. Ten ducklings was a truly ugly duckling.

Ross was hacking his way through the billing entries for that month's box rentals, and incidentally keeping his eye on the safety-deposit counter while the regular clerk was at lunch, when a six-duckling came to the counter. She was bad news. If you were even tempted to throw her a mercy fuck, you'd want to put a rug over her head first. All of that went through Ross's bottlecap-sized brain as he pushed himself up from the desk and dragged his lard-ass over to the counter.

The woman was small, dark-haired, olive-complected. She had a mole by the corner of her mouth, a notable mole, nearly black, and another one beside her nose. And she wore over-sized glasses, the kind that are supposed to turn dark in sunlight, but always made your eyes look yellow when you were indoors. She handed him a key and he took it, ran it through the file machine, found her card, and brought it to the counter for her to sign.

But she was no longer looking at him: she was looking at the television that the bank had screwed to the ceiling of the lounge area, where visitors waited while their spouses or friends went into the vault. The TV was permanently tuned to CNN Headline News, which at that moment was showing the wreck of a bloody-red Jaguar that had plowed halfway through a cement-block wall.

'Ma'am?' Ross said. 'Ma'am, can I help you?'

The woman apparently didn't hear him as she drifted closer to the TV, listening, looking up at it, her mouth half-open.

'Happened last night,' Ross said helpfully. He'd already seen the loop a dozen times. The ugly duckling watched until another story started, this one involving a dog getting oxygen from a fireman, then turned back to the counter. He dropped her from six ducklings to four: she had a really nice ass, like a gymnast's. She seemed dazed.

271

'Hope it wasn't somebody you knew,' Ross said.

'No, no. I just wish they wouldn't show so much violence on TV,' Rinker said. She signed the card and pushed it across the desk at him. He noticed that her hand was trembling, and he hoped it wasn't some weird foreign disease.

Lucas had been patched up in the emergency room and sent home. The patching had been messy. A slug had burned through the skin on the side of his neck, leaving a groove, which was sewn closed. A fragment of lead – he'd been hit by a storm of ricochet fragments – had pierced the skin on his skull, behind his right ear, but hadn't reached the bone; the fragment was removed with tweezers, and two stitches used to close the wound.

'Just like that Wooden Head guy,' Sherrill said happily. She'd cheered up a lot when the doctors said that he wasn't badly injured.

Another fragment had struck his hip, which also made Sherrill happy.

'Hit in the butt,' she said.

'Hip.'

'Looks like a big butt to me,' she said. 'Your hip is over here, on the side.'

More fragments were taken from his side and legs. To get at one, just over his kidney, the doc had to make an additional small cut. The wounds in his legs were all superficial, but nasty; three got stitches. When it was done, they gave him a sample pack of ibuprofen and told him not to play basketball that weekend.

'That's it?' he grumped. 'Don't play basketball?'

'Well, we also extend our deepest sympathy,' the doctor said.

Lucas got down from the examining table, put on his pants, tottered to the door. 'You know what hurts the most?' he asked Sherrill. 'I really *dove* into her apartment. She was blasting away and I really racked up my elbow and ribs. I'm gonna be sore for a week.'

'Better than the alternative,' she said.

He *was* sore for a week, and hobbled by the feeling that all the stitches were about to unravel. But the stitches came out on Thursday, and by Friday, when Malone came to town with her FBI team, he was beginning to loosen up.

'No sign of Rinker,' Malone said. She was sitting in his visitor's chair, wearing a somber blue suit with a red necktie. 'But we'll get her.'

'I don't know,' Lucas said. 'She's smart, and she had nine or ten years to figure out how to hide. She could be here in the U.S., up in Canada, Australia, India, the Caribbean, and with her Spanish, anywhere in South America. God only knows how much money she had by the end.'

'We put her out of business, anyway. I just wish I'd been here for the shootout with Carmel.'

'Really? Why?'

'I mean, if I coulda gotten wounded like you did . . . you know, not too bad, but go to the hospital . . .'

'Excuse me, but I think you left your brain out in the hall,' Lucas said.

'You're just an ignorant local cop,' Malone said. 'You know what it's worth to be an FBI agent wounded in the line of duty? And if you're a woman? My God, I'd be up there.'

'Like an under-assistant deputy director, or something.'

'At least,' she said. 'So . . . how're you feeling?'

'Not bad. I could probably manage a foxtrot, if somebody pressed me on it.'

'Consider yourself pressed,' she said.

On Monday, Sherrill went to the FBI office to make a statement. When she came back, she dropped into Lucas' visitor's chair and said, 'I just talked to Malone.'

'Yeah?' He was peering into the thick black volume of the Equality Report. He was on page five-twenty-nine, less than a hundred to go. Pushing a boulder up a hill would have been a snap compared to the Report. 'Does she still think she's gonna catch Rinker?'

'I don't know exactly what she thinks,' Sherrill said. 'When I talked to her Friday afternoon, she was like really quick, incisive. Executive – maybe that's the word I was looking for. Really tightly wound, you know?'

Lucas turned the page, kept reading.

'But this morning, I mean, she was a lot looser. Hair was a little messed up, you know – she actually giggled once. Lipstick wasn't quite straight.'

Now Lucas looked up. 'What?'

'Giggled. Like, girly-giggled. In fact, she looked like somebody who'd had her brains foxtrotted loose.'

'Detective Sherrill, aren't you in the middle of a case? I mean, I've got to read this report.'

'That's what I thought,' Sherrill said.

273

* * *

The commission had nine members: the chairman, a desperately fading politician named Bob, once known in the State House for his fine ethics, and viciously ridiculed in the same institution after he lost his seat to a twenty-six-year-old spitballer; seven members of affected constituencies; and Lucas. After the routine *Roberts Rules of Order* opening, the meeting devolved into a nasty fight about whether adding to the list of minority or disability statuses would dilute the authority of prior assertions of those statuses . . . or that's what Lucas thought somebody said.

He wasn't sure. Passing through a bookstore earlier in the day, he'd discovered that Donald Westlake had revived the 'Richard Stark' Parker novels, and Lucas had *Backflash* buried in the pages of the Report. By the end of the meeting, he was more than halfway through, just finishing a chapter that ended with the word *Asshole*. He agreed.

The night was straight out of a country-and-western song, one of those smooth warm evenings made for rolling around in a hay mow with a farm girl. Even the traffic seemed subdued, as though people had abandoned their cars to walk.

Lucas' neighborhood was quiet, with only occasional cars rolling along the boulevard between his house and the bluff that dropped to the Mississippi. As he pulled into the driveway, he realized that he needed milk and cereal, if he wanted to eat at home the next morning; and he'd noticed a slight puffiness around the waist that needed to be trimmed away, and eating in a diner wouldn't help that. He thought about it, and decided to leave the car in the driveway. He popped the door, swivelled, reached back to pick up the copy of the Report and the novel, started to climb out of the car . . .

And saw her coming.

She was coming fast, from the corner of the garage. And though it was dark and late, he knew exactly who she was. He could just make out her height, and the smooth way she moved, a small woman, like a dancer. She was handicapped by the car: she had to clear around it. She had expected him to drive inside, and then she would have had him trapped between the Porsche and the big Chevy Tahoe parked on the other side of the garage. But she was ready and he could see her hand up with her gun and he reached desperately for his .45 and at the same time threw up the Report in front of his face and the explosions started, the night-flashes.

He was going down as the Report came up, and the Report flew out of his hand of its own will and he concentrated on clearing his holster, which wasn't made for fast draws, concentrated on jacking the slide, and he triggered the first shot blindly. The shot went into the car at an upward angle and punched through the windshield. He hit the ground and rolled, fired again, still half-blindly, just trying to slow her down, to shake her, saw another flash, felt a slug pluck at his suit, fired at the flash, rolled back toward the car and fired under it at where he thought she was, sensed that she was moving, fired again . . .

She was running.

He could feel it, maybe hear it – later doubted that he could hear it; the gun blasts, which he hadn't heard at the time, must have been deafening – and he fired in the general direction she was running, the slug going through the front of the house.

Then he was after her, running through the wonderful warm night. She was dressed all in black, but he could see her, in the lights of the house windows and the porches, running crazily across his back yard, crashing through bushes, over a chain-link fence. He was running as hard as he could, handicapped by his loafers; one of them came off as he cleared the fence. She swivelled as she ran and fired two more quick shots at him, wildly, but he ducked away, purely by instinct, lifted the pistol but saw window lights behind it and held off, still running . . . She crossed another fence, a higher one, and now he was only a hundred feet back, and then . . .

She ran up a ladder that was leaning against the back of a low rambler, kicked the ladder sideways and ran up the roof. He risked the shot this time – it should hit the Mississippi or the far river bank – but it was a bad shot and then she was over the ridge of the roof and out of sight. He tried to run around the side of the house, but hit a garbage pail and went down, got up, ran another few feet and hit a lawn-mower and went down again, got up and ran out onto the lawn . . .

She was gone.

The homeowner was at the door yelling, and Lucas screamed, 'Call the cops. There's been a shooting, call 911.'

He had to pick a direction and he picked north, since that had been her tendency. He ran hard for a hundred feet, kicked off the second shoe, stopped at the street corner, looked wildly up and down, started to run west, turned back . . .

Nobody there.

She was gone.

The St. Paul cops arrived three minutes later.

Malone, looking businesslike again, in a light tweed jacket and carefully ironed, pleated-front blouse, said, '. . . valuable information. We know she's still in the States, which suggests to me that she wasn't planning to leave. We'll get her.'

'Maybe,' Lucas said. He was fiddling with a yellow No. 2 pencil; since the crime lab had taken the Report away, he didn't have anything to fiddle with.

'Have some faith,' Malone said. 'After all, you're the only guy who ever survived her.'

'Ah, it was a complete fuck-up,' Lucas said. 'I fired five shots, and never hit her. She fired more than that, and never hit me. We must've been five feet apart for a couple of seconds . .'

'You're *complaining* about her bad shooting?'

'Well . . .'

'She would have put a couple right through your brain if you hadn't had that Report, and hadn't managed to throw it up in time.'

'Fuckin' Report,' Lucas grumbled. 'Now I miss the goddamn thing. Took two in the heart for me.'

Malone pushed up out of her chair. 'Listen, I'm heading back to D.C.'

'Really? I thought you were gonna be here for a while.'

'Too much going on back home,' Malone said. 'I'm flying out tomorrow morning.'

'Well, jeez,' Lucas said. 'Uh, you think you'd have time tonight, you know, we could go foxtrotting again?'

Winding down.

Kissing Malone good-bye at the airport.

Careful at nights.

Carmel, then Clara Rinker. Out of his life, he hoped.

A week after the visit from Clara, Lucas sat in his office, re-reading a note from Del. A woman had been referred to him through hippie friends: she claimed that her abusive husband was actually a Russian spy, a mole. When Del checked, the guy had no past that went back before 1974. He was carrying the name of a Montana boy who'd died in 1958. What should he do?

Shit, Lucas didn't know. Call the State Department?

The phone rang, and he picked it up.

'Took me a little while to get switched to you,' Rinker said.

He picked up the accent instantly; could almost smell the french fries and beer at the Rink. 'Bureaucracy,' Lucas said. 'Are you all right?'

'Yeah, but you scared the hell out of me. I took a little glass in my shoulder, from when that slug went through the car window.'

'What can I tell you?' No way to trace this; no way to call anybody, no way to let anyone know he was talking to the new Number One on the FBI's most-wanted list.

'I never touched you, did I?' she asked.

'No, but you screwed up a perfectly good Ermenegildo Zegna sport coat,' Lucas said. 'I gotta find a place to have it rewoven. And I had these nice slacks, Italian slacks, they're ruined.'

'Aw. Too bad. I'll tell you what – the thing that got me was the flash from that weapon of yours. What was that, a .45?'

'Yeah, exactly.'

'I couldn't see anything. I was hiding by that evergreen of yours, the one by the garage.'

'Juniper . . .'

'Yeah. My eyes were so adjusted to the dark that when you flashed me . . . there was nothing I could do but keep pulling the trigger. I couldn't see anything. Never thought of that – but heck, it was my first time for a gunfight.'

'You got lucky. You didn't put that ladder up there, did you? As a way out?'

'Nope. Just luck.'

'Damnit. I almost killed myself trying to run around that house. I hit a lawn-mower, scraped a piece of skin the size of a dollar bill off my shins.'

'C'mon, Lucas. All you've done is whine.'

'What I'm saying is, if you'd gone that way, you would've hit them. I would've been all over you.'

'And now you'd be dead, instead of sitting in an office.'

'Maybe not,' Lucas said, a little steel in his voice.

After a moment of silence, Rinker asked, 'That FBI chick that came into my bar with you? I saw her on TV.'

'Yeah?'

'Yeah. She said I'm a monster.'

'What? You're insulted?' He laughed.

'Yeah, yeah . . . You ever nail her?'

Lucas sighed and said, 'Jesus,' and then, 'Yeah. I guess I did.'

'Congratulations. She looked like she needed it.'

'That's kinda catty,' Lucas said. 'She's a really nice woman. We were just talking about you, in fact. Where in the hell are you?'

'You'd tell,' Rinker said.

'No, I wouldn't.' Of course he would.

'Philadelphia. I just cleaned out a safe-deposit box. My last stop – and I thought I'd give you a call, as long as this pay phone was right here.' He could hear the cars in the background. 'I wanted you to know, I was really pissed about Carmel. She could have been a good friend. I don't have any of those.'

'I don't think so,' Lucas said. 'For Carmel, friends were expendable. Look at Hale Allen. I mean, Christ, she thought she was in love with him, and bang! She kills him . . . or was that you?'

'That was her. He was screwing around on her.'

'Aw, come on, Clara, what she was doing to him was the next thing to date-rape. The guy had no ability to resist. She killed him in one minute, and she'd have done the same to you, sooner or later.'

'All right,' Rinker said. Then: 'You still after me?'

'If you come back here, I'll kill you,' Lucas said.

'Maybe. And what if I don't come back?'

'I won't be after you, but there's still the Feebs.'

'Who?'

'The FBI. They're putting the screws on Wooden Head.'

'I hope they send him away for a hundred fuckin' years,' Rinker said. 'He tried to get me killed.'

'I was a little worried about that,' Lucas said. 'When we hit your apartment, we found blood on the floor. We thought maybe your Mafia pals had decided you were too much of a risk.'

'They did, but I talked them out of it.'

'We ever gonna find them?'

'Who?'

'The two guys in tweed,' Lucas said.

'I'm gonna ignore that question.'

'Okay. Well, I didn't really think you were dead. I just didn't think you'd come back. After me. I thought that was sort of . . . unprofessional.'

'Really? My counselor at Wichita said I was too goal-oriented. I decided this one time, I'd forget the goal, which was to hide, and just let it all out. Express myself. For a friend. In her memory.'

'That was thoughtful of you,' Lucas said. 'I'll tell you what . . .' And he laughed again.

'What?'

'We had fifteen people looking for you at her funeral.'

'Really? I was a thousand miles away.' But she was pleased.

'We didn't want to take the chance. It was like a Chinese fire drill out there, cops scrambling all over the place, trying to stay out of sight, TV guys taking pictures of them . . . Big scopes. Hiding in poison ivy . . . I wore a Kevlar outfit that was so goddamn hot I almost died of heat stroke.'

'That's flattering, anyway.' She sighed, and said, 'Well, I gotta go. I've got so much to do.'

'Heading out to where? Costa Rica, Mexico, Chile? Those are the top three guesses,' Lucas said.

'Not bad, but they should have included the coast of Venezuela – lot of Americanos down there, everything's cheap. Life is easy . . .'

'I'll tell them.'

'Do that. Gotta run,' she said. And just before she hung up, 'I'm faster than you.'

'No way, sweetheart.'

She laughed, a light, southern-belle sound. Her laughter was cut by the *click* of the phone going down.

Somewhere in Philadelphia, Lucas thought, right at this minute; getting into an unremarkable car, headed for an obscure destination. Number One on the most-wanted list.

Number One with a bullet.